Turning Point

Turning Point

Lara Zielinsky

P.D. Publishing, Inc.
Clayton, North Carolina

ISBN-13: 978-1-933720-19-7
ISBN-10: 1-933720-19-0

9 8 7 6 5 4 3 2 1

Cover design by Lara Zielinsky/Barb Coles
Edited by Day Petersen/Medora MacDougall

Published by:

P.D. Publishing, Inc.
P.O. Box 70
Clayton, NC 27528

http://www.pdpublishing.com

Acknowledgements:

There are an incredible number of people without whom this book would never have left my head and reached your hands. From the very beginning, the members of my online fiction group, LZFiction, encouraged me to keep writing through some pretty dark and troubled times. I would have been absolutely lost without the keen eyes of dedicated editors, Day Petersen and Medora MacDougall, who, along with Barb and Linda, believed in the merit of this work enough to honestly help me make it better.

Dedication

For all those who believed I could, but mostly for the love of my life who has supported me every step of the way. John, I'm so glad we found each other to walk this life together.

Chapter 1

Parking her Mercury Mountaineer beside the mailbox at 134 Alaca Drive in Altadena, Brenna Lanigan pensively studied the cream-colored brick home trimmed in earthy dark brown. Nothing special indicated that one of television's most popular stars lived there. Set on a large corner lot, it was typical of the surrounding homes. Six-foot-high privacy fencing enclosed the back yard. The red and white "Beware of Dog" sign nailed to the fencing gave her pause. Tidy beds of annuals lined the stepping stone walk to the front stoop. Somebody in the house obviously gardened. Brenna thought of her own gardens. She could be pulling the weeds on her dahlias.

She realigned her hands on the driving wheel and considered leaving. She could forget about putting herself in this awkward situation entirely. It was Saturday afternoon. She should be grocery shopping. She could be visiting Kevin in Michigan.

She wished her sons had not had dates last night.

She wished...for an excuse.

There was none. One by one, her castmates had accepted their invitations to this party for the son of another member of their ensemble. As the "lead" on the television series *Time Trails*, she could not be the only absent figure.

She sighed and checked her appearance once more in the rear-view mirror, not sure what to expect of a party at the home of Cassidy Hyland. She had only appeared with the woman at official Pinnacle public relations events, and even then, she interacted with her as little as possible. She tugged nervously at the short blue ribbon holding her auburn hair away from her face, her frown deepening. *What if I took "Dress: casual" wrong?* She looked critically over her short-sleeved jersey, dark blue jeans, and cross-trainers.

Looking again at the handwritten script on the party invitation, Brenna recalled her frustration at learning the woman had a son, much less one turning five on this early autumn day. She could not picture Cassidy Hyland tending a bloody knee or wiping a child's runny nose. The image did not fit with her first impression. Since Cassidy's arrival, Brenna had tried to learn as little about the woman as possible. Clearly she had succeeded.

She had been furious when the producers at Pinnacle Pictures decided the series could use an injection of pure sex appeal, thereby implying she herself had none. Hyland was thirty years old, long-legged, thin and blond, the epitome of the Hollywood starlet. She was in demand for high-value movie scripts and celebrity appearances, while Brenna was five foot five, forty-one years old, and hadn't had a big-budget movie project offered to her in two years. Following a supposed one-time appearance in a double-episode arc in April of 1999, Hyland joined the *Time Trails* cast full time. The costumers and the directors made the most of her "assets" by giving the younger actress a figure-hugging uniform that was slightly different from that of the rest of the cast, explaining she had come from a different branch of the new military structure.

From her first set call, Hyland had displayed almost inhuman poise. Incisive ice-blue eyes pinned Brenna in the scenes they shared. She stood regally tall, stalked with the sleek grace of a panther, and looked unaffected by the hours and hours under the stage lights. Flawless honey-blond hair framed her cream complexioned face. By the end of a twelve- or fourteen-hour shooting day, Brenna was tired and worn, disarrayed in body as well as mind. She felt like a wrinkled old woman next to the golden glory of Hyland, a veritable angel...

Brought to earth to make my life a living hell. Brenna sighed. The writing staff loved the sparks of tension as the two characters set out in very different ways to get things done, and they constantly staged them in close, tense exchanges.

Resolutely, Brenna gave the blonde bombshell who had exploded into her life as cold a shoulder as possible. However, ignoring that statuesque frame standing less than an arm's length away in most of their scenes was impossible. She found herself tongue-tied or abruptly turning away to avoid her. Early morning one month ago, Brenna found the party invitation tucked in the edge of her makeup mirror. She was not over her feelings of resentment toward the producers, but she suddenly realized she was being unfair to the woman when she overheard the rest of the cast cheerfully accepting their invitations.

So why am I here, almost an hour late, just staring at the house? Her hesitation smacked of fear, and Brenna despised being afraid of anything. She gripped the door handle and shoved it open, stepping out onto the grass easement. *So what if it's the first non-production-related event where you're going to be in the same room with her? Suck it up.* Hurrying up the walk, she rang the bell before she could change her mind.

She remembered leaving the child's gift on her front seat at the same instant the door opened.

Cassidy Hyland's small home buzzed with the joyful laughter of children; adult voices filled her living room. She smiled with pleasure at her success. Her castmates did not seem put off by the number of her neighbors, parents of Ryan's playmates, also attending the party. Though, she sighed, one important face was still missing. She had tried several times to break through the ice that existed even off camera between herself and Brenna Lanigan, nominal leader of the *Time Trails* actors. She had understood from the beginning that Brenna's opinion mattered to most of the other actors and that they were only following her lead in leaving Cassidy mostly shut out of whatever socializing they did away from the set. She'd hoped that a birthday party for a child would be something so non-studio that everyone would see her as just another person.

Rachelle Cheron had been the first to arrive, with her daughter and husband, then Rich Paulson, along with Sean Durham with his son, followed quickly by Terry Brown and his daughter. Each had accepted enthusiastically while between takes at various times in the past month. With everyone else here, Cassidy hoped that she could be an accepted member of the troupe now. It had been more than a year, after all.

There was a light tap on the window separating the kitchen from the screen porch. Cassidy looked up to see her neighbor, Gwen Talbot, mouthing the word, "Cake?"

Realizing she was holding up things over a clearly false hope, Cassidy put down the tray of juice cups and turned to a nearby drawer to withdraw the cake knife.

"Can I carry something?"

Startled by the warm, rich voice that reminded her of smoky jazz clubs, Cassidy spun, knife still in hand. "Brenna?"

"Um, hi. Rich let me in." Brenna backed up and gestured toward Paulson, just closing the refrigerator door, beer in hand. "I hope I'm not too late."

With a tap of the bottle's neck to his receding hairline, a twinkle in his brown eyes, and a grin in salute, Rich was gone. Cassidy took the opportunity to watch him go and spend the few seconds collecting herself. Lowering the knife, she took a step back and slowly turned to Brenna.

Brenna Lanigan, swirls of gray in otherwise midnight blue eyes, was a beautiful, petite woman. She had brown hair pulled back in a low ponytail, but if Cassidy wasn't mistaken, the red highlighting was from the woman's Irish-American heritage, natural, rather than from a bottle. She had always appreciated genetics over Hollywood facade.

Taking in the other woman's attire, she was pleased Brenna had understood this was an informal party. She wore a sweatshirt with cropped sleeves bearing a New York University logo. One smooth, slender hand rested against the kitchen's island countertop. The fingertips of Brenna's other hand were tucked into the front pocket of figure-hugging, navy blue jeans. "You look like you had a good night's sleep."

"I...yes, I did. Thank you."

The woman displayed a slow, surprised smile that Cassidy appreciated after being served up a year of cold shoulder. Perhaps this could be the start of a change between them. "You're just in time for cake," she said genially. She recalled the woman's two teenage sons. "Did Thomas and James come with you?"

"I had to start them cleaning the gutters," Brenna replied.

"Is that a normal chore?"

Brenna shook her head. "Punishment. They missed curfew last night."

Cassidy absorbed the information with surprise. "That's pretty rough. Didn't you miss any curfews as a teen?" Brenna frowned at her. *Oops, too familiar,* Cassidy thought. In an attempt to recover the situation, she pointed to the kitchen doorway. "Um, cake?"

Brenna gestured for Cassidy to go first, then picked up the tray of juice cups and followed.

"Bren!" Rachelle Cheron came to her feet from the couch. A woman of exotic almond coloring and angular features framed with ebony, short-styled loose curls, Chelle smiled widely and easily. "So you didn't go to Michigan this weekend."

Brenna shook her head. "The boys had dates last night." She accepted a one-armed hug and inhaled the scent of baby powder from Rose, the eight-month-old in Chelle's arms.

"I don't envy you. Girls today can be predatory," Rachelle said. "After all, your boys are related to a *star*."

At the emphasis on the label, Brenna shook her head with chagrin. "I don't remind them." Studying Rachelle and Rose, Brenna wondered how the little girl would grow up to view her mother's job. Thomas and James certainly were not shy about sharing their negative views.

Brenna pinched a smile on her features and turned away, taking in the whole of the living room space as she looked for a place to sit. There was the brown stuffed leather couch where Rachelle sat with Rose. Behind her were two stuffed chairs in matching brown leather, one occupied by another woman — a brunette unfamiliar to Brenna — holding a cup of punch.

She caught the soft sound of music and noticed the entertainment center set off to the side behind the couch. A shadowbox on the wall held several figurines — some Disney characters and others clearly Hummel or similar. Brenna reached up toward a beautiful figurine of dancing children wearing homespun overalls. The effect of bare feet and heads tipped back in open laughter was enchanting. A hand brushed Brenna's shoulder. Startled, she looked back into Cassidy's pale blue eyes capturing her with curiosity.

"Cake?" Cassidy asked.

Brenna looked around to realize they were alone. Everyone else had already left the living room for the porch. "Yes. I'm sorry."

"It's all right. I don't have time for a proper tour, but perhaps another time?"

Tongue-tied, Brenna could only silently follow her hostess out to the porch, stepping through the sliding glass door. Out in the fenced yard, Brenna spotted Terry Brown following Rich Paulson toward the porch.

The dark-skinned Terry was another actor from *Time Trails*. He played Creighton, Susan Jakes' hatchet man. He was an expert at killing people — not in the traditional sense, though he could do that in a pinch — but as a computer expert who could wipe away records, making someone disappear from history before they took him or her out physically as well. He was also their "cover" man, inserting their impersonations into databases so that their presence would not upset the timeline while they were trying to restore it.

Paulson's character, Dr. Pryor, handled the team's medical needs. Both men were as level-headed and personable as their characters, with lengthy résumés as character actors.

Jacques Cheron, Rachelle's husband, brought up the rear, along with a man Brenna did not recognize. She was surprised to realize that it was probably someone from the neighborhood. All talked easily and looked comfortable, dressed in jeans and pullover shirts or sweatshirts. The atmosphere reminded Brenna of her own large family gatherings as a child. Again she marveled at the simplicity. She had never expected to find Cassidy like this.

Looking at her hostess, she noted the woman's soft, grass-green, scoop-neck cotton blouse as she talked quietly with a portly woman standing beside her. What Brenna had thought were slacks were actually dark green jeans. Knife in hand, Cassidy stepped up to the other end of a wooden picnic table covered in drawing paper where some of the children were drawing with crayons on the space in front of them. The half-sheet cake in front of her on the table was decorated with colorful handmade whorls and a stick-figure boy and dog. A boy with blond hair climbed onto the bench at the end and leaned on thin arms over the cake.

"Time for cake?" he asked.

"Yes." Cassidy tucked his shirt in where the tail of it was dangerously close to the icing. Brenna was surprised to realize that he was Cassidy's son. He looked small for five years old.

A dark-haired boy built considerably thicker than Ryan climbed up next to him and yelled, "Sing!"

Brenna smiled and joined in a discordant, yet joyful rendition of "Happy Birthday" to Ryan.

Cassidy cut the cake, occasionally nudging her son's hands away from the blade as he reached to move pieces by hand. Paper plates began to circulate.

Ryan scooped ice cream rather messily, though Cassidy did not appear to mind. She handed Ryan his plate, then another to the boy next to him. The two jumped off the bench and pushed their way out into the yard to sit on the grass and eat. After being served, many of the other children followed.

Brenna stepped up for her piece of cake and overheard the portly woman speaking to Cassidy. "The cake's a hit. That recipe I gave you turned out really well.

And I love the decorations."

"Thanks, Gwen." With a warm smile that crinkled the skin at the corner of her eyes and lips, Cassidy leaned forward and pressed her lips briefly to Gwen's cheek. Brenna wondered who this neighbor was to be treated with such casual intimacy.

"Brenna?" Cassidy's voice brought her eyes back up. "Do you want ice cream?"

Jerking her head up as she tried to formulate a response, the first thought Brenna had was that Cassidy's eyes looked different in the sunlight. *Softer*, Brenna thought. She was more used to the defiant expressions she encountered when they were in character. She reminded herself, *Cassidy is not Chris Hanssen, and I'm not Susan Jakes*. Brenna tried to remember that she was here because Cassidy had invited her. It was time she related to the woman on a personal level. She cleared her throat. "Yes, thank you."

Passing a paper plate of cake and ice cream, Cassidy made introductions. "Brenna, this is my neighbor, Gwen Talbot. Gwen, this is Brenna Lanigan, from *Time Trails*."

"Hello. My son, Chance, is Ryan's shadow there." Gwen pointed out the boy next to Ryan where they sat in the grass. The bigger boy was swiping a finger of icing from the top of Ryan's slice. Beside them, Sean had his son, Kieran, sitting next to him and was supervising the messy consumption of cake and ice cream by the two-year-old.

"It's very nice to meet you, Gwen." Brenna stepped back, looking around for a place to sit.

"Sit here," Cassidy suggested, pointing to the bench opposite Rachelle, Jacques, and Rose. "The kids seem to prefer the grass."

"I can see that," she said with a half smile. Clearing aside a few crayons, she settled onto the bench, looking up to see Rachelle sharing small bits of cake and the occasional smear of ice cream with Rose.

Brenna moved aside as Gwen settled to her right, then was unsure where to go when Cassidy settled to her left, having at last served herself a piece of cake. Cassidy's thigh was firm and warm against hers. She resolutely ducked her head to her food.

Always to be counted on for livening up a social occasion, Rachelle started small talk about the L.A. County park system. Cassidy joined in as she described the new installation of fitness stations at her own neighborhood park. Feeling the body moving against her own, Brenna considered getting up, but she became entranced by the voice and the long fingered hands with which Cassidy was illustrating her points.

"You don't work out at a gym?" Rachelle sounded as surprised as Brenna felt.

"Ryan and I can go through the park together. At a gym I have to leave him with the sitting service. I try to limit that."

Brenna asked, "What do you do with him while you're at work?"

"Ryan's in preschool at Gwen's elementary school, so she keeps him with her until I get home."

Quite neighborly, Brenna thought, aware she'd had no such offers from her neighbors. Then again, she tried to keep to herself, and her neighbors in Pacific Palisades, many of them in the business like she was, did the same. Cassidy, it seemed, lived in a more working-class neighborhood. She studied Gwen again and watched the woman respond, "Chance gets time to play with Ryan, so it works out for everyone." The dark-haired woman shrugged as her voice trailed off.

Glancing over her shoulder back to Cassidy, Brenna ducked away from the intense smile Cassidy beamed at her neighbor. "I couldn't have done this without her," Cassidy said.

A small clock on the fireplace mantle chimed the hour, drawing everyone's attention. "Time to send the children home," Cassidy murmured as she extracted herself from the picnic table bench. At the sound of the doorbell, Cassidy went to let in the first of the other children's parents. For a while the house filled with the commotion of greetings and farewells tossed among the adults and eager children showing off their prizes from the party.

Terry straightened from dusting grass cuttings off his daughter's jeans. "Great party, Cass. I had a good time."

"Glad you could come," Cassidy said with a smile. "Nice to meet you, Becca." She offered her hand to the young girl.

Becca's brown eyes widened, and she blinked, hiding her face before turning to grin up at her. "Can I come back?" The girl's eyes followed when Cassidy raised her face to Terry's.

Cassidy directed her question to him. "Perhaps we can all get together sometime?"

Terry nodded as he warmly held both Cassidy's hands in his dark ones and then turned to Brenna. "It was good to see you, Bren." She nodded. Terry prodded his daughter out, though she tried to cling to Ryan. Cassidy, Brenna, Rachelle, and Jacques, holding Rose, remained in the foyer.

"Thanks for a great party," Rachelle said, adjusting the shoulder strap of her baby bag. "I'll see you both Monday morning." She looked first at Cassidy, then Brenna, and nodded at some personal thought before she stepped out, followed by her husband.

Brenna stood alone with Cassidy on the front step. Ryan hugged his mother's hip and waved goodbye to the guests.

The sound of a car door opening and slamming shut caught Cassidy off guard. She had been trying to think of something to say, something that would convey how much she appreciated Brenna's attendance at the party. The other woman, also startled by the sound, spun around, turning her back toward Cassidy to assess the new arrival.

Stepping out of the house to stand behind Cassidy, Gwen grasped her arm, tense and alarmed, but Cassidy patted the hand and Gwen withdrew. She frowned at the tall man with conservatively trimmed blond hair. "Mitch," Cassidy said, "what are you doing here?"

He nodded curtly to Brenna as she passed him going to her car, then snapped his attention back to his ex-wife. "I came to see my *son.*"

Cassidy saw Brenna hesitate, look back, then resume her walk to the curb. She said quietly but forcefully, "You're supposed to call first."

"You're not alone." Crouching, Mitch pulled his left hand from behind his back, revealing the wrapped present he had been concealing. Ryan let go of his mother's leg and sprinted to his father's open arms.

Damn, she thought with heartfelt disappointment, both for Brenna's departure and her ex-husband's arrival. Familiar wariness rose like bile in her throat as Mitch pulled Ryan to him in a tight hug. Then Mitch's green eyes fixed on her.

Chapter 2

Script pages turned amid the group of actors seated casually on the floor of a set sparsely decorated and liberally painted in green tones. The Vortex room.

"All right. Let's try the basic marks." Director Mike Malley, his own script copy in hand, started pointing out places. "Bren, here. Will, out of frame. Terry, you're starting here. And Rich, you're there."

Rising to her feet from downstage left, Brenna shrugged her shoulders at Will Chapman as the actor folded up his script and stalked off stage right, pushing past Cassidy as the blonde unfolded from her Indian-style position downstage right.

Brenna saw Cassidy absently rub and rotate the shoulder Will had knocked into. Will, she recalled, had not been at Cassidy's home the other afternoon. Clearly he was ticked off about something. Brenna was surprised to see him taking it out on Cassidy.

Mike wasn't done with his stage directions. "Chelle, you cross front, but let's have you coming left instead of right." Chelle took her position. "All right, lighting check."

A scurry of technicians with light meters stepped into everyone's space, positioning their meters as needed, shouting notes to the overhead lighting grips. The walk-through would allow the light team to take their readings and check for any overt glare or bad shadows caused by the actors' relative heights and the lamp positions. The cast, used to the routine by now, stood quietly, glancing over the current script page.

When the stage was cleared, Mike called, "Begin."

"All right, everyone. You know the mission. Lieutenant Raycreek's made the calculations. We're going in, making the correction, and getting back out again. Is that clear?"

Time Squad Commander Susan Jakes looked in turn at each of her team, dressed in their Time Squad jumpsuits, a sleek, futuristic black with colored armbands denoting their respective ranks.

The camera and lighting grips measured distances and took notes for the framed close-ups, each actor taking a moment to nod as he or she would when the cameras rolled.

Trailed by a grip, Rachelle crossed the stage reciting her line. She held out her right hand. Empty now, during filming it would hold a remote-control-like prop. On cue she now "handed" that to Brenna.

Time Agent Luria Dewitt reported, "I've set the circuits, Commander."

Sean Durham dusted his hand through his blond hair and tapped his script, which would be replaced by another prop, an information disk, during shooting.

Time Agent Jeremy Dewitt questioned, "Are you sure this is the right place? It doesn't look like one of Heatherly's usual hits."

Susan's reply was confident. "Mark did the calculations himself. I had him check them after Robinson's last orders."

Luria nodded. "Well, good thing I packed my dancing shoes. Looks like our target location is a rock 'n' roll club."

Rich smiled at Cassidy as the woman stepped up next to him, reaching out for his "file copy", looking down at the script.

Time Agent Chris Hanssen asked brusquely, "Has CE Creighton completed the insert?"

"Yes."

"What's our cover?"

"Lu," Susan said, nodding toward Luria, "and Jeremy are a couple looking for good games. You and Doc will 'fleece' them to make them look inviting to Baxley. Be sure to do it where he can see you."

"Who's our target? What did he do?" She lifted a file photo, a grainy black and white of a man in a 1950s-era suit and fedora.

"Baxley's your basic time jumper, an opportunist. We've traced his interruptions through two time streams. Mostly gambling scams. We've gotten the warrant, so it's time to bring him in." She looked around at the others. "Any other questions?"

There was no reply. Chris continued to look pensively at the rather handsome face.

"All right. I'll be site coordinator. We have 72 hours."

Rachelle, Sean, Cassidy, Rich, and Brenna stepped around an "X" on the floor by the shadows of the crossbeams of an overhead lamp.

"Mark?"

Followed by a lighting grip, Will Chapman stepped up to a mocked-up panel, his back to the other actors.

Lieutenant Mark Raycreek cast a silent look over his shoulder, turned away from the team, and pushed forward on a handlebar-style switch.

"And...break!"

Libby, the lead grip, pulled her luminosity meter from around her neck. "We got all our reads."

"Great. We'll set up for the transmission site on the alley set next door." Mike looked at his watch. "Well, maybe we'll do it after lunch. Take an hour, folks."

Brenna started off the stage, walking past Will's position just as the huge man turned. As she bounced off his shoulder, she looked up at him, catching a sour expression. "Something wrong, Will?"

"Would be nice to get something to do for a change. I flip switches and read off-screen quite a lot."

"The nature of the beast, right? You'll get another episode."

"I damn well plan on it."

Surprised at his vehemence, Brenna turned to watch him storm off in the other direction. He sidestepped Rich, but though there was plenty of room to go around Cassidy, who was next to him, Will clipped her right shoulder. Rich grasped Cassidy's other shoulder to steady her and guided her as they turned behind Sean and Rachelle.

"You coming, Bren?" Rich asked. "We're off to the catering table."

Brenna declined automatically. "No. I've got a few calls to make." She saw his lips quirk in dismay as his eyes darted to Cassidy. She reluctantly turned around. "Never mind. They'll wait until the dinner break." Rich's smile reappeared as she came alongside them.

Listening to the other cast over their sandwiches thank Cassidy again for the weekend party, Brenna joined in with, "How long have you lived there?"

"Just this last year."

"It's very homey."

There was a brief silence as the rest of the cast, Cassidy, and finally Brenna, realized how atypical such a civil comment was between the two women. "Thank you," Cassidy said quietly.

Following lunch break, the crew and cast were back on the sets, breaking off into rehearsal pairs as the main set was configured for the first full scenes to be shot that night. Taking this first day to rehearse by herself, memorizing lines away from the distractions of the set, Brenna started for her trailer. Cassidy's voice interrupted her.

"Brenna?" When Brenna turned and Cassidy saw her frown, she took a step back. "I'm sorry. I forgot you had some calls."

"Actually, I'm just going to rehearse."

Cassidy pursed her lips; Brenna fidgeted with the script pages in her hands. "Would...would you like to rehearse together?"

From the venturing tone, Brenna knew that Cassidy had worked herself up to ask. A month ago she would have not even tried to meet the woman halfway. Something felt different though; Brenna found she was actually curious to see how Cassidy rehearsed. She nodded. "All right. Where would you like to start?"

"I thought, maybe, well, the argument we have in scene 7B about really having to take in Baxley."

"What's wrong with it?"

"There's not a lot of room for understanding in the dialogue."

"They're not supposed to understand each other. Susan's by the book. They get in, they get the guy, and they get out."

"But Chris wants her to think about it. She's emotionally involved."

"Susan isn't. So she'll ask 'Why?'"

"Because the world isn't all black and white," Cassidy snapped. She swallowed and took a step back. Brenna realized only then herself that the taller woman had invaded her personal space. "Um, sorry."

"Don't be. Characters get carried away."

"Do you think we could shade the argument a little differently?"

Brenna was intrigued. This was perhaps an opportunity to reveal more of Susan's layers to the audience too. "If we don't change dialogue; we'll have to do it all in the blocking."

Cassidy smiled. "Let's go to the set then."

Brenna found herself eagerly following.

Commander Susan Jakes paced, occasionally looking at the junior officer, Lieutenant Chris Hanssen, who stood stiffly beside a craps table. It was the middle of the night, and the two women were alone in the community dance hall.

"Commander," Chris started.

Susan spun, slapping her right hand at the air. "No!"

"He wants to stay here."

"That's what he tells you. He's playing you."

"Just put a tracker on him."

"And let him keep amassing his private little fortune? No."

"It isn't a fortune. And he doesn't want to go back to work for Heatherly."

"What the hell makes you believe him? We've seen more than our share of turncoats, Hanssen. The minute the Squad lets this one get away—"

"I believe him. Have you talked to him?"

"No. And I'm not going to. You're going to bring him to the recovery coordinates tomorrow on time."

"Heatherly has an assassin waiting for him if he comes out in the open."

"Damn it, Hanssen, I should have recommended you for the records department instead of reconnaissance when you first came on. You're not seasoned enough. You're not seeing clear—"

"Then why didn't you?"

Susan blinked. The quiet interruption stymied her a moment.

"You had full control over my assignment to this squad. So why didn't you put me in Creighton's place? My tech skills are equal to his."

"Creighton thought you'd make a versatile member of the on-site team."

"You didn't trust me."

"No, I didn't."

"But you gave me a chance." Susan frowned. "Give him a chance to prove himself."

"Why does he want to stay here? This is ancient history."

"He likes it."

"He likes it?"

"Actually, he said he'd rather die among friends than people he's never known."

"We can't make a judgment on that here. That's for others to do."

"Is there nothing I can say?"

When Commander Jakes shook her head, there was a sadness about it. Chris Hanssen straightened up. Brusquely the commander issued her final order, "Be at the rendezvous spot. With Baxley in custody."

Brenna turned and walked away from Cassidy. As she reached the edge of the set, she turned back. "We ad-libbed in the middle there."

"It was easy because the emotional arc rings true. They do disagree." Cassidy crossed to her. "But the lines suggest that Chris is turning Susan's opinion, just a little."

"We can't ad-lib for shooting without approval."

"I know. So, how can we convey some of the lines without words?"

The two women sat down in a pair of chairs near the camera lines and pulled out their scripts to consult and scribble.

Brenna walked past the central sets of *Time Trails*, headed for her trailer to relax until her after-dinner shoot of several C.U.s, or close-ups. She had just finished an interview about her upcoming fan convention appearance with Terry. She reflected on the give-and-take she had experienced while rehearsing with Cassidy. She felt like she had stretched muscles she hadn't used in years. It was a tiring, but good feeling. She smiled.

"Ms. Lanigan?"

Am I ever going to get to my trailer today? Irritated, Brenna rolled her script in her hands. "Yes?" But when she turned and saw a pre-teen boy standing nervously about four feet away, she forcibly relaxed. "Oh, hello." He scuffed a foot against the floor. She affected Jakes' patented glare and stern tone, forcing down her smile as he squirmed. "Did you sneak away from a tour?"

He straightened like a green military recruit. "Ah, uh...No. I mean, NO, Ma'am! I'm here with my Uncle Bill. He...William Doherty...um...he wrote the script, and he thought I'd like to see it being made while he's in another story meeting."

Brenna grinned and put a reassuring hand on his shoulder. "That's okay. I've brought my sons once or twice. You're all right back here as long as you stay out of the way." She started to turn away but stopped when he spoke again.

"Would you...please?"

The boy presented her with a small book pulled from his back pants pocket. He wiped his hands on his jeans — no doubt to wipe away the sweat — before passing her the small notepad-sized autograph book.

"All right." She smiled as he fumbled with a pen, then passed it to her. His shyness was endearing.

"You...you said you have sons?"

She pursed her lips to stifle a chuckle. Apparently he was bold enough to start small talk with her. "Yes, two. Thomas is seventeen and James is fifteen. What's your name?"

"I'm..." He swallowed. She patiently waited. "My name's Ricky. I mean...could you make it to 'Rick'?"

"Sure." She signed, "To Rick, love, Commander Jakes" and passed it back. "Here you go."

"Oh, man! I can't believe...Yes!" Rick whooped and was quickly shushed by a dozen people nearby. He lowered his voice and finished, "Thanks, Commander!"

As the boy bounced away, Brenna wondered who else he would sneak up on before the end of the day. She looked forward to listening for the random whoops and hollers from distant parts of the soundstage.

"That was sweet."

"Hmm?" Brenna looked up from the pen still in her hand. In his excitement, the boy had forgotten to reclaim it. Over her left shoulder, she saw Cassidy step around the edge of a temporary wall. Unnerved by the idea of Cassidy watching her, she explained, "The writer brought his nephew to the set."

"I heard."

"You didn't come out."

"He'll find me later."

"I was just thinking about that."

"I wonder who else he's gotten today."

Brenna shrugged as Cassidy walked up next to her. "I didn't see him around before lunch, so...maybe I was the first."

"Appropriate," Cassidy said with a smile. She nodded toward the set where several of the actors and the director were going back over their placements and working through the apprehension scene again. "Are you going to your trailer? I just spent twenty minutes repeatedly darting after our 'bad guy' for a one-minute fifteen-second onscreen result."

"Yes, I was. So, did the—"

To Brenna's surprise, Cassidy sighed and rubbed her feet, releasing them from a pair of dress heels as soon as she sat down in a nearby canvas chair. "I wish I had a longer dinner break. I could really use my foot bath. But I'm first up for the C.U.s."

Brenna could not recall Cassidy expressing any discomfort before and wondered if it was because she had not bothered to notice or if the woman was in an atypical amount of pain. Cassidy continued massaging her stocking-covered foot. *Well, there's time enough to correct that now.* Brenna rolled up her script and patted it against her own thigh, snapping her gaze up to Cassidy's face. "I might have something to help there. Why don't you come to my trailer to sit for a few minutes? Besides, I forgot to leave Ryan's present on Saturday, so I can give you that, too."

"You don't have to."

"I do. I had it with me, but in...I left it in the car."

"Oh." After another brief hesitation, Cassidy nodded. "All right." She bent over to put the heels back on. With a sigh, she stopped. "Forget it. I'll walk in stockings."

"I think I have a spare pair of slippers."

Cassidy's head snapped up in surprise. "I...thanks."

Brenna realized where Cassidy's eyes were staring — at the casual hand she had put on the other woman's arm, which she quickly withdrew. She covered her quandary about why she had done something so intimate with a quipped, "Sure."

Brenna in her boots and Cassidy in her stocking feet walked around to the back of the soundstage and out the door to a line of trailers. Each cast member had one. They walked to the second to last one on the left.

"I don't think I've been in here." Cassidy took the last step up into the cozy trailer. She eyed a refrigerator and Formica-topped folding table. Brenna's "home away from home" was littered with photographs and books. A hand-crocheted afghan lay haphazardly over the back and arm of a small recliner. She noticed a book half-tucked under the old beige version of a script page and picked it up as Brenna disappeared into the second half of the trailer, tossing over her shoulder, "Have a seat."

When Brenna returned, Cassidy held up the book with a questioning look. "You read this?"

Brenna laughed. "I have to know a little bit about the science of some of this stuff or I'll never say it right." She took the book from Cassidy's hands and laid it aside, glancing at the star-speckled cover of Hawking's *A Brief History of Time.*

"Yeah, but him? Seems a little dry. I read Feynman myself." She offered a wry smile. "You're right, though. We've got to sound somewhat convincing when we do this."

Brenna presented her with two pairs of slippers. "Go on. Blue cotton or Bullwinkle J. Moose?" Cassidy hesitated, then reached for the brown character slippers. "I figured you for a Bullwinkle fan," Brenna added as Cassidy dropped to the couch to place them on her feet.

"You did?" She sighed in relief as the thickly padded interior hugged her aching feet.

"I just took one look at you and said, 'Bullwinkle.' Though as you can see, I brought the blue ones in case I was wrong."

"Always prepared? I find it odder that you would like Bullwinkle," Cassidy admitted.

Brenna shrugged. "I grew up watching this earnest moose that seemed to mess everything up."

"Though things usually came out right in the end."

"Serendipity." Brenna smiled.

"Or his buddy Rocky." Cassidy chuckled. The two women fell silent for a moment.

"Oh, mmm...Here." Brenna reached around behind the edge of the couch, just out of Cassidy's line of sight, and withdrew a wrapped box. About twice the size of a shoe box, it was covered in paper printed with party hats in a menagerie of colors. "For Ryan."

Taking it, Cassidy nodded and set it beside her on the couch. "I'll give it to him tonight."

Brenna shifted. "I can rewrap it, if...would you just tell me?" She leaned against the arm of the small stuffed chair where she sat across from Cassidy.

"What? You want me to open it? I'm sure he'll love it."

"I haven't bought for that age in years, Cass."

Cassidy hesitated at the woman's earnest expression, surprised by the unexpectedly vulnerable admission and the way Brenna had shortened her name. Since she did not want to ruin the cute paper, Cassidy asked, "What is it?"

"A stuffed animal."

She considered that. Her son did sleep with a worn stuffed crocodile.

Brenna went on with a tone that sounded abashed. "I saw it at a specialty toy shop when I was in Mount Clemens."

"What kind of animal?"

"Well, really a...a monster." Brenna shifted and crossed her left leg over her right and steepled her fingers together over the knee. "There's this story...I've always loved it. About a boy and the monsters he meets in a land of make-believe. Maurice Sendak wrote it."

Cassidy smiled. "I know that one. *Where the Wild Things Are*," she identified. "Right?"

Brenna grinned. "Yeah. This was a handmade toy modeled after the cover illustration." She shrugged. "I wasn't sure you'd think it appropriate. I did include a copy of the book, if you don't already have one."

Cassidy picked up the wrapped box and studied it. "Ryan doesn't have it." She set it down. "I know what I'll be reading to him next." She smiled at Brenna and saw the woman exhale.

"If we get out of here at a reasonable hour," Brenna said.

"You mean midnight isn't reasonable?" Cassidy's gamble at making a joke paid off. Brenna tipped her head back and laughed until tears appeared in her eyes.

"Oh God. I'm sorry. You're right. Midnight is not reasonable. So, when do you read to him?"

"I try to read to him at least twice a week. Sometimes it's just Saturday and Sunday afternoons. Sometimes it's after getting a lucky break here and being home around ten."

"It is hard to have a young child and work these hours."

"And teenagers are better? I seem to remember you saying that yours were out past curfew. The anxiety would kill me."

"Thomas and James are generally pretty good — and helpful now that Thomas also drives."

Cassidy nodded. There did not seem to be much to add. They fell into silence, and she ran her hand over the couch cushion, tracing the simple maroon linear print, unable to avoid contemplating a nap. She even yawned. Quickly she stifled it, as she was quite sure the change in Brenna's attitude toward her was not yet up to offering to let Cassidy nap on her couch.

Brenna suddenly moved, jerking Cassidy's attention to her. "We had better head back." Cassidy bent over to remove the slippers. "Keep them."

"All right," she accepted and stood. Collecting the wrapped present and the costume boots in her arms, she stepped back as Brenna held open the door. As she stepped into the daylight, she came close to Brenna, acutely aware of the other woman watching her pass.

Brenna waited at the bottom of the steps to Cassidy's trailer while she dropped off the gift and slippers and put her boots back on, though Cassidy had invited her to enter. But it was together that they walked back to the soundstage.

Chapter 3

It was late Friday, near the end of their last scheduled day of shooting the season's tenth episode, *Crap Shoot*. After a late dinner break watching the stars come out and eating a snack on her trailer steps, Brenna was back on the soundstage. She looked over to where Cassidy worked with Will Chapman in a concluding scene. She and Cassidy would have the next one.

The rehearsal for the scene was still fresh in her mind, practiced Wednesday morning with Cassidy after the woman had been to costuming for her shooting of two stunt scenes with the B camera team.

Previously Brenna would have only done the rehearsal with Cassidy with the other actors and the director for the regularly scheduled run-throughs. But Cassidy had approached her with an idea, and they followed through the rest of the week, consulting together on several scenes. The episode had finally come together with a fabulous amount of character development, prime among them the relationship between Chris and Susan.

In the plot, Baxley had taken advantage of Hanssen's mixed feelings about bringing him in, building an elaborate story. When the time came to take him in, there was a firefight. Jeremy Dewitt had to shoot Baxley, who was holding Chris hostage in a room filled with "normals", their term for those living in the timeline they had intercepted. Dozens of people could have died. Chris' fight with Susan now proved that the commander had been right. Regulations also meant that the young officer had to be reprimanded for her misjudgment.

In the end, they didn't rewrite a single word in their four scenes together. To Brenna's surprise, they managed to convey all of the nuance with simple body language. All it took was simply letting herself react to Cassidy's very mobile features — letting herself see, for the first time, the skill and knowledge with which Cassidy Hyland played her character. When they had played this final scene through at the pre-shoot rehearsal, the director had been very pleased and congratulated them both on the development.

Having finally recognized Cass as a member of the *Time Trails* team, both on- and off-camera, it felt right to Brenna that their arguments came out with a softer edge. Cassidy's smiles off-camera were more frequent now, and Brenna realized that the other woman also had been unhappy. While her presence could still have negative repercussions for Brenna's career, she recognized that it was not Cassidy's fault. Letting that go made her feel as if a weight had been lifted from her own shoulders.

The director's call for action drew Brenna's attention from her thoughts to the unfolding scene. On stage, Will Chapman portrayed Lieutenant Raycreek. As the second-ranking officer in Susan's Time Squad, it was his job to inform Chris Hanssen of the punishment Susan had devised for her disobedience.

Raycreek slammed the ball around the court walls, forcing Chris to chase it. When she stopped to catch her breath, he continued to drill: "You disobeyed her, Chris. You'll be on restricted duty until she thinks she can trust you again. You knew that going in. Why did you do it?"

"I believed it was the right thing to do," Chris replied defensively, panting.

"Sometimes it's not right or wrong that you should be concerned about, it's doing the prudent thing," Raycreek countered, starting another round of the game. "Rules and regs protect everyone."

"It's prudent to stand by and let someone die?" Chris sneered. She missed another shot. "Your game," she conceded sullenly.

"He played you for a fool, Chris. If you had listened to your commanding officer, you wouldn't be in this situation right now," he offered coolly, then walked toward the doors.

The stagehands used a pulley to open the doors, and Chapman walked out of camera view.

"Cut. Excellent."

Chapman spun his racket in his fist and strode quickly off the other side.

It was clear to Brenna that Cassidy's energy was flagging. Will had taken her all over the court with his shots, certainly more than was required for the cameras. Inhaling, Brenna started for the doorway to take her place for the next sequence. Around her, the camera crew, microphone, and lighting grips adjusted their equipment for the closer up angles coming in her one-on-one scene with Cassidy.

Concentrate, she prodded herself, hoping to finish this in just the necessary number of takes required to get all the right angles. She felt the telltale warmth of nerves dampening her palms, so she paced, trying to shake it off.

Cassidy had a moment to breathe as well. Since she would not be required to be in exactly the same position for the opening of the next scene, no one jumped to chalk the floor as she stepped away. She joined Brenna behind the doorway for a few moments of respite from the hot lights. "Brenna?"

"Ready to get off your feet?" Brenna asked.

Cassidy drew closer, decreasing their visibility to the others as she gave a tired smile and sighed. "Absolutely."

Her voice, soft as it was, drew the attention of another actor. Jeff Liverpool, the now dead Baxley, walked up and interposed himself. "Hey, Cassidy, it's been great. Thanks." He cast a look over her costume once, then offered his hand.

"Mmm hmm," she replied, forcing a smile as she looked away from Brenna. Patiently she shook the hand of the man she had spent the most camera time with over the previous week.

Brenna caught Cassidy's shake of her head as the actor turned away. She thought she also heard a breath of relief. When Jeff was out of earshot, headed for costuming to get out of his clothes, she nudged Cassidy's arm. "Trouble?"

"Not any more."

"What happened?"

"Oh, that's right," Cassidy started wryly. "You had that interview with *TV Cult Times,* so you missed the fifteen takes it took to convince him not to pinch my butt when he was holding me hostage."

Brenna bit her lip to hold back a laugh and shook her head. "It's such a cute butt, though."

Cassidy blinked. *Where on earth did that come from? Exhaustion?* When she opened her eyes again, she saw Brenna sauntering away to the water cooler tucked against the wall of the soundstage. Deciding to extend the joking, Cassidy called, "So's yours." Brenna spun around and shook a finger at her while sipping from her paper cup, barely hiding a grin. Even though she wondered why Brenna had bantered with her in such a teasing way, Cassidy could not deny she was relaxed again by the time the director's voice reached them both.

"All right, last one of the day, folks."

Cassidy stepped out onto the gym set again, and he looked over at her. "Let's see how few takes we can do, hmm?"

She displayed a thumbs up and stood on her mark at the service line, stretching to loosen her body.

"Action!"

The stagehands used pulleys to open the doors, and Brenna swept inside, racket in hand.

Commander Jakes hesitated when she saw the room was already occupied. The blond head swiveled toward her. When the azure eyes fell on her, Jakes straightened her uniform, a telltale "I'm not sure what I'm doing here" sign.

"Commander?" Chris Hanssen's voice was low, a little tired but clearly questioning. She straightened from the beginning of a solo game. Considering she might be in for another reprimand, Chris drew herself up into an "at attention" posture, tucking her hands behind her back.

"I didn't expect to find anyone here." Jakes swallowed.

"I'm working some of the stiffness out of my arm."

That drew Jakes' attention to the bandage on Hanssen's left arm. "Are you all right?"

"Yeah. The doctor patched me up."

The women were silent, looking at anything other than each other. Something occurred to Susan and she finally, reluctantly looked at Chris, "Did Lieutenant Raycreek deliver my decision?"

"I am relieved of duty for one month."

"Do you understand why? You could've been killed, Lieutenant, many of the non-coms as well. We cannot reverse the orders once we're on the ground. I thought you understood that. When I said no, I meant it."

"What if his story had been true?" Hanssen bristled. "It would be an innocent man that is now dead. We still don't really know. We'll never really know."

"You've got time on your hands. Read his file again, Chris. He lied to you."

"So he lied to me. Don't tell me you haven't believed a lie once or twice," Hanssen shot back.

"You don't know anything about my service record." Jakes stepped forward and glared hard at the woman whose gaze was just a bit higher than hers. "When you're in command, you can give the orders. In the meantime, I'm in charge here."

"You don't give a damn about the fact that a man died."

Jakes snatched the ball from Chris' fingers, and Chris flinched. "Everyone's life matters to me." Catching her breath and trying to diffuse her frustration with the younger officer, she repeated softly, "Every life." There was a quality of regret.

Chris' body language softened slightly, but she still barked, "Second thoughts, Commander?"

"Cut." The director interposed himself loudly, drawing both women's attention. "Too angry. More contrite. Remember you're inviting a connection here."

Cassidy nodded. "Sorry."

Brenna's hand slipped over hers with a squeeze. "Where from?" she asked Mike, stepping back from her mark.

"Let's start at the service line. Start your marks there."

"Okay." Brenna took several steps back while Cassidy adjusted her position as well. She looked over Cassidy's form and, catching blue eyes on her, she smiled briefly. "I'm ready whenever you are."

Cassidy nodded and turned away. Mike stepped off the stage and slipped back behind the number one camera. "Action!"

"You don't know anything about my service record." Jakes stepped forward and glared hard at the woman whose gaze was just a bit higher than hers. "When you're in command, you can give the orders. In the meantime, you follow orders."

"You don't give a damn about the fact that a man died."

Jakes snatched the ball from Chris' fingers, and Chris flinched. "Everyone's life matters to me." Catching her breath and trying to diffuse her frustration with the younger officer, she repeated softly, "Every life." There was a quality of regret.

Chris' body language softened slightly, and her tone was conciliatory. "Second thoughts, Commander?"

Jakes' voice also softened. "I know you won't believe this, but I was almost willing to give Baxley that chance." She came back alongside Chris. "Until he took you hostage." She exhaled.

The two women stood side by side for a long moment, each counting two beats. Cassidy jumped when Brenna's hand landed on her shoulder. Their gazes met across that shoulder.

"I told Jeremy to shoot."

Cassidy's stomach quivered, and she could not look away from Brenna's very direct, very blue gaze. She could not remember her line and backed away from Brenna abruptly.

"Cut!"

Mike's voice swiveled her head around sharply; Brenna's hand squeezed her shoulder, then dropped and skimmed along her spine.

"Bren, too soon. Cass, why so jumpy?"

Brenna shook her head. "It's my fault. You're right, it was too early." Cassidy looked to her questioningly.

The director seemed uninterested in placing blame. "Whatever." Mike turned away, stepping back down. "Let's just do it again. From 'Second thoughts'. And, action!"

Chris' body language softened slightly, and her tone was conciliatory. "Second thoughts, Commander?"

Jakes' voice also softened. "I know you won't believe this, but I was almost willing to give Baxley that chance." She came back alongside Chris. "Until he took you hostage." She exhaled. "I told Jeremy to shoot."

"There wasn't any other way?" Chris sounded confused.

Jakes shook her head. "It was up to Baxley to trust you, or us, to get him that hearing. If he had...maybe we wouldn't be here right now." She lifted her hand to the woman's shoulder. After a moment, her hand slid away. Hanssen looked up toward the blank gym wall as Jakes walked out.

Cassidy finally took a breath when she heard the doors slide open and then shut again. She poised herself and studied the ball for a long moment before serving it against the wall with a resounding thud.

"Cut! And print!" Cass watched Mike turn to the crew and wave his hands. When she turned back to talk to Brenna, the other woman had already disappeared. Taking a steadying breath, she walked gingerly on aching legs to her trailer to clean up.

Brenna stepped from her trailer, still wiping a towel over her chin and cheeks, removing the last remnants of the thick stage makeup. "God, I need a shower," she groaned. As was typical, she could feel the ache in her legs and back, not to mention her feet, now that being "on" had been turned off for the day. Stopping on the pavement, she rubbed the back of her calf through the loose tan cotton pants. Relief spread into her sneaker-covered foot, and she lifted the other to rub at her ankle.

"Looks like you need your slippers back."

Cassidy walked up stiffly, obviously still aching from the shoot as well. Brenna noted the loose pale green cardigan over a white cotton tee shirt and jeans and the white cross-trainers she held in her left hand. Looking down at the woman's feet, she chuckled. "Seems you're wearing them."

The taller actress lifted a foot and balanced, removed one slipper, and held it out. "A compromise," she proposed. "You get one. I get one."

Brenna shook her head and waved it off. "I'm glad you've enjoyed them. What's on tap for your weekend?"

"Time with Ryan. I have tickets to the A's game tomorrow."

"He likes baseball?"

Cassidy put the absurd slipper back on her foot and nodded. "Loves it."

"Maybe you can bring Ryan to one of Thomas' high school games." That earned Brenna a smile.

"Sounds nice. What about you?"

"Me? I'm headed out tomorrow for Mount Clemens."

"Family?"

"My husband, Kevin," Brenna confirmed, "is attending a charity fundraiser."

"Are you going to appear as the Commander?"

"No. It's hard enough..." She shook her head. "Just me." The blonde nodded. Brenna sensed they shared an acute understanding about the line drawn between family and screen — and about how it sometimes just didn't seem to separate the two worlds enough.

Before she could respond, they were distracted by a car peeling across the lot. A brown LTD jerked to a halt, and the tinted passenger window rolled down. "Cass?"

Recognizing the voice of Cameron Palassis, one of the show's writers, from inside the shadowed recess, Brenna nodded, looking from Cassidy to her boyfriend. "Hello, Cameron."

Leaning out, he offered her a nod. "Brenna." He tilted his head again toward the blonde. "Are we going out tonight?"

"Cameron, I said..." Apparently sensing a conversation coming that she should not overhear, Brenna started to retreat. "Wait," Cassidy called after her. "Please?"

Brenna was pinned in place by blue eyes and nodded tightly, remaining still. She watched the younger woman step off the curb and lean into the car window. Unintentionally, Brenna overheard the tense exchange.

"Cam, I'm tired. I haven't spent time with Ryan all week. Not tonight."

"I could come by...We'll...put him to bed and go out?"

"No." Cassidy stepped back onto the curb. "I'll call you tomorrow."

Brenna saw Cameron's baffled expression, but as he drove away she watched Cassidy instead. The woman's posture was hunched, but she quickly recovered with a shrug of her shoulders before turning back to face Brenna.

"I'm sorry."

Brenna shook her head. "It's not my business."

"I just..." Cassidy fell silent again. "I don't know. Maybe I am too tired." She brushed her long fingers through her loose, straight locks and rubbed the back of her neck.

Worried that the other woman might fall asleep at the wheel or something equally dangerous, Brenna asked, "Would you like to get a coffee before heading home?"

"No." Cassidy shook her head. "I'll be fine. Go on. Have a good weekend."

Brenna nodded. "All right." Stymied as to how, or if, to help further, she turned and walked into the parking lot. She unlocked the door to her SUV and opened it, leaning on the frame for a moment, watching as Cassidy crossed the dark empty lot and got into her blue compact. Once behind her own wheel, Brenna sat a few minutes quietly pondering her day before turning the ignition over and driving the forty-five minutes along L.A.'s dark surface roads toward home.

Chapter 4

The woman half-asleep on the couch stirred as Cassidy stepped inside her door. "Cass?" She rubbed the head of the sleepy Dalmatian next to her feet.

"Yeah, it's me, Gwen." Cassidy took off her sweater, hung it over a hanger, and tucked it back into the small closet by the door. "Sorry to be so late. We lost a lot of time with reshoots today."

"Hey, no problem. Ryan's a great kid. I fed him with mine and then brought him over here, leaving Lou to watch ours. He's bathed and been in bed since eight-thirty."

Sitting next to Gwen on the couch, Cassidy looked at the clock over the mantle and winced. It was after ten o'clock. *Where did the time go?* She leaned back and pressed the heels of her palms against her eyes.

Gwen noticed her footwear. "What on earth have you got on your feet?"

"Huh?" Cassidy sat up and looked down, unfocused, and then she blinked, bringing the furry brown blots into focus. "Oh, yeah. Slippers. I was on my feet in every scene. I didn't feel like even wearing sneakers after I finished today."

"Since when do you own a pair of slippers sporting a moose head?"

Rubbing her eyes tiredly, Cassidy said, "They're not mine. Brenna gave them to me."

"No kidding? Is that finally smoothed over?"

"I guess so. You remember she was here at Ryan's party last Saturday." Cassidy slipped off one of the Bullwinkles, curled her foot under herself, and studied the wide-eyed simpleton face. "We're getting a chance to talk more between takes since we aren't up to our necks in stunt shoots. We've been rehearsing together, too. There was this scene we did—"

Interrupting with a yawn, Gwen patted Cassidy's knee and stood up. "Well, that's as much as I've heard you talk about work right after you come home. Though it's incredibly fascinating, I've gotta go."

"Thanks again." Cassidy reclined against the arm of the couch as she watched her friend leave. Once the door was closed, she sighed and propped her chin on a fist. Her body began to relax into the cushions, and she reluctantly pushed off. *I better check on Ryan. Then,* she promised her muscles, *bed will follow.*

Rubbing Ranger's head as the Dalmatian walked alongside, Cassidy went to her son's bedroom and nudged the door wider. The night light next to his bed illuminated his face. Leaving the dog in the hall, she crossed to the bed and crouched, brushing away the long bangs from Ryan's forehead.

"You need a haircut, buddy," she whispered with a smile before kissing his cheek. "Maybe tomorrow before the game, hmm?" She adjusted the stuffed animal in his haphazard grip and then backed away, firmly closing the door.

Cassidy made a brief stop in the bathroom, changing out of her clothes into a roomy oversized tee emblazoned with the St. Louis Arch, a present from the city's mayor when she went back to her hometown to be the marshal of the Independence Day parade. The gold-painted, six-inch-long stainless steel Key to the City was tucked under her winter sweaters in a bottom dresser drawer. She had been flattered to be honored by the city, but she wondered why, when she had been a National Merit Scholar as a senior in high school, that accomplishment had not been worthy of the same attention.

She flossed and brushed her teeth, then worked a densely bristled brush through her hair. Though she had removed her stage makeup at work, Cassidy gently washed her face again and applied moisturizer. In her bedroom, she pulled down the covers and crawled between the sheets. Consciously relaxing her back, she stretched up over her head and turned on the radio. Rachmaninoff played as she drifted to sleep.

"Hey, Mom." Thomas Lanigan, Brenna's seventeen-year-old son, looked up from the couch as his mother stepped inside. He crunched a few chips and took a sip from the soda perched on the side table. "How'd it go?"

"Pretty good. Is James still up?"

"Yeah, playing Playstation in the game room."

She heard a guttural yell and glanced at the television in front of him. "Off." He gave her a sheepish look as he tapped the remote sitting next to him. The offensive wrestling program vanished. "Please tell me you've eaten dinner." She leaned over the side of the couch and snatched up a chip with a grin. "It's been a long week. I won't find just chips and soda in those veins, will I?"

"Nope. We had the leftover penne from Tuesday. James scarfed the leftover casserole from Wednesday night."

"Anything left in the fridge for me?" She walked into the kitchen, and Thomas followed, leaning on the counter as she ducked her head inside the refrigerator. "Oh hey, not crazy about my quiche?" She pulled out the aluminum pie pan filled with half a quiche.

Thomas shook his head. "Figured you'd prefer it."

"You're right. It's light enough for this late." She cut herself a slice of the vegetable and cheese dish and took the refrigerator chill off with a few seconds in the microwave. Grabbing a fork, she returned to the living room, Thomas tagging behind. She kissed his cheek as he sat on the couch next to her.

James stepped in from the bedroom wing. "Glad you're home, Mom." He patted her shoulders as he leaned over and kissed her cheek. "Can I go over to Marcie's?"

Brenna laughed. "You've got to be kidding. It's after ten. We've got a plane at eight."

James frowned but nodded. "Well then, I guess I'll hit the sack. See you in the morning."

Watching Thomas flip on the television again, she called over her shoulder to James, "No telephone, either."

Her younger son groaned but called back wanly, "Yes, Mom."

"Good." She kicked off her shoes and tucked her feet under her on the couch, nibbling on her quiche. "Video games, huh?"

Thomas lifted his shoulders and looked away. "He's really nuts over her."

She reached over and rubbed her knuckles over the strong line of his neck. "How are you and Cheryl doing?"

"Fine. There's a dance I'm taking her to at school next weekend."

"I've got a convention appearance."

Thomas frowned. "Can't you just leave us here?"

"Alone?"

"Yeah. C'mon, Mom. We're old enough to watch ourselves for a weekend."

She pursed her lips, chewing her quiche while she considered. "I'll think about it."

"Thanks." She ruffled his hair as he shut off the TV and sprang up from the couch. "I'll get some sleep now."

Brenna finished her dinner quickly. Returning to the kitchen, she cleared the dishes from the sink into the dishwasher and set it to run. Then she ducked into her bedroom and the master bathroom, scrubbed her face, and brushed her teeth.

Changed into a slip gown, the slim straps faintly caressing her shoulders, Brenna curled up under the covers, adjusted pillows behind her back as a support, and flipped on the television. She paused with a finger over the channel-up button as she recognized the set on the screen. She laughed when she recognized it as an episode of a sitcom she had guest-starred on several years earlier. Her character swept into the scene, startling the principals out of a heated kiss. Brenna critically observed that she might have been smirking a little more than required. She sighed. More than twenty years in acting, and she was still uncomfortable and self-critical. She wondered if she would ever get over watching herself. Mercifully it was the last scene, just before the news.

The news report was depressing, and she was about to switch off the set when the sports preview mentioned the Oakland A's baseball game. She waited through the evaluation of the team's chances and hoped, for Cassidy and Ryan's sake, that the game would be enjoyable. Turning off the set, Brenna crossed her arms over the top of the covers and studied the ceiling, replaying the week in her head.

You should have held those slippers for her birthday. Yeah, but she looked so miserable. Okay, but now you're going to have to come up with another present.

She wondered how Cassidy's son had liked his gift, then decided wryly that she must be turning sentimental. Maybe it was the fact that *Time Trails* was supposed to end in April. It was the longest running set she had worked continuously since *Lantry Place*, the soap opera where she had started her career at age eighteen.

She closed her eyes and rolled onto her side, curling around a pillow. Parades of co-stars followed her into sleep.

Phhhfffftt. Phhhhffffftt. Looking around, disoriented for a moment, Cassidy finally reached for the cell phone vibrating on her belt. Beside her, as she flipped open the phone, Ryan jumped up excitedly as the batter stepped up to the plate, yelling, "Home run! Home run!"

Patting his back, she spoke into the phone. "Hello?"

"Cass?"

When the batter connected, the shouts around her drowned out anything further that was said. She glanced toward the field and saw the runner skidding safely into first base. As the cheering dwindled, she heard, "Where the hell are you?"

Cameron, she identified. "At a baseball game," she explained patiently in the break in the noise.

"I thought we were going out."

"Tonight." She tucked the phone against her ear more tightly. "Cam, this is my time with Ryan."

"Then we won't go out. Or we'll take him with us. Where would he like to go? I haven't seen you in nearly two weeks, Cass. I miss you."

"You see me every day on the lot."

"C'mon, Cass. I mean *see* you."

She placed her hand over the phone and glanced toward Ryan, who was oblivious, bouncing excitedly and wildly cheering the game action. "All right. After the game, I'll talk to Gwen and see if she can watch him for a couple of hours. Movie?"

"Dancing," he countered.

"I've been on my feet all week." She sighed. They constantly had the same argument, and she was tired of it.

"Just as a prelude. Then we can go back to my place...take a dip in the Jacuzzi?"

Cassidy pondered the invitation and brushed her fingers over her son's freshly cut mop of hair. She relented. "All right."

"Great. I'll pick you up at seven?"

"Okay. See you then." Before he could add anything, she flipped the phone closed and slowly replaced it in her belt pouch, snapping the cover shut.

"Mommy?"

She looked down to see her son looking up. "Mmm hmm?"

"Can I have a cotton candy?"

Following his finger-pointing, Cassidy spotted the pink and blue swirls of spun sugar parading toward them up the near aisle. Feeling bad that she was going to leave him alone for another evening, she nodded. "Sure." She stood and called out, "Over here," to get the hawker's attention. He smiled, and she waved a bill, flashing a single finger. He nodded back, and soon a blue swirl of cotton candy was being passed along the row toward her.

She had not settled to the bench before Ryan was leaping on her, giggling and hugging. "Thank you!" Encouraging him to sit, she smiled and kissed his head as he tore off a large chunk and stuffed it into his mouth, instantly staining his lips and tongue blue.

"I love you, Ryan." With another brush of her hand over his head and a pat on his shoulder, Cassidy turned back to the game.

The trio from California stepped out of the flow of humanity off the gangway and fell into a cluster with two teenaged girls and a well-dressed older man in a dark blue sport coat, matching trousers, white shirt, and tie. Brenna threw him a playful smile and then turned to the girls. "So, how's life?"

From behind, her husband of fourteen months, Kevin, swept her up in a hug, kissing her cheek. "Ignoring me already?" He chuckled. She turned in his embrace and kissed his cheek. "That's better."

"Good to see you again," said Eleanor, at fifteen the elder of the two brunettes.

"You, too." She reached out and grasped the girls' hands. "So, what's on the agenda?" She looked from father to daughters.

"You two can bum." Marie pushed at her father's arm. "We're taking Thomas and James to Toppers."

The park name sounded familiar, but Brenna had not been there since childhood. "Is that the amusement park on the north side?"

"Yeah. You've been?"

"A few times." She passed her boys each a twenty. "Have fun. Be careful on the transit."

"We'll be fine, Mom."

"Meet back at the house at eight."

"Aren't you two going out tonight?" Thomas asked.

Kevin placed a hand on Brenna's shoulder. "Charity dinner and auction, over near the college."

"Well, we'll see you tomorrow, then," Eleanor said cheekily, earning herself a laugh and a kiss on the cheek from Brenna.

The two adults accepted the bags and watched the kids leave, as only teens can — helter-skelter, half-chasing one another and leaping for the escalators and the exit. "So," she said at last, "to the home front?"

"Looking to put your feet up already? I thought we'd check out the new artist showing at the Guggenheim Gallery."

Brenna pursed her lips and then shrugged. "Can we at least get a good Irish before we set out?"

Offering his elbow, he waited for her small hand to tuck into the crook, then patted it. "I think I know just the spot."

She smiled winsomely. "I was hoping you'd say that."

Twenty minutes later, ensconced in a car headed to downtown Mount Clemens, Brenna leaned on the open window and rested her temple in her palm.

"It's good to see you," he said. His right hand found her left on the side of her seat. She looked over to see him focusing on the road. "Missed you."

"What's been happening?"

"Ellie broke up with Kyle, I think. I couldn't get more than two words out of her about it, though."

"Just give it time," she suggested. "She looked in good spirits. Maybe she's adjusting."

"Yeah, but you can talk to them."

She patted his arm and laughed. "Just get in touch with your feminine side."

Kevin parked behind a small pub painted green and dubbed "Biscuit and Jug". Brenna grinned widely. "I don't think you've brought me here before."

He chuckled. "There's a pub in Mount Clemens you haven't been to?"

"At least with you, farmer's boy," she shot back with a saucy smile.

"Ah, really, Brenna m'dear, ye wound me." He pantomimed an arrow shot to the heart and then tucked her against his side and entered the pub.

She liked the smells immediately, detecting both hops and cue chalk. "A finger of the Irish," she said to the bartender, who sported a scruffy face of whiskers. "On ice."

"Two," Kevin said when the bartender's eye turned to him settling onto the neighboring barstool.

When they received their drinks, she clinked her liquor glass against Kevin's. "To time off."

"Time off," he echoed.

She rotated around, scanning the room, locating the dartboard and the pool table nestled in the back corner. "Indulge me?" she asked over her shoulder.

"You'll whip me."

"Saying I haven't already? Come on. Get out of that stuffy jacket and give me a game."

"Isn't that...?"

The sharply whispered phrase caught her attention.

"Nah, it couldn't be. This is Mount Clemens."

"I heard she's married to some fellow here. You think that's him?"

"She wouldn't go for him. Must be some bigwig giving her the city keys or something."

Brenna suppressed a wince on Kevin's behalf and turned around. The speakers, a couple of college-age young men, stood before her.

"Hey..."

"Hello," she offered back politely.

"You're Commander Su...I mean, Brenna Lanigan, aren't you?"

It was useless to deny it. "Yes."

"Oh, man. Yes! The guys will never believe this!" The dusky blond, who reminded Brenna a lot of Sean Durham, snatched a napkin off their table and dug in his pocket for a pen. "Would you sign this?"

She signed quickly and passed it back.

"So, is that guy your husband?"

"Yes," she said. "Kevin?" She looked back, and finally Kevin stepped forward, looking the younger men up and down.

"Hello," he said slowly, offering a hand. One took it. "Kevin Shea, running for councilman," her husband said.

"Ah, geez." The young man pulled his hand away fast. "Politics? So geek, man." Brenna watched his expression change when he looked back to her. "Well...nice to meet you," he said, nudging his buddy past them to the door.

When they were alone again, Kevin looked at her. "Now, did I just throw a damper on that or what?"

"Don't mind them," she said, though she was disturbed by their reaction. "Come on. Table's open. Let's play one game, and then we'll go."

"All right."

Chapter 5

"Cameron! Cassidy!"

Turning in Cameron's embrace, Cassidy spotted a bearded male waving his sport cap from a table just beyond the edge of the busy dance floor. Hanging on the man's arm was a giggling brunette, also waving. "It's Angel and Lynn." Angel and Lynnette Corteñas were a couple she and Cameron frequently paired up with for dates on the town.

Cameron brushed his hand down her back as she stepped away from him. "We only just got here," he said with a frown, scanning the room.

She nodded. The blues beat of the music was pleasant, but she preferred to just sit down and have an evening of good conversation rather than dancing. "We haven't seen them in weeks, though."

"He lost his job out at Viacom two weeks ago."

"Has he found anything new yet?" she asked, leading him in the general direction of the Corteñas. When Cameron shrugged, Cassidy said, "Then we definitely have to spend some time with them." She spun away from him and moved quickly up the two steps to the table where Lynn was standing to greet them.

"Cass!"

"Good to see you." Cassidy smiled, and the two women shared an embrace. Turning, she accepted a warm hug from Angel. "Angel." She kissed his cheek with a grin.

Cameron stepped up next to her and clasped both of Lynn's hands in his own. "So, what brings you two out tonight?"

"A little change of pace from the house," Lynn said, glancing significantly toward Angel. Cassidy realized that meant that he had yet to find work. "We've been renovating," the brunette said.

"Renovating? Now?"

Angel nodded, sitting down as he gestured for Cassidy and Cameron to join them. "A few adjustments were necessary."

"Tightening the belt already?" Cameron asked. "I heard Viacom's severance packages were pretty good."

"Not that...well, not just that," he corrected. "It's...Lynn's pregnant."

Cassidy watched the look of anxiety and pleasure fill the expectant father's face. She caught Lynn's nod and wan smile. Reassuringly, Cassidy reached across the table and grasped her friend's hand. "That's wonderful." Lynn looked up, and Cassidy squeezed her friend's hand again. When Lynn blushed, Cassidy leaned close and whispered, "It really is. If you need something, call."

The brunette nodded before turning back to her drink — a sparkling cider. "Angel's got a lead at Tri-Star."

"Something will come up." Cameron looked away and waved at a waiter. "Molson Ice," he requested. The waiter nodded. "Thanks." He turned back. "Movement is the nature of the business. No worries."

Sipping at her ice water, Cassidy thought about her own situation. She wondered where she would be in a year when *Time Trails* was finished. Musing her way through the regular cast, she wondered where everyone else would go as well.

"Cass?"

She looked up to find all three of her tablemates studying her. Cameron had spoken.

"Just listening to the music," she said, noting the tune currently filling the club.

"Want to get back out there and dance?" Cameron asked.

She shook her head, running a finger in the top of her water. "It's late. I'd like..."

While she spoke, Cameron had turned around and straightened, wrapping his fingers around the back of her chair. "Oh, hey, someone I was hoping to see. Cass, come on." He grasped her arm and stood, pulling her up with him. "Hey, Angel, buck up, buddy. Lynn, it's great about the baby. Call sometime."

"Cameron," Cassidy said as they stepped away, "you didn't have to be so abrupt. Who'd you see?"

"Griffin Torend. Come on." He waved at someone as they moved through the throng on the dance floor. "Hey, Griff!"

"Cam!" Griffin Torend was forty-something, wearing clothes meant for a much younger and trimmer man. His gray khakis were tight around his waist, and the cotton blend shirt with breast pockets stretched tightly around his torso. They stopped next to him. "So this is your girl, eh? Nice. Mmm. Nice to meet you." He offered a hand.

She nodded. "Hello."

Cameron slid his arm around her waist and patted her hip. "Cassidy Hyland, my gem on *Time Trails*. Cass, this is Griffin Torend, casting agent for dozens of star-tups."

"Right now I'm looking into the cast for the next series," Torend said, "and a few more conventional projects for J-TV."

Wanting to return to Angel and Lynn rather than spend time talking business, Cassidy tried to bow out of the meeting graciously. "Well—"

"Got anything new lined up yet?" Griffin asked, cutting her off.

Despite having been thinking about that very thing, Cassidy stepped back. She had a gut feeling she did not want to discuss her future with this man. "I'm too busy doing my best in my current role."

"Business mind, my dear."

Cassidy felt her molars compress together in the back of her mouth. *God, I hate people treating me as though I have "dumb blonde — handle with care" stamped on my forehead.* She quickly doused the anger boiling up inside her.

"Thank you. I already have an agent." She disengaged from Cameron's elbow and excused herself. "I'll be right back." Though Cameron frowned at her, she shook her head and headed for the restroom corridor, tired and feeling a distinct itch from being around Torend.

With a sigh, she sank onto the small couch in the outer lounge of the ladies' restroom. *Come on, Cass. Cam obviously thought you'd appreciate a contact.* She had never expected to encounter someone who actually made her jaw hurt from restraint. She rubbed the sore muscles in her cheeks and dropped her head into her palms. "I haven't hidden out in a restroom since I started on *Time Trails*," she lamented softly.

Right after her introduction in the series, she abhorred going out because of the mob scenes her appearance generated. However, she had done it, knowing the consequences if she did not. Suddenly lonely, all Cassidy wanted to do was curl up under a blanket with Ryan and a good book. She stood up, turning directly into a pair of young women who were leaving the restroom. "Excuse me."

"Oh my God!" one of the two women squealed, and Cassidy swallowed, freezing in place. On Cassidy's left, hands wrapped around her upper arm in a vise-like grip; a blonde whose hair was liberally streaked purple went wide-eyed. Reflexively, Cassidy grabbed for her slender shoulders as her brown eyes rolled back in a faint.

The girl's friend hovered as Cassidy carefully moved the limp woman to the couch. "You're so cool. So normal," she gushed.

Cassidy didn't make any acknowledgment, concentrating instead on assuring herself that the fainter had regained her senses. Deciding to forestall another attack, she apologized. "I should have been looking where I was going. Are you all right?" The woman — whom Cassidy judged to be in senior high or college — nodded.

"Yeah. Hey, look, I'm sorry. Karen and I just moved into the neighborhood to go to school. I didn't expect...*You!* You're probably my favorite person on TV, y'know?"

Cassidy pulled her wrists from the woman's urgent grip and swallowed again. "Really?" She forced her tone to sound interested.

"Oh yeah. I just loved the poignancy of the ending scene between you and Commander Jakes in *Conspiracy of One!*"

Cassidy blinked. That episode must have aired just recently, she realized, probably in reruns. It had been her first episode, a two-parter, when she had not yet known that the *Time Trails* assignment was going to pan into a full-time part. Her character, Chris Hanssen, had lost everyone in her air squadron in a massive dogfight. Headquarters had ordered her reassigned to Jakes' unit. She had been a fighter and now was out of her depth, cast among what was supposedly a group of desk jockeys. But when she discovered they were really a group of Time Marshals, she had wanted to go back in time to stop the deaths of her squadron mates. Jakes had firmly stood in the way. Their first moments on screen together were nothing but fighting.

Ultimately, at the memorial service at the end of the two-parter, Jakes had looked as devastated as Hanssen. Hanssen, the character, had not yet learned the reason for that, though Cassidy knew it had to do with Jakes having been a peer of the air squad's commander. The toe-to-toe between Jakes and Hanssen, both hurting and angry, had bristled. They hissed and circled like a snake tangling with a mongoose. The process had both energized and unnerved Cassidy for hours on end.

The women in the restroom grinned at her, bringing her back to the present. "You are so cool."

"So, you ever kissed her? Bet she's hot."

"Kissed?"

"Yeah. You mean that isn't where all that tension is going?"

Cassidy blinked. "No."

"Damn waste then. Lots of rumors have Sue and Chris in liplocks after hours."

Taken by surprise, Cassidy sat down on the couch. "Well, it's not in the script, as far as I know."

"Oh, okay. Even if it were, you probably couldn't tell us. Gotcha." Karen fished around in her small handbag for a moment, coming up with a pen and a scrap of paper. "Would you sign this?"

Frowning at the pad, Cassidy hesitated. Her policy was to not sign autographs during her off-time. However, she needed to let the women go, realizing she could not ask any questions about their assumptions or she'd seem to be fishing. Which she would be, but she wouldn't want to seem to be naïve about her own character. She took the paper and qualified her actions even as she signed, "I don't usually do this."

"Gotcha." Karen took back the pen and paper and studied it. "'Thanks for the chat. Cassidy Hyland. Damn, this is so cool!" The two women, deep in hushed conversation, quickly left the restroom.

A few minutes later, Cassidy returned to the dance floor. She found Cameron and tapped his shoulder. "Time to go," she said firmly, loud enough to bring his head around. "It's late."

Cameron nodded. "I'm done here." He had apparently sat down for a deeper conversation with Torend. Reaching across the table, he shook the man's beefy hand and stood. "I'll call you next week, Griff."

"Right. Nice to meet you, kid."

She nodded politely but turned away quickly and followed Cameron to the exit. Stepping into the brisk night air, she rubbed her arms to warm up. Out at the car, he unlocked her door, pulling it open for her. His hand brushed her arm, but she did not move. "Something wrong?" he asked, when she brushed the hand away.

"I want to go home, Cam."

"Sure. Some music on the couch..."

Feeling disquieted and restless for no reason she could pinpoint, she shook her head. "No. Take me home. My home."

"I thought you didn't like to do anything in the house with Ryan?"

She swallowed. "I don't."

He dropped his gaze away from her, but when he looked up she could see he had come to a decision. "Fine. Go on. Get in."

He ducked into the driver's seat, and she breathed out slowly. She had never before felt the need to cut a date short. She sighed. Maybe she was PMSing or something.

"...welcome to Mister Kevin Shea!"

Applause filled the gymnasium of the brand new Milburn County Boys and Girls Club. For the dedication celebration, the sports space had been set up as a dining hall. Brenna looked up as Kevin's hand slipped over her bare shoulder as he passed behind her to the podium. While he adjusted the microphone, his brown eyes searched hers out, and she offered an encouraging smile. He turned back to the crowd and waved at a few people in the front tables, as he waited for quiet. Finally the last few handclaps died away.

He grinned at the gathering. "Ladies and gentlemen, eighteen months ago a group of students from Tillek College came to my office and told me stories of collecting children after school and trying to find them a safe place to play and study. They had a proposal, and my business agreed to sponsor the project. But, eh...I just got the building permits; *they* got the place built." He pointed to a packed table near the front and gestured for them to stand.

The applause resumed as the young adults rose slowly to their feet, the Greek letters proclaiming their sororities and fraternities on the front of shirts emblazoned with the words "Tillek College Greek Council". Some looked unsure, and Brenna's heart went out to them. She too liked public service work, but moments in the spotlight unnerved her, as it was doing to them right now. The thought made her smile wistfully as she thought how she had deliberately stepped on stage time and time again. Despite the butterflies. Her reverie was interrupted by the call of her name.

"...Brenna Lanigan." Kevin had continued his remarks and somehow worked his way around to introducing her. She started to rise to acknowledge him when he turned to the audience and added, "You might know her better as Susan Jakes, the commander in *Time Trails!*"

The college students stood and howled, clapping and stomping loudly. Only by the grace of God, she thought, was she able to keep the mortification from her face. She painted on a thin-lipped smile before quickly sitting again. She grasped her napkin and pinched it between her hands and then held it over her mouth. When Kevin moved behind her, she remained seated, despite his hand on her back, the signal to rise again. She dropped her head and barely shook it.

"Bren?" he whispered, leaning over and pressing a hand to each shoulder, before kissing her left cheek.

She carefully held her hands together on the tabletop, wishing she could defuse her temper but knowing she did not have that luxury while in public. Finally the applause died away and the emcee stepped back up as Kevin returned to his seat.

"Thank you, everyone, for joining us for this dinner. Now, if you've stuffed yourselves enough," a low trickle of laughter started at the college students' table, "it's time to pick up the cards for the auction. We've got it built, but now we've got a mortgage to pay," he added.

As the auction items were dragged out, Brenna stood up from the table. Stepping backward, she turned into her husband directly behind her. Looking up at Kevin's sport-jacketed frame, she realized she was glaring only when he ducked his head to the side.

"What's that for?" he asked.

"When can we go?" she said by way of answer, catching a curious look from a young man walking toward them and schooling her features carefully.

"It's a chance for us to socialize. Forget about the week. Spend a little time with friends."

"Friends of whom?" she asked grimly. She turned away from him as the young man from Sigma Chi stopped about four feet away. "Hello," she greeted, showing her teeth with a brief smile.

"Hello, Ms. Lanigan." He looked over his shoulder, apparently seeking encouragement from his friends. She glanced past him and watched several of the students nod briskly and offer nudging gestures. She tracked to his eyes as he turned back to her, and she waited patiently for the request she could sense coming. "I...well, my friends and I would like to say thank you for coming. Many of us are avid fans of your show."

He offered a sheepish grin; she took a deep breath and refreshed her smile. Kevin remained at her back, and with that acute awareness she had developed on stage, she realized he was focused on her young admirer even more than she was. She reached out and put a hand on the young man's arm. "What's your name?"

"Me? I..." He stumbled over his own tongue, and Brenna would have laughed if she were not so upset. "Mike...I mean, Michael Turncot." He let out a nervous laugh as she took his hand and shook it. "I'm with the Greek Council."

She nodded. "I can see that, Mike." *Time to put on a good show, Brenna.* "You did a lot of work here. Why don't you introduce me?" she offered, loud enough to draw the attention of the other young adults. "Congratulations."

"Thank you." A young woman dusted her hands on her Delta Delta Delta shirt tail, before offering it. "With all the work you do, this must seem like such a small project."

"Small projects make the biggest differences, I've found," Brenna said sincerely.

Kevin remained close by, but her irritation ebbed as she focused on the volunteers. They relaxed around her when it was clear she admired them in return. She walked through the facility with them, talking about the work itself, the setbacks, and the time they thought they had lost their grant. She commiserated about the time an entire corner of the infant structure had collapsed under an unexpected snowfall the previous November.

"Thank goodness no one was hurt," she exclaimed. "Really, what you've accomplished is remarkable."

"Your husband had a lot to do with our success. He donated the supplies and kept up with the permits," someone said. "Kept telling us the project was important enough to keep going."

"He's right. So, tell me more about the programs you're going to run here."

The students answered all at once, and Brenna heard a cacophony of responses. "After-school studying and activities for school age children. Athletic clubs. Basketball, soccer in the field out back, and a day camp program in the summers."

"How are admissions handled?" she asked.

"Parents are referred by the local public aid office. We've already got forty-five children in the borrowed office space near the sports center at the college."

Someone offered her a drink, and Brenna took it with a nod of appreciation. Sipping briefly, she identified it as clear soda. "I'm really impressed. I'll keep an eye on your progress. If you'll excuse me, though, I should find my husband." She brushed a hand through the fall of her hair against her shoulders and stepped backward.

Mike, who had brought her into the small group, led her out, and up to Kevin, who was chatting with a slim man in pinstripe pants and a double-breasted, blue-black vest smoothed over a crisp, white cotton shirt. The gentleman nodded past Kevin, acknowledging Brenna's arrival.

Kevin turned and smiled, holding out a hand. She put hers into it and allowed herself to be drawn forward and introduced. "This is my wife, Brenna Lanigan. Bren, this is Senator Josiah Birmingham, chairman of Michigan's Democratic Party."

"Senator Birmingham." She held out her hand, and the senator bent over it and squeezed lightly. "A pleasure."

"My pleasure," he said. "And who's this?"

She introduced her young escort with a genuine smile. "Mike Turncot, Tillek Greek Council president."

"Senator." Mike turned to Kevin, who smiled. "Mr. Shea, the council would like to invite you to speak at our Pan-Political Rally on the twenty-fourth. Would you consider it?"

Kevin smiled. Brenna could tell he was quite pleased with the invitation, though he sounded terribly formal when he shook Mike's hand and said, "I'd be delighted, young man."

Brenna felt a chill go through her as Kevin leaned forward, shaking Mike's hand again. "Very delighted."

"That's was some fun, right?"

Brenna sighed. "No, I was very uncomfortable."

"You seemed to be having a good time with the students. The senator thought you were perfect."

"Perfect? Was I being sized up for something? Kevin, this was supposed to be just a social outing, with a bit of charity benefit." She could feel her face growing hot with anger.

"It was."

As the car idled at a stop light, she looked at him. He looked straight ahead. She noticed his fingertips tapping on the steering wheel. "But that wasn't all. What is it?"

"The party money is being spread around. They've been talking to me."

With foreboding she asked, "About what?" Kevin didn't answer. "What did they want you to do with your *celebrity* wife?"

"It wasn't like that. They want me."

"But I'm a particularly sweet bonus? For what?"

Kevin turned into the driveway and shut off the engine. "I don't know yet." She narrowed her gaze at him. "I don't!" She pushed her way out of the car, entering the house quickly. Kevin followed in her wake. "Bren," he started.

She turned around a few steps away from James and Ellie rising from a checkerboard. "Good night, Kevin."

The children left their game. Brenna stepped into the hall bathroom, staring her own anger down in the mirror. Kevin was out of sight when she emerged again, and she heard the telltale noises that said he was in the bedroom. She settled on the couch, grabbing a magazine from the coffee table while waiting for him to return to the living room. When he did come out, it was to offer her a brief kiss and remind her to turn out the light when she came to bed.

"Kevin." Her voice stopped him in the corridor.

"Yes?"

She looked up at him as he paused in the doorway. "Please don't do that again."

"Darling, I didn't..."

"You did." She kept her voice even. "You have me, not a fictional character."

"Someone was bound to mention it. Consider it diffusing the tension."

"Whatever you might have thought, it made *me* tense, Kevin. I'm not going to be Susan Jakes forever. We've talked about this. I thought you understood."

He leaned against the wall, bracing his frame against that of the hallway. "Derek thought it would be a good idea."

Now it comes out, she thought with a sigh. "And you went along with it to get that invitation to the Pan-Political Rally?"

"That segment is important."

"I won't go with you to the rally," she said quietly.

"Your father is coming."

"He'll be all the support you need. You'll be fine."

"Are we?"

She fingered the magazine in her lap. "Yes," she said, not looking up at him.

He stepped close, put his big hand on her shoulder, and bent to kiss her cheek. She accepted it and pressed into it briefly before he pulled away. "Coming to bed?"

She rubbed her hand over his before it left her shoulder. "You go. I'll be in later."

Chapter 6

Greeted by Peter, the north entrance guard, Cassidy Hyland drove through the gate and pulled to a stop in a space near the far end of the Pinnacle cast lot. The sun was already breaking through the Los Angeles smog. She should have been there almost two hours earlier. As she pressed the remote lock on her key chain, she spun round and bolted for the support trailers where her makeup awaited.

The crunch of gravel under the tires of another vehicle turned her head as she hit the sidewalk with full-length strides. She was stunned to see Brenna Lanigan stepping out of a taxicab. She waited for the compact woman to reach the sidewalk. Jogging toward her trailer, Brenna did not look up until the last second before they collided. Cassidy grasped Brenna's arm to steady them both, letting go when Brenna's gaze darted to her face. "Are you all right?"

"Plane was late," Brenna mumbled. She started past Cassidy, then stopped and turned around. "You didn't come looking for me, did you?"

"No. I'm late, too," Cassidy explained. "I couldn't drag myself from bed this morning. Then Ryan didn't feel well, so I had to take him to the sick care arrangements I have."

"I hope he gets well soon," Brenna offered.

"Thanks." They strode toward the studio set together, almost perfectly in step. "How was Michigan?"

"Cold." Brenna shook her head as she pulled open the door. Cassidy grasped the side, gesturing for Brenna to enter first. "My flight was postponed because the overnight temp was twenty-eight with freezing rain."

"I'm sorry."

"You can't control the weather." Brenna shrugged. "I wanted coffee on the plane, but because of the delay, they weren't serving."

Cassidy watched her uneasily run her fingers through her hair, presumably fixing it. Though if she'd been asked, Cassidy would have said that even tired, Brenna looked good. She exhaled and felt her cheeks. They seemed too hot, probably with Ryan's fever.

"Did I hear someone asking for coffee?"

Cassidy turned to the approaching voice. "Morning, Cam."

Beside her, Brenna hesitated, then offered, "Cameron."

"You two are awfully late for your calls, aren't you?"

"I had a flight delay," Brenna responded. "And apparently Ryan is sick," she added, to Cassidy's surprise.

"Well, Sean's directing this one, as you know; he's been looking for you both for thirty minutes. The gang's all here."

"Thanks." Brenna turned away.

Cass began to follow her, when Cameron touched her arm. "Yes?" There was deliberate coolness in her voice.

Cameron had the grace to look sheepish, then his expression cleared. "Would you like to try doing something tonight?"

"No. I'm going to talk to Sean about going home early so I can take care of Ryan."

"Awful short notice."

"I'll talk to Sean about it," she repeated, turning away and feeling better for having asserted her parenting above other things. The image of Ryan crying and rubbing his runny nose and coughing through a sore throat that morning flashed through her mind. It made it easy to ignore Cameron's grumbling as he walked toward the executive offices.

"You're going home?"

She had forgotten Brenna's presence. Turning now to the other woman, she saw that Brenna had moved off a few feet but still waited. The unconsciously supportive gesture warmed her. She nodded. "Ryan is really sick."

"I'm sure Sean can rearrange things. We can just do our scenes later in the week."

Brenna's lips pursed together in a tight line, but then she smiled gently, again warming Cassidy with the sense that an understanding was passing between them. Cassidy rubbed her throat as she cleared it.

Brenna stepped closer. "Are you sure you're okay?" She held the door for Cassidy to enter the soundstage area first.

"Yeah, I'll be fine." Cassidy wiped her brow.

Brenna pulled her toward the coffee pot. "Here." Pouring two, she fixed hers with sweetener. When she held up the fixings, Cassidy said, "Cream only."

Coffees in hand, the two settled in chairs near the set. After a fortifying sip which soothed her throat, Cassidy asked, "Did you have a good time Saturday?" When Brenna did not immediately answer, Cassidy figured she was debating whether or not to share. "It didn't go as you had hoped?" she guessed,

"Forget it. How did baseball go?"

"Oakland lost."

"Was Ryan upset?"

"No. He was already blue by then," she replied. Brenna gave her a look of confusion. "He was stained blue from the cotton candy. He was so amused by that, he forgot about the game."

Brenna giggled, surprised by the mental imagery. *Oh, it feels so good to laugh.* "I remember when mine would do things like that."

"Are you two ready to get down to this week's episode?"

They both turned to see Sean Durham with a sneaker-clad foot propped on another nearby chair. He queried them both with a raised eyebrow. His green eyes crinkled over a suppressed smile as he crossed his hands over his bent knee and studied them.

"Sorry, Sean. We ran into each other running late," Brenna said easily.

They both glanced toward the soundstage. Behind Sean, Cassidy could see the other actors walking through a blocking sequence on the medical bay set.

"I wouldn't have even noticed you except Rachelle kept stopping her dialogue, wondering what you two could be discussing so intently."

Cassidy took the opportunity to make her request. "I need to ask for the day off, Sean. Ryan was sick this morning."

"Do you have temporary arrangements so that you can stay at least until first break? If we get through the read-through, I can rearrange the shoot a little. Maybe you could come back early tomorrow for most of your close-up work? Shooting those out of order won't make much difference." He looked away, obviously already mentally rearranging things. He even grabbed at the pen tucked behind his ear and the script in his hands, thumbing through already-tagged pages.

Left alone, though the man was still standing right in front of them, Brenna smiled at Cassidy and patted her arm. The blonde exhaled in relief. "Told you it could happen." Brenna looked at Sean and grinned.

"Well, come on. Let's get you two your script copies. No filming until after lunch, so you can skip costuming." Sean dropped his foot from the seat of the chair and stepped back, spun around, and headed back to the set.

Cassidy stood. "I'm ready."

Brenna came up behind her and idly patted Cassidy's shoulder. "All right, let's get the job done so you can get out of here."

As Brenna walked ahead, Cass felt the residual warmth on her shoulder. She watched Brenna walk confidently onto the set, take a script copy from Durham, and give Rachelle a warm hug.

"So, Ryan is sick?" Rachelle asked as Cassidy walked up. "I'm sorry. You should be home to take care of him."

Cassidy knew that Brenna had already updated the other two on the situation. "Where are Will and Terry?" Cass asked.

"Working with the stunt team. They've got a full-fledged B plot this time, an explosion in the Vortex lab."

"Inside intrigue," Brenna mused before she realized what Rachelle's explanation meant. "You've read already?" She flipped ahead through the pages.

"Some," Chelle admitted to Brenna. "We were beginning to think something had happened to you."

Brenna ducked her head, pleased to have been worried about but quick with assurances. "Delayed flight. I had planned to leave last night, but freezing rain grounded flights until morning."

Joining them, Rich interjected, "You haven't even been home, have you?"

Brenna shook her head. "I gave Thomas the keys and took a cab here."

"God," Chelle commiserated. "You should go home and get some sleep."

Cassidy silently echoed that thought. She found traveling difficult. Brenna had to have been up continually since Sunday morning. When her flight was grounded, she likely stayed up waiting for the first flight out, just to be here for a six a.m. set call. Her respect for Brenna rose another notch.

Sean appeared again, mercifully offering a tray with juice and sweet rolls. "Now do you think we can do some full read-throughs?"

"Food? God, I'm yours!" Brenna scanned her script pages as she sipped. "From the top?"

"From the top," Sean confirmed. "And, Cass, listen close. In this one, you're going to spend a lot of time being me."

Cassidy's face paled. "What?"

"Yep. It's called *Brains and Brawn*. We get knocked through a vortex and end up with our bodies switched."

"So you're me?" Cassidy asked. "And I'm going to be you?" Chris Hanssen might not like being part of Susan Jakes' Time Squad, but she was the antithesis of Jeremy Dewitt. The guy loved the role of card sharp, or gunslinger, or sports figure. Whatever action was to be had in a particular case, he wanted to be in the thick of it. Cassidy was uncertain she could carry off the swagger of someone so confident.

"And you get to kiss me." Rachelle took Cassidy's hand to hop off the exam bed.

"I what?" Cassidy just stared around at the other actors, digesting the situation.

Sean cleared his throat, drawing all attention back to him. "All right, let's read scene 4 B."

It was the middle of the last day of filming *Brains and Brawn*, the gender-bending body switch episode. Most of the major work had been done over the last five days.

Though Chris and Jeremy had been sent to handle an extraction, that mission had been abandoned as soon as they discovered they'd swapped bodies. Dr. Pryor had gone after them and, despite an accident with the Vortex equipment, had been working on unswitching the pair in a rudimentary medical facility. He was soon joined by Susan, who risked herself to get important data to the doctor. While they assessed the problem, Chris and Jeremy had traveled back to the Time Squad's headquarters to await the doctor's remedy.

Out of consideration, Sean held the "big" scene until last, rightly figuring Rachelle and Cassidy's ease with each other would increase over the week's work. But right now, standing outside the set of Commander Jakes' office, Cassidy was pacing to try and shake off her nervousness. Her palms were soaked with sweat. She had called her agent and asked about the possible angles, fallout, or benefits, of the kiss.

"*Coudreau gets great work.*"

Great, I'm being compared to a character on Friends. *Lisa Coudreau's kiss, though, had been a stunt kiss — the actress in her own character.*

This would be Chris' body, but supposedly with Jeremy's spirit inside it. The way Sean and Rachelle portrayed Jeremy and Luria the couple's relationship was deep and solid. There was nothing timid in their touches, no hesitation as they went from moment to moment.

Cassidy wasn't a novice, but kissing Rachelle or being kissed by her — they had tried it twice — had set her head swimming. She had been unable to complete her lines in fourteen rehearsals.

There was a buzzer. Time was up.

A buzzer sounded. Anxiety making her run her fingers through her hair, Commander Jakes looked up from the pile of papers on her desk of papers. "Come."

The doors opened to reveal Chris Hanssen attired as Jeremy Dewitt, a lost look on the blonde's usually self-assured features. Beside Jakes, Luria, who had obviously been crying, turned. "Chris?"

Controlled by Dewitt's thoughts, Hanssen's body jerked at the misidentification. "The test didn't work."

Cass delivered the line dryly and dejectedly, obviously pushing forward Dewitt's depression at the situation.

"We will keep trying, Jeremy," Jakes assured, rounding the desk with a purposeful stride. She stopped at the slouched shoulder and tried to get "him" to look at her. She started to reach for the shoulder, paused. "I..." She dropped her hand. "Would you like to sit down?"

When "he" wouldn't, Jakes led the way over to the leather-padded bench against the view port wall. "Don't give up hope. There is a way."

Luria walked up. "Jer?" She used her husband's nickname. "It

will work."
     "I hope so." "Jeremy" looked at her, pained.

One second Cassidy was staring at Rachelle's full, dark lips, watching her speak, and the next second, Rachelle's hands were on her cheeks. Rachelle's chocolate brown eyes swept her face before she moved to meet Cassidy's lips with her own.

Luria gave her husband a reassuring, even desperate kiss.

Cassidy's grip reflexively tightened on Rachelle, as she felt she was going to fall.

"Now, let's go try again." Commander Jakes put a hand on "Jeremy's" back and propelled "him" out the door. "I want my officers back." Luria was close on their heels.

"Cut, and print that." Assistant director Kim Swanson ducked out from behind camera one and waved the two women over. "That's a wrap."
     Having been in an earlier scene, the "test" Chris/Jeremy had referred to, Rich Paulson walked up. "That was fantastic. And perfectly timed," he complimented.
     "Thanks for the shove," Cassidy said to Brenna.
     "No problem. We worked it out in blocking while you were back getting reset in makeup."
     "I'm sorry."
     "It was a gamble. I'm sorry that we couldn't get it changed. Network floated the idea, and the demographic seemed to love it."
     "So it was a stunt."
     Sean stepped out from behind the camera. "Yeah, I'm sorry. I didn't think you'd have a block about a five-second kiss."
     Next to Cassidy, Rich looked at the time on a nearby wall. "Bren, are we seeing your kids tonight for the Halloween party?"
     "Yes. I'm on my way out to meet them."
     "This will definitely end the day on an up note." Rachelle turned. "Cass, are you coming?"
     Cassidy shook herself and answered quickly, "I have to grab Ryan. I'll be back in a little over an hour."
     "Are you going to be in costume tonight?" Brenna asked.
     Cassidy nodded. "I'm switching to my own instead of staying in this one. But it is Halloween, so I thought it best. What about you?"
     "I'm staying in costume, too." Brenna hesitated, then added, "What you did was just an amazing performance, Cass. Even with the blocking changes."
     "Rachelle, too."
     "Mmm hmm." Brenna ducked her head and walked off set. Cassidy turned in the other direction, headed for wardrobe.

Chapter 7

A little more than an hour later, Brenna led a band of children from the front gate to the Pinnacle offices. Guardians and other volunteers from the Los Angeles Kids Experience (LAKE) trailed behind. She guided them to the offices first.

Time Trails producer Victor Branch had been alerted by the gate guard and stood at his office doorway. In a gray business suit, he was dressed typically except for a plastic tiger face mask pulled down over his features. He growled impressively. "I see you brought my dinner, Commander."

Several of the youngest children cowered, some older ones laughed. He tipped up his mask and dropped to a crouch, drawing a bag of candy out from behind his door. The children spotted it, and small plastic orange bags were presented in short order. Giggles of delight filled the corridor as the youngest opened their bags to "Aunt Brenna" and yelled, "See what I got!" before dancing out of the doorway to let others partake of Branch's bounty.

Hands resting lightly on her upper arms, Brenna smiled, occasionally reaching down to brush fingers over soft cheeks and kissing others until the candy distribution was complete.

"What do we say to Mr. Branch?"

"Thank you, Mr. Branch!"

Victor laughed, ruffled the hair of a few of the nearest children, and waved Brenna to him as she gestured for the other adults to lead the children down to the next office area. "Nice group of kids," he said. "These are the ones you work with?"

"One weekend a month, I help out with their fundraising," she answered quietly. "I'm glad you agreed to host the Halloween party. They'll enjoy themselves in a safe place."

"No problem. I'll trail with you down to the soundstages."

"Who's still on set?" Brenna asked.

"Rich has been helping the props guys. Cassidy just got back with her son. Chapman was here earlier. Interview, I think." They walked behind the group as the children were greeted by more executives and writers in partial costume. Then Ginger Vitano appeared. Victor's personal secretary had dressed as a fairy godmother, complete with wings. Waving her wand, she helped lead the tour to the party area on the other side, collecting actors from several of the soundstages along the way.

Victor and Brenna chuckled as the wide-eyed youngsters listened to the few rules: no touching props, no straying from the group, and absolutely no stepping through a closed doorway.

"Aunt Brenna, does she mean it? She'll turn us into frogs if we do bad?"

Brenna washed the smile from her face. A look of disapproval shaped her features as she affected Susan Jakes' sharpest tone. "Regulations must be followed at all times."

"Well?" asked Ginger. "You already have pretty full bags of candy, but are you ready to get to the fun?"

"Yes! Yes!" The children bounced up and down, their costumed feet padding over the floor with a rustling sound.

"All right. Commander Jakes," Ginger waved her wand, "would you lead the way?"

"This way," Brenna said, pushing wide the double doors that led out of the administrative building to the rows of large soundstages. She strode firmly, listening to the chatter of the children behind her, unable to keep from smiling.

She checked the light above the door before entering *Time Trails'* primary soundstage. On the far side a tent had been set up covering tables of food. However, a trip through an area filled with gory games and Halloween decorations was part of the tricks before the treats she knew her castmates were planning for the children.

Hearing Rich's easy lilt rather than the Doctor's brusque tone and seeing fewer lights on, Brenna knew that they were having a post-shooting discussion, not a filming moment. She rounded the corner of a set wall and grinned as she found Rich and Cassidy, Ryan in her lap, seated casually on the edges of one of the exam tables, sharing a laugh. She caught the punch line to Rich's joke.

"With a gleam in its eye, the cat said, 'I'm no mouse.'"

Cassidy and Ryan both laughed. Just then Cassidy caught sight of Brenna and the collection of children staring at her from around the black-clad legs. The children's wide eyes made her consider putting on her character's austere expression, but then she caught Brenna's smile and let her own smile come back.

Children suddenly swarmed in, in a chorus of "Hi!", "Cool!" and "Got any candy?"

Brenna was dragged forward until she was almost on top of both Rich and Cassidy. "Hi, guys," she said simply.

"Looks like you brought the whole L.A. school district with you," Rich said.

"Just half," she replied. "Think you can handle them?"

"Yep." He grinned, tight-lipped, lifting a prop. "Have you had your shots?" he asked the children.

Screeches and giggles greeted his mock threat, and he swept one of the kids up onto the exam table, pretending to scan her pixie tails with a wand-shaped prop. "These growths out of your head, are they normal?"

"Yes!" She put her hands on her hips and glared at him as he tugged one.

He lifted the girl down, and Cassidy set Ryan down, issuing an invitation. "Who's ready to bob for apples? Or paint a pumpkin face?"

Hands went up, and voices cried out, "Me!"

"Commander Jakes?"

"Lead the way," she said, patting Ryan on the back as he stared at the large group of kids.

The two women fell into step side by side, with Rich behind. A figure suddenly sprang from behind a wall, arms outspread, a black cape over his shoulders and arms, face covered by a bat mask. "I've got you now!" issued forth in an impressive Dracula imitation. Not expecting it, Brenna squealed and leaped sideways, stumbling into Cassidy as the children behind them screamed and fell into each other.

"Hey! Hey!" The mask came off revealing Sean Durham's surfer-dude good looks. "It's okay. Just me."

One of the kids asked, "Who're you?"

The actresses righted themselves, helping each other. Cassidy's hand remained on Brenna's arm as they listened to the children's reactions.

Another child elbowed the questioner and loudly whispered, "He's a vampire!"

Cassidy laughed and patted Sean's shoulder as the now foursome of actors led their merry troupe to the far side of the soundstage and out into the lantern-lit tent where the rest of the cast had assembled.

The main attraction was the center table, laden with soda, punch, and barbecue foods. Over at the far edge of the tent, Cameron and Victor sported aprons and spatulas and stood over grilling meat. The children swarmed the table, with some of the younger ones getting help from a cast member in filling their plates with hot dogs, hamburgers, and potato salad. Nearly everyone picked up a candied apple from the bin at the end of the table.

The group settled on the ground, devouring their food. Brenna circulated a few minutes, checking on everyone. Rachelle waved her over.

"How's things?"

"Fine. You're in costume, too." Brenna crouched next to her. "You didn't have to do this."

"The kids are worth it." Rachelle smiled and accepted another shy, but interested study of her costume from a curious child. "I'm surprised you haven't brought them through before."

"Trying to keep some of my life separate, I guess."

Rachelle chided, "These kids are great." She finished off the last of her potato salad, scrambled to her feet, and trashed the paper wares. She smiled and patted Brenna's shoulder, then turned away and announced that her "booth" was open. "Who's ready for the haunted tent?" Cheers went up. "Everyone grab a buddy."

Children scampered about, seizing hands. As Brenna watched, Will Chapman was surrounded by half-pint admirers. Four grabbed his hands and arms, and he laughed. As sour as he had been lately, the laughter was quite a shock. Terry Brown and the two guest actors from the current script were soon dragged toward the decked out entrance to an adjoining tent.

Thrust into the lead, Brenna was the first to step into the dark opening, followed by her collection of children. Halloween decorations leaped out at her, and props rounded out the garish appearance. A sharp-looking weapon danced in mid-air, and someone piped in non-English language chant music. Several children screamed when stagehands, sporting alien makeup courtesy of the set's makeup artists, burst through openings and scowled in the red and ultraviolet lighting.

Brenna was laughing when she emerged from the other side, having had to pick up one of the smaller ones who had gotten frightened. Child in her arms, she turned to watch the rest emerging.

"That was so great!"

"Too cool! Can we do it again?"

Brenna shook her head. "There are other games."

"All right!" As a pack, the children raced into the main tent again, sizing up the carnival games.

Stagehands and cast members manned the booths, handing out bean bags and baseballs and fishing poles for carnival-style games. Props had been stacked into pyramids for several knockdown-type games.

There was face painting by the makeup crew and miniature pumpkin painting. Brenna took out a pile of Vordt statuettes with several baseballs, then slipped off to the side and sipped a soda while watching the happy mêlée. Sensing someone at her shoulder, she turned to find Cassidy. "Hi." She scanned down the still-costumed woman. "I think you can take off the boots."

Cassidy shook her head. "It's all right." She carefully leaned against the tent pole. "Nice thing you have here." She glanced away.

Following the other woman's gaze, Brenna noticed Ryan at a booth fishing a prize from the murky Vortex pool. "The guys in Props are gods," she responded. She leaned closer to Cassidy and pointed out Chelle passing out the stuffed animals and other toy prizes for winning at the games. "Look at all that stuff."

Smiling, Cassidy pointed toward the apple-bobbing cauldron where a line of children waited their turn at the wet game. As they watched, a ten-year-old boy came up with a mouthful of apple. One of the volunteers offered him a towel and sent him with a ticket to Chelle's booth to claim a prize. "Where are Thomas and James?"

"They'll be here in about twenty minutes. Thomas had weight training, then he was going to drive them over."

"I'd be white as a sheet letting them drive alone," Cassidy admitted.

Smiling, Brenna made a show of patting her cheeks. "I use heavy makeup."

A little girl rushed toward them. Brenna caught her before she could run into Cassidy. "Hi!" the girl enthused.

Brenna crouched to be at eye level. "Hello there. Having a good time?"

"The best!" The girl's arms flung around her neck, and she felt the fluffiness of a stuffed toy on one cheek just as a wet kiss pressed against her other cheek. "Thank you!" the girl gushed before running off again.

Brenna put her hands to her face, hiding the heat, and nodded after the girl was gone. A hand moved softly across her back, and she dropped her hands hastily.

Cassidy observed, "These kids mean a lot to you."

"Yes." She glanced up nervously only to find comprehension. Inhaling, she stepped away. "Sorry."

"Nothing to be sorry for."

Their gazes met, and suddenly the noise around her muted to the borders of Brenna's awareness. "All right," she said, startling herself with her own voice.

Cassidy smiled slowly, holding Brenna's gaze.

"Mom!"

Brenna's head jerked around, and she spotted her sons standing at the entrance to the tent. Thomas wore his baseball uniform, and James wore a biker's leather jacket and black leather pants. He even had a metal-studded black leather cap pulled cockeyed on his head.

"Yours?" Cassidy asked quietly. "I like the leather look."

"My rebel with a cause," Brenna offered cheerfully. She left Cassidy's side to greet her sons. All three were swarmed when she wrapped an arm around each and kissed their cheeks.

"Kisses for me, too!" yelled the children.

Brenna distributed her kisses judiciously, making sure she caught each cheek once before sending the children off to more games. Sean Durham waved at her, but children still swamped her. "Thomas, would you go take over at the slot track? Sean's got a plane to catch."

Thomas went over to the slot racing table where Sean had been directing the various racing heats of wooden track cars. Brenna had promised to find a stand-in for him so he could head out early for his flight to Boston and the convention there.

Thomas lined up the cars, and Brenna kept an eye on him while she relieved Rachelle at the prize table. Two circuits of the track later, the blue car had won. Thomas passed a prize claim ticket to the winner, lined up the cars again, and started the next round.

Handing fishing poles to the youngest children so they could catch prizes from the Vortex pool, Cassidy scanned the cheerful tableau, confused by her emotions. Her eyes strayed frequently to Brenna. She was witnessing a side of Brenna that she'd suspected had existed, but which had been held secret. Judging by Rachelle's surprise, Cassidy realized that it was something Brenna had hidden from the entire cast, not just her. She wondered why. Most of them had a charity or two that they spoke for or worked with. Brenna seemed particularly watchful and engaged with this group, she realized, observing as the other woman accepted another hug from a little girl as she gave her a prize in exchange for her winning ticket. She had a distant, wistful look on her face as she closed her eyes and wrapped her arms around the smaller body.

Out of the corner of her eye, Cassidy saw one of the volunteers look at his watch and set down his ticket bucket. He stepped from behind the table and strode across the tent. Her heart sank as she realized the evening was about to end.

Brenna knew it too. Noting his approach, she stepped from behind the prize table and listened as he spoke to her quietly. She frowned but nodded, then stepped to the center of the room and stood by the decimated food table. "Could I have everyone's attention?"

Cassidy smiled painfully. It wasn't Jakes' voice, but Brenna's own rich contralto that quelled the mayhem of the room. The effect, however, was the same: All stopped and turned their eyes toward their leader.

"Has everyone been having fun?" Cheers from the children filled the room. "I'm glad. But now, it's time to say goodbye." Moans and groans and some tears came.

A pair of arms slipped around Cassidy's thighs. A young boy had latched on. She dropped a gentle hand to his dark hair and brushed the tight curls, causing him look up. His chin pressed into her thigh muscle as he hugged more tightly. She asked, "Would you like a buddy to walk with you to the bus?"

He nodded but said nothing. Cassidy guessed he was just about Ryan's age and took his hand in hers, separating him from her legs so she could move. "Come on, Ryan," she called out, drawing her son away from the abandoned game tables. He ran up and caught her other hand. The boys eyed each other around her hips. "This is my son, Ryan," she said. "What's your name?"

"Isaiah."

She smiled and patted his shoulder. "Nice to meet you, Isaiah."

Walking toward the exit, she noticed all the others in the cast and even the executives found themselves in similar situations. She shrugged at Cameron, who was trying to prevent a little girl from climbing into his arms. One of the guest actors swung a boy onto his back, and Cassidy shook her head in amusement. Terry had a boy on the end of each arm. Both looked to be about eight and wore glasses, clearly very taken by the brainy member of the Time Squad. Finishing her survey, she turned her gaze to Brenna, who had a boy and a girl clasping each hand.

The auburn-haired woman smiled back and started to lead the way out. "All right, everyone, to the bus."

Filled with sugar, the children skipped and dragged their companions along the set interiors. They bounced with enthusiasm through the Vortex set and scampered about, shouting to one another as they separated into a "good guys" and "bad guys" game.

Cassidy stood amid the rest of the cast, arms crossed over her chest, watching the children run around, laughing and even cheering on her own son, as Ryan stood in the middle of the transversal platform and, clearly mimicking Susan Jakes, ordered, "Go!" She felt eyes on her and looked to the side to find Brenna studying her, a puzzled look on her face. Raising her eyebrows and nodding toward the mêlée, Cassidy expressed her amusement without words.

Brenna shifted, and Cassidy, thinking she was going to push through the crowd toward her, felt a rush of anticipation. However, the other woman did not join her. Instead Brenna grinned and turned away. Holding her hands like a megaphone around her mouth, she ordered in a perfect "Jakes" voice, "At-TEN-SHUN!"

Forty-three children ground to an instant halt.

"Time's up. Move 'em out."

Their wide eyes fixed on the transformed Lanigan, who suddenly appeared, with every gesture, to be the *Time Trails* leader. It startled Cassidy, who was surprised to realize that before now she was not sure she could have told the difference between the two. She was really getting to know the actress separate from her character. The revelation made her smile.

The children quickly lined up and began marching like a drunken military platoon out the doors held open by Terry and Will. The line broke when the children spotted the bus idling. They raced to get seats.

Snagging Ryan, who tried to follow the other children onto the bus, Cassidy spun around with him in her arms and almost slammed into Brenna. The other woman caught her before either of them could stumble. Cassidy complimented her restoration of order. "I've never seen anything like that."

"Commander's skill," Brenna said with a grin. Cassidy felt the woman's hand just barely brushing her own arm where she held Ryan securely against her hip. Looking at Ryan, Brenna added, "Jakes has taught me a few things over the years."

"You, too, hmm?" Cassidy smiled. She turned around to watch the last of the children escorted onto the bus by the volunteers. After passing blown kisses and hand slaps through the open windows, the cast members slowly trailed back toward the soundstages. Cassidy squared her shoulders and turned around.

"Where are you going?" Brenna asked.

"To help clean up."

"I can do that. You should change and take Ryan home."

"We're a team," Terry said, coming up within earshot. "Besides, more hands get it done faster."

Brenna looked from Terry to Cassidy and back, then over his shoulder to Rachelle, Will, and Rich standing around expectantly. "Well, I guess that settles that."

"Commander's overruled," Rich Paulson teased with a grin.

The actors and Brenna's sons trooped back to the tent, grabbing trash cans from behind the set walls along the way.

Cassidy set Ryan down next to the food. The tired boy was asleep before the group finished. Within an hour, the grounds behind the soundstage looked as though the party had never taken place. Props had been returned to the Property Department, and the tents were pulled down, bundled, and delivered to the catering truck. Tied trash bags stuffed the bins outside against the walls of the building in wait for the night cleaning crew. The tables — folded up, thanks to Rich and Terry — were stacked inside the soundstage against an interior wall, and everyone was given an assortment of the leftovers.

Balancing Ryan on her left hip, Cassidy stepped into her trailer and put the bagged leftovers into her mini-fridge, keeping one caramel apple out for Ryan. Carefully she set the boy, still sleeping, on the far cushion of the couch. Then, with relief, she sat next to him and propped her feet over the arm, preparing to push off her shoes.

"I told you that you should have taken them off."

The voice startled Cassidy. She hadn't known anyone else had walked to the trailers. She distinctly remembered Terry and Rachelle heading for the makeup room. Brenna had not only come out to the trailers, however, but she now stood silhouetted in Cassidy's open doorway. Surprising her further, Brenna reached out and, wrapping warm fingers around her ankle, tugged off Cassidy's shoe.

"I'm sorry. I didn't mean to startle you."

Cassidy reflexively caught first one tossed shoe, then the other, as Brenna quickly removed them. Dropping her feet to the floor and flexing them, Cassidy bent over and rubbed her toes. "Thank you. Did you need something?" She started to rise.

Brenna noticed Ryan on the couch then. She seemed to catch herself before bending over and stroking his hair. Cassidy froze, warily watching the other woman's manner with her son and wondering what had Brenna so preoccupied. It seemed she might never learn when Brenna abruptly straightened and fidgeted.

"You're probably anxious to get home. It can wait." Brenna turned to the door.

"No. Go ahead and sit. I just need to put this up and change into something else."

"But...?" She glanced pointedly at Ryan.

"I doubt he'll wake up," she assured.

"All right." Brenna stepped back into Cassidy's trailer and closed the door. "I wanted to ask you something."

"Go ahead. Ask." Brenna moved to the couch, and Cassidy watched her drape an idle hand over Ryan's back.

Ducking away to change, she heard the question, "Would you be interested in joining me at the next event?"

Popping her head back out, she asked, "What?"

"Well, I was just...You looked like you had a good time tonight. We...I thought..." She finished in a rush, "There's an overnight camping trip in the mountains the weekend before Thanksgiving."

Turning away to finish changing, Cassidy collected her thoughts. When she reappeared, she wore a gray pullover sweater, jeans, and Nikes. "Don't you have enough chaperones?"

Brenna shook her head. "It's not that. Not just that," she corrected. "I...thought you and Ryan might enjoy yourselves." At his name, Ryan stirred slightly. Brenna missed Cassidy's surprised reaction as she concentrated for a moment on gently rubbing circles over the small boy's back. "He's sweet, Cass."

"Ryan could come?"

Cassidy's response drew Brenna's eyes back to her. She sounded shocked. "Of course." *What was so odd about inviting her son along on a camping trip?* Cassidy continued to study her. Brenna had felt less scrutiny from the children patting her hips and asking why her pants didn't have pockets. She shifted self-consciously and cleared her throat. "Um. Well?"

Cassidy straightened her shoulders and leaned back on her palms on her writing desk. Brenna likened the posture to surrender. "Sure, we'd like to join the trip."

Brenna exhaled in relief, suddenly aware how much she had hoped for a positive response. "It'll be fun and relaxing. We're planning s'mores, campfire songs, and storytelling."

"Singing, hmm?" Cass smiled.

"You have not lived until you've heard all fourteen verses to 'I lost my poor meatball' sung by a group of sleep-deprived kids." Brenna chuckled.

"Sounds like fun. It's settled then."

Brenna opened the door as Cassidy lifted Ryan. The boy settled against his mother's generous chest with a mumbled grunt. *Positively endearing*, Brenna thought.

Chapter 8

Thomas watched his mother at the stove stirring a saucepan of sizzling chicken strips. When the phone rang on the wall next to her, startling her, she stepped away from the food, caught his eye, and gestured for him to continue with the preparation while she grabbed the cordless handset.

"Oh, Kevin. How's Mount Clemens?"

Recognizing his mom was speaking to her husband, Thomas glanced over his shoulder and watched her. She tucked the receiver between her ear and shoulder and fished in the silverware drawer for the flatware.

"No," she said into the phone. "You caught us at lunch." There was a pause as she listened, fishing for the butter knife. Coming up with it, she spoke again into the receiver. "Yes, I know it's late, but I had gardening to do."

She moved out of earshot to the dining room table, circling it and laying the settings while still talking. Thomas studied the chicken, moved it off the burner, and stirred the stewed tomatoes, checking the pasta with a quick taste. He moved to the cutting board, intermittently watching his mother while he chopped the salad ingredients. His mom suddenly sat down at the table and grabbed the handset firmly off her shoulder. The raised volume of her voice made it possible for him to hear.

"No. I told you I wouldn't."

Uncomfortable, Thomas concentrated on his task, trying to ignore the conversation even as his mother's voice lowered in volume but intensified in emotion. He stopped cutting and looked at the salad ingredients. The cucumber, his mother's favorite addition, was missing. Leaning into the refrigerator, he found the hydrator empty. "Hey, Mom, there's no cukes."

Silence greeted his statement. Returning to the cutting board, he looked into the dining room and saw her still sitting. The phone was on the table; it was her face that concerned him. She had it covered with one hand. The other hand rested against the tablecloth in a balled fist. "Mom? Are you okay?"

She was still for a breath, then moved her hand away from her face and quickly stood, turning her back on him and walking down the corridor toward her bedroom.

In that split second, Thomas realized his mother had been crying. He looked down at the phone she had abandoned on the tabletop. Picking it up, he found it had been turned off. A sizzling sound caught his ear. He returned the phone to the wall before finishing the meal prep. Just as he was placing the salad and three bowls on the table, James wandered in from the driveway, carrying his basketball under his arm.

"Hey, bro. Where's Mom?"

"Her room. Help me finish here?"

"Sure thing. She reading?"

Thomas shrugged. He did not think so, but he decided against sharing his suppositions. James set the basketball down and collected the pasta bowl, taking it out to the table. When he returned to the kitchen, Thomas was pouring sodas. "Take the other two bowls. I've got the drinks."

James looked toward the bedroom hall. "Aren't you going to call her?"

Thomas shook his head. "I don't think she's too hungry." Though James was only two years younger, Thomas recalled their parents' divorce more vividly. The phone call worried him. When the three of them had left Mount Clemens two weeks earlier, he sensed something had changed between his mother and Kevin but had thought little of it. Now he was concerned. His mom did not cry.

His silence tipped James. "Okay, so tell me what happened?"

With a sigh, Thomas confided, "Kevin called. I think they had a fight."

Tucked where they were in the kitchen talking, Thomas and James did not see their mother return to the dining room. Settling into her chair at the table, she heard the end of their conversation. She acted surprised, though, when they came out with the glasses and the pasta dish.

"Mom?" James sat in his seat on her right against the sideboard. Thomas took the seat to her left.

She grasped their hands, smiled, and dropped her head. "Grace?" Thomas offered the prayer, though she could tell he was still studying her.

"Thank you, Lord, for the fullness of your bounty. Amen."

"Amen," she echoed, as James did the same. Thomas did not let go of her hand immediately. Brenna squeezed his hand, then tugged hers free, picking up her fork. "Thank you," she said quietly.

"Anytime, Mom."

"Were you planning to go out tonight?" She looked from one to the other, wondering what they would say.

As James started to respond, Brenna caught a quick head shake from Thomas that silenced him. Thomas drew her attention and filled in quickly, "No, Mom. What would you like to do?"

Touched, Brenna almost relented and excused the boys to their own fun, but then she remembered the upcoming camping trip. "Why don't we go get some more things for the campout?"

"Hey, that would be cool," Thomas agreed.

She smiled. He had been excited about the trip since agreeing to take some of the adults and older kids up into the ridge for a guided climb.

"So where do you want to go?" Thomas asked. "I need a few more things for the climb anyway."

"There's a new warehouse-style store on Riordan Avenue."

James was surprised. "That's all the way into Alameda."

"I know."

"Oh, okay. Sure, whatever," James recovered.

"You don't have to go," she allowed.

"Maybe we can take you out to the movies on the way back," Thomas suggested.

Brenna smiled tightly at Thomas' concern. He had obviously overheard more than she'd thought. No typical teen would offer to take his mother out to a movie. She grasped his hand. "Maybe we'll just rent something."

Lunch was finished quickly, and the dishes put in the dishwasher before the trio piled into the SUV. Thomas asked to drive. Brenna kissed him and laughed. "Not on my life."

Thomas was smiling as he slid into the front passenger seat and buckled up. Clearly he thought his mission had been accomplished.

"So what stuff do you think we ought to get for the kids to do?" she asked as they left the neighborhood and merged onto the highway toward Alameda.

Cassidy studied her son, asleep beside her, as they lay on her bed for his afternoon nap. The radio played softly as she lightly rubbed his back with one hand and read script pages in the lamplight. His copy of *Where the Wild Things Are* lay across the covers just beyond her right hand. Putting down her script, she reached for the colorfully illustrated book, lifted it, and studied the cover for a long moment.

Opening the pages, she perused the pictures, but her mind wouldn't stay on the fanciful monsters, instead drifting constantly to the woman who had presented the gift. Then there was last night's unexpected invitation to go camping.

Lightly brushing her fingers through Ryan's hair, she murmured, "Camping, huh? I think you'll like it. Certainly you'll have a lot of fun with the other kids." She leaned back, looking at the ceiling. "I wonder if Brenna will bring her sons."

She wondered if the teenagers found camping fun. She thought about the last time she had ventured into the mountains. About eight years earlier she had gone on a winter ski trip to a Denver cabin with a group of college friends. She remembered spending most of the slope time on her rear end, pride damaged more than anything else. The nights had consisted of keeping warm under blankets that barely covered anything. Efforts to keep warm had led to other interesting pastimes.

Maybe she ought to call Misty and catch up.

Mentally cataloging her camping supplies, Cassidy realized she would need several things. A glance toward the clock revealed that it was only one-thirty. Maybe she could cut Ryan's nap short at two, drive to the new Sports Warehouse on Riordan, and pick up what they needed. Until then, she decided, she could read the latest script. She wasn't in any frame of mind to memorize lines, but at least she could give it a read-through and get a feel for the overall picture. After last week's surprise, Cassidy was leery of her character taking on anything else right away.

A while later, satisfied that Chris Hanssen was back in the realm of standard sci-fi fare, she reached the closing scene and set the script aside. A glance at the clock prompted her to wake Ryan. "Come on, buddy," she whispered. "We're going to get you some camping things."

"Camping?"

His green eyes blinked open, and she smiled, kissing his cheek. "Yes. Do you remember Ms. Lanigan?"

"Mmm hmm."

"She invited us to go with the bunch of kids from the Halloween party up into the mountains in a couple of weeks."

"So why we gotta go shopping now?"

"Because I've got the time." She coaxed him with a bribe. "If you behave, we'll go for ice cream afterward."

"Ice cream? Mmm." He sat up and rubbed his eyes. "Can I have chocolate? Two scoops?"

Cassidy stifled her laugh. *Bribery works.* "We'll see, after we go shopping."

"Okay." He scrambled off the bed, stood there in his sock-covered feet, and declared, "I'm ready to go. Come on!"

"Put on your shoes. I'll be right out." She stepped into her bathroom, ran a quick brush through her hair, and slipped her feet into a pair of sandals. Stepping back out, she asked, "All right, ready?"

Ryan looked up from the floor where he was tying his shoes and nodded.

"Come on." On the way to the front door, she snapped up her purse from the side table. She buckled him into his booster seat in the back before getting behind the wheel. After allowing a jogger to pass behind the car, she pulled out of the driveway.

Chapter 9

Grand opening banners were displayed all around the large store. The aisles were crowded. Cassidy grasped Ryan's hand firmly in her own. *Most of the county must be here.* Her son was captivated by the displays. She repeatedly had to tug him back against her side while reading the aisle listings to find their particular objectives.

Buffeted as she moved into the appropriate aisle, Cassidy searched the shelves until she found the lanterns. She found battery-operated, gas, and candle lanterns, all rated by lumen output and designed for different conditions. Checking that Ryan remained at her side, she pulled down a boxed gas powered light to read the labeling more closely. She scooted closer to the shelving and grasped her son's shoulder as a family with a cart tried to maneuver past.

"Excuse us," the man said, shifting the front end of the cart away from her feet.

His gaze stopped on her briefly, and Cassidy watched a puzzled half-recognition flash in his brown eyes. She smiled faintly, and he nodded, taking his family past without any further exchange. Cassidy lifted the box back to eye level and continued reading. The lantern's bowl was open at the top without a guard screen. She shook her head and replaced it on the shelf. She wasn't going to risk Ryan sticking his hand inside out of curiosity. She liked the idea of the gas over the batteries though, for longevity, and continued searching for another model.

"Mommy?"

She felt a tug on her jeans and looked down into Ryan's upturned smile. "Yes?"

"Can I see the animals?"

"Animals? Where?" She looked around. He tugged her pant leg again, and she followed his outstretched arm. At the end of the aisle, just visible through the throngs of people, was a display of woodland animals. Cassidy suspected it was the entrance to the hunting section and shook her head. "No, Ryan."

"Mommy, please?"

She crouched and rubbed his shoulder. "They're not real, honey."

His eyes gleamed with excitement. "Toys!" Tugging on the hand holding his, he pleaded, "I'll just look. I promise."

Cassidy shook her head and stood. "No, now wait." She fished behind the front row of the display and withdrew an unbattered box containing the lantern she had selected. "All right. Now let's go find you a sleeping bag."

She tucked the box under her left arm and reached down to take Ryan's hand in her right. They navigated the aisle and emerged near the display that had caught his attention.

Pausing for a moment, Cassidy studied the animals and realized the animal carcasses were real, preserved, and posed. Glass eyes seemed to follow her as she looked away. "Come on," she said to Ryan, who was transfixed. She scanned the aisle labels and moved two down against the wall of the warehouse building, which proclaimed "sleeping bags".

The crowd was thinner there, and Cassidy breathed a little easier, scanning the labels of the bags for something warm enough for a mountain winter night. Ryan pointed out a sleeping bag covered in Rugrats figures. The fleece was too thin, though, more suited for a summer than a winter trip, and she shook her head. Ryan pouted. She pointed out one which advertised a thicker woolen lining covered in Barney renderings. He turned up his nose at the purple dinosaur, and Cassidy continued looking. A plain blue one received the same disdain.

Ryan sat down on the bottom shelf as she moved away a little to look at others. *At least he isn't throwing a tantrum*, she thought, counting her blessings and continuing to look along the shelves for something that would suit her requirements and his. She tried very hard to compromise where it was reasonable to do so. Her mother had always told her to pick her fights carefully. So far the advice had proven sound. Ryan was well-mannered and generally aware of the feelings of others and did not cry out for every trendy thing.

She found a Disney Dalmatians bag with enough lining and turned to suggest it to him, figuring he would like it because it looked like their dog, Ranger.

Ryan was no longer seated on the shelf.

The aisle was nearly empty. One bearded man in fatigues was looking at the tarps, and a pair of teenaged boys checked out the waterproofing sprays, but no Ryan.

"Ryan?" Calling out as she went, she hurried down the aisle to one end and looked among the throngs for her son's three-foot-tall form. There were children everywhere, but each was attached to a parent or seated in a cart. Quickly she moved toward the other end of the aisle. "Ryan!" Stumbling into another patron, she dropped her lantern.

"Oh, I'm sorry." The speaker, a woman, leaned over to pick up the fallen box. "Let me help you get that."

The voice? Cassidy stopped and focused on the person in front of her. "Brenna?" She met curious blue eyes as delicately strong hands closed around her forearms.

"Cassidy?"

"I'm...Excuse me. I have to find Ryan." Cassidy looked past her castmate and scanned the aisle, dimly noting Brenna's sons straightening up behind their mother.

"Ryan is missing?" Brenna questioned sharply. Cassidy's gaze jerked back to hers. "How long ago?"

"A few minutes, maybe. I don't know," Cassidy admitted.

"Thomas, James, fan out. You both know what he looks like."

"No problem, Mom." Cassidy caught a nod from the lankier Thomas. "We'll find him," he assured her. She nodded back.

The teens spread out, each taking an aisle and calling out the boy's name. Brenna drew Cassidy back into the quieter aisle. "Cass? Where did you last see him?"

Her heart was pounding, and she fisted her hands together to focus. "We were here looking at sleeping bags." She took a deep breath. "He didn't like what I'd chosen, so he sat down to sulk."

Brenna nodded. "Okay, was there something that caught his attention?" Cassidy shook her head. "Anywhere in the store?"

Cassidy paused. "The animals."

"The what?"

"The animals displayed in the hunting section." Cassidy strode away quickly; Brenna kept up. "The taxidermy display," Cassidy clarified.

"Oh." Cassidy had stopped in front of it. Brenna was confronted by a ten-point buck and, on faux wood set at various levels, raccoons, and birds, even a rabbit. "Oh," she said again in a faint voice. She swallowed against her suddenly queasy stomach. "Let's take a look through here," she went on quickly.

Their search turned up no sign of Cassidy's son.

Meeting back at the animal display, Brenna asked, "Okay, do you have a picture?"

"What?" Events were eroding Cassidy's control. The blonde's voice was curt and distracted as she continued scanning their immediate area.

Brenna spoke with quiet, calm direction. "You need a picture of Ryan. We're going to the management."

As Brenna's hand rubbed lightly on her back, Cassidy took a deep breath and let it out slowly. She searched through her purse for her wallet and Ryan's birthday picture. Shaking fingers pulled it out of the plastic, and Brenna's hand closed over hers.

"All right. Let's find the office."

Cassidy looked up hopefully as Thomas jogged toward them. He shook his head, admitting defeat. She stopped. "Do you think..."

Brenna met her gaze with determination. "No, it's just a big place. We need more people to help look." Looking around, she spotted the office sign behind the Customer Service desk. "Over there. Let's go."

"All right." Cassidy admitted to herself that she felt infinitely calmer with Brenna beside her.

Brenna tugged Cassidy forward through the service line. "We have a missing child to report."

The clerk, whose name tag identified her as "Jessie", looked over from the customer she was helping with a catalog and brushed her braided bangs out of her face. "We don't have any kids here."

"My son's missing," Cassidy supplied.

"We need to see the manager," Brenna insisted. "Now."

"Okay. Just hold on." Jessie went into the back. Brenna watched her enter a doorway down the short corridor.

Brenna's hand closed over Cassidy's again as the blonde patted the counter surface impatiently. "Relax. You're going to have to remember what he was wearing."

Cassidy blanched. Had it been a red shirt or tan? Was he in his blue jeans or black ones? She looked away from Brenna's face to see a thick-waisted man in short shirtsleeves and a red tie step out of the office and walk out behind Jessie.

"Here's the manager, Mr. Dunwald."

"Mr. Dunwald, my friend's son is missing. If we give you a picture, could you ask your staff to help us look for him?"

He held out his hand. Brenna placed the picture in it. While looking it over, he asked, "How long has he been missing?"

Cassidy looked to Brenna, finding her encouragement calming. "About...um, a...half hour I think."

"What's his name?"

"Ryan Hyland."

"How old?"

"He just turned five."

"How tall?"

She breathed slowly. "Thirty-nine inches at his last checkup." She hesitated. "I think."

"All right. We'll go call for him over the intercom. Does he know enough to report to a clerk?"

"We've never been here before."

He shook his head. The clerks, Brenna noted, were all wearing green vests. She squeezed Cassidy's hand again, drawing her attention. "What if he tells Ryan to go to someone in a green vest," she whispered.

Cassidy nodded. "That'll work."

The manager asked one more thing before turning around to catch up the intercom microphone. "How long do you want to wait before we call the police and report a kidnapping?"

Cassidy's face went pale at the blunt question. Supportively, Brenna wrapped her arm around the taller woman's lower back. "Make the announcement," she ordered him sharply. The manager shrugged and turned around.

"Attention, customers. Would Ryan Hyland report to a clerk in a green vest please?"

He turned back to the two women. "Why don't you sit in my office until we have word?"

Brenna nodded to Thomas, who disappeared back into the aisles to continue looking. "Come on," she said to Cassidy. "Thomas will go and keep looking. We'll sit down for just a couple minutes. That's all it will take." The manager opened the counter door and gestured them back to his office.

Thomas skidded to a stop in another aisle and pushed his hair from his face. "Hey." He drew the attention of a skinny man in overalls balancing two oars in each hand. "Have you seen a kid about this tall?" He held out his hand waist high. "Blond hair? Looking a little lost?"

The man shook his head. "Nope."

"If you do, would you please take him to the front desk?"

"Sure thing. What's the kid's name?"

"Ryan."

"Okay."

"Thanks." Thomas dodged around another patron and found himself near the back of the store. A layaway area was there, along with the restrooms. There was not much else there, and the area was empty of people. He turned around, starting back, when he looked left, then right, and spotted his brother, hands on his hips and looking up a ladder laid against a set of shelves, leading to the top. "James!"

His brother brushed a hand across his freckled cheeks and then waved Thomas over. "Any luck?"

"Nothing. You?"

"Do you remember that time I was, oh heck, I must've been about Ryan's age? I followed Dad up onto the roof when he was cleaning the gutters?"

"Shit. Yes. You think he went up there?"

"We won't know until we get up there and look around. He could be stuck on top of one of these things."

"So why isn't he hollering?"

"Come on. I had the idea. Let's give it a shot first, then think about the logic. This is a five-year-old we're talking about."

Thomas sighed, pushing his fingers through his hair. He was tired, but his mother clearly wanted them to do as much as possible to help. Looking for Mrs. Hyland's son was the least they could do. Certainly she wasn't in any shape to do it herself, he thought, remembering the fear he'd read in her face at the manager's suggestion that they place a kidnapping report. "All right. Let's go." He grabbed the base of the ladder, steadying it as his brother climbed up quickly.

"Hey! You kids get down from there!"

Thomas turned around to see a freckle-faced clerk who looked about his age jogging toward them. "We need to get up there and take a look around."

"You could get hurt. And it'd be my neck in a sling."

"Well, listen. We're looking for a little boy. Maybe you've seen him?"

"That the 'Ryan Hyland' they called for over the intercom?"

"Yes."

"We've got a policy not to let on that the person being sought is underage. Predators, y'know?"

Thomas nodded quickly, waving off the protocol talk. "Yeah. Sure. Fine. Have you seen him or not?"

"He wasn't around when the announcement came in, or I'd have called in. He was climbing the ladder earlier. I shooed him away. Told him to go back to his parents. He looked at me, cried and ran off."

"Which way did he go?"

The clerk pointed back over his shoulder. "That way."

Thomas and James exchanged hopeful looks and dashed away. "Do you think it could be that simple? We're just a few steps behind a five-year-old wandering the store?" James asked.

"We'd better hope so."

"I wonder how Mrs. Hyland's doing," James said, as they rounded the nearest corner and drew up short on the rear loading dock. "Whoa!"

Thomas grabbed his brother's arm and prevented him from falling off the edge. They looked down. No Ryan on the outside asphalt. Looking around, they tried to figure out where to go next. Thomas spotted a dark opening to the side of the dock. "Look, over there!"

James scrambled over to the hole first and looked inside. There was a notice on the wall, which he read aloud. "'Stand clear — compactor.' Where the heck's the safety stuff they always have around?"

"I don't know." Thomas leaned against the side and looked down. "Ryan!" he called into the opening. "Ryan, can you hear me?"

There was no answer. James grabbed his brother's shoulder and tugged him backward. "I think we'd better report to Mom," he said worriedly.

Thomas considered. Whether Ryan was down that shaft or not, they needed help to look. Big help. "Yeah, let's go."

Chapter 10

In the manager's office, Cassidy fretted. "What's taking so long?"

Brenna laid her right hand over Cassidy's. "They're looking for him. Thomas and James are, too. We will find him."

"It's been over an hour. Maybe the manager's right. He didn't run off; someone kidnapped him."

Aware of the tension in the taller woman, Brenna sympathetically rubbed her shoulder. "I won't lie to you. The longer he's missing, yes, the more likely it is that someone coaxed him away. But you have to have faith."

"Ryan knows not to go off with strangers," Cassidy reasoned, finding some measure of calm. In the next moment, though, she recalled, "We haven't practiced his safe word in a while. What if he doesn't remember it?"

Brenna's expression told Cassidy that she wanted to give the reassurances she sought. The door of the manager's office started inward. She pushed abruptly to her feet, Brenna immediately doing the same in front of her, standing between her and the doorway. The manager's head appeared around the door frame. "Ms. Hyland?"

She answered quickly. "Yes."

Dunwald stepped all the way inside and closed the door. Something in the careful way he shut the door and the way the latch resounded in the silence made Cassidy bite her bottom lip nervously.

"I am sorry. We haven't located your son. I just called the police. We will have to file a missing child report." He moved around and sat down behind his desk. "Since your son disappeared from our store, I'm going to ask you to fill out an incident report here before the police arrive."

"Why?" Brenna asked sharply. "She's going to have to tell the police the exact same thing."

"You can use it to write your statement for the police. Our headquarters requires their own on file." He fished a form from the low filing cabinet drawer behind his desk and slid it across the table along with a pen. "Here you are."

Cassidy reached for the pen; Brenna snapped up the paper and scanned it. "We'll just fill them both out at the same time, all right? Show the police in when they get here."

The manager looked from Brenna to Cassidy and then frowned. "Of course," he agreed stiffly before withdrawing.

He was gone only a few seconds when there was another knock. Leaving the form on the desk, Brenna stood quickly and opened the door. Jessie stood outside. "Yes?"

"There are two boys at the desk who say that their mom's back here."

"That'd be my sons."

"I don't want to let them back here," Jessie explained. "Could you come out front?"

"All right. Just a minute." Brenna closed the door and turned around. Cassidy's forehead rested in her left palm as she bent her elbow against the wood laminate surface. "Cassidy, I'm going out to talk to Thomas and James. Maybe they've found something."

The blonde stopped in the midst of lifting the form to read it over. Brenna could tell from the line of tension in Cassidy's back that the other woman was barely holding herself together. Tears of empathy pricked her eyes. Not questioning, just knowing she needed to do so, Brenna tucked her arms around the younger woman's shoulders and pressed her cheek against the top of the blond head. "I'm sorry," she murmured.

Cassidy turned in her arms suddenly and wrapped her arms around Brenna's waist, startling her when Brenna felt a cheek press against her breasts. "Oh God..." Tears dampened Brenna's stomach through her thin shirt.

"I know. Oh, I know." Brenna spoke against Cassidy's hair and brushed her fingers through the soft locks. Instinctively, she pressed a kiss to the top of Cassidy's head and then reluctantly pulled away, crouching a little to catch Cassidy's gaze. "I'll be right back. I promise."

"Thank you." Cassidy wrapped her arms around the back of the chair, resting her chin on the top edge for a moment before drawing a deep breath and turning back to the form. "I'd better look at this."

"You might want to wait," Brenna suggested ruefully. "It's probably more of a liability protection for the store than an incident statement for the police report." She left Cassidy looking at the form, her gaze scanning the text dubiously.

Brenna found her sons pacing at the service desk. "Hey," she drew their attention.

"Mom!" James rushed up as she stepped from behind the counter. "We've got to get the police."

"They've already been called," she assured him. "What'd you find?" she asked, dropping her voice as she caught glances from other patrons around them.

"We don't know. Out back there's a loading dock, and a big hole compacting the boxes and stuff."

Brenna drew a deep breath. "Any signs that Ryan was there?"

"Not that we can tell." Thomas shook his head when she shot her gaze up to his. "I called for him, but we can't see anything."

A commotion drew Brenna's attention to the store entrance. "Good, they're here. I want you to show the police where you were. We only need one to talk to Cassidy in the office." She nudged both boys over to the officers and introduced herself.

"We're here about a missing child report. Where's the mother?"

Brenna checked the officer's badge. "Lieutenant Taylor, the mother is in the manager's office. My boys have been looking for her son and have a place they'd like your men to check first."

"We need a statement from the mother."

"Listen, it's a trash compactor that's open in the back," she said firmly. "I'll take one of you to meet with Ms. Hyland, but I want someone to check out that compactor."

The officer waved over his partner. "Murph, you, Jefferson, and Maxwell go with these kids. I'm going to talk to the mother."

Murph, whose badge read "Sgt. Murphy", nodded his dark head. "Got it. Okay, boys, lead the way."

Thomas and James guided Sergeant Murphy through the store. When curious onlookers started crowding them, the other two officers behind started running interference, urging people back from the threesome.

"So, how long has the kid been missing?" Murphy asked.

"We've been looking for at least an hour," Thomas supplied. "This way." He turned at the end of an aisle and stopped at the back storage area. "The loading dock is through here."

With Murphy, the two boys stepped out onto to the loading dock, and Thomas pointed to the left. "You think he might've fallen down there?" the sergeant asked.

"We couldn't see anything," Thomas said. His brother pressed up against his back and peered over his shoulder.

"We'll check it out. Now, get back. Maxwell," he called to one of the other officers. "I need your light."

"Yes, Sergeant." Immediately one of the officers stripped a long black tube flashlight off his belt and crossed to where Murphy was dropping to his stomach. "What'cha got?"

"Kid maybe fell in here." He waved the light to his right. "Shine it down there. Straight down."

The tube was long, going deeper into the ground than the four-foot drop to the surface of the truck driveway. The light only bit faintly at the shadows, illuminating not much more than nothing. Murphy rolled over and sat up. "We're going to have to get down to the other end of this thing. Open it up where they pick out the pieces for the trash pickup."

"I'll find a clerk who knows the way." James was off and running before any of the officers could stop him.

Murphy wiped his hands on his uniform pants as he stood. "Let's take the stairs down. Maybe we can get to the room without a clerk's help."

Thomas tagged along because frankly he did not want to face his mother without the officers, especially if the news wasn't going to be good. He was tired enough to contemplate the worst.

They found a set of short stairs that led to the basement level and a series of storage rooms. Pressing his ear to one, Officer Murphy heard the whir of gears and immediately stepped back. The doorknob turned in his hand, and he shoved inward, shining Maxwell's flashlight around the dark room.

The far wall was dominated by a set of metal doors. Another officer behind him located a light switch. Flipping off the flashlight, Murphy tossed it back to Maxwell, who returned it to his belt. "All right, let's open it up."

They checked the latch mechanism and slipped the restraining pole from the catches. The doors swung wide. The officers jumped back out of the way as bits of boxes spilled out, littering the floor around their feet.

"Okay, start digging around."

Thomas looked at the mess. "He can't be in there, can he?"

Murphy, who had begun digging in the darkness of the bin's interior, looked over at him suddenly. "Kid, you better get out. We'll do this." The teen's shoulders slumped. Murphy left off his task for just a moment, crossing the room. He laid a big hand on the slender shoulder. "You did a hell of a job. You don't have any worries. You did everything right."

"Well, I...I'll just be outside then."

"Go on back to your mom. Catch that brother of yours if you run across him and sit tight."

He opened the door to show Thomas out and glanced out into the corridor.

"On second thought, make sure no one else comes down here 'cept the ambulance when it arrives."

"You're calling one? Even if..." Thomas blinked. "I know. I know. Think positive."

The officer thumped Thomas across the shoulder. "Got the right attitude. Now, go on."

Thomas ran to the stairs and halfway up before he just stopped, sat down, and took a deep breath to calm himself.

On the first floor, another pair of patrolmen worked to clear the store before the ambulance team arrived. "All right, everyone, time to go. Sorry for the inconvenience, but we need order here."

"KTLA News." A middle-aged man in a staid suit and tie, microphone in hand, pressed forward through the crowd. "We heard on the scanner there's a missing kid. Possible accident?"

The officer right next to him groaned and turned his back. Over his shoulder, he ordered, "Outside. You'll have an update as soon as we do."

The reporter shrugged off the hands of the crowd pushing at his shoulders. "Just point out the manager."

The manager, with Cassidy and Brenna, stepped out of his office at that moment, with Officer Taylor.

Yelling past the policeman's blocking shoulder, the reporter announced, "Don Deering, KTLA News! Which of you is the mother of the missing boy?"

Cassidy's head shot toward the voice when she heard "mother," though she had been talking to Officer Taylor. Brenna beside her, grabbed her arm in warning. She turned toward her.

"Ma'am, I want to talk to you!" Deering, his cameraman, and another reporter whose shirt was imprinted "KRDV Radio 940" shoved their way through the crowd.

Lieutenant Taylor stepped in front of them. "You were ordered outside, gentlemen. Now move."

"How long has the child been missing? Do you suspect foul play? What's the expectation here?" Both reporters peppered Taylor with questions, occasionally glancing toward the two women making their way with the manager back into the safety of his office.

Taylor grabbed the radio reporter's lapels and picked him up. "No questions until this situation reaches a resolution. Now," addressing both reporters he added, "do I move you, or you remove yourselves?"

The reporters and cameraman retreated to the open doorway of the store, camera lenses trained on the interior, focused on the back of the retreating officer.

"We're here at Sports Warehouse where the grand opening celebration has been marred by the disappearance of a child. More details as they unfold. Stay with KTLA, your team in the city." He motioned to his cameraman. "All right, Randy. Cut. Let's check the crowd and see if anyone's seen anything."

The reporter and cameraman mingled, chatting up the gathering crowd. "Anyone know what's up inside?" Deering asked nonchalantly.

"Missing kid got himself stuck in a hole out back of the store, I heard. Saw the cops heading out that way as we were coming out."

"Out back, you say?"

"Yep, I was by the service desk when the redhead told that officer to check out the trash compactor."

"A trash compactor?"

"Yeah."

"No kidding." Deering got a gleam in his eyes.

"What's the press doing here?" Cassidy whispered to Brenna as they grasped hands, stepping back into the manager's office.

"You can always count on them showing up." Brenna studied Cassidy's face with concern. "How are you doing?"

"Tired. Worried. No, scratch that. Scared to death. I'm really glad I've got a friendly face in all this." Cassidy gave her hand a quick squeeze. "Thank you. The officer's questions were unnerving."

"Just remember, you didn't do anything wrong."

"I let him out of my sight in a crowded store. Whatever happens is my fault."

Brenna patted Cassidy's shoulder. Leaving her hand there a moment, she spoke softly into Cassidy's ear. "We're parents, Cass. We're not perfect. Just keep positive. We'll hear something soon."

The musical interlude from *Eine Kleine Nachtmusik* suddenly erupted between them, scaring both women into jerking apart. The refrain sounded again, and Cassidy reached for her belt and the cell phone attached there. "Hello?" she said timidly into the mouthpiece. "Cameron?" she said faintly, then looked at Brenna. "I...hold on." She covered the receiver with her hand. "Brenna?"

"Do you want me to talk to him?"

Lieutenant Taylor saw her with the phone. "Who is that?"

"A friend of hers," Brenna answered.

"We're having enough trouble with the crowds here. Don't bring anybody else onto the property."

"But..."

"No. Tell whoever whatever you want, but we've got enough problems. Already we're having trouble bringing up the ambulance."

Brenna frowned. "Where is Cameron? I could go get him."

Cassidy's "He's at my house" was almost lost under the policeman's emphatic words, "If you leave, you're not coming back inside, lady."

Brenna pursed her lips, itching to retort. She left the choice up to the person who mattered most at the center of this fiasco. She grasped the other woman's arm, holding her attention. "What do you want to do, Cassidy?"

"Don't go. I'll...he shouldn't worry. I'd like you to stay." Brenna nodded. Cassidy returned to the phone. "Cam, I got held up at the store for a bit longer than I thought. I'll be there soon, I hope." She absently shook her head at the phone; Brenna felt her hand gently squeezed as Cassidy continued to talk. "No. No, just wait there for me."

There was a long silence while Cassidy obviously listened to Cameron. Finally she murmured, "Bye," cutting the connection with a firm snap of the receiver.

There was a knock at the door, and Taylor opened it. "Murph."

The officer sent with her boys walked in, and Brenna stood up. "Sergeant?"

"Your boys are resourceful," he complimented. "We checked the compactor."

Cassidy rose quickly behind Brenna, her hand planting itself on the shorter woman's shoulder. "Compactor? Just what exactly do you think happened to my son?"

"Ma'am?"

Lieutenant Taylor made the introductions. "Sergeant Donald Murphy, this is the boy's mother, Ms. Cassidy Hyland. She and her friend and those boys looked for Ryan before we were called in."

"Well, Ms. Hyland, we were checking out the back loading area and the compactor. We went down to open it up—"

"Trash compactor? Show me."

Cassidy's grip on Brenna's shoulder started to hurt. Though understanding her friend's anxiety, she peeled the long smooth fingers from her collarbone and grasped them, meeting scared blue eyes. Brenna spoke for them both. "Can we go with you to the area?"

"Nothing there. That's good news."

Sharply, she corrected him. "The boy is still missing. Good news will be when he's found."

"I...well, yeah, of course, I just meant..."

"Come on, Cassidy."

Sergeant Murphy looked to his superior, who shrugged. "I...It can't hurt, I guess. All right." He watched the blonde straighten her shoulders, and he stepped back, half into the hallway. "You know. You're familiar somehow. I..." He caught a glint of steel in the redhead's eyes as he tried to recall. The two of them together clicked in his head. He looked back at the missing child's mother. "Shit, you're from the television."

The two women were just passing him, entering the corridor to leave the Customer Service desk. The blurted words drew significant attention from the photographers gathered outside, being held back physically by other officers. The two women dropped their eyes away from the burst of shouted questions and distant flashes.

"Are we looking at a kidnapping, sir?" Murphy asked his superior. "We didn't find any sign that the kid had been near the compactor."

Taylor shook his head. "I honestly don't know. But I didn't expect we'd be dealing with celebrities," he confided as the women moved quickly, now with a pair of officers ahead and behind, toward the back of the mostly empty store.

Chapter 11

Brenna followed a step behind, letting Cassidy work out some of her anxiety as they strode quickly through the store. Still, she cautioned, "We don't have to do this."

Cassidy turned and stopped. "I have to know. I have to see it for myself."

"They said he wasn't there."

"Maybe he was...for a moment. I just have to look."

It was the anguish plainly shown that made Brenna concede. "All right."

They entered the loading dock with the officers who pointed out the compactor shaft. Cassidy stepped close but stopped just before she could look down. "Bren."

Brenna was instantly at the other woman's side, her hand reaching out as Cassidy's reached back. "I'm here."

As their fingers slid together, Cassidy took a steadying breath. "Thank you."

"I told you he wasn't in there," Murphy said, coming up beside them.

Still holding Brenna's hand, Cassidy looked around the floor and noticed a small red object. She bent and picked it up. It was a small Lego piece, like the ones her son kept in his pockets despite her attempts to get him to leave them in the car or in the house.

"What'd you find?" Brenna asked, peering around Cassidy's shoulder.

"It's a Lego," she said quietly. "He was here." She squeezed the plastic bit hard in her hand and closed her eyes. "He was here."

Looking down the shaft, she shivered. Her eyes scanned the edge of the loading dock, and she backed up suddenly. Brenna grasped her hand, trying to stop her.

"He isn't down there, Cassidy. Have faith."

Cassidy stumbled into a pile of boxes along the back wall of the loading dock. The stack was upset when she tried to right herself. A childish yell sounded from elsewhere in the pyramid of cardboard. The officers leaped together into the debris before Cassidy or Brenna could scramble to their feet.

Boxes flew everywhere. Someone hollered, "Got him!" One of the officers rose from the floor, kicking away cardboard and holding Ryan aloft. He was mussed and crying.

She dropped to her knees weakly. "Ryan!"

They brought him over to her, and she sat with him on the floor, hugging him and crying. Brenna crouched over her shoulder, steadily rubbing it. Ryan tried to pull free, at the same time pulling at his mother's neck and hair and crying. Brenna's hand brushed over his head soothingly. She brushed at her own wet cheeks and leaned in, pressing a kiss to Cassidy's cheek in her relief.

Thomas and James raced up, and the officers let them through. In aggravation, Thomas started, "Where in the hell—" A sharp look from his mother tempered his tongue, and he finished more calmly, "Where'd you find him?"

"Playing among the boxes," Brenna said.

"We checked here, I swear we did. Called for him." Thomas crouched down next to Ryan, who was finally beginning to snuffle in his mother's arms, both of them calming. "Why didn't you answer us?"

The boy's blue eyes looked up owlishly, and he pouted. "You didn't use the secret word," Ryan said plaintively. Cassidy's tears renewed against his head on a choked-off laugh.

Brenna, brushing at her own tears, gave a watery laugh as well. She dusted her fingers through the mop of blond hair that looked so much like his mother's. "Honey, I think Mommy's going to refresh your memory how that all works." She offered to take Ryan so that Cassidy could stand. The younger woman took her hand instead of passing over her son, and Brenna found herself lifting both from the floor. The effort resulted in Cassidy steadying herself against Brenna for several seconds.

The police escorted Brenna, Cassidy, and their sons back to the office. Cassidy apologized profusely for making such a stir, still holding Ryan like she would never let him go.

Brenna finally coaxed Cassidy into giving Ryan to her boys for the moment. "We ought to get the report done quickly so you two can get home." Passing Ryan to her sons along with her car keys, she warned them, "Go directly to the car. Don't talk to anyone."

"We'll escort them, ma'am." Maxwell and Murphy, who was throwing an arm around Thomas' shoulders, pulled them together as they guided the boys out of the store.

Twenty minutes later, with most everyone dispersed except a few diehard reporters, Cassidy and Brenna emerged. Cassidy shook Lieutenant Taylor's hand. "Thank you," she said with a weak smile.

"You're welcome, ma'am. Just glad there was a happy ending."

Cassidy was too relieved to speak. She followed Brenna to the parking lot.

"KTLA TV." A reporter approached them. "Don Deering here. So, Ms. Hyland, isn't it?" She nodded absently. "Your boy's all right?"

"Yes," she said, accepting Ryan back from James. Deering reached out and rubbed the fur of the stuffed raccoon Ryan clutched to his chest.

"Don't you think safety measures in the store should have been more stringent? Certainly there was a real danger he could have fallen into that trash compactor?"

Cassidy blanched as the vivid fears resurfaced. Brenna stepped forward, taking Deering's hand off Ryan. "He wasn't hurt, and everyone's fine. I suggest you go back to your station and leave the two of them alone. Now."

Deering shrugged but persisted even as Cassidy was opening her back door and securing Ryan in his car seat. "She ought to decide that, don't you think?"

Brenna, who had a hand on Cassidy's back, felt it stiffen. She patted the muscles and stepped away from the car, drawing Deering's eyes to her. "Mr. Deering, I'm going to say this once: We don't need your attention or the attention of your camera. Now get out of here before I have the police remove you."

Deering looked her up and down, and she was never more thankful for her alter ego: A quick placement of her hands on her hips and a glare made him reconsider pushing the issue. With a dispirited wave of his hand in front of the camera lens, the reporter turned his back and walked over to the closest police officer, his cameraman following.

Brenna caught a grimace from Taylor, but the officer quickly straightened up and delivered a summary which was probably considerably dryer than the reporter would have liked. Taking a deep breath, Brenna finally released her own tension. She turned around to see Cassidy slipping into her driver's seat. There was a tug on her shirt.

James whispered, "Mom, she's in no shape to drive."

Brenna looked more closely and saw that Cassidy's hands were shaking. Bending to the window, she knocked on the glass. Cassidy jumped. James was right. She motioned for Cassidy to roll down the window. "Hey, listen. Why don't I drive? Thomas can follow us."

Hands squeezing the wheel, Cassidy nodded reluctantly and got out, moving around to the passenger seat. Brenna waved to Thomas, who jogged over. "I'm going to drive them."

"Where to?"

Brenna slid into the driver's seat and gently touched Cassidy's arm. "Do you want to go home?"

"Please."

"All right. Thomas, follow me." She reached out the window and patted his cheek. "Be careful. I love you."

"See you in a few minutes," he said confidently, turning away.

With Cassidy collecting herself en route, Brenna soon pulled into the Hyland driveway. Thomas pulled in behind. Cameron was just getting out of his car at the curb. "What the hell happened to you? I heard a report over the radio that Ryan was missing."

"He was," Brenna confirmed. "But we found him." She pointed to the back seat. Cassidy had gone around to the other side and let Ryan out of his car seat, taking him inside.

Watching Cassidy disappear inside her home with Ryan, Cameron asked, "How'd you get caught up in all this?"

Brenna shrugged. "I was there."

"You and Cassidy were shopping together?"

"We happened to be at the same store."

"You live on the other side of town."

Cassidy emerged from the house. "Cam, leave her alone. She was there, and I'm glad for it." She turned to her friend. "Thanks, Bren. I've sent him to his room. I'll talk to him later, when we're both a little less traumatized," she explained when they both looked at her. "Cam, I know you wanted to go out tonight, but I'm not good company right now. Call tomorrow?"

"I'll make you some dinner."

"I can't. I have to talk to Ryan."

"All right," he conceded. He looked toward Brenna and frowned. Turning back to Cassidy, he leaned in and took her elbows in his hands, pressing a kiss on her cheek.

The teenaged boys walked up. "Well, Mom, ready to go?"

Intent on Cassidy as the blonde stepped away from Cameron, Brenna offered, "Don't be too upset with Ryan, Cass."

Cameron got into his car. Brenna saw him watch them for a long moment before driving away. She turned back to Cassidy, who was looking at the ground, rubbing her hands over her face.

Brenna took a deep breath, reached out, and clasped the other woman's hands between her own. Their eyes met, and Brenna felt her stomach twist. Seeing Cassidy so exhausted, she wanted to offer to do something more — like watch Ryan while the young woman slept. She stifled the offer before it could reach her lips; Cassidy had requested to be alone. "Call me if you need to talk."

Impulsively, Cassidy embraced her, and Brenna felt the warmth as their cheeks touched. They separated slowly before relinquishing their mutual grip.

Cassidy turned and entered her home, while Brenna followed her boys back to thejr car. Still pensive, she leaned against the passenger window and quietly thought over the afternoon's events, while Thomas drove home.

Chapter 12

Arms crossed over her chest and leaning against the open glass door, Cassidy watched Ryan run in the backyard with Ranger. The dog was chasing the unexpected "prize" of her son's afternoon escapade — a taxidermy raccoon from the sports store's display. Though he had scared her and several L.A. police officers, Ryan appeared unaffected after being missing for more than an hour.

She watched him stop and turn, catching sight of her in the doorway. He waved and smiled, falling down as the dog leaped at the toy. He laughed as the dog licked his face and then the stuffed animal. She wasn't sure about the sanitary implications, but clearly there was no way she would be able to get the "toy" away from the pair any time soon. Cassidy shook her head.

Thinking about the afternoon quickly took Cassidy's mind down paths she felt better forgotten. Looking into that compactor had scared her nearly witless, despite Brenna's hand in her own to steady her. She closed her eyes and offered up silent thanks that they had found Ryan among a collection of boxes rather than at the bottom of that shaft.

I should have kept a hold on his hand, she berated herself. If she had, he wouldn't have gotten away from her to go look at the animals and consequently gotten lost. Brenna had pointed out that holding on wasn't always possible. She sagged. As the sunset lent an orange haze to the day's end, Cassidy wished for some of that confidence now.

Abruptly she sat up. "I could just call her." She realized that just speaking with Brenna would probably cheer her up. "Ryan!" she called. "Time to come in for dinner."

He ran toward her, and she had to sidestep him and the dog as they barreled through the doorway as a pair. She stepped into the kitchen, sending him to the bathroom to wash up while she put on a couple of hot dogs to boil and retrieved the bag of chips she kept rolled up on the top of the refrigerator. Warming the buns in the microwave, she had a hot dog, complete with ketchup, ready as Ryan slid into his chair at their small kitchen table.

He dug in immediately. She reached for the phone, going so far as to pick up the receiver before scanning her phone list and realizing that she did not have Brenna's home number. Undeterred, Cassidy dialed Information, her hip resting against the counter as she waited for the recording. "Los Angeles," she responded to the prompt. "Lanigan, Brenna." The computer reported the entry as unlisted and disconnected her. Looking at the phone, she muttered, "What now?"

She considered who might know the number and realized that there were very few options: the studio, which was closed, or someone on the coordinating production staff. She blinked. *Of course. Cameron.* She wondered why she had not thought of him first but chalked it up to stress. *Except you saw him just a few hours ago,* memory prompted. Quickly she punched up his number.

"Hello?"

He sounded tired. "Cameron. Hi." She settled to the table, brushing her fingers over the surface. "I have a request."

"You need a day off? No problem. I'll arrange it."

"No, I...I'm okay. I just need a phone number."

"Okay. Sure. Who?"

"Brenna's."

"Lanigan? Why?"

"I need to talk to her."

"Something wrong?"

"I'm sorry, but I really just...Brenna'll understand." There was a long pause before she heard the flutter of papers being turned.

"I...I'm sorry I couldn't help you today. All right. Here's the number..."

She copied it to her list and initialed the entry: BL. "Thanks, Cam. I really appreciate it."

"Ryan is all right, though?"

"Yeah. I'm just..." Cassidy couldn't explain it. Instinct told her Brenna was the only one she could talk to about this. "Sort of a 'you had to be there' thing."

"All right. Well, I...I'll see you at work on Monday?"

"Catch me at the lunch break?"

"Will do." In the silence, Cassidy could hear his breathing over the line. "Well, um, have a good night."

"Thanks." She pressed the disconnect button and immediately dialed the number. Disappointment filled her. The line was busy.

Script loose in her palm, Brenna curled up on her couch, throw pillow against her stomach as she tucked up her bare feet. She could still hear James cleaning the pots from their dinner and filling the dishwasher. Thomas had excused himself to his bedroom to call his girlfriend. She looked at the clock. Twenty minutes already. She sighed, wondering what they could possibly be talking about after spending a whole week together at school.

She acknowledged that she wanted to use the phone and that probably also explained her own distraction. For the last hour she had repeatedly reached for the phone to call Cassidy, only to pull back. Certainly the woman had had a trying enough day; she wouldn't want to bring it up again. But Brenna couldn't get it out of her mind. She kept thinking about just how bad things could have been and wondered at the fate that had put her at the store just in time to help.

Thomas came in and sat down, flipping on the television. As he settled back, he looked over at his mother at the other end of the couch. "Mom?"

"Hmm?"

"Do you mind?"

She shook her head, then straightened a bit. "I just can't seem to get today out of my mind."

"It was totally weird, but everything turned out cool."

"Yes, I know." She leaned over and rubbed his shoulder. "I'm really proud of how quickly you jumped in to help."

"She's a friend of yours." He shrugged as if that explained all.

"She's different from other women I've had as friends," she answered, wondering exactly what she meant by that — and exactly when she had decided Cassidy was someone she could call "friend". She did not have many of them. She shook herself. "I'm just really glad nothing serious happened to Ryan."

"Now that's a cute kid," Thomas agreed.

"He is." Brenna laughed. "I wonder if Cassidy was able to clear things up with him about the 'secret word.'"

James came in, drying his hands on a towel. "That was the weirdest thing I think I'd ever heard."

"He is only five," Brenna reminded her son, reaching up and extending her hand for him to grasp. "I remember you at that age. Remember when you climbed up on the porch railing, convinced if you just spread your arms, you could fly?" She covered her face. "Luckily you only sprained an ankle instead of something more serious." James rolled his eyes, and she chuckled. "See. Kids and risks — natural companions."

"Thanks, Mom," he groaned and left.

Thomas stood. "Are you deserting me, too?" she teased.

"I've got *Hamlet* to read for school."

She nodded. "All right."

"See you in the morning." He kissed her cheek.

"Good night."

After Thomas left, Brenna found her thoughts drifting back to Cassidy and their last moment together on the woman's front lawn. "I'm going to call her," she resolved, reaching for the portable phone on the table. Looking at the keypad, she paused. *What's her number?* Brenna couldn't recall, though she thought the invitation from Ryan's birthday party had it for the RSVP. Of course, after the party, Brenna had tossed the card. She sighed. *Who else would know the number?*

"Cameron!" Hopping up, she checked her desk and pulled the writer's number from her Rolodex. Quickly she punched in the sequence and put the phone to her ear, walking back to the living room couch. Halfway there, she pulled it away and disconnected. *Busy.*

He's probably talking with Cassidy, she reasoned, trying hard to ignore the disappointment coiling in her stomach as she sat down with the script and tried to concentrate.

Stepping out of the bathroom where she had just turned off her son's bathwater, Cassidy looked at the script on her bedside table. *I should work,* she thought, picking up the pages. Reclining on the bed and trying to focus, she rehearsed the dialogue different ways in her head.

Giving up because she was too distracted, she reached for the remote and turned on her TV, keeping the volume low. The background noise frequently helped her concentrate.

"New at 10 o'clock, it was a busy day for a grand opening. It all went awry for a local celebrity and her son when crowds spelled a danger every parent fears."

Cassidy set aside her script and turned up the sound. She caught a piece of news clip — her carrying Ryan, flanked by Lieutenant Taylor and Brenna. "God, I thought this was over," she groaned, reaching for the phone to call the station and request the story editor.

It rang before she could start dialing. After a moment to collect herself, Cassidy picked up the receiver. "Hello?"

"Hey, Cassidy."

"Rich?" Surprised by Rich Paulson's voice, Cassidy blinked, then put the receiver back to her ear. "What's up?"

"That's my question. Just heard a news brief. You had a little excitement this afternoon? Everything all right?"

Cassidy brushed her fingers through her bangs and pulled them back from her face. "Yeah. We're both fine. It was nothing really."

"Not what the news said. Ryan almost fell into a trash compactor?"

"There was an open one near him, but no...he didn't."

"Well, that's good news. I wanted to check on you, I guess."

"Might've been different if Brenna hadn't been there," she said.

"Brenna? Our Brenna?"

"Yeah, we were both shopping for camping equipment when we ran into each other."

"How's she doing?"

"Fine. She was great. Her boys, too."

"I'm glad you had some help." There was a long pause. "Well, I just wanted to call. Guess I'll let you go."

"Thanks. Really."

"Good night."

"Good night." With a half smile, she set down the phone, wondering who else would call. Slipping from the bed, Cassidy returned to the bathroom.

"All right, Mr. Prune. Bedtime." She pulled Ryan from the tub and wrapped a thick towel around him. Perched on the toilet, she rubbed him down and patted his face dry. He rubbed his eyes tiredly. "So, did you have enough fun for one day?"

"Mmm hmm."

"All right. Can we have a better day tomorrow?"

"Mmm hmm."

She picked him up and brushed her nose against his cheek. "I love you."

His arms wrapped around her neck. "I love you, too, Mommy."

She carried him into his bedroom and helped him into his pajamas. Tucking him under his covers, she knelt by his bed. "Please don't run off again, okay?"

He put his arms over the top of the covers and nodded emphatically. "Okay."

She stifled a chuckle and ruffled his hair. "Sweet dreams."

Retreating to the door, she turned off his light. He turned on his side, and she paused for a lingering look. *Thank God for you, Brenna.* Any longer and Ryan might have come looking for her. He might have actually fallen into that compactor. Her need to talk to the other woman suddenly acute, Cass returned to the bedroom and dialed the number Cameron had given her. "Hello? Brenna?"

Across town, phone to her ear, Brenna unfolded suddenly on the couch with a huge exhalation of relief. "Cass, are...is everything all right?"

Cassidy took a deep breath, feeling real relief flood her for the first time in hours. "Yeah, I just... It's okay that I called?"

"Absolutely." The redhead curled back in the cushions and pulled the pillow into her lap as she spoke. "How's Ryan? Any lingering effects from his adventure today?"

"Not a thing. I think he's still unaware just how much trouble he caused."

"Did you try to explain it to him?"

"Yes."

"Well, you'll just have to watch him more closely for a while. You've got an adventurer, like James was. Still is, really," Brenna mused.

"Really?" Cassidy curled up on her bed and relaxed into the pillows. "Tell me about it?"

"When he was about Ryan's age, he tried to fly off a porch railing," Brenna reminisced. "He was always the one halfway down the street when I called them in for dinner." She chuckled. "Thank God, he doesn't drive yet. I'll never see him once he does." She choked up a bit. "But," she suddenly sounded more assuring than reminiscent, "that's what we raise them up to do — be able to walk away from us, hmm?"

"And be safe," Cassidy agreed. "Yeah. So why is it so damn scary when it happens?"

Hearing the other woman's exasperation and completely understanding its source, Brenna hugged her pillow tighter, let out a half-chuckle, and sighed, feeling better than she had in hours. "I don't know," she admitted ruefully.

Cassidy felt warmed beyond belief. "You were so positive for me today. I...don't know if I'll ever be able to thank you."

"You needed someone," Brenna offered quietly.

The line was silent between them for several breaths. Cassidy closed her eyes and inhaled as the unexpected connection soothed her. "You were perfect for the job." She heard Brenna's soft intake of breath.

For her part, Brenna didn't want the call to end. She looked around the couch and table, spying her dog-eared script. "Well, so...um, you want to practice a few pages?"

"Over the phone?" Cassidy put her hand over her mouth to quash the laugh bubbling up. The idea of reading script pages at one another over the phone in the middle of the night was absurd. However, she didn't want to hang up, either. "All right." She reached for her script and heard through the line as Brenna did the same. "Where do you want to start?"

Brenna started reading; Cassidy recognized the section and flipped there, picking up her response.

A long, strange day came to an end on a high note.

Chapter 13

Script under his arm, Sean Durham trotted onto the set and settled at one of the round tables where several other cast members already sat. The new script called for a bar setting, and the props people had recreated a speakeasy from the 1920s. "They're about to break," he said. "Who's going with me to get the trays?"

"You want to eat here?" Terry Brown raised an eyebrow.

Cassidy elbowed him. "I'm partial to this place. Cozy." She looked to her right and smiled at Brenna, just sitting down. "Don't you think so?"

"Yep." Brenna grinned back, looking around at the atypically costumed group. Many of them wore Prohibition-era, semi-formal attire. "Wonder if we could convince the writers to let us stay here. I like the change of clothes."

She laughed, running her fingers over the jacket line of her blue skirt suit. She cast a sidelong glance at Cassidy, who wore a torch singer's elbow-length gloves and long, slinky white dress, complete with sequins. With the woman's blond hair pulled up off her cheeks but falling down her back, the effect was stunning, like looking at an alabaster or marble statue, despite the rouge defining her cheekbones. "Hmm?" She caught Cassidy's eye and cocked her head.

The blonde nodded. "I'd go for it."

Rachelle Cheron paused as she was settling onto a chair. "Oh, um, Cass, didn't see you this morning, but I wanted to say how glad I am that everything is okay with Ryan."

Cassidy nodded sheepishly, tracing idly on the table with her sequin-gloved hand before intertwining her fingers and looking toward Brenna. "Thanks to Brenna, I didn't go nuts."

"Brenna?" About half the table, unaware Brenna had anything to do with the situation, looked straight at the compact woman.

"I was just in the right place at the right time." She looked at Cassidy, then ducked her head. Taking the attention off both of them, she pointed to Sean. "I think that's enough. Engage your afterburners and get us our lunches. Best speed," Brenna said with a tossed thumb over her shoulder. "I'm hungry." She winked at him.

"Aye, aye, Ma'am!" He stood and saluted before leaving.

In their *Time Squad* uniforms, Rich Paulson and Will Chapman finally stepped up to the bar set, leaning on the table sections between the others. "So, how's it going?" Will asked.

"Not bad," Brenna said. "How's shooting?"

Rich grinned. "Four more scenes."

Thinking quickly, Brenna calculated. "What, then? Another five hours or so? You might make it home for dinner."

"If we can get through everything in a minimum of takes," he said with a nod.

Curious, Cassidy asked, "What's tonight?"

"My anniversary." Rich smiled.

"Congratulations," Cassidy said. "How many years? Are you doing dinner?"

"Twenty-nine years. And yes, we're going to dinner. Then dancing. And a play at L.A. Playhouse. I don't have to be here tomorrow. I checked." He grinned.

"Nice to see someone having some fun," Will added.

Just as Sean reappeared, his arms weighted with trays and a collection of juice and soda cans, a stagehand appeared. "Ms. Hyland?"

Cassidy, who had just taken her choices from the pile, turned around. "Yes?"

"Phone call for you. You can take it over there."

"Who is it?"

"Wouldn't say. Said it was important, though."

"All right." She stood, catching Brenna looking at her while nibbling on the corner of her tuna fish sandwich. "I'll be right back."

Will dropped into the chair Cassidy had vacated and dug into his meal. Looking briefly at Brenna, between bites he said, "So, part of the weekend had some excitement for you?"

"Yes." She sipped her Diet Coke. "How about you? What'd you do this weekend?"

Around them, other conversations started up.

Will shrugged. "I flew out to Phoenix and visited my sister."

"Family event?"

"Nah, just a visit. Haven't seen her much. She's expecting her first baby in a couple of months. We haven't had a chance to talk."

Brenna nodded. "Sounds nice. How's the weather out that way?"

"Nice." They fell silent. He studied her for a moment longer before turning back to his meal.

Brenna glanced up at Cassidy, just at the edge of the set wall, as she talked on the phone. Looking agitated by the conversation, the blonde paced. Brenna continued to eat but kept an eye on her, her own stomach twisting in concern. She considered that it must be a reaction from the weekend. She had become deeply involved in a very private pain with the younger woman. The connection lingered a little bit, she supposed. When she looked at Cassidy again, her heart constricted.

Cassidy's face was ashen. She had covered her mouth to prevent whatever she was feeling from coming out. Brenna snapped to her feet as Cassidy hung up. Intercepting her at the far edge of the stage, she put a hand on her arm. "What's up? You're white as a sheet."

"It's the makeup," Cassidy joked, with obvious forced effort.

Unexpectedly hurt by the dismissal, Brenna realized that was also why Cassidy had tried the joke. The blonde had been hurt by the phone caller. "What is it?" she coaxed. With a glance over her shoulder toward the others, she nudged Cassidy behind the stage wall.

Taking a deep breath, Cassidy searched Brenna's face before finally deciding to share. "Mitch heard," she said briefly. "He wants to see Ryan."

Brenna shook her head and leaned against the wall carefully. "Mitch? That's your ex, isn't it? He has visitation, right?"

"Yes."

"Nothing happened. Ryan is fine. I'm sure he just wants to see that."

"He's never agreed with my having custody," Cassidy explained. "All he needs is a good reason to challenge."

"This isn't a good reason," Brenna assured her.

"What isn't a good reason?"

Brenna and Cassidy, who had huddled close to talk, looked outward, startled. Cameron and producer Victor Branch had wandered over from their offices. "Hello," Branch said when their gazes fell on him.

"Hi," Brenna returned.

"What's up?" Cameron queried again.

Cassidy's answer was unexpectedly short. "Nothing." She moved quickly away from the group.

Brenna could not stifle her surprise.

Cameron posed his question again directly to Brenna. "What's happened?"

"Cameron, I shouldn't get in the middle of things."

"You seem to be doing that lately anyway. Why stop now?"

Brenna was stung by the cutting remark. She pushed aside the wave of indignation with a deep breath and turned away. "Nice to see you, Victor," she offered in parting.

"Um, yeah. Bye." Victor looked from Cameron to Brenna, then back to his writer. "What the hell was that all about?"

Cameron watched Brenna settle next to Cassidy. The women resumed eating in silence while the rest of the cast animatedly conversed around them. "I wish to hell I knew."

"Cameron."

The two men looked up to see Will Chapman coming toward them. "Hello, Will." Cameron became even more uneasy; conversations with the actor seldom went well lately. "What's up?" he said carefully.

"I wanted to talk about a scene coming up. Instead of sending Pryor out again, I can recover the team this time. I've got an idea to restage it," Will suggested. "It'll give more punch to the action, an undercurrent I think the fans will appreciate."

"No," Cameron said sharply. "The story stays as is."

"So you'd rather write flat shit than build a story with some character, Cam?"

"You're the flat one, Chapman. Dull as a board. Your dailies put half the exec team to sleep."

"Then give me something to do!"

"You get what you can handle."

"Cam," Branch interrupted. "We'll discuss it later." He saw the director come around the edge of the set. "We'd better go."

"All right, everyone," Gerry Hifer, the new episode's director, addressed the group at the table. "Break's over." Cameron and Victor left, the latter dragging the former away with a bit of effort, and the cast cleared away their lunch mess, quickly sweeping everything into the trash cans.

Brenna stepped out of her uniform with relief and pulled on her thick robe. Hanging the costume carefully, she sat at the small mirror and brushed her hair, loosening the spray's hold on it. There was a knock at her trailer door. "Come in."

"Ms. Lanigan?"

"Kyle?" She turned around to face the guest actor, Kyle Masters, cast to play her office boss. It was strange for her to be playing a secretary in the current episode's pre-women's lib era. Playing the demure was tough; Susan's in-charge attitude was part of her nature. It did not vanish overnight. "What's up?"

"We didn't get a chance to talk today. I was wondering if you'd like to go to dinner. Read a few lines," he offered hesitantly. "Work on our rapport?"

"I can't do dinner," she said, "but I'll read with you for a little while."

"Thanks. You all are a pretty tight-knit bunch," he said. "Saw you during the lunch break."

She nodded sagely. "It's hard to come into that, I know. I've had to do it myself a few times."

"And...Cassidy, is it? She's a bit of a chilly personality."

"Not really. You just caught her on an off day. By the end of the week, you'll see." Cassidy's performance had been rougher then usual during their run-throughs after lunch. *Mitch's call really rattled her.* Brenna resolved to find out more, to see if she could help at all. She shook the other woman's troubles out of her head and returned her attention to Kyle. "Well, ready to read?"

Cassidy stepped into her trailer just as the phone rang. Picking it up, she answered, "Hello?"

"Hello."

Recognizing her ex-husband's voice, Cassidy sat down hard. "Um...hello, Mitch." Distracting herself, she slipped off the high heels. Reaching for the Bullwinkle slippers, she held them in her lap for a long moment, the soft fluff comforting. "I'm sorry about earlier. I...You just caught me in the middle of working. Came out of left field."

"I still want to see Ryan."

"Nothing happened."

"This time. What about next time?"

"There won't be a next time," she insisted.

"You can't know that. Who's with him right now?"

"Gwen. You know her."

"Yeah, and I know she's got three of her own to look after."

"Mitch, don't. Please."

There was a knock at her trailer door. "Come in."

Cameron stepped up and stood in the doorway. "Hi, Cass."

She held up a hand, motioning him to silence. "I'll have to talk to you later," she said into the phone. "A writer just walked in." She hung up, took a deep breath, and turned to Cameron. "Hi."

"Just wanted to come by and see how you were doing. Who was the phone call?"

"Mitch heard about this weekend. He wants to visit Ryan."

"So he wants to visit with his kid. About time he shared some of the responsibility. As long as he stays away from you." He moved toward her.

That Cameron could suggest letting Mitch have Ryan for any time filled Cassidy with so much anger and fear it made her curt. She stepped out of his reach. "I'm still in costume. Excuse me." She slipped into the second room of her trailer, emerging a few minutes later, straightening a pullover sweater over her worn jeans.

He smiled and held out a hand. "Dinner?"

"I'm going home." The flat statement was not an invitation to join her.

Cameron overlooked her coolness. "I'll meet you there."

"Mmm hmm." She walked out of her trailer before he could say anything more.

The parking lot was almost empty when Cassidy reached her car. She was still trying to calm herself as well as to understand why she had gotten so upset with Cameron. Noise a few spaces away drew her gaze up from the pavement. Brenna was getting in her car. She called out, "Good night!"

The other woman turned from pulling her car door closed. "Cass? I didn't think you were still here."

"And you..." Cassidy noted how tired the other woman looked and regretted bothering her. "What kept you late?"

Stepping out of her SUV as Cassidy came closer, Brenna pointed toward another section of the lot. "He did." Cassidy glanced over and saw a silver car driving away. "Kyle wanted to practice our scenes again."

"So, is Jakes getting along with her boss?" Cassidy asked with a twinkle in her eye. "Should Chris offer you a love song the next time you come into the club?"

"No. Please don't." For a moment, Brenna wondered about Cassidy's singing voice. She had not had a chance to see the woman rehearsing the numbers she was doing in the episode. Brenna shook it off. "Did you resolve things with Mitch?"

"Not yet. I'll call him tonight after Cameron leaves."

"Entertaining tonight?" Brenna's voice was uneasy.

"I need to find a balance between spending time with Ryan and with Cameron."

"I know the feeling."

Cassidy nodded. "I guess you do."

"Well," Brenna said quietly, reaching out a hand, "Good night."

When their palms touched, both stepped forward. Cassidy suddenly threw her arms around Brenna. "Thanks for everything," she whispered in Brenna's hair, inhaling the distinct scent of muscle ointment. She closed her eyes and squeezed lightly. Happiness tingled along the nerves in her back as Brenna's hands moved lightly up her spine before the two pulled apart. When she met Brenna's eyes again, they were lightly crinkled by an uncertain, but pleased smile. She felt a similar one shape her own lips. The change in their relationship felt incredibly good.

"You...you're welcome," Brenna said, and Cassidy was surprised to hear a mild huskiness in the voice.

Cassidy could say nothing, being caught up in the depth and breadth of swirling cobalt. Following a deep breath, Brenna slipped from Cassidy's arms. She clasped Brenna's hand for a moment longer, suddenly reluctant to let the other woman leave.

Brenna's voice was soft in protest. "I...should go." Cassidy released her hand. Brenna looked up and nodded. "Take care of yourself."

"I will." Cassidy stood in silence, watching Brenna slip behind the wheel and drive off the lot.

Chapter 14

"Come on, Cass. Sit down. Relax." Cameron patted the couch where he'd sat after turning on her stereo with an easy-listening CD.

Cassidy finished up the last dish and dried her hands. "Something to drink?" she asked.

"Sure."

She fished in the refrigerator and discovered the remnants of a bottle of white wine. She was moving it to the counter when Cameron entered the kitchen. Stepping aside when he reached into an upper cabinet for a pair of glasses, she felt his hand slip over her upper back. "Sorry," she said, moving away.

"No, I was just getting the glasses." Cameron turned to her. "What's wrong? You've been jumpy all night."

Cassidy shook her head and shrugged. She was both keyed up and exhausted, her mind filled with thoughts she could not seem to put in order. "Tired, I guess."

He poured and handed her a glass, then guided her to the couch, kissing the back of her neck before she sat down. "Well, day's over now." After setting his wine on the low table, he turned her around and put his hands on her shoulders. "Massage?"

"No, it's okay." She sipped the wine and tried to focus on the evening. Unfortunately, the only thing she kept thinking about was her conversation with Brenna in the parking lot after work. And the hug. She wondered what the other woman had thought of her at that moment — and just when she had realized Brenna needed that hug as much as she had.

She leaned into Cameron's body reluctantly and wondered why. With a rueful sigh, she sat up straight. "Thanks," she said politely as his hands slipped from her shoulders.

"Is it the call from Mitch?" he asked. "Why didn't you tell me when he first called?"

"What?" Cassidy, who had not been focusing, looked at him in confusion.

"At the studio, during lunch. That call you got — it was from Mitch, wasn't it?" Her forehead briefly furrowed. "Oh. Mmm hmm."

"You said it was nothing."

"I couldn't deal with it then," she said. "We were heading back into shooting."

"You told Lanigan about it."

"She asked."

"So did I."

"Mommy?"

Cameron and Cassidy turned to see Ryan in his footed pajamas, peering at them from the bedroom hall, his stuffed monster doll hugged to his chest.

"What is it?" Cassidy held out her hand to her son.

"Can't sleep. Can you tell me a story?"

Cassidy looked over her shoulder at Cameron, then back at her son. "Not tonight, buddy," she said quietly. "I'll give you a hug, though."

"Okay." Ryan climbed onto her lap and turned into her chest. She closed her eyes and reveled in the sensation as she wrapped him securely in her arms and kissed his hair.

Cameron's hand moved between her arms, and he patted her son's back. "There you go, guy," he said. "One bona fide Mom hug."

Cassidy loosened her grasp but was pleased when her son did not immediately get down from her lap. She absently stroked the monster toy, thinking of the woman who had given it to him, while her other hand lightly drew circles on Ryan's lower back. Looking up, she saw Cameron looking pensive.

"Back to bed," she said, keeping her mouth from showing the regret she felt as her son left her lap. She stood and walked him back to his bedroom. Pulling the covers to his chin, she kissed him again. "Good night."

When she returned to the living room, Cameron was sitting back against the couch sipping his wine. "So, are you ever going to tell me what happened Saturday?"

"I told you," she said, resuming her seat. "Ryan got away from me, and it took a while to find him."

"Somebody take him?"

"No. Cam, I got the third degree from Mitch; I don't need you to cross examine me, too."

Cameron eased back and lifted his hands in the universal symbol of surrender. But he couldn't resist one last question. "How'd Lanigan get involved?"

Ruminating, Cassidy leaned back. She remembered the wariness on Brenna's face when they ran into one another in the store aisle and how it was just as quickly set aside when Cassidy revealed her problem. Brenna had taken thorough command of the situation, dispatching her sons. Cassidy smiled. "After the Halloween party at the studio, she invited me to go camping with her charity group. Saturday, I realized there were still a few things I'd need. It seems we both had the same idea to check out the new warehouse store. She was there to pick up a few things for the trip herself."

"She invited you on a camping trip?"

"Yes. Next weekend."

"That was nice of her."

Cassidy thought Cameron's tone didn't sound like he thought it had been. Her response was defensive as a result. "Yes, it was. We haven't talked much—"

"She's done her best to *ignore* you. You've—"

"But that's been changing. We've become friends."

He scoffed. "Since Saturday?"

"You don't think it could be that simple?"

"Nothing with that woman is *that* simple. What's she getting out of it?"

"She said she thought Ryan and I would have some fun."

"Press gonna be there?"

"No, a bunch of underprivileged kids. Damn, Cameron, can't you just be happy for me?"

Cameron shifted on the couch and even pulled his arms down from around the back of the cushion as he rubbed the knees of his trousers. "She's never made a gesture like this before. Doesn't that just seem...weird to you?"

"I'm flattered she wants to spend time with me *and* Ryan," she responded pointedly.

Cameron straightened and shot back, "Don't start. I like Ryan just fine, but I'm dating you, not him."

"Cameron, we're a package deal."

"Why are you picking a fight with me?"

"I'm not picking a fight."

"Speaking of picking a fight... You should thank me. Today, Chapman wanted to rewrite a scene. Branch got him to cut our 'discussion' short at lunch, but I still found a sheaf of script pages on my desk. After one look, I ripped them up."

"Why? Maybe Will had an interesting idea. You let Rich pitch you ideas all the time."

"Paulson doesn't want to write scenes where he's kissing you," Cameron replied.

"Chapman wants to kiss— But Raycreek and Hanssen have nothing in common."

"He doesn't care about that. He knows you're the ratings grabber, and he wants in on the action."

Cassidy sighed. "I really thought I was beginning to be part of the team. Brenna—"

"Brenna's been all over you lately."

"I worked hard to get her to acknowledge me," Cassidy objected. "That's why I appreciated the invitation to go camping."

"We could've gone to Napa or something."

"But Ryan couldn't come along on a winery tour."

Cameron stood abruptly. "Fine. Forget it. Go camping."

Cassidy said nothing. Leaning on the arm of the couch, she rested her head on her crossed wrists, watching as he collected his coat. "Will I see you tomorrow?" she asked to his back as the door opened.

"Maybe." Cameron's terse response followed him out.

Worn emotionally, Cassidy rose from the couch and went to her bedroom, stopping at Ryan's door with a quick glance inside to see that he was safely asleep.

She decided to unwind in the bathtub. Opening the taps to the clawfoot tub in the master bathroom, she returned to her bedside table and picked up the script. She shook her head and put it down. *You want to unwind.* Pinning up her hair, she stepped out of her clothes, slid into the warm water, and stretched out in lavender bubbles.

Breathing deeply, she ignored the phone when it suddenly rang in the bedroom. Whoever it was, however, disconnected as soon as her answering machine picked up. A beat later, she remembered she had wanted to call Mitch. Shaking her head, she closed her eyes resolutely. *Tomorrow. From work. Maybe Brenna would be willing to sit with me while I try to reason with him.*

The thought of Brenna brought Cassidy back to their hug. Her body flushed at the memory. In that instant, when Brenna had presented her hand, Cassidy had seen the same "this is absurd" expression on Brenna's face that she figured she'd had on her own. When she initiated a hug instead, Brenna had leaned into the embrace. Remembering the contact, Cassidy crossed her arms over her chest and submerged in the water. The warmth soothed her prickling skin. *What an incredible feeling of belonging.*

Cameron's words bubbled to the surface along with her released breath. *"Brenna's been all over you lately."*

What did he mean by that? Was it just a professional thing, some form of manipulation, or something more personal? When she surfaced, she scolded herself for being fanciful. "Ridiculous. You are overanalyzing again, Ms. Cancer Ascendant. It was just a hug." She grabbed her sponge and scrubbed her skin until it held a rosy glow.

When the water had cooled, she pulled the plug, stepped out of the tub, and dried. After pulling on a nightshirt, she pulled up her bed covers and curled around a pillow. Sleep claimed her quickly.

Inside her front door, Brenna was surprised from behind with a hug from Thomas as she turned around to put up her coat and keys. She jumped, then returned the embrace. "Good to see you, too," she said with a chuckle. "What's up? Besides you, that is?"

"I thought you were stuck at another all-nighter."

"No. I ended up in a conversation in the parking lot, then took surface roads instead of the highway." Putting her purse down, Brenna thought back to the hug. *And I needed time alone to think.*

Thomas nodded. "Sure. Are you hungry?"

"No. I'm just going to bed. You should, too," she told him with a kiss. "Why are you always up waiting for me?"

Thomas shrugged. "I'm usually still doing homework." She looked askance at him. "Well, okay. It'll sound kind of stupid, but sometimes I think you could use someone to talk to. I like being that someone," he added sheepishly.

Moved by her son's admission, Brenna patted his arm. "You're going to make some young lady very lucky, Thomas. Thank you."

"Mom," he groaned as she leaned against him and hugged him.

"Where's James?"

"Right here."

She hugged her younger son, who appeared at her shoulder from the bedroom hallway. "I missed you guys," she said. "Are you looking forward to our weekend away?" They both nodded.

"Good night, Mom."

"Good night." Brenna entered her room and flipped on the late news to watch as she changed. The reminder to vote in the elections the next day brought Kevin to mind. She had already sent in her absentee ballot, but she ought to encourage him on his important night. She reached for the phone, then remembered it was going to be two a.m. in Mount Clemens. She arranged her pillows and curled up, hoping the bed would warm quickly as she snuggled deeper into the mattress.

"Thanks for everything," Cassidy whispered in Brenna's hair.

Brenna's eyes opened as the soft voice played in her head. She had been looking at her own hand, wondering why a handshake was not what she wanted to offer, and then suddenly they were hugging. Awash with pleasure, Brenna realized she had not wanted to say goodbye in the first place.

She took a quick breath of relief and met Cassidy's gaze. Surprise and curiosity were mirrored there. Stepping closer to the other woman, Brenna felt Cassidy's arm brush against her hand as she lifted it to waist height. She remembered how warm the skin of Cassidy's cheek felt as it lightly touched her own. She could smell the scent of lavender caught in Cassidy's hair, present even after a long day. Her arms went around Cassidy's back; Cassidy's fingers spread and slid up Brenna's back. She closed her own eyes and moved her hands up a little. Cassidy's arms squeezed briefly before the two pulled apart.

When she met the blue gaze again, there was a faint smile. She felt a similar one shaping her own lips. The change in their relationship felt incredibly good. "How was that?" Brenna asked. She was surprised to hear a mild huskiness in her own voice.

"Perfect," Cassidy said absently.

She backed reluctantly from Cassidy's hands and their grasp lingered for a long moment. She hesitated. "I...should go. Take care of yourself."

"I will."

Brenna's heart had been pounding so hard afterward that she needed the extra drive time to relax. Just the memory now sharply raised her heart rate. Closing her eyes tightly and balling her hands against her chest, she wondered what the next day would bring in her changed friendship with Cassidy.

Chapter 15

"Action!"

Brenna and Kyle were ushered inside by the doorman, and Brenna gave up her rain slicker and hat, revealing a ladies' skirt suit in a very flattering dark blue.

With her boss, Virgil, Susan Jakes entered the nightclub set in this altered timeline. He had coaxed her to dinner while they worked on an office project. "Are you sure we can spare the time away from this project?" she asked.

"I appreciate that you want to get it finished, but taking a break isn't a crime," he answered, taking her coat.

"How can we talk in this noise?" Susan asked.

He smiled at her. "Don't you like the music?"

Susan studied the woman crooning into a microphone and swaying to the pianist's music as she sang. When she didn't answer, her escort shrugged. "Something to drink?"

Jakes shook her head. "No. It's all right. Should we sit?"

"Perfect." He smiled.

Surreptitiously Susan kept track of the other Time Squad operatives. Chris was the singer, Creighton kept the liquor flowing behind the bar. Their waiter, Jeremy Dewitt, showed them to a table near the stage.

Chris' blue eyes brushed over them as she moved across the stage, beginning another song:

> No, you don't know the one
> who dreams of you at night,
> and longs to kiss your lips
> and longs to hold you tight…

Finishing the stanza, she paused, turned back, and found Susan Jakes studying her. "You, you just don't know me," she crooned, watching as Jakes' escort grasped her hand where it rested on the table. "You'll never ever know, the girl who loves you so…" Chris dropped her gaze back to the couple in the front row, finding Susan's eyes. *Mind on the mission*, she reminded herself. She paused for the handful of beats between the stanza and the next refrain, looked at Virgil, and then growled seductively.

"Cut!"

Cassidy immediately softened the line of her shoulders and laughed. Brenna reached over and tapped her on the arm, and she turned to the Commander. "Yes?"

"Don't do that!" Brenna said with mock distress. "You're acting like a jealous lover."

"Just trying to distract him from guessing we know each other already." She laughed again. "But I could do jealous, if you like."

Kyle Masters stood. Half a day with the blond actress he had thought was ice cool had quickly shown him her playful side, which, as the day wore on, she had thrown his way once or twice. "I'll flip you for her. Someone have a quarter?" He caught one tossed from off set. "Heads she stays in this time frame with me; tails she goes back with you."

Cassidy nodded, catching Brenna's shoulder in a quick hug. "You have to come back! What would I ever do without you!"

Brenna laughed uneasily, and Cassidy felt the other woman tug away gently. Reluctantly she let go, watching Brenna move away with her head down. She was obviously thinking very hard about something as the post-camera smile had evaporated, replaced by...*Anxiety?* "Bren?"

Brenna turned at the soft call, but just then, Hifer walked up. "Are you three finished?" He chuckled. The trio suddenly looked up and laughed, separating. "Go on, back to your marks."

"Scene 18 B. Take 12." On their cue, the trio replayed the scene, finally finishing it to Hifer's satisfaction.

"All right, everyone. Take five. We're going to set up for the scene with Terry." The dark-skinned actor stepped up. "Ready, Terry?"

Terry nodded, and Brenna watched him sink into character; it was a palpable change. His eyes went shallow and dark, and the musculature and veins in his neck and arms became more pronounced. *Damn,* she thought. *He's going for scary.*

Cassidy stopped at her shoulder on her way off to the side. "What's up?" the blonde asked against her head.

"Look at Terry," Brenna said softly. Her head close to Brenna's, Cassidy turned and caught sight of Brown, pacing the portion of the set where his character worked. He was so caught up in character that he was muttering to himself and stalking, ignoring the lighting and sound grips moving the booms around to illuminate the area properly.

"Damn. That'll give me nightmares," Cassidy remarked. "He should've worked on my last movie. I didn't have anything on him as a vampire."

Brenna chuckled at the image of Cassidy as a vampire. "I'll have to go to the opening of that now," she teased.

"It was fun." Curious about Brenna's earlier withdrawal, Cassidy slipped an arm over the smaller woman's shoulder and watched gray-blue eyes look uneasily at the hand trailing over her costume. "I liked the fangs," she said.

"Cass, I..." Brenna eased out from under the touch.

"Horror movies scare you?" Cass asked in a playfully low voice. "Look. No sharp teeth." Brenna's eyes met hers, and Cassidy gave her a full grin, showing her very white, very straight teeth. Cass released Brenna as Hifer stepped toward them.

"All right, everyone. Places."

Brenna went over to her mark with Kyle, and they leaned across the table toward one another; Cassidy returned to her mark, and Terry stood behind the bar. "Action!"

The dark-skinned actor became frenetic; Brenna was transfixed. Standing behind the bar, he smashed a bottle against the bar. With an animal-like growl, he jumped onto the bar surface and began raving, then he leaped onto the stage and grabbed Cassidy.

Brenna started toward him.

"Let her go!"
Creighton lunged away from her, dragging Chris with him. He grabbed the microphone and held it like a knife against her throat. Chris' face filled with fear when Creighton held her close with one hand and growled his lines into her face. "Stop singing!"

"Would you prefer a different song?" Chris' voice was a weak, breathless plea.

Jakes was only a step away when Chris pulled free of Creighton, who was restrained by several patrons. Creighton's strength gained him his freedom, however. Suddenly a real knife was in his hands, and then, just as suddenly, he plunged it into the chest of another patron. He started shaking and then turned and rushed headlong through the gathering crowd and into the night.

Jakes grabbed Chris' upper arms as the singer backed up into her. Tension rippled through the muscles under her hands and just as suddenly, Hanssen turned into her shoulder, grasping Jakes' left arm with her own right hand. They both knelt to see to the murdered man. "Are you all right?" Jakes asked Chris.

"Yes. I... Thank you." Hanssen and Jakes huddled close for a long beat. Chris reached out and checked the man's throat for a pulse. "He's dead."

"What the hell happened? We were supposed to stop a murder, not cause one."

"I'll go check behind the bar, see if I can find any clues."

Susan patted her back. "Go on. I'll cover for you." She stood and steered her "date" away from the dead man.

"Cut!" Hifer ended the scene.

Terry stepped out and took a bow to the applause of the camera crew, then looked toward Brenna and Cassidy, offering a wide smile. "Ladies, my Hyde imitation."

Glad to have a diversion from her still-racing heart, Brenna threw a prop to Terry.

He caught it, raising it in an exultant fist. "I would like to thank the Academy," he began.

Cassidy leaned against a console, laughing.

"One take, and damn, I'll take it. Next scene up," the director said. "Terry, go take a break. Everyone else...let's belly up to the bar."

"Does he do that often?" Kyle asked as Brenna, he, and Cassidy fell into step together on the walk over to the second soundstage.

"Nail a scene in one take? Not on your life." Brenna laughed. "But damn, he did, didn't he, Cass?"

The blonde nodded. "I'll give his name to my last movie director. Terry's got the sequel locked up." She shook her head and took a deep breath. "I thought I was the only horror film vet."

Brenna shook her head with appreciation. "Terry's gotta have a few on his résumé somewhere."

They sat at a bar table and worked into the short filler scenes, bantering with Sean Durham for a few minutes. They talked about their later scenes, relaxing with sips from their stage drinks — filtered water. The lighting and sound crews climbed around the set like flies on a screened porch.

The sound of flipping script pages brought their attention back to Hifer, who was going over the planned angles with the camera crew. One of the extras playing a bar patron came up. "Hey, George." Cassidy waved him over to the empty fourth seat at their table.

He sank into the chair. Gratefully he sipped at the cup at his place. "Man, this is great."

"The water or the job?" Brenna asked.

"Both."

Shaking off the energy lingering from the shoot, Brenna settled back and watched the two men chat quietly. She looked over at Cassidy, whom she found looking back, over the rim of her water cup. Her blue eyes really were very pale, almost clear. "How'd it go with Mitch last night?"

"I, uh, actually...didn't call him yet. I'm going to at the dinner break." Cassidy hesitated, then stirred her water idly with a finger as she spoke softly, "Would you consider being there?"

Brenna startled. "Me? Why?"

"Well, you were there Saturday. I...Mitch might want to ask you a few questions."

Nodding, Brenna sipped her drink while thinking. "All right." She wanted to ask about Cassidy's evening with Cameron but wasn't sure it would be appropriate, so she chose a safer topic. "How's Ryan?"

"Doing fine. He had a little trouble going to sleep last night, but your birthday gift is his favorite toy at the moment, and he cuddled in with that."

Brenna smiled, remembering the *Wild Things* monster she had picked out. "I'm glad." She slid her hand across the tabletop and squeezed Cassidy's.

The director stepped up to the table. "Just business," he said. "Without the sound I could've shot the last five minutes. Keep it up, just put the dialogue in."

Brenna looked up at him and nodded, withdrawing her hand from the tabletop. "Will do." She caught Cassidy's nod at the director out of the corner of her eye, and Kyle and George's as well.

"All right." He stepped back to the camera line. After a few checks on the lenses, he called, "Action."

"We can't let them lynch Creighton," Jakes said. "We all have to get out of here together."

Hanssen considered aloud, "I'm a co-worker at the club. What if I asked to see him?"

"You...you show up from the hiring agency and tell me you're my new secretary," Virgil said. Jakes reached over and squeezed his hand. He squeezed back. "Now, you tell me you're not even from here."

Jakes looked at Hanssen. "Are you certain you can do this?"

Hanssen looked back with firm determination. "We all go, or no one, isn't that what you said? I can do this." Their gazes held for several beats.

Susan nodded. "All right. You know when we'll intercept the line. I expect to see you there, Lieutenant."

"Cut!"

Brenna leaned back and smiled. *Nothing like having a good rapport with the people you work with.* That had been devastatingly simple.

The director looked at his watch. "Well done. That's dinner, folks. It's five o'clock. Keep this up and we'll be out of here by nine."

"Are you going to make that call?" Cassidy stopped walking, and Brenna caught up to her in the back lot near their trailers. The evening lighting bathed them each in separate pools of lamplight.

"Yes," she replied. "Thought I'd call Gwen then and check on Ryan."

"Missing him?"

"Yeah."

Brenna shrugged. "Do you have to stay?"

"I have a scene over at the warehouse set after dinner."

"I've got mine with Kyle." They stepped up into Cassidy's trailer, and the blonde offered a bottle of fruit juice. "Thanks." Brenna sat down on the small couch. "Are you sure you want me here?"

"It won't take long. Then I thought maybe we could talk about the camping trip."

"All right."

Cassidy set aside her own fruit juice. She sat at the desk, picked up the phone, and punched in her ex-husband's number. "You know," she said while waiting for the call to ring through, "I don't ever remember a day going this easily."

"Me neither," Brenna admitted. "Nice, though."

"Hello, Mitch. It's Cassidy."

Brenna saw Cassidy's shoulders stiffen. What was it about Mitch Hyland that got his ex-wife so nervous? Offering encouragement, she reached out and squeezed Cassidy's knee.

"Yeah," the blonde continued. "I guess you could come for a visit. This weekend okay?" She nodded at the receiver. "That'll work. Do you want to meet at the house?" She nodded again.

Brenna leaned back and smiled when Cassidy looked toward her. "Well, no, I don't think we should do Disneyland." Cassidy shook her head. "It's too much of a day. Ryan will just get overexcited." Another pause. "The park with Ranger would be better." Finally the conversation was coming to an end. Cassidy said, "Yeah, see you Saturday," and pulled the receiver away from her ear, straightening her hair and disconnecting the call.

"So, Saturday in the park. Good. Mitch'll get a chance to see Ryan, and you can show him things are fine. Why didn't you want to do Disneyland?"

"Nothing really against it, but Disneyland...well, it's where we used to go on our dates."

"Afraid of seduction?" Brenna asked with a half-serious questioning tone in her voice.

"No. Afraid of losing Ryan in a crowd again," she admitted.

Brenna sobered. "True. I think you've had enough excitement in that department to last a while."

"That's why I'm looking forward to the camping trip," Cassidy said. "It'll be fun, but no crowds. And I think Ryan will enjoy the outdoors."

Brenna smiled. "We've done this about three times a year since coming to L.A. Just a chance to get out of the city for a weekend. When I started working with these kids, taking them on a camping trip once in winter and once in late spring was my first suggestion. Thomas is quite the mountain climber."

"Mountain climbing? I haven't even been camping in years. I'm looking forward to it." Cassidy shifted from the chair to the couch, settling next to Brenna.

"Have you been in the mountains at all?"

"A couple of ski trips to Denver when I was in college."

"We won't see any snow this time out."

"Yeah. Now when the snow hits, I like a fireplace and an endless supply of Irish coffee or mulled wine," Cassidy mused. "How about you?"

"The same."

They were interrupted by a knock. "Yes?" Cassidy got to her feet and opened the door.

"Ms. Hyland, have you seen—" The stagehand looked past Cassidy. "Ms. Lanigan? Mr. Hifer says you're needed on set."

"All right." Brenna rose from the couch as the young man dashed away. "I'd better go."

"I'll come watch until I get my call."

"I thought you were going to call Gwen, check on Ryan."

"Oh, right. I'll be there in a minute, then."

Brenna stopped at the door. "Don't you dare make faces at me," she warned.

"Would I ruin a love scene?" Cassidy grinned.

"Speaking of... What was that business singing to Virgil and me? It wasn't in the original blocking."

Cassidy held her door open. "I know."

Brenna stopped on the stoop and looked up. "What is it?"

Cassidy smiled. "I like the way our characters are connecting. I thought I could extend it a bit. Do you mind?"

"The characters," Brenna echoed. "Um, no. That's...that's fine. I probably should, too." *What is going on*? She felt like something was changing — too fast or in a direction she could not determine.

The lighting in the alley was very low.

Susan Jakes moved closer to Virgil and stroked a hand across his chest. He smiled, and she looked into his features. "I'll miss you," she said, a little bewildered.

"Are you sure you have to go?" he asked.

Cassidy watched from the side of the stage, arms crossed over her chest pensively. Despite knowing she had a job to do in another time and place, it was clear Susan was strongly drawn to the man the team had come to save. *Damn*, Cassidy thought. She felt her cheeks heat as the two actors kissed. *She's good at this.*

Chapter 16

Brenna caught the phone in her trailer as it rang mid-morning. "Hello?" She tucked the receiver between her ear and shoulder as she settled on the couch and pulled off her costume boots. "Kevin?" Leaning back, she briefly pulled the phone away, studied it, and then tucked it back under her ear. "You've never called me on set. What's wrong?"

"It's official. After a very close recount, I won the election," he said. "The party bigwigs are frantic. They're contesting the presidential results in Florida."

She could hear the smile in his voice. She smiled genuinely. "Congratulations. I'm glad yours came back more quickly." He had worked hard on the campaign. She heard music in the background. "Celebrating?"

"Yes." There was a long pause. "I miss you."

Wriggling her toes in relief at their release from the tight confines of the boots, she massaged them distractedly. "Miss you, too," she replied automatically.

"Could you fly out here this weekend?" he asked. "For a private celebration."

His voice had dropped, and she felt an expectant shiver. "I have a convention appearance. ... It's in Vegas. ... I know," she added quickly. "You're not crazy about that, but we could have some time together."

The line between them was silent for a long time. "I fired Derek."

The name did not ring a bell for Brenna. "Who?"

"The staffer who suggested I take advantage of your celebrity. I was stupid to listen to him."

"Yes," she said. She closed her eyes and felt the hot sting of tears. "You were." The feelings of betrayal hit her hard again.

"It won't happen again."

"It won't?" Brenna whispered to keep her tears from him.

"Bren, I love you. Please come to Mount Clemens."

She covered the receiver and breathed deep and slow. Pained, she said, "No."

He did not answer immediately. "I need to make it up to you." His voice was quiet, regretful.

She drew a short breath. *An apology?* "It hurt," she admitted. "Still does. Tom did the same thing to me. Tried to make me choose," she told him honestly. "I need my work, but I need to be me, too."

"I know you like the work."

"I *love* the work. But I won't be used to get you votes, or favors, or anything else."

"I was losing in that district. I lost the demographic vote at the university in the end anyway. Made up for it in the retired—"

"Kevin!" She wiped her face, aware that she was smearing the heavy makeup. "Polls aren't everything. I have to mean more to you than a few votes."

"You do," he protested.

Awash in emotion, she sucked in a deep breath. "Then," she said on a watery inhale, "how could you hurt me like that?"

She ignored the knock at her door, waiting, wanting him to answer so she could heal. The slight in Mount Clemens had, she thought, been resolved. Brought up again, she realized how, left untouched, it had only festered.

"Bren, come home. Please?"

She shook her head. "I can't. Not right now." She took a deep breath, trying to collect herself. "I'm sorry. I have to go." Taking a deeper breath as she pulled the phone away from her ear, she tapped the button and set the cordless receiver back in its cradle. Standing, she turned to find the door already open and the doorway occupied. Cassidy stood there, backlit by the sun, and Brenna felt tears prick at the back of her eyes. *Damn.*

"Bren? Are you all right?"

Sidestepping the question, Brenna asked, "Something up on the set?" She had to close her eyes when Cassidy's shadowed with concern. She raised her hands as the blonde came closer, taking the final step into the trailer. "No."

Cassidy's concern deepened. Long fingers slipped over Brenna's wrist and pulled her hand away from her cheek. "I'm sorry about this. Gerry needs you back on set."

Brenna nodded, trying to put her smile back in place as she moved toward the door. Cassidy's hand caressed her shoulder. Drawn by the touch, Brenna looked up into a face that showed understanding.

"You'll need a quick run through makeup." Fingertips traced Brenna's cheekbone.

Two new tears tracked down Brenna's cheeks before she could turn away. Quickly she left Cassidy alone in her trailer.

Not seeing anyone in Makeup, Brenna slid in front of a mirror in the corner and repaired her face herself. Voices reached her from next door.

"Chapman still wants this?" The voice belonged to Cameron Palassis; his voice was hard.

Picking up the cake of base, Brenna was surprised to hear Victor Branch respond, "He will want to be written out if he doesn't get more to do."

"How are we supposed to explain this to the audience?" Cameron shot back.

"He doesn't care. It's just the one scene for now, anyway."

"You damn well know he'll want a whole script on the subject later."

"Demographics might like it. They liked Raycreek and Jakes for quite a while."

"Until their off-screen breakup soured the on-screen chemistry. Chapman doesn't get along with anyone now, especially Cassidy."

Brenna was shocked. *Will is demanding a script change or he'll walk? God, we're only a few episodes from the whole thing being over anyway. And he wants to be written in with Cassidy?*

Brenna admitted to herself that she had not been an advocate of focusing so much attention on Chris Hanssen at first, but after a year and after all the plot lines which had seen them thrown together, Jakes had a stake in this, too. From Branch's words, though, it didn't sound like Chapman wanted more professional interaction between his character and the lieutenant. They had specifically mentioned Jakes and Raycreek's affair. She sighed. *And how badly that went.* She frowned. *Is Will angling for a romance with Cassidy?*

Palassis was right. Other than the odd scene here and there, Chapman's Mark Raycreek barely spoke to Cassidy's Chris Hanssen. There were very few grounds to support a closer relationship.

The two men moved away from where she sat. She finished reapplying her makeup and went out to her soundstage, her mind still reeling with questions. *What scene does Will want changed?* she wondered. Then she wondered how, or even if, she could or should stop it.

Terry Brown and Will Chapman were conferring at a cafeteria table when Brenna arrived for her own dinner break. "Mind if I join you?" she asked, looking between the two as she held her tray.

Terry gestured to the seat across from him. "Of course." Will's gaze was polite as she settled.

"Terry," she started easily, hoping to feel Chapman out. "How's the shooting?"

"Coming along."

She looked at Will, who had turned to his meal. Uneasy, she wondered what to say. An imp prompted her to joke. "How's the base line coming, Lieutenant?" she asked with a light smile.

"Just a few minor rewrites to the history books, Commander," he replied in kind, after a hesitation. Brenna nodded. "Something on your mind?" he asked.

"I've just been thinking about the end of everything," she said quietly, projecting a vague note of melancholy. "This will all be over sooner than we think."

"I keep trying not to consider it," Terry said honestly. "I've enjoyed myself."

"We certainly have been through a lot together."

"I think about it all the time," Will added. "Where everything could've gone, what's next."

"Do you really? I'm going to miss the entire company," Brenna said, biting into a sandwich. "We've done something special here."

"It's just a job, especially now," Will countered. "Certainly the writers have squandered the real possibilities."

"What possibilities?"

"Storylines that matter to the social conscience or the science conscience. For crying out loud, we're a science fiction program. Where's the 'out there' stories? Instead we get—"

"We have social commentaries," Brenna interrupted. "That's the whole premise behind changing history."

"Today's issues are so much more personal — cultural but impacting on the individual," Will insisted.

"What are you talking about?"

"Situational ethics; conservative, liberal; inclusion, exclusion; love's many forms."

Brenna frowned. "We're not *West Wing*."

"No. With our science-fiction setting, we could be a lot less threatening than something like that."

"Is that what you would suggest to Cameron or Victor?"

Will shook his head. "No, I didn't suggest a political storyline."

"What did you suggest?" she prodded pointedly.

"Some changes."

"What would piss Cameron off so much?" Brenna asked. "I...overheard him talking with Victor."

Terry looked askance at Will.

"I thought a scene we're doing could use a little emotional punch."

"That doesn't sound so bad," Brenna said.

"Cameron didn't like it. But don't worry, I have other ideas." He tapped her plate. "You should get back to eating. Don't you have more shooting?"

Realizing he wasn't going to share anything further, Brenna returned her attention to her meal. She only vaguely heard the cafeteria doors open. A prickling sensation caused her to straighten and rub the back of her neck, drawing her gaze toward the doors.

Stepping in with Cameron at her side and out of costume, Cassidy entered the cafeteria. The blonde's hair was loose against her sweatshirt-covered shoulders. Brenna noted the college logo — University of Missouri. Light eyes swept the room and found hers, the smooth chin dipping in acknowledgment. She nodded in return greeting. Terry turned to observe where she was looking.

Cassidy took a couple of steps toward them before Cameron's hand on her arm stopped her. The two then turned into the buffet line, collecting up trays and utensils.

"Looks like she's done for the day," Will observed.

"It'll give her a chance to get home and see Ryan before bed," Brenna commented idly. She lifted a hand and gestured the two toward the table as the cashier handed them their change. Her gaze continued to follow the tall woman as Cassidy smiled and sat down in the chair to her left. "Going home?" Brenna asked.

"After this." Cassidy nodded to both men across the table. "Terry. Will." Cameron settled next to her. She shifted toward Brenna to make room at the table that normally seated only four. Their hips touched. Brenna inhaled sharply, drawing Cassidy's eyes to her face. "How much longer do you have?"

"I should make it out of here by nine," Brenna guessed, "if everything goes according to schedule."

Cameron leaned forward, looking around Cassidy toward Brenna. "Shooting going well?" He directed his inquiry to Brenna as well as Terry and Will.

Terry replied with a brief nod, "The usual."

"That's great." He looked at his food, then up at Cassidy for a moment.

Cassidy addressed Terry. "Aren't you going to the Vegas convention this weekend?"

"Yes. So's Brenna."

Brenna met Cassidy's questioning look. "We're flying out together. Friday night."

"What are you planning to do with Thomas and James?"

Brenna shrugged. "I'm going to give them a chance to spend the weekend alone. They asked for it."

"Did you set down the rules yet?" Cassidy teased.

"That's planned for tomorrow." Brenna chuckled. The two women shared an understanding grin that excluded the men, something they knew — strictly one mother to another.

In the brief silence that saw everyone return to eating, Will and Terry exchanged nods that made Brenna uneasy. "Well," she said, standing and briefly dropping her hand over Cassidy's to draw the other woman's attention. "I have to get back. Have a good night."

"Take care," Cassidy replied.

The look they exchanged warmed Brenna, reminding her of Cassidy's concern in her trailer earlier. She nodded at the others, then discarded her tray and left the cafeteria, very aware of blue eyes on her back.

Chapter 17

Adventurously, Ryan hauled himself around a wood-and-steel frame jungle gym on the north side of Constance Park. Ranger leaped beneath him, barking enthusiastically.

"So, things are going well?"

Cassidy tore her watchful gaze from her son to meet the hazel green eyes of her ex-husband. "Yeah." They sat together on a gray steel bench set in the sand nearby. Her eyes swept his frame, realizing he had not changed much in the year since their divorce. He was still the physical fitness hound she had met at a beach bar when she first arrived in Los Angeles. Most people would never think he was a paper-pusher for one of the largest investment firms on the West Coast. His eyes settled on her, as if questioning her answer. "And Ryan likes the neighborhood," she added.

Mitch nodded and pressed his hands against the seat, flexing his arms. He released the tension and sat back again. "You and that writer fellow still getting along?"

Cassidy hesitated, surprised to hear her ex-husband talk of Cameron when he had been adamant that the man's name never be mentioned in his presence. Trying to hide her hesitation and cover her surprise, she added quickly, "It's been busy lately, with lots of stuff to do as the series closes down."

"Really? Not seeing much of each other?" Mitch crossed his arms over his chest and nodded toward the playground. "So when you do get together, you get side-tracked? Is that how you lost track of Ryan in the store?"

"Cameron was not at the store." Cassidy shook her head and set her jaw. *Okay, so we're finally going to get to it.* The few pleasantries they had exchanged on the walk out from the car had just been a lull. She squared her shoulders and wished Brenna was there. She envisioned the compact woman as she had confronted the nosy reporter at Sports Warehouse. She smiled at the memory and then asked the question that had been bothering her. "How did you hear about it?"

"You remember Booker?" Cassidy nodded, recalling Mitch's college roommate. He had spent a lot of time in their home while Cassidy and Mitch were married. "He caught the newscast. Thought I should know." He flexed his shoulders, and Cassidy moved a few inches away on the bench. He grasped her right wrist. "I should've heard it from you."

Cassidy shook her hand from his grasp. "Nothing happened!"

"A hell of a lot could've happened. What if he'd been kidnapped or really fallen down that compactor?"

Cassidy winced. She had envisioned many horrifying scenarios, only holding the inner demons at bay with Brenna's help. Brenna had been so convincing that it was just a minor mishap; her faith had held Cassidy's world together. She nodded toward the play equipment. "Ryan is fine. He's the first thing I think about every day."

The green eyes searched her face. "Are you going to take up another project when you finish *Time Trails*?"

"Something will come up."

"Can you really provide for him the way he deserves?"

"We settled this in the court hearing. I'm not giving Ryan to you. He needs his mother, not a nanny."

Mitch shook his head. "When you don't know where your next gig is? So what happens in a year when you're yesterday's news?"

Cassidy exploded. "If there's anything useful I learned from you, it was investing. I'm doing fine. Better now that I don't have to deal with *hospital* bills," she replied scornfully.

Mitch's eyes darkened dangerously. She eased away a cautious foot or so but held his gaze.

"I'll take you to court again. Ryan is *mine*."

Cassidy wasn't cowed. "I won't give him up."

His voice dropped as he stood up. "I intend to get him eventually."

Over my dead body, she thought, but she wisely didn't say it. She had once. The results had been three weeks on crutches. Cassidy felt his big frame towering over her five-feet-eight inches like a boom about to fall from set rigging. She watched his eyes go dark and started to take a step backward, then realized that was exactly what he wanted — he was feeding on her fear. "I won't come back to you, Mitch. It's over." Resolutely she shook herself and started to her feet.

He grabbed her arm, coming to his feet as well. "It's never going to be over. We will always have Ryan," he shot back. "I will always have a place in your life. The minute you're nobody, you're both mine again," Mitch challenged. "All I gotta do is wait, and you'll crawl back." He stepped back, relaxing out of the menacing stance and chuckling at her wide eyes. "I see I've made my point."

Cassidy swallowed, consciously slowed her heart rate, and licked her suddenly dry lips. "You've made your point."

She caught movement out of the corner of her eye and looked toward a jogger moving past their location. The line of Mitch's shoulders softened further as the jogger gave them a curious glance. Gaining several steps away from her ex-husband, Cassidy crossed the path and searched the jungle gym. "Ryan!" she called, finding him hanging upside down on the monkey bars, knees bent around the crossbeam. "Hey, buddy, are you ready for some lunch?"

"Is Daddy coming with us?" Ryan asked. He rolled himself over and, while his mother reached out to spot him, dropped to the ground.

Mitch strode up behind Cassidy as she dusted Ryan's pants free of sand. "Absolutely, wouldn't think to miss it. Do you want hot dogs and ice cream?"

"Ice cream! Yay!" Ryan sprang past his mother and leaped into his father's outstretched arms. Green eyes shot her an unmistakable message over Ryan's head: *I got him.*

With a shaky hand, she patted Ryan's back and encouraged him to get down and walk between them. Ryan reached out and grasped one parent's hand in each of his own, looking up at them as they exchanged looks with him and with each other.

"Lunch!" he yelled happily, skipping briskly and gleefully dragging his parents along.

Cassidy's heart skipped several beats. She held on as firmly as she dared without hurting Ryan or letting Mitch's grip take him from her.

The cacophony that met their entrance made Brenna jump a little as she and Terry Brown were announced onto the stage at the Vegas convention. The two were in street clothes. Terry wore a black tee shirt with the show's tagline, "All time stops here", and a pair of blue denim pants. Brenna had opted for black slacks and a hunter green silk blouse, very different from the black jumpsuit uniform with purple arm-bands she regularly wore on the set. The convention hall was packed, standing room only, and the two actors were the center of attention.

Terry took the microphone from the emcee and passed it to Brenna. She grinned as a bouquet of roses was thrust up from the foot of the stage, and she bent over to accept them. On the other side of the bouquet, she found the face of a boy who looked to be about twelve. He flushed bright red when she passed a kiss to his cheek with her fingers before taking the roses with a mic-enhanced, "Thank you." She straightened to more cheers and stepped back, handing over the microphone to let Terry speak first.

"It's great to be here," he said. "Just caught a vortex for a short stay. You know how much our commander likes tunnel travel."

That raised a laugh, and Brenna grinned, then put her hands on her hips in her favorite Jakes pose and gave Terry a glare. "Creighton should be careful. He might just find himself dropped in The Lost World instead of the tunnel home," she joked to applause.

They hugged, and Terry gave her a kiss on the cheek. He stepped back and ges-tured at the audience. The emcee waved at them from what was now the front of the question line, a queue of hopefuls who had questions at the ready for them. "Looks like it's time for questions."

First up was a girl with a round face, big blue eyes, and tied-back blond hair. She asked Commander Jakes if she missed her mom because she traveled so much.

With a reassuring smile, Brenna said, "Someday I hope to get everything just right and see her again." She nodded to the mother who patted her daughter on the shoulder before drawing her away from the line. For the benefit of the rest of the audience, Brenna added, "Changing official time has left me very little *personal* time." There was a roll of knowing laughter, and she stepped back, watching the next questioner come forward.

Terry answered a question about why he didn't take the second spot when Chapman's character Raycreek had mutinied in an episode two years earlier. "You want me to face off with her?" He hooked a thumb toward Brenna. "I don't have a death wish. She's tough."

"Is Commander Jakes going to find a new romance?"

Brenna answered lightly. "Isn't she still smarting over Raycreek?" she asked. Two years ago while she was briefly involved with Chapman, they had taken it on-screen for a few episodes. The storyline had sizzled, then fizzled. The arc that brought Cassidy in, in the spring of 1999, had fractured the team, ending the rela-tionship both on- and off-screen. Brenna had married Kevin just four months later.

Turning more serious, she asked, "Besides, who else is there?"

A cacophony of suggestions rose up. She heard several people suggest she give Raycreek another chance. *Nope*, she thought. *That boat has sailed.* She raised her eyebrow in shock at Terry when his character, Creighton, was suggested. "But he's married!"

"So what?" someone shouted back. "Maybe you'd rather she get with Hanssen?"

That rattled Brenna. *Where would they get that idea? Susan in love with Chris? What will these fans think of next?*

"I think maybe Jakes is just a little busy running from crisis to crisis to settle down," she responded finally. *How about that?* She covered her eyes. Factions of the audience began arguing among themselves.

Searching for serenity, she pictured Cassidy, out of costume, the blonde's hair loose around her cheeks, and her face filled with the concerned expression she'd worn when she inadvertently overheard Brenna's conversation with her husband.

That brought to mind Mitch, Cassidy's ex-husband. She wondered how the woman's meeting in the park had gone. Distracted, Brenna did not focus on the next several questions addressed to her. She only hoped the answers she gave made some kind of sense.

Finally the organizers brought the audience under control. There were more questions asking for spoilers. They didn't have information themselves, so Terry and Brenna truthfully shrugged. "Your guess is as good as ours. Maybe better." Before long, Brenna and Terry were taking their last questions to repeated standing ovations.

When they were motioned off, Terry and Brenna stepped into the wings. Inhaling and exhaling to dispel her tensions, Brenna looked up at a pat on the shoulder from Liza Garnet. She played one of the big-wig types on the show, returning from time to time with dire pronouncements about the future of the Time Squad. The dark eyes smiled back. "Don't let 'em shake you. Remember, it's just a role."

Terry's hand on her shoulder drew Brenna's attention away as Liza walked out on stage to thunderous applause. "What did I say?" Brenna asked him. "Was it bad?" *Maybe I was more disconnected than I thought.*

"Not bad at all," Terry said without elaborating. "Come on. Let me take you to dinner."

Brenna frowned but nodded. "All right."

They entered the elevator and slipped up to their adjoining rooms. Brenna washed up but decided against changing. Terry knocked a few minutes later and presented himself in a black leather jacket pulled over a yellow polo shirt and black slacks. She reached over and grabbed her own soft black leather jacket and stepped into the corridor, locking her door behind herself and tucking the key card into her purse. "Ready?"

"Ready," he said, offering her an elbow. "What are you interested in?"

Brenna considered that. "How about something fun? Fondue?"

He laughed. "Messy. I like it."

Contemplating the cheese melts and the bits of beef, an indulgence she rarely allowed herself, Brenna led the way out to the curb and hailed a cab.

"I've never seen anything like it," Brenna praised, lifting a forkful of sizzling steak from the boiling oil. Dipping it in a bowl of spicy steak sauce, she let the excess drip before popping it in her mouth. She regarded Terry across the table. "You can do scary really well. Cassidy was shaking."

"I had a chance to play Jack the Ripper on stage two years ago during the hiatus. Enjoyed it," he said with a smile, dipping a chicken strip in a béchamel sauce. "You've got a theater background, too, but you haven't done anything on the breaks. Why not?"

"Between spending time here and in Mount Clemens, my boys' schedules, and trying to hold it all together, who has time?"

"Would you be interested if there was, say, a local playhouse production to do?"

"How local?"

Terry smiled. "Mine."

She laughed. "Yours?" He frowned. "I didn't mean it like that," she assured him.

"Just, I didn't know you owned a playhouse."

"Part owner. I went into it with some friends."

"That's great. What's the playbill this season?"

"We're currently casting for *Juniper Falls*, a locally written play." He paused to drop a vegetable piece into some melted cheese. "I could pass you the script if you want."

"Oh, I couldn't. Where would I find the time?"

"You ought to consider what you're going to do after we wrap," he prompted.

Brenna speared another strip of steak and dropped it in the sizzling oil. "Kevin wants me to come to Mount Clemens."

After a telling pause during which she felt her cheeks warm, dark eyes met hers across the table. "You don't sound like that's what you want."

"I should," she said, finding it convenient to check on her steak and then changing the subject. "So, tell me more? Where is it? Who are your partners?"

Terry bit into another piece, but otherwise did not seem fazed by her topic shift. "It's in Fullerton. We converted a vineyard press house about three years ago. We've had a few nice reviews. Small company, pretty stable. We like local writers over getting name projects. A labor of love," he finished with a smile.

Brenna smiled warmly, pausing as she contemplated the memories she had of theater life. Starting out in New York, at eighteen, those days had been scary and exciting. "Sounds wonderful."

"Will you consider coming out? At least see a performance? Meet the company?"

"All right. Just one night. Sometime." She speared a strip of meat and settled it against the hot rock. "You'd make a good salesman." She laughed lightly.

"My wife will appreciate knowing I have another occupation to fall back on," he joked, making her chuckle deepen with genuine pleasure. "You'd like the work."

"I'd love the work," she acknowledged finally. "I miss live performance."

"You did have fun on stage today." Terry paused. "You...were relaxed for a change."

"Are you saying I'm not usually?" Brenna speared a strip of yellow pepper, sinking it in the bowl of oil. "Tell me more about your playhouse."

"So you are interested?" He reached over and picked up his drink.

"Maybe," she granted with a nod, sipping from her own glass.

"Well, that's one down, one to go," he said idly.

"Who else are you asking?"

"I'd like to get Cass before she gets another offer." Terry shrugged. "Her range is impressive. Like her singing last episode."

Brenna remembered she had not had to work hard to remember to stare at Cassidy. The woman's voice had been mesmerizing. Brenna paused with her fork in her mouth, then slowly chewed and swallowed. "She surprised me."

"Why?"

"Well, we all know why she was brought on board," Brenna said frankly.

"We've had some good moments together," Terry observed. "Off-screen as well as on."

"Until recently I haven't seen her much away from the set," Brenna said. "I enjoyed the birthday party she hosted."

"My wife and I have gone over a couple of times now. One time the power went out. We walked over to a corner hot dog stand. Ryan ate himself silly with hot dogs, soda, and chips while playing with my daughter in the yard with that Dalmatian of theirs. Cass even got down on the ground and rolled around some herself."

Brenna imagined Cassidy wrestling with her son on the ground. She was sud-denly unable to speak as the image of Cassidy "letting go" blew coherent thought away.

"I understand she had quite a fight to keep him," Terry went on, drawing her attention. "That's why I'd love to see her stay in town and work at the playhouse. I doubt she really wants to uproot and move somewhere else."

Brenna nodded. "Mitch, her ex, was planning to visit this weekend. He heard about the incident at the store."

Terry steepled his hands, then folded one over the other. "Was she upset?"

"Shaking like a leaf. Do you know why?"

He pursed his lips, clearly withholding something. "Maybe on Monday we can ask how things went." He waved over a waiter and requested a refill on his beer. When he turned back, he asked, "So, what do you want to do for our entrance on stage tomorrow?"

Brenna shook her head. While Terry had shrugged off the concern about Cassidy, she found herself unable to do the same. "I think I'm a little tired. How about we wing it? I'd like to get back to the hotel. Get some sleep."

"Sure."

She finished a last bite of fondue, then laid a credit card over the check the waiter brought with Terry's beer before he could. "Thanks for the conversation and the company," she offered in explanation.

While he drained the beer, she sat quietly pondering their conversation. When he set the empty glass down, they gathered their coats and wended their way out of the restaurant.

Blasted by the chill of the open refrigerator, Cassidy searched for something for Ryan's bedtime snack. She tried to shake off the afternoon's unease but found it impossible. Each time she closed her eyes she saw Mitch playing with Ryan, tossing a baseball with him, or helping him drink from the park fountain or Ryan laughing as Daddy jogged with him through the sprinklers. Every time it happened and the boy raced back breathlessly to her side giggling, she would catch Mitch's significant look, and her heart sank a little further.

Finally she had been able to call a halt by pointing out that Ryan had to bathe and get to bed. Her son had been upset, but Mitch did not have any argument he could offer up without making himself look foolish. They had driven back to the house, and Mitch had let Cassidy and Ryan off in the driveway. Then he pulled out and drove away.

"Mommy?"

"Ready for bath time?" She turned to see her son coming off the porch where he had taken the dog into the yard.

"Okay." He headed for the bathroom, and she followed.

She swallowed as she asked, "Did you have fun today?"

"Yeah." He grinned, pulling off his shirt as she bent past him and twisted the water spigot. "Daddy's a lot of fun."

"Don't we have fun?" she asked uneasily.

Ryan tried to explain himself. "Sure, but...he's...Daddy."

Now nude, Ryan stepped into the warm bubbles, holding her hand so he wouldn't slip. It was an unconscious request for support, and after the emotional rollercoaster of the afternoon it warmed Cassidy's heart. She reached for the wash-cloth and soaped it, then washed his back and chest. She splashed him lightly, and they both giggled when bubbles covered his nose. He wiped them away with wet hands and then patted her cheeks with his bubble-covered palms.

Once she had his hair washed, she stood. "Play for a little while, then after snack and story, I'll tuck you in bed."

He immediately grabbed for the collection of toys in a bucket by the side of the tub and splashed them noisily into the water. Smiling, she stepped out of the bath-room and returned to the kitchen. She poured out two small glasses of milk and set a plate of chocolate chip cookies between them on the table before returning to the bathroom. "Snack time."

Ryan stepped out of the tub and wrapped up in a fluffy dark green towel. She lifted a corner of it over his hair and dried vigorously, to his delighted giggles. "What's for snack?"

"Cookies and milk," she answered. He pushed past her. Only with quick hands did she grab him and pull on his pajama top and bottoms. "Now, you're ready," she said with a laugh. Scrambling back to her feet, Cassidy followed her son to the table.

An hour later Ryan was fed, his teeth brushed, a story read, and covers tucked to his chin. Cassidy retreated to her room and lay across her bed. Tension gathered in her neck and shoulders as she tried to dispel her anxieties.

Mitch was just playing on your fear, she told herself. *It's a bluff because he knows you get like this.* Deciding a bath might help, she checked on Ryan once more and then went into the bathroom. Adding salts instead of bubbles, she leaned back and closed her eyes, letting the aromas soothe her while she concentrated on pleasant thoughts.

Next weekend will be fun, she told herself. She immediately smiled, thinking of the hiking and campfire fun. Mountain climbing, she recalled, was also on the agenda. She shrugged. She had never climbed, but she was in good shape. She had really enjoyed the children at the Halloween party and looked forward to more time with them. Ryan would enjoy the time with other children, as well. She welcomed the opportunity to chat with other adults about things that had nothing to do with work. Particularly, she looked forward to getting to know Brenna with both of them letting their hair down.

Despite the times they had recently shared, Cassidy knew there were more depths to discover in the intriguing woman. She closed her eyes and pictured Brenna's tear-stained face two days earlier in the woman's trailer. At the sight of Brenna's pain, Cassidy's protective instincts had flared sharply. Her fingers tingled in memory of the briefly comforting touch she had offered.

"Good night, Brenna."

"Sleep well. See you in the morning." Closing her door, Brenna hung her jacket and sat down on one of the beds. Eyeing the phone, she thought, *Should I?* She shook her head against the sharp tang of concern that dampened her palms. *This is so weird. She's a grown woman, able to take care of herself. You're getting too involved, Bren.*

"Oh hell." She reached for the phone and dialed quickly before she could change her mind.

"Hello?"

She hurriedly identified herself when she heard Cassidy's voice on the line, sounding soft and tired. "It's Brenna. I didn't call at a bad time, did I?"

"Brenna?" Cass' voice was light, incredulous.

Leaning back against her pillows, Brenna smiled. "Yeah. You sound good."

"So do you."

There was silence, and Brenna just listened, intent on the other woman's breathing for some sign that she really was okay.

Finally Cassidy asked, "What's on your mind?"

Brenna temporized. "I was... Terry and I were talking and I remembered you were supposed to see Mitch today. I... How did it go?" Cassidy exhaled, and Brenna's throat clenched.

"It went." Now Cassidy's voice was flat.

"Not good?"

"I was reminded of why I left him," Cassidy said. "He's...scary when he wants to be."

Brenna felt her heart rate speed up slightly, remembering the feel of Cassidy shaking in her grasp during filming. To have access to that sort of fear... Anger on Cassidy's behalf burned behind her eyes. Rubbing at them, she offered, "I'm sorry I couldn't be there. How's Ryan?"

"He loves his dad."

"How are you?"

"I just finished a bath to unwind."

"Good."

Both women fell silent, trying to figure out what to say. Cassidy finally prompted, "This is long distance. How's the convention going?"

"Makes me wish we had another year at this. The fans are really into it."

"Yeah, I know. So what questions did you get?"

"Standard fare." Brenna thought a moment. "I did get one new one, though."

"Yeah?" Cassidy had not done a con in about eight months and wondered what the fans were thinking up now.

"There's a group that wants Jakes to have another romance." Brenna wondered why she was having such a hard time with that. Liza was right; it was just a role. "Some want her to go back to Raycreek. A few...want y— Hanssen."

"That's new." Cassidy's voice was playful. Brenna pictured her relaxing, phone pressed to her ear, and waited for more. "What does Commander Jakes think?"

"I haven't..." Curled on her bed, Brenna pulled her knees up and pondered the question. "It's pretty ludicrous."

"I don't know. We have a strong enough friendship for it to make sense," Cassidy pointed out. "And the audience obviously has fewer biases than the studio would credit them with. There won't be a ripple, I think, when Luria kisses Chris in *Brains and Brawn*."

"Susan couldn't do that," Brenna said quickly. She passed her hand over the bed covers to still the tingling in her fingertips and quickly changed the subject. "I'm glad you're all right."

"Bren?" There was a long pause before Cass spoke again. When she did, she had apparently changed her mind about what she wanted to say. "Never mind. See you Monday."

"Yes. Sleep well." Brenna held the phone listening as Cassidy broke the connection first. Setting the receiver back on its cradle, she rolled onto her stomach, fisting her hands under her chin and wondering why she was so unsettled. *Cassidy's all right. So's Ryan. Now,* she sternly told herself, *call your sons and then go to sleep. You've got a long day tomorrow.*

She called her home number and waited two rings for it to pick up. She recognized the "hello" from her youngest. "James?"

"Hi, Mom. How's Vegas?"

"Fine. How are you two?"

"Thomas is out with Cheryl at the dance."

"Not back yet?"

"Curfew's not for another hour."

"Oh, that's right," Brenna said, checking the bedside clock. "Well, you get some sleep. I'll be back by dinner tomorrow night."

"Having a good time?"

Brenna thought about the day's events. "Yeah, it's been a good day. Next weekend ought to be even more fun, though."

"Yeah. You know... Did Ms. Hyland ever get what she needed from that store?"

Brenna frowned. "I have no idea."

"Well, we've got lots of stuff. If she needs something, she can just borrow it."

"They could share with us." Her lips quirked in a smile. "Always room for one more in a tent."

"Yeah."

"You get some sleep. I love you," she told him. "Tell Thomas I called."

"I will. We're fine. Really. Stop worrying."

"Don't deny me my ulcer, okay?" she said with a laugh, hearing him laugh in return. "Better. Now, good night."

Still chuckling, he replied, "Good night," and disconnected.

Energized, Brenna rolled onto her back and sat up. *It's too cool for a swim, but maybe... Yeah.* On light feet, Brenna left the bed, changed into a pair of shorts and tee shirt, and headed downstairs to hunt up the rec room. Maybe after a light workout she could get some sleep.

Chapter 18

On Monday the set overflowed with activity. Pinnacle had granted press passes to dozens of media outlets for interviews with the cast and crew about the final season of *Time Trails*. Seeing that everyone on the set for the morning shooting was already present amid the chaos, Brenna Lanigan strode into the menagerie with an undaunted smile. She waved to Terry Brown, already in full costume and makeup. He was being questioned by a bored-looking interviewer, and Brenna hoped the copy eventually proved kinder than the reporter's expression portended. She caught Terry's eye and offered a thumbs up before ducking around the corner.

"You look like you already had your morning coffee," Will Chapman commented, slipping into his chair as the head of makeup, Brent Eastland, shook out a hairdresser's cape and secured it around his neck.

Brenna shook her head and laughed. "I had a chance to eat with Thomas and James this morning before taking them to school."

Will nodded and closed his eyes. Eastland applied his base and watched carefully as Brenna applied her own. "You don't have many scenes to run through today."

"Stunts with the second unit, then interviews." In the mirror, she saw a reporter peering in the doorway, an elaborate 35mm slung over her shoulder. "And here's the first one," she said softly. She turned in the chair and greeted the woman by rising slightly and holding out her hand.

"Melissa Peregrine, *Sci-Fi* magazine. Ms. Lanigan?"

"We can talk as long as you can keep up," she allowed, using Jakes' all-business inflection. "I have thirty minutes before I'm due on set."

"Yes, ma'am."

She caught the younger woman's straightening shoulders behind her in the mirror and touched up her base to hide her amusement. *God, I do love making them jump.*

Peregrine started off with a question that Brenna expected. "You're coming to the end of five years with your character. What's changed most about Susan Jakes?"

"You have to know where she started. I think initially the producers were concerned whether the show would fly with the commander being a woman. They were concerned about a woman being able to project authority," Brenna mused. "Once I was established, I think they took a deep breath and, after watching the dailies and watching this character evolve through me, they have pretty much entrusted her to me. They've let the woman in the commander come out, more fully integrating her. I think they discovered women really do lead differently than men."

Will nodded as he pulled off his smock. "In the long run, we've benefited from having a female in charge. The dynamic has been risky, but it paid off, I think. Brenna's a big reason why."

Brenna flushed, and when Will leaned over, she kissed his cheek. "Jakes is philosophical, but she's also capable of taking great — and occasionally questionable — risks."

"Only occasionally?" Will quipped. "I don't know about that. But questionable? I'll certainly second that." He was laughing as he left.

Brenna turned back to Peregrine. "While she has always been a devoted commander, over the five seasons Jakes has evolved. I think she's more relaxed, more confident. I don't think that confidence was really there at the start, just the potential for it. However, she's seen her toughest decisions result in incredible goodness. Her team is a family, with her as the matriarch, with all that entails about mutual respect and love. Regarding the 'dangers' of time, she's more thoughtful, more reflective."

"Will Jakes go down in history as one of the greats?"

"Unquestionably, she will. It has taken me a long time to understand her influence, and mine, as a role model."

"Is that the biggest achievement of Brenna Lanigan — to let people know that women can do anything they set their mind to?"

"I've taken my influence on young women seriously. I've tried to be vigilant about it, to share as much as I can of myself and my philosophy with them so that they understand that the sky's the limit."

The two left Makeup; their voices softened as they neared one of the soundstages. Peregrine prodded, "How has it been as an actor? Seventeen-hour days for the birds?"

"The work has clearly been a once-in-a-lifetime opportunity. I will always treasure the relationships I've developed in this foxhole."

"That sounds like you've been in the trenches of a war zone."

"Trenches?" She contemplated the intensities of filming. "That's a good metaphor."

"So when the series is over, do you expect to suffer post-traumatic stress?"

"That kind of let-down is very specialized, so I'd have to say no. I've left other jobs before..." Brenna gave her answer some thought. "But this one is special."

The reporter looked at her in puzzlement. "Aren't all roles 'special' until the next one comes along? What do you see happening after this?"

Passing the warehouse set, Brenna did not answer the question but stopped and listened to the actors' exchange.

Chris was trying to get Creighton to believe he wasn't insane and that she would get him out before the lynch mob got there. Brenna listened to Cassidy's voice, rounded by Hanssen's careful diction — caring while being simultaneously urgent. Mindful of the fact that sound levels were very sensitive, Brenna caught Cassidy's eye across the distance and mouthed, "Nice job," and smiled broadly before ducking her head and walking out of view.

The action surprised Cassidy and she stumbled over her next line, causing a break in the action. A grip checked their poses, and Cassidy once again grasped Creighton's arm and delivered her line. As soon as the director called cut, she left the set and followed Brenna. She held her breath, watching Brenna perform her own stunt for a chase through a darkened building.

Standing next to Peregrine, Cassidy focused her eyes on a catwalk over the stage. Rushing forward, Brenna limberly vaulted the railing and dropped about eight feet, the fall being filmed in front of an aqua green screen. Post-production would make the drop look like a considerably greater distance. When Brenna finally rolled to her feet and Cassidy could draw breath, the young woman flashed a thumbs up before ducking away.

Brenna chuckled as she caught her breath. She looked up at the collection of stunt actors that had been chasing her and flashed them the same thumbs up. "Good work, Brenna," called the second unit director. "Ready to do it again for the reverse shot?"

"Again?" She groaned in disbelief. The evil look she shot at the director prompted laughter from somewhere beyond the lights. Shielding her eyes, Brenna identified Rachelle leaning casually against a set wall. "You want to do this?" She gestured to her position. "Come on. I'm sure a wig'll be enough to let you pass as me from behind!"

"I'm smaller than you," Rachelle shot back, chuckling.

"Not many people can say that." Brenna laughed and stepped off the sound-stage toward Rachelle. She found herself next to Cassidy, who had returned with a bottle of water she offered to Brenna. With a grin she took a healthy gulp just as they were cornered by the *Sci-Fi* reporter.

"Are you hoping for any particular developments before things completely wrap?" Peregrine asked, catching Brenna's attention again.

Brenna passed back the water bottle with a mouthed "thank you" to Cassidy before answering. "I'd like to see some of the interpersonal stories wrapped up." She nodded toward the nearby set. "I think we've certainly discovered that messing around with time, even if you have completely altruistic reasons, doesn't let people really *live*. I mean if someone can come along, a grandchild maybe, and arrange it so that his grandfather doesn't just not die in the battle but becomes a decorated hero, it diminishes the sense of success in the ordinary trials of life. That young man isn't living *his* life, he's living someone else's."

"So you don't think Susan Jakes has been one of the good gals?" Peregrine asked.

"Oh, undoubtedly, but it hasn't been because of things she's done with the time-line. Her real contribution has been how she's affected the people she met."

"Jakes certainly did a lot to reshape Chris' outlook on both the Time Squad's mission and her own life," Cassidy interjected. "She was not exactly a fan when they first met."

"And vice versa. Susan likes a tight team, and Chris did her best to be outside of that most of the time," Brenna pointed out, catching Cassidy's hand as it swept across her shoulder.

Looking up from her pad, Peregrine asked, "What are biggest issues that remain for Commander Jakes?"

"The characters have grown, but we haven't managed to reveal much of that in close scenes. There's always so much action..." Brenna hesitated, trying to find the best way to explain. The squeeze of Cassidy's hand on her shoulder gave her a moment of peaceful clarity. She smiled and looked back at Peregrine. "It's hard to say, other than Luria and Jeremy, whether any of these characters would want to stay together if the Time Squad were to lose its mandate."

Cameron Palassis leaned in around a corner. "Heard chatter. Interview?"

"Mr. Palassis, I'm Melissa Peregrine, *Sci-Fi* magazine. What sort of stories do you have on tap? The kind Ms. Lanigan was describing?"

"It's an action show. There's at least one last big showdown coming. A familiar enemy will reappear." Cameron shook his finger at Brenna, and she frowned.

Peregrine caught the reaction and jumped on it. "Not thrilled?"

"If the action has a science fiction heart, it's all right. But stories have to have emotional connection to the audience. And the characters have to mean something to each other. We have what amounts to six lonely characters. A few recent episodes explore what they are like inside when they are out of the uniforms. I like Susan. I think we should give the audience a sense that these characters will live beyond 'the end.'"

Cassidy pressed Brenna's shoulder and grinned toward Peregrine. "Triumphant into the sunset."

"With a threat or an unsettlement looming."

"In other words, an opening for a movie plot." With another grin, the tall blonde squeezed Brenna's shoulder, and the smaller woman reached up and squeezed back.

Clearly sensing something from the two women, Peregrine asked a more directly pertinent question. "What of Hanssen's dedication to Time Squad? From rogue ne'er-do-well to respected officer. Jakes has had a definite hand in that."

"Hanssen's almost all the way in, I think," Cassidy said quickly. "All that remains, I guess, is for her to believe in the value of her own life as much as she has believed in that of others."

"Jakes could help her with that," Brenna added. "It's one way to show how their relationship has matured — her progression from stern leader to friend."

Peregrine tapped her pad with her pen. "I'm seeing a friendship between the two of you. Which, if rumor is to be believed, is quite a change. Things weren't easy on the set when you first arrived, Ms. Hyland."

"No," Brenna admitted before Cassidy could speak. "It was...a very uncertain time." She cast a wry glance at the blonde, who nodded in understanding. "As actors, we're thrown together in many situations that can force revelations of ourselves, maybe even parts we don't like and never share with anyone else willingly. It's a pressure cooker. Adding new ingredients upset the whole balance."

"And now?"

"From the beginning, Chris and Susan weren't set to be friends." Brenna looked at Cassidy, recalling some of their conflicts. She wondered if she could ever make up for some of it. She felt she wanted to say more as her gaze intersected Cassidy's. Hesitating over exactly what to say, she suddenly heard Peregrine's pen scratching on pad. Brenna jerked back to the reporter. "But that's the nature of the beast," Brenna concluded quickly. She disregarded the shiver that ran down her spine at Cassidy's smile.

Clearly frustrated by the half-response, Peregrine asked a more direct question. "Would you work together again?"

"I'm game." Cassidy smiled.

"Maybe after a *short* break." Brenna shook her head. "I need to find more time for my personal life. I haven't managed it very well."

"Do you like Ms. Hyland's suggestion about a movie?"

"Not right away. I'd like to do a play, maybe. But I want to just take some time. I'd like to give my time, my heart, and my life to my loved ones." She looked toward Cassidy, who slowly let out a breath.

"We'd all like that, I think," Cassidy said. She nodded and left for her set.

"I'd like to be little Brenna Lanigan for a while, remember who she was. Jakes has become bigger than life. At least bigger than my life."

"Everyone's smaller than the bigger-than-life Commander Jakes," Will said, stepping out from behind the opposite wall from where he apparently had been watching. Surprised, Brenna caught the teasing in his tone and put her hands on her hips, smiling as she saw another camera flash go off.

The interview was concluded when the director called Brenna back for a second take. Pulling herself up an access ladder behind the set wall, she stepped back out onto the catwalk. The stunt actors crowded just off the walk behind her, and the second unit director called, "Action!"

One breath, then a second, and Brenna bounded forward, grasped the railing, and threw herself over. She was thankful for her rock-climbing experience, which had cleared her of any inhibitions or vertigo. Once down on the ground, she remained sacked out on the air mattress, arms splayed and eyes closed, waiting until her heart started again and the director called, "Cut."

Stagehands pulled away the mattress, and she took her mark directly beneath her jump point and completed filming the end of the jump. On cue, she crouched, then stood. Spinning clockwise, she ran off stage left, ducking imaginary attacks from above.

She ran into Cameron coming around a corner of the soundstage. The two tumbled together until she could recover her feet. "Sorry," she said, reaching down and grasping his hand to haul him up. More flashes went off, and she sighed.

Cameron dusted himself off and straightened his pants and oxford shirt. "Having a good time?"

"Just dandy," she drawled. "If you have a chance later, maybe you could explain about the big returning enemy you dropped like a rock in my interview."

"The ideas are only just beginning to form. A lot of the staff is working on it." He glanced up and spied Branch, who was also mingling with off-set cast and crew. He waved to him. "Victor?"

"Yeah?" The producer offered Brenna a smile; she nodded back. "What's up?" He directed the question at Palassis.

"Are we set with the finale yet?" Cameron asked.

"Of course not."

Cameron turned back to Brenna. "We'll cover a lot of ground over the next several episodes, Brenna. Those interpersonal relationships you were talking about? They'll get covered."

"Ms. Lanigan?" A set grip located her standing between the two taller men. "You're needed on your mark."

"Thanks." She glanced at Cameron, offering a final word concerning the one thing that had continued to bother her since the previous week. "Listen, I don't know what Chapman asked you to do, but I want you to reconsider. For Cassidy's sake." She returned to the soundstage, setting for another angle on the stunt shot.

Cameron frowned and then sighed. "I guess she overheard."

"Funny that she'd come to Hyland's defense like that, though," Victor commented. "Certainly a lot of changes in the last several weeks."

"Yeah." Cameron ruminated on it for a moment longer and then looked around. "Have you seen Cass?"

"Just came from there. She's back on the set. She was in Lanigan's interview for a while," Victor said with a shrug. "You sure you want to talk to her right now?"

"Damn straight."

As Branch watched Palassis stalk off, Will Chapman walked up, patting his sweating face carefully with a soft towel. "What's with him?"

Branch shook his head. "Brenna and he squared off about something. Finale, I think. But there's something else going on with him. I wish to hell I knew what. He can't even manage to concentrate on the new series pilot at the moment."

"Really?" Will raised an eyebrow in question.

Seeing Cameron leaning against a set break watching the soundstage where Cassidy was among the filming cast, Branch confided, "Cassidy's got him not knowing if he's coming or going, and I don't think she knows it."

"She doesn't," Will said, patting Branch on the shoulder. "But I'll change that."

Chapter 19

Cassidy completed her stunt and heard the second unit director call, "Cut." She stood and stretched to the little extent she could. Though the dress was less binding than her Time Squad jumpsuit, it was still a dress. *Like those women detectives in the TV shows in the 80s who ran after crooks in high heels because some studio execs felt that sneakers were too "manly".* She sighed.

Despite the wall of activity that separated her senses from what was happening in the off-stage area, Cassidy got the distinct impression she was being watched. She tried to shrug it off. It was a curious reporter, perhaps. But the sensation persisted, and she turned, aware of a flutter as she hoped to see a specific face. She stifled a surprisingly strong wave of disappointment when she spied Cameron leaning against a set wall. Hoping the lighting angle concealed her response, Cassidy looked around once, still hoping to spy Brenna. She slowly stepped down from the slightly elevated decking of the soundstage.

"Hi, Cass." Cameron crossed the three steps separating them and grasped her arms just above the elbows, leaning forward with obvious intent to kiss her.

Cassidy could not put her finger on why the attention felt wrong, but she was uneasy as she broke off the touch of their lips.

Cameron lightly squeezed her elbows — *a warning?* — then dropped his hands. His smile was forced, surprising her and causing her a little alarm. His voice came over the uneven thudding of her heart.

"I thought we could talk over a late lunch," he said. "You don't have another set call today. Wanna go someplace off site?"

"I have interviews." She intently watched his expression, which only twitched briefly, adding to her confusion.

His composure broke slightly as they moved aside to allow a stagehand bearing props to pass. Struggling to regroup, he smiled suddenly. "What about this weekend? We could take Ryan and go up the coast, maybe to Napa. I..." His voice trailed off as he shrugged.

Cassidy sipped in a breath slowly and let it out just as carefully. Cameron took a step back. "It sounds like that would be a nice trip." She had a previous commitment that she preferred to keep. "But Ryan and I already have plans."

Cameron straightened and, though he wasn't an imposing figure, she had to quell the dismay roiling in her stomach. His gaze narrowed, and she fought her impulse to look away. Cameron seldom was ever truly angry with her, an appealing trait after the white-hot flash point that had been Mitch.

Cameron's voice was low and deliberate. "Where?"

"I told you we had a camping trip."

"When?"

"This weekend."

"No. When did you tell me?"

She searched her mind for a date reference, then answered, "Two, maybe three weeks ago. Do you remember when Mitch called me at work? That night."

He looked puzzled for a long moment, then shook his head. "Well, would you like some company? Maybe I could go with you."

Cassidy shook her head. "Cameron, you couldn't stand having that many kids around."

After a moment, he nodded. "When do you leave?" His tone was flat.

"Saturday at dawn."

"Dawn. When will you be back?" Cameron was squeezing his hands repeatedly.

"Look, I have to go." Filled with unease, Cassidy backed away. When he remained focused on her, she looked away, ostensibly adjusting the fit of her costume. She spotted a reporter standing about five feet away, patiently waiting for his interview. Thankful for a reason to cut short their exchange, Cassidy called, "I'm ready."

The reporter was a thin man in his mid- to late-thirties, with dark hair; his smile was clearly admiring. "Any place you'd prefer to do this?" He stepped back to let her move away first. As she passed Cameron, she felt the reporter's notepad gently touch against her lower back.

Behind her, Cameron stalked away.

Cassidy tried to relax, but Will was edging into her personal space at the conference table. Still, she had to admit he was interjecting supportive additions to her answers to the reporter's questions. The reporter had already, in her opinion, covered the typical questions. The appearance of her co-star fueled a change in the direction. One she hadn't expected.

"Do you think your character has made any connections with the other team members? Do they still resent being bunked with a screw-up?"

"Resentment? No, I...think we've gotten past that." Cassidy caught a raised eyebrow from Will and added, "With most of them."

"Definitely with Commander Jakes," Will injected.

He caught her eye, and Cassidy thought there was a message there she was supposed to catch. She frowned and dropped her head briefly, aware of a heat in her cheeks. When she had controlled it, she looked up. "There has been a different edge between Jakes and Hanssen as they're working out their differences or at least coming to an understanding. I've learned a lot working with everyone, but Brenna in particular. She's—"

The reporter's follow up interrupted Cassidy's thought. "Why do you think that is?"

Will supplied the answer. "Female bonding. Audiences eat it up. It's closed out nearly all the males."

He shoved off the table, the intensity of the maneuver startling Cassidy. Her chest tightened at his abrupt and dismissive tone. *Damn.* She had finally begun to feel part of the company, with the banter, the lunches, and the clincher, Brenna's openness in talking with her. She didn't want to lose that.

"Will, wait." She pushed to her feet, waving the reporter to stay seated. "Wait here," she commanded sharply. Will turned. She looked into his features. In a low voice she asked, "What is wrong with you?"

"What?"

His exclamation was muted, in deference to her own lowered voice, she guessed. "I..." She searched for words. "Why are you being like this?" It sounded petulant even to her ears, but she hoped for an answer.

"It's no secret."

"I can't change the scripts," she replied sharply. "I try to be part of the team, but you're making no effort at all."

"You can't change things, but he can." Will's accusation accompanied a glare directed somewhere over Cassidy's left shoulder. Turning, she jumped when she saw Cameron only a few feet away. "Right, Cameron?" Will's tone was baiting.

"What?"

"Hanssen and Raycreek would make a good match, don't you think?"

Though the question had been posed casually, Cassidy could see Will's eyes harden. A focused glare nailed Cameron as he walked up.

Cameron did not look away from the challenge. He snapped, "No, I don't think so."

Cassidy flinched. "Cam, I—"

"Stay out of this," he told her sharply. He turned back to Chapman, shoving a finger in the bigger man's face. "Stop your bellyaching. There's auditions going on right down the street." He waved in a gesture of "out there". "You can walk away anytime."

Stung by Cameron's sharp dismissal, Cassidy watched silently as Will straightened to his full height and crossed his arms over his chest. His expression was supremely confident. Standing firm in the face of Cameron's fury, which was washing off the writer in almost visible waves, Chapman suddenly appeared mountainlike. Immovable. Granite hard. The smile he wore promised unpleasantness. She tried again. "Will..."

He glanced at her briefly, only shaking his head before returning his gaze to Palassis. "I don't like being window dressing," he said. "Scenes with Cassidy could change that."

"You will never touch her," Cameron shot back. "Never."

Suddenly Brenna was pushing between the two men. She did not touch either one, but awareness of her presence diverted them from their enmity.

Looking up at one then the other, Brenna warned, "Not here. Not now." The rest of the reporters swung their attentions toward the tense group. "I don't give a damn what your differences are, but you can't do this here!"

"Haven't you heard, Cassidy?" Will blurted. "They say you'd rather have Jakes than Raycreek."

Cameron became incensed. "The fans are always making up some kind of crap. Fuck that and fuck you. Come on. Let's get out of here." He stepped toward Cassidy, his body rigid, angry. Brenna stepped back to remain between them.

Cassidy recognized the signs of impending violence. "No," she said sharply. Thanks to her restroom encounter, she had an idea of what was fueling the rumors, but she wanted to hear more. "Why? Just because Luria kissed what appeared to be Chris they think *I'm* gay?"

"Even before that."

Cameron fumed. "Come on."

"Because the number of scenes you have with any male can be counted on one hand. Or they're your father figure, like Dr. Pryor."

"But the storylines..."

"And who do you think writes the damn storylines? This jackass who thinks you're too hot to be on the same set with most of us. Who thinks we'd lust after you."

"Cameron?"

"I am not letting him get his hands on you."

"Excuse me? Cameron, they're co-workers. I... What's wrong with..." Cassidy found no words to express herself, leaning into Brenna, looking from one man to another as if both had escaped from an asylum.

"I'm protecting you!"

Cassidy recoiled from his vehemence. Clearly defeated by that single reaction, Cameron threw up his hands, then shoved a finger into Chapman's chest. "Fine. You want scenes, Mr. Macho, you got 'em." He cursed and pushed through several reporters on his way out.

Cassidy and Brenna held their breath as Cameron stormed off. Abruptly, and still keyed for violence, Cassidy sank into the nearest chair and dropped her head into her hands.

Brenna pushed into Chapman's personal space. "I never figured you for such a bastard," she said harshly. "That was completely uncalled for."

He pursed his lips, looking in the direction Cameron had gone before responding coolly, "It was a bit more of a dust-up than I had figured on, but it worked. He showed his true colors." Turning away, he strode toward the edge of the set.

Hurting for Cassidy, Brenna spat after him, "So did you." Will paused at the edge of the set and gave her a look she could not interpret, eyes narrowing almost angrily, then just as abruptly he shrugged and resumed walking away.

Confused but pushing him from her mind for the moment, Brenna turned and grasped Cassidy's shoulder. Rich, who had walked into the mess without warning, now stood absolutely frozen. Converging from the other direction was a sea of reporters, microphones, pads, and pens at the ready and asking loud questions.

"Rich, run interference." Brenna nodded toward the press.

He looked from her to Cassidy, who was trying to hide her face in her hands. "Uh. Sure." He drew the reporters after him with promises of sneak previews. Smartly he played off the entire scene as a rehearsal, insisting it was all part of the storylines coming up. "If you'll come with me, there's more on another set for you to see."

There were grumbles as Brenna continued to "act" concerned over Cassidy who had seemingly withdrawn in shock. Finally when the reporters were on the other side of a closed door, she squeezed Cassidy's shoulder. The blonde started.

Brenna kept her voice low, to soothe Cassidy as well as not be overheard. "It's all right. You needed an out. I just made you one."

Rising to her feet, Cassidy inhaled shakily. "I have never been so humiliated." Her baffled voice caught on the question. "He's demanding I do a scene with him just to prove Chris isn't gay?"

"I used to think Will was just a harmless, bored actor," Brenna admitted as Cassidy eased out of the chair. "But that was purely self-serving."

"It's not really like it is even today's news. I had heard rumors; I just didn't put a lot of stock in them." Cassidy reminded, "You also mentioned something from the convention in Vegas."

Brenna flushed. "I... Well, how would Chapman have heard? I...didn't talk about it."

Cassidy shrugged and exhaled. "I don't know. I don't want to think about the numbers game, politics, any of it. I wish I wasn't here right now."

Brenna caught Cassidy's shoulders and ushered her gently toward the exit. "Let's get you out of here, at least." They walked together out the back of the soundstage, looking around cautiously for unwelcome press before they locked themselves in Cassidy's trailer.

Anxious to be gone, Cassidy pushed the gown off one shoulder and struggled to pull it off. She had trouble with a catch and tried to force it. Brenna's hands closed over her fidgeting ones. Cassidy met a sympathetic expression, and her adrenaline shock faded, giving way to tears.

"Relax," Brenna whispered. "You'll need that costume for the scenes you have to shoot tomorrow. It's not the dress that you're mad at."

Cassidy drew a ragged breath. She finished the buttons and turned around. Brenna tugged the bodice off her other shoulder, and her fingers momentarily touched bare skin. Cassidy shivered and dropped her head. "Thank you." She hoped Brenna understood her gratitude was not only for the help with her costume.

"You're welcome."

The inflection promised Cassidy that Brenna knew what she had meant. She lifted her eyes in time to see Brenna lean away and snap up a loose tee shirt.

"Here."

With a quick pull, Cassidy was covered again. Then she dropped to her couch, laid back, and covered her face to compose herself. Brenna perched on the edge of the cushion next to her, resting a hand on Cassidy's thigh. "Take a deep breath. It's over."

Dropping her hands and opening her eyes, Cassidy looked for forgiveness. "Brenna, I'm so sorry. I hate scenes. I can't believe he did that. I should tell Cameron—"

"Don't take any of this on yourself. Cameron is the one who should apologize. Instead he stormed off to do God knows what. Hell, for that matter, Will needs to make a trip to a confessional," she said quietly. "All you've ever done is your best with what we're given — Cameron's writing, whatever motivates it. You've done a remarkable job, making what could have been a flat character very appealing." Cassidy was silent, but Brenna easily read surprise on the expressive features.

"Do you think so?"

"Yeah, I do." Brenna smiled gently and patted her leg. Just as Cassidy began to register the warm hand on her thigh it was gone, and Brenna quickly spoke. "You'd better finish getting dressed."

"Brenna, I..." As Brenna started to her feet again, Cassidy felt Brenna's gaze become her whole world for a lingering moment. Abruptly, Cassidy said, "Cameron and I are through." She had no idea why she felt the need to say it, but she knew she wanted Brenna to know.

Brenna abruptly turned away. "Go home. Get some distance from this. Get some sleep."

"What about the reporters?" Cassidy pushed to her feet.

Despite the butterflies flying through her stomach, Brenna was calmly reassuring. "Check the *Variety* copy in the morning." She brushed Cassidy's arm. Brenna drew Cassidy's warm hand to her chest. "There won't be a word about this." Cassidy looked dubiously at the door. "I promise," Brenna said, drawing the woman against her. She put her arm around Cassidy's back. "I don't want dozens of reporters following us into the mountains this weekend." She leaned back and smiled uncertainly into turbulent green-blue. "That is...if you still want to go."

Cassidy took a deep breath and smiled back. "Yes, I still do."

Chapter 20

The sunrise was a sea of golds and reds on the eastern horizon when Cassidy pulled into Brenna's driveway Saturday morning. Her headlights illuminated the other woman, flanked by her sons. All three wore jeans and hiking boots. Brenna had her hands on her hips and a welcoming smile on her face. It was a unique sensation Cassidy felt, as though the rest of the world were already far away. As soon as she turned off her engine, Brenna was at her door, grasping the handle, and looking down at her over the side. The expectant expression made her concerned. "I'm not late, am I?"

"Not too bad," Brenna replied, closing the door after Cassidy emerged. She glanced into the back seat. Soundly sleeping, Ryan was tucked among the bags in the back. "Why don't you get a cup of coffee? I'll move Ryan, and Thomas'll put your stuff into the back."

"Thanks." Wearing her own jeans and trailblazer boots, Cassidy stretched and then rubbed her face tiredly. "You mentioned coffee?"

"On the kitchen counter. Go on inside." Brenna gestured to the house, then leaned into the car.

Cassidy did not move immediately for the house. She watched nervously as Brenna pulled Ryan's limp form against her chest. Absently, Brenna pressed her lips to his hair, and Cassidy swallowed, aware of a surge of warmth that washed through her. Undoubtedly thinking herself unseen, Brenna allowed a fond smile to brighten her expressive face as she moved Cassidy's son to the backseat of her own vehicle.

The emphatic sense of caring from her friend warmed Cassidy immensely. She had done the same with Cassidy over the last week. Not a whiff of the confrontation had appeared in any news source. At work Brenna kept close tabs on her and even listened in on interviews, ready to provide a diversion if the subject arose.

For her part, Cassidy had spent much of the week evaluating a variety of things. Her relationship with Cameron was at an end. She had not seen him once on the set since the mid-morning break when she told him they were through.

Thoughts scattered from the topsy-turvy week, she entered Brenna's kitchen and was drawn immediately to the fragrant smell of coffee. She poured some into a mug she found upside down next to the maker.

The break with Cameron had been coming for a while. Will's public lambasting of the writer had only made the propitious moment appear. Cassidy liked spending time with Ryan; Cameron had never wanted children. She preferred socializing with a small group; he preferred public venues such as conventions, premieres, and awards ceremonies. Then there had been the little things, things Cass now realized she had glossed over. He also had not bothered to attend Ryan's party or bring him a present.

She sipped the coffee thoughtfully. *Now that's just petty. After all,* she castigated herself, *you were far from perfect, too.* She thought about all the times she had declined his dinner invitations because of a late work schedule or an early set call the next morning. Resentment had been inevitable, she realized, as they both continually were not there for one another.

There was something else, too, she realized. Over the last several weeks, she had begun to regain a sense of purpose and self-determination that had apparently been subverted, first by Mitch and then by a well-meaning Cameron. She took another sip, nodding to herself.

Cassidy leaned on her elbows on the counter, eyes surveying the interior of her colleague's home. The furnishings were elegant but practical, and they energized the room with vibrant color and texture, much as Brenna herself effortlessly did in any space she occupied.

She moved to the back, looking out on the yard, noting the gardens and a deck that looked new. The dominant furniture was an A-frame wooden swing that made Cassidy think of lazy Missouri summer nights. She leaned against the wall, sipping her coffee and studying the dew-draped trees.

"Like it?"

Brenna's voice drew Cassidy around to see the other woman unconsciously mimicking her pose — hip perched against the entry to the kitchen as she gazed toward the taller woman. She straightened but was caught and held by a pair of smiling blue eyes. "The coffee's delicious. Thank you. You have a fabulous view from here, too."

Brenna let out a breath she had apparently been holding and straightened as well.

This isn't Hanssen and Jakes, Cassidy thought, even as she found conflicting signals rushing through her body and her skin tingled. She finished the coffee, more to have something to do than out of any need for the fortification of the caffeine. Brenna walked up alongside her and gazed out on the horizon as well. The woman's presence offered warmth that Cassidy found hard not to move toward. *Why do I feel like Hanssen when she's about to do something reckless?*

"The boys have finished moving everything." Brenna's voice was quiet, as though she were distracted.

"Is it a long drive?"

Brenna's shoulders moved in a shrug. "Couple of hours."

Cassidy felt the tightness in her chest slowly unfurl, spreading warm tendrils through her arms and legs. "I'm looking forward to putting L.A. behind us."

Pouring the rest of the coffee into an insulated bottle, Brenna nodded with a smile that intrigued Cassidy. "Me, too. Let's go."

Brenna pressed the remote to open her garage door and watched in her rear view as the blonde drove into the shadowed recesses. They were storing Cassidy's car in the Lanigan garage for the weekend. Brenna closed the garage and waited for Cassidy to get into the front passenger seat and secure her belt. "Everyone set?" Finding Cassidy's gaze on her, Brenna covered the tightness in her throat by turning around and looking at the three boys in the back seat. Ryan still slept, his head resting in Thomas' lap and his feet on James' knees. Brenna's eldest shifted carefully to avoid disturbing Ryan as he made sure the boy's seat belt was secure.

"All set," Thomas responded.

She caught Cassidy's nod and put the Mountaineer into gear. "Then we're off."

The pre-dawn lighting was peaceful, and for a while silence settled among the group as Brenna concentrated. Once they were on the highway headed north out of the valley and into the foothills, Brenna reached for a CD from her glove box. The motion was a little blind as she focused her gaze on the road at the same time.

"What are you looking for?" Cassidy asked.

Straightening up, Brenna offered sheepishly, "I thought a little music?"

"Tell me what you want, and I'll get it for you. I don't mind."

"The CDs are in the glove box." Brenna shot a quick look at her passenger. She wondered what Cassidy would think of her music collection. "I... Well, see if there's something you like."

She felt their age difference acutely at that moment. As Cassidy thumbed through the titles, she was keeping her opinions of the selection to herself. Brenna worried nervously at her bottom lip as she returned both hands to the wheel. Certainly the thirty-year-old wouldn't have the same tastes. Brenna was more than ten years her senior. She glanced into the rear-view mirror to recheck her position amid the light morning highway traffic.

She held her breath as Cassidy slid a CD from its case, into the player, and adjusted the forward speaker volume. Curiosity changed to surprise when Brenna heard the opening promenade of an original cast recording of *Allura*. She had caught the obscure musical during a trip last year to New York City.

Cassidy adjusted the volume again, raising it to catch the voices of the singers. "I've never heard this," she ventured.

"It's something I caught on stage last year. I had a chance to speak with the producer afterward, and I asked for a recording."

"What's the play about?" Cassidy leaned back with her elbow in the window, head resting in her palm, gaze fixed on Brenna.

"It's a love story between a dancer and his partner."

"Period or modern?"

"Period. 1920s," Brenna said.

"Like our last story. So, was it accurate?"

"More or less."

"What drew you to see it?"

"The lead actor was a classmate of mine in high school."

"Really?"

Brenna nodded. "We were...an item, I guess, and worked in all the drama productions together, went to Homecoming and Prom together. That sort of thing."

"So you went to see him in his first Broadway play?"

"Oh no, not his first, but the first I'd seen, yes. He and I were both stage struck. He has been in New York since we were eighteen. He got steady work; I didn't. After leaving a soap, I drifted away from New York, bitten by the big-screen bug. I came to L.A."

"Do you want to go back?"

Brenna nodded solemnly. "Someday. Maybe after *Time Trails* is finished, I'll find an apartment in New York and try my luck again."

"I have no doubt you'll make it." Cassidy smiled, her hand covering Brenna's on the gearshift for a moment.

"You think so?"

"I've seen you act, remember?" Cassidy chuckled.

Brenna's smile returned. She pulled her hand from beneath Cassidy's and brushed her hair from her face as she chuckled, too. "What are you going to do?"

"When *Time Trails* is over?" Cassidy dropped her head and studied her hands in her lap. "I haven't had any offers yet. But," she added quietly, "I really haven't been looking."

"Because of Cameron?"

"Yes."

"I'm really sorry about how things turned out."

"Don't be. He's just... We didn't have the same priorities."

"That makes it hard to make a relationship work," Brenna acknowledged, feeling guilty about not speaking with Kevin in over a week.

"The hours. The pace." Cassidy sighed. "Why do we do it?"

"Because we love those hours, that hectic pace," Brenna responded with a wry twist to her lips. "Thomas knows." She glanced over her shoulder and asked with a smile, "Don't you?"

"Mom's a nut case less than a month into hiatus," Thomas provided, which made Cassidy laugh. "Short vacations are okay, a weekend here or there, but longer than a couple of weeks and she's climbing the walls. She built the deck last summer."

Cassidy laughed again. "Handywoman, huh?"

"My set-building days left me with a few skills," Brenna supplied with a blush.

"I'd say so. I saw the deck and that swing. Nice work."

Brenna was warmed by the compliment. She dwelled on it for a few moments, almost missing their turn off. At the last possible opportunity, she changed highways, heading more east than north.

When they arrived at the park entrance, Brenna displayed their pass and was waved inside. The ranger gestured them forward. "Follow the road ahead. Parking for the hiking trail to the campground is the second one on your left."

"Thanks," Brenna told him, then pulled away from the station.

"You really do come here a lot," Cassidy commented as they drove into the park.

"Yes, we do." Brenna rolled up her window and looked in the rear view, noticing Ryan had finally stirred. "Just in time," she said with a smile, reaching back between the seats to tickle a sock-covered foot.

Cassidy leaned between the seats and brushed his hair smooth. "Sleep well, buddy?"

He nodded. "Could I have juice?"

"You're thirsty?" James asked. The youngster's blue eyes lifted quickly to the dark-haired teen, and he nodded. "Mom, is it all right if I pull one of the juice pouches for him?"

Brenna deferred to Cassidy. "It's all-natural."

"That's fine, thanks," Cassidy said. "It'll help him wake up."

"That's what I thought," Brenna replied as she pulled into the lot. Parking, she looked around and spotted Mike Connell, the charity director. "Looks like we aren't the first."

Brenna tossed her keys to Thomas while she went to catch Mike's attention. "Good morning."

Connell was a tall, spare man with brown eyes, curly brown hair, and a face worn from years in the sun. He wore a wide-brimmed hat and a leather jacket over what was really a skydiver's jumpsuit. "Hey, Brenna."

"Thomas is here," she said before he could ask. The two of them were conducting the central attraction of the weekend — a rock climb up a fifty-foot rock face. "I wanted to introduce you to a friend first." She waved Cassidy over. The blonde had the hiking pack half on when Thomas spotted his mother beckoning and quickly helped her finish.

"I remember her from the Halloween party," Mike noted, holding out his hand and shaking Cassidy's. "Good to see you again, Miss Hyland."

"Cassidy, please." She shifted awkwardly under the weight, and Mike reached back and held the pack's support beam above her head while she adjusted the balance. "Thanks."

Brenna watched the woman push her hands through tousled blond hair and swallowed against her suddenly dry mouth when the blue eyes met hers briefly. *She looks relaxed. That's good, right?* Brenna had worked hard the last week to keep news of the blowup from leaking out and was pleased to see that her efforts had paid off. Seeing the way Cassidy had been torn up by being thrust into Will and Cameron's pissing match, she had needed to do something. She dragged her attention away from Cassidy, where it was straying far too often. "How far to the campsite?"

"Second change in the tree line," Mike supplied. "About an hour up the side. It's not too steep and a pretty basic hike. It will put us next to the feeder spring and just below the rock face we're climbing tomorrow."

"Sounds good." Brenna shook his hand again and returned to the car and efficiently secured her own backpack. Primal energy flowed through her as she adjusted the belly strap. "Thomas, how are you doing?" She glanced toward her sons and found both Thomas and James already wearing their packs, kneeling next to Ryan.

"I want one!" the little boy pouted.

Cassidy started forward, but Brenna grasped her hand, stopping her.

"They'll find something small for him to carry," she assured. "I promise they won't give in to his request for a pack."

As the two women watched, Brenna's sons performed a negotiation worthy of Commander Jakes. Soon Ryan had his *Wild Things* monster tied to his back with about six feet of tent rope. He was grinning ear to ear as he reached for his mother's hand.

The five joined the gathering crowd, children and adults of various ages and sizes, a host of them wearing long-sleeved LAKE logo shirts and carrying packs with personal utensils and sleeping bags. Adults carried tent bundles. Brenna and Cassidy had split the materials for their own tent between them. Thomas and James had done the same for the tent they would share with Ryan.

Mike moved to the front of the group and welcomed everyone. "All right. Everyone ready for the best weekend of your lives?"

Cheers rose throughout the group, and Brenna looked at Cassidy, who was scanning the surroundings with a quiet, expectant smile. *I am so ready for this,* Brenna thought as the group started out. She fell into step next to the taller woman. She heard Thomas and James behind them, already chatting with other teens. Between her and Cassidy, Ryan darted every which way, trying to take in the whole atmosphere at one time. Brenna pointed out birds and squirrels, and a frog jumped away from their path as they continued through the woods and the trail began to angle upward.

The sun found Cassidy's face and lit the pale skin with a soft golden fire as her eyes met Brenna's. Thudding in her chest, Brenna's heart sped up in response. She dusted her hand through Ryan's hair as she looked ahead on the trail, wondering what waited around the next bend.

It was nearing nine o'clock when the group reached the campsite. While the youngest children played tag, the older ones assisted in setting up camp. Despite the cool November temperature, the exertion had them all sweating very quickly. Wielding a hammer, Brenna had just finished sinking the first stake in her last tent when she stood, stretched, and pulled off her outer shirt. Tying its arms around her waist, she returned to her work in her tan cotton tank top, arms bare and glistening.

Steadying a pole for a tent across the way, Cassidy studied the loose fall of auburn hair concealing Brenna's face from her view. She considered the smoothly muscled arms and could easily picture the other woman laboring on her deck. Familiar energy swept her through her loins. She recalled watching Susan kiss Virgil and sighed.

Diverting herself from the budding feelings, Cassidy took a deeper breath of the pine-scented fresh air. Out here it felt like anything was possible. She worried fretfully at her bottom lip as she moved to hold the next pole. She was assailed by a strong vision of brushing Brenna's sweat-dampened hair away from those high-colored cheeks and—

"Ouch!" Cassidy blinked and looked down to where the man she was helping had just rapped her booted foot with the stake hammer.

"Sorry," he offered.

"It's all right, Gerry." She patted his dark shoulder absently and wriggled her toes. The sudden impact had hurt, but thanks to her footwear's thick leather and sturdy construction, she could already feel the ache subsiding. She judiciously moved her feet back as he resumed his hammering, fighting down a blush as she felt Brenna's eyes on her from across the clearing.

Brenna's color was high, and her smooth skin was highlighted by wet sunlight. Cassidy stole another glance toward the working woman and sighed again. Brenna had made a lot of adjustments over the year they'd worked together. When the actress eventually told Cassidy how much she respected her work, her reaction to the revelation had surprised her. The more she thought about it, though, the more she realized that Brenna's respect was something she had desperately wanted.

Gerry proclaimed the assembly finished, and Cassidy let go of the last pole. Brushing her palms together, she dropped onto a log. Sitting by one of two unlit fire pits, she pulled off her own outer shirt, using it to wipe the sweat from her face and neck, thankful that she had already pulled her hair into a ponytail.

A thin towel suddenly draped across her shoulders, sliding down into her hands. She looked up to see Brenna sitting on the log beside her. Cassidy returned her friend's quick smile. She lifted the towel to her face to mop at the sweat, pausing abruptly at another scent already on the towel. *Brenna.*

"Want to go for a swim before lunch?" Brenna asked.

Despite the evaporation of sweat from her back and shoulders, Cassidy still felt hot. "I could use the chance to cool off." She dropped her gaze quickly from the warm glow of Brenna's sun-touched, smiling face. She squeezed the towel reflexively, not sure why she was suppressing the sudden urge to grasp Brenna's hands, which were fidgeting in her lap.

We're friends, right? Friends could touch, and no one would think anything of it. The two of them had even touched in comfort before. However, she knew her earlier daydream had not had mere comfort in mind.

The opportunity fled, as Brenna stood in the next moment. "I'll round up the kids."

Her hand brushed across Cassidy's damp shoulder, sending conflicting waves of chill and heat along the nerves. Mopping at her face, Cassidy watched Brenna walk away and wondered what the hell she should do. Clearly the gesture was an invitation. But to what?

Cassidy thought about Hanssen being gay, about the idea of her wanting Jakes. Jakes and Hanssen were fantasy. This was reality. *Does that make a difference?* Cassidy was not sure.

Walking away from Cassidy and the curious pale blue eyes that had followed her all morning, Brenna reached a cluster of trees where the younger children were racing about. Catching one girl under the arms and swinging her around, she announced loudly, "Swim time!"

Shrieking, the children raced to their tents in a mad scramble, eager to be the first dressed and into the water. Mike stepped from his tent, already clad in plaid green swim trunks. The teens, Thomas and James among them, loped over more sedately, also ready to change.

Brenna caught a wave from James and waved back, fretting when she realized her arm and chest were still tingling from her light contact with Cassidy's shoulder. As she walked toward their tent, Cassidy approached from the other side. She found herself studying the other woman's figure.

So, she's physically attractive, Brenna. You knew that a year ago.

In the beginning, Cassidy's physical beauty had scared Brenna, professionally and personally. She agonized for months over what she had done, or not done, to lose the confidence of the production staff. Why had they brought in someone younger, taller, and a former model, to boot? Looking at Cassidy now, she felt no jealousy. It also was not protectiveness filling her chest, since she wanted to wrap much more than her arms around the younger woman.

Brenna was feeling very energized, she realized. While working on the tents, she had found her progress constantly disrupted by side glances toward Cassidy. Checking on the first-timer's progress, or so she told herself. However, it was clear that Cassidy was fine. *Very fine*, she noted, tracing the backs of her legs, the way her hair had worked free from her ponytail. It was insane the way she had tracked drops of sweat from Cassidy's hairline down her cheek, throat, and onto her collarbone before tossing a towel across the lean shoulders. She wanted suddenly to be very active, very sexual, but couldn't understand why a woman she was just barely beginning to know — and had until recently largely ignored — would be at the center of the whirlpool of emotions.

She and Cassidy reached for the tent flap simultaneously. When their hands touched, the vibration ricocheted through her body. It came to a stop deep in Brenna's groin, where it crouched like a wild cat coiling to pounce. She quickly pulled back. She motioned Cassidy inside, pacing outside as she tried to bring her reactions under control.

Aware of the necessity for propriety, but reveling in the chaotic feelings sweeping her body, Brenna was surprised when Cassidy suddenly reemerged and straightened up before her. Her gaze swept the trim body, noting the sleek black one-piece suit.

"Your turn." Cassidy stepped out of the way.

Just as the tent flap started to fall, Brenna felt a fleeting touch on her back. Startled, she looked back, but Cassidy was looking off into the distance. Then the canvas obscured everything.

Brenna bit off a gasp as she hit the surface of the cold spring. Diving shallowly, she came up and tilted her head back, letting the water wash the hair back from her face. She stroked evenly to the shallow side, where the youngest children were being supervised by adult partners.

Screeches and nervous laughter arose as little toes hit the cold water. She stood and stretched against the sandy bottom, watching Cassidy coaxing Ryan into the water. Abruptly, he jumped. When he came up spluttering, his mother tucked a hand under his stomach. He laid out, arms and legs splashing in a sloppy crawl stroke.

Thomas swam past Brenna, briefly diverting her attention. He had partnered with a young black boy, probably ten years old. Thomas paused frequently to check his buddy's progress. She smiled, and her chest filled with pride. *He's growing up so fast,* she thought, watching her eldest child stand and shake the water from his hair. Thomas was beginning to look a great deal more like his father. Thinking about Tom made her think about Kevin and their fight. Resolutely, she pushed the issue aside.

She moved through the water toward a sputtering boy whose head had dropped beneath the surface. Grasping him under the arms, she helped him clear his face and directed him back to his partner. The boy's uncle waved to her as she moved off again.

A splash behind her drew her around to see that someone had brought a volley-ball, and a group of adults and children were siding up, batting it back and forth among themselves. Mike leaped up, intending to intercept the ball but missing, land-ing heavily in the water. The resulting wave smashed into Brenna. Staggered, she snatched at the ball he had missed and smacked it back with the heel of her hand. Mike laughed, as did others.

As the game continued, Brenna heard splashing coming closer and turned again, expecting to find another child in need of a hand. Instead she found Cassidy — walking along, keeping a firm palm under Ryan's stomach as he propelled himself forward, his puffed cheeks regularly dropping into the water. Finally, he tried taking a deep breath and swallowed some water. Catching him around the stomach and pulling him up, Cassidy waited for him to stop coughing, unalarmed. Her gaze lifted from him and found Brenna. "Hi."

"Hi." *Hi?* Brenna castigated herself for the singular response. *Come on, for cry-ing out loud, talk to her.* "He swims pretty well," she noted. "Lessons?"

"No. Just the waterproof baby class at the Y when he was two."

"Oh." Brenna fell silent, feeling like a teenager at a prom. The rush of sensation she experienced in Cassidy's presence was both exciting and terrifying, and she exhaled slowly.

Howls and loud splashing drew the women's attention to the rocks. Brenna spotted James leading off a series of wild cannonball jumps, each splash bigger than the last as the group's teens hit the water.

"James!" Brenna shouted. Her worry subsided when her son surfaced. The joy-ful expression on his face demonstrated he was fine and eager for another run. He looked at her, shrugged, and slowed his steps for about three paces before he ran to the end of the line of kids. Brenna shook her head, decided against starting a battle of wills, and splashed the water surface lightly in her distraction.

"Lessons?" Cassidy asked, her voice sounding in Brenna's right ear at the same moment Ryan's small hand grasped Brenna's forearm.

Brenna inhaled and exhaled to release the shiver of reaction the double assault had on her senses — one innocent and the other unintentionally seductive. Cassidy had a warm throaty voice when she talked softly. Shaking her head, Brenna fought to just answer the question, trying to avoid letting her own voice go equally soft in response. "No, just pure gumption."

"I wonder where he gets that from," Cassidy mused, her eyes dancing with laughter, though not so much as a chuckle passed her lips.

Despite the flutters in her stomach, Brenna bantered back, "Oh really?"

Cassidy nodded. "You've got more guts than ten people put together. I really believe that, especially after this week."

Brenna flushed under the praise. "Just trying to help," she said quietly.

Cassidy did not respond. In her curiosity, Brenna looked back. She found a softening light staring at her. She felt as though the gaze were swallowing her whole. *Are you feeling what I'm feeling?* She almost opened her mouth to voice the question and then suddenly clamped her jaw shut as a voice in her head warned, *Don't go there.*

It was barely audible over the pounding of her heart.

Two hours later, the springs were abandoned to cries of "I'm starving!" and the crowd descended on the campsite. The portable grills were lit and hamburgers and hot dogs set to cook. Brenna monitored one, and Mike monitored the other. Both had helpers to pass the paper plates of buns back and forth to the campers. Next to her, filling the plates, Cassidy was silent. Taking her cue from that, Brenna focused on the meat.

After a while, Cassidy asked, "Want to trade? You could go eat."

"No, I'm all right." Brenna flipped over another patty and then looked up. "Why don't you make yourself up a plate and go sit. I've got this."

Cassidy scanned the groupings, apparently considering who to join. Brenna watched Cassidy's face slip into a bemused, indulgent smile that lit up her fair features. Brenna followed the gaze and saw what had her attention.

Thomas had coaxed Ryan into his lap, and the two were alternating bites of hot dog and chips. The boy, with a young version of his mother's intense look, painstakingly pulled off bites and fed them to Thomas, who playfully snapped his teeth over each morsel.

"I've never seen him do that," Cassidy marveled.

Brenna laughed. "Thomas did it to get him to eat. He was probably too excited to settle down."

The two women watched a while as the interplay between their sons continued, then Cassidy turned to make up a plate for herself.

Brenna watched the bent head, aware of the smile still playing on the full lips and the corresponding tightness in her own chest. Flexing her grip on the spatula handle, she suddenly realized her hand was hot. "Ow!" Brenna jerked back from the flames that had licked her palm. The spatula dropped with a clang. A cold wet paper towel was suddenly pressed around her injured hand as she gripped the wrist with her left hand.

"Are you all right?" Cassidy asked, carefully supporting Brenna's hand while she removed the paper towel to look underneath at the angry red skin.

"I... Yeah." Brenna grimaced as Cassidy turned the injured palm up, stretching the skin near her wrist painfully. "Ow." Cassidy immediately stopped pulling.

"There's no blistering yet," Cassidy reported, the relief plain in her voice. "We can put a salve on it and wrap it up." She wet the paper towel again and pressed it against the tender redness. "Does it hurt much?"

"It's numb," Brenna admitted worriedly. "I'll go find some first aid cream."

"Go sit. I'll bring your lunch over. Hot dog or hamburger?"

"Burger with ketchup." Brenna grimaced again as the light pressure keeping the towel in place aggravated the abused skin. "Damn," she cursed under her breath.

Cassidy went to work on the two plates, pulling the rest of the burgers and dogs off the fire and following quickly as Brenna looked for a place to sit. She settled on a grassy spot just outside those circled around one of the unlit fire pits. Cassidy was at her side quickly.

Caroline, another chaperone, noticed Brenna's predicament. "Burn?"

Brenna nodded, and Caroline jumped to her feet to grab a first aid kit. The hand was salved and gently wrapped. Throughout the treatment, Brenna felt Cassidy's hand on her shoulder. Though she felt absurd for having done something so careless, Brenna appreciated the quiet presence.

The emergency handled, Brenna accepted her plate from Cassidy, balancing it in her lap and eating awkwardly with her left hand. When she looked up from her hamburger, she found Thomas studying her, Ryan still in his lap, secured with a big hand. Thomas' head tilted in question. Shrugging, Brenna offered a twitch of her injured hand conveying that the pain was minimal. Her son nodded and returned to entertaining Ryan and a young girl next to him with the "disappearing potato chip" trick.

A scavenger hunt took up the afternoon. Still nursing her hand, Brenna declined to lead a team. Her son, James, and his team, the Blue Bombers, found all thirty items first, earning a grab bag assortment of movie tickets and coupons, as well as baseball and other trading cards.

When her hand began to throb and itch, Brenna gave up on trying to keep a public face and retreated to her tent to rest and read. The noise of the zipper opening drew her attention as Cassidy stepped inside and hunched over, crowding Brenna for a moment before folding up on her own sleeping bag.

The taller woman stretched out, offering up a sybaritic sigh. Rolling over and propping her head on her hand, she took a deep breath and exhaled. "I haven't had this much fun in months." She nudged the book in Brenna's hands. "What are you reading?"

Turning it over, Brenna presented the front. "*The Red Tent.*"

"Enjoying it?"

"It's pretty good." Brenna started to turn the book back. Its spine bumped her injured hand, and she winced.

"How's your hand?" Cassidy wrapped her fingers around Brenna's hand.

Brenna felt as though she had swallowed her tongue. "It's sore," she managed in soft protest, withdrawing from Cassidy's touch.

The other woman nodded. "I'll rewrap it while you tell me what the book's about."

"It's biblical fiction, about Jacob's four wives and his only daughter, Dinah. She's the narrator." As she talked, Cassidy retrieved the first aid kit from her own supplies and applied more burn salve. Brenna's eyes watered at the renewed pain.

"I'm sorry," Cassidy offered, brushing Brenna's lower arm soothingly with her thumb.

Putting down the book, Brenna wiped her eyes with her uninjured hand. "It's not your fault."

"I know. I feel bad all the same." She held Brenna's hand gingerly in her lap as she took pains to wrap the gauze without further aggravating the skin. "Tell me more about the book."

Watching Cassidy's hands move around her own, Brenna had lost her train of thought. "Oh... Um..."

"How do they handle jealousy?" Cassidy prompted.

"Culturally, it's very different. There seems to be a lot of negotiating going on."

"Humans just can't help being jealous," Cassidy said thoughtfully. "Monogamy just...is, I think."

"Many ancient cultures practiced polygamy, but like you, I have a hard time seeing how it would all work. That's why the story's fascinating, I guess. It seems to work for them."

"Is that a recommendation?"

"I could loan it to you when I'm finished." As Cassidy let go, Brenna flexed her rewrapped hand, making only a mild face. "Thank you."

Cassidy leaned back, tucked the kit back inside her bag, and crossed her hands under her head, staring up at the tent peak. "Best I can do."

Rolling onto her side, Brenna could see Cassidy struggling to explain herself. "It'll get better."

"I know," she said finally. "Do you think you'll be all right to climb tomorrow?"

"Not without my gloves, which I was planning to wear anyway."

"I should probably go take your place in the dinner prep," Cassidy said suddenly.

Brenna's bandaged hand on her arm forestalled her. "It's only four o'clock. Relax."

Cassidy relaxed back against her sleeping bag. "You don't mind the company?"

"Go on. Sleep." Brenna watched Cassidy's eyes close as the blond head turned into the cushioning of the bag.

"I am a little worn out. Must be all this fresh air," Cassidy mumbled.

Brenna's right hand lay between them. It was covered gently. Book forgotten, Brenna leaned back and watched the gentle rise and fall of Cassidy's chest, soon drifting off herself in the quiet.

Chapter 21

"Mom? Ms. Hyland?"

Cassidy stirred as the call came again from outside the tent. She flexed her wrist and arm and found an unfamiliar texture pressing against her palm. Focusing, she realized she was holding Brenna's injured hand in her own. Gently she released her grip and tracked up to the other woman's profile, finding the distinctively featured face turned toward her. A sharp pang of desire made her breath catch.

Is it possible to fall in love in a day? She shook her head. *This has been building for a lot longer than a day.* What she had always felt as admiration was finally blossoming, having been buried under work and their intense and adversarial relationship for weeks, probably months.

Cassidy grasped Brenna's other arm and shook gently until Brenna stirred. Blue eyes blinked open, capturing her, and she gasped.

"Cassidy?"

The husky voice flowed over her senses with a shocking tenderness. "It's dinner call," she guessed, drawing away quickly as Brenna sat up.

"Boy, I really sacked out." Brenna sighed, rubbing her cheeks with her palms and wincing as she aggravated her burn.

"Mom?"

Brenna glanced to the tent opening. With a sigh she shifted to it, unzipping it. "Dinner, I guess. Hmm?" she invited over her shoulder to Cassidy, who had not moved.

Looking away as Brenna exited the tent, Cassidy tried to pin her emotions down and contain them. She knew what lust was about. She had even experienced it in the context of a woman once. This was different. The urge to touch, yes, but more...the desire to hold and cherish was also present. At last she released a long breath and followed Brenna into the evening air.

Brenna's son, James, stood a few feet away, looking at the women as they emerged, straightening their sleep-wrinkled clothes. He held Ryan by the hand.

Stepping forward, Brenna brushed her son's hair from a cheek and kissed his temple. "Thanks," she said.

"You were sleeping?"

"Yes. That's not so strange." Brenna ruffled her son's hair. "I've had a long day." She looked at Cassidy with a wry expression. "And I'm not as young as I used to be."

Mike hailed them from the grill. "Corn on the cob? Fish?"

Giving James a parting pat on the back, Brenna led the way to Mike, took two plates, and passed one to Cassidy. "Thanks. Did we miss anything?" Carefully, Brenna picked up the cob in her left hand and bit into the kernels, enjoying the sweet savor on her tongue.

"Not really. Thomas and I double-checked the equipment for tomorrow. Most people relaxed in their tents for a little while." He turned a pair of fillets. Spearing one, he held it up. "Fresh fish? Can't beat it."

Biting into the one delivered to her plate, Cassidy agreed. "Delicious."

Seated on a log by a now-lit campfire, Brenna and Cassidy listened to the hum of conversation around them, content for the moment to be quiet. An orange glow lit the western sky as the sun set.

Caroline slid over. "How's the hand?"

Brenna flexed her bandaged hand, able to stifle the wince. "Not so bad any-more." When she dropped her hand and looked up, Cassidy's deeply concerned gaze intersected hers. "Really," she insisted.

Unnerved by the fire that began flickering behind the concern in pale blue eyes, Brenna felt the need to escape. "I think I'll take a walk."

She handed her plate to Caroline and set out of camp. Passing the main table, she plucked an apricot from the basket of fruit. Aimlessly, she turned onto a path that would take her higher up the mountain. Determined to sort out her feelings, she followed the narrowing path, trying all the while to dispel the image of kissing away that doubting look from Cassidy's face.

She's a woman, her inner voice pointed out. Brenna was surprised to find that the inferno inside her did not dim for a second.

You're married. All right, that caused a brief flicker. However, her heart soft-ened again at another visit from her memory: Cassidy's face as they hugged in the Pinnacle lot the week after Ryan's mishap in Sports Warehouse. The fires roared back to life.

Brenna was forced to acknowledge that it was desire she felt — not protective-ness, not simple friendship. Her belly was thick with it; her chest ached with it. Her breaths shortened. *I can't be feeling this.*

She felt like turning tail and running. Her heart pounded, her head throbbed, and her knees shook. She couldn't move. Sinking to the ground against a tree, Brenna closed her eyes against the images that would not stop now that they had come forward to be recognized.

The crack of dry wood breaking brought her head up sharply. Twilight shadows concealed the face, but it wasn't necessary to see; she knew who had followed her.

She dug her hands into the tree behind her and rose slowly, steadying herself in the maelstrom of emotions assaulting her, challenging her conscience. *Should I flee again? Or is it time to stop running?* She studied Cassidy's silhouette. The other woman's head was tilted, her shoulders rounded. She hesitated, but then stepped for-ward.

All contrary arguments were crushed under the weighty evidence of a reality far more powerful as Brenna realized, *I do feel.* "How did this happen?"

"So you *do*...I wondered if it was just me." Cassidy stepped hesitantly forward into a beam of moonlight that pierced the canopy of trees.

Brenna held her breath. *What will she ask of me?*

Neither knew who reached out first, but they fell into a hug which became an embrace, their heads turned into one another's shoulder. They inhaled in surprise and sensation, and their lips touched lightly. The tiny flames in their souls licked up through their chests and joined where their lips melded in a nascent, delicate kiss, the faintest brushing of their lips one against the other. The sensations — warm, cool, and dewy soft, like rose petals brushing against their sensitized skin — rocked them both.

Brenna gasped for breath, and Cassidy reluctantly let her go.

"We can't do this," Brenna said huskily, though this was exactly what she had wanted since that morning in the car.

"You want this," Cassidy countered softly, knowingly. Her palm warmed Brenna's cheek as the other woman fought against the desire to lean into the caress. "All day...I saw you. I watched you."

"I know. But this isn't some fantasy, some role." Brenna's words sounded unconvincing, even to her own ears.

Cassidy shook her head. "No, you're right. It's real."

Brenna's eyes widened, her expression worried, hopeful, and alarmed in quick succession. Palms tenderly held her cheeks, and Brenna's stomach flip-flopped as warm, full lips brushed hers again.

"It's very real," Cassidy assured her quietly again. Leaving behind a layer of cool air filled with a scent of passion that made Brenna shiver, Cassidy disappeared into the darkness.

What the hell do I do now? Brenna leaned weakly against the tree that still held her somewhat upright. Traitorously, her body shook with the desire to run after Cassidy.

A woman of forty plus years shouldn't be reduced to a puddle of mush from a single kiss.

Ah, hell, who am I kidding? This wasn't about what should be. As she had told Cassidy, there certainly seemed to be something here.

So what do I do now?

Go after her.

Brenna stumbled away from the tree and through the darkness, trying to find a path out.

The chaperones and children had gathered around the fires, each carrying sticks stripped of their bark. Several adults were armed with bags of marshmallows, graham crackers, and chocolate bars. The shadows were deep; it was hard to see people until you were right on top of them. Rubbing her face to hide her emotional turmoil, she stepped into the milling group. Where she promptly bumped into Mike.

"Oh, hey. Saw you go off earlier. Everything all right?"

"Yes," she said. "I just went to stretch."

"Sure. Here's your stuff." He supplied her with the s'more makings and pointed out an unoccupied log by the furthest fire.

As she passed each group, she looked at the fire-lit faces. She worried when she did not see one in particular. *Did Cassidy even come back?* She looked back at the woods, worried that the blonde might be still out there somewhere. *And you hurt her.*

With children crowding around her, Brenna settled to a log. Someone prompted from the darkness, "Sing-a-long!"

Suggestions were passed around and Brenna listened. Finally *Little Rabbit Fufu* was selected. She started to sing and do the hand gestures for the story-song, the children mimicking her and the other adults.

> Little rabbit Fufu
> Hopping through the forest
> Sneaking up on field mice and
> Batting them over the head
> (spoken) Along came the Good Fairy, who said...

By the second verse, Brenna's eyes had adjusted to the firelight, and faces took shape across the campfire. Her heart skipped a beat. Head down, helping her son with the song's motions, Cassidy was singing softly. Brenna's awareness shrank down to the other woman's voice. It was very different with the folk song than it had been during her role as a lounge singer in their last episode. She thought she heard a rawness that suggested Cassidy had been crying. She rubbed her own throat as it tightened. Scared about what that meant, Brenna returned to the song:

> Little rabbit Fufu,
> I don't want to see you ...

There were middle verses, but Brenna had not heard them in years. Falling silent, she listened as, amazingly, about a dozen others did keep singing. Cassidy was among them. Brenna shook her head and joined in the ending of the song:

> Along came the Good Fairy —
> Who turned him into a goon.
> Which just goes to show you:
> 'Hare today and goon tomorrow.'

Groans echoed all around. Brenna watched Cassidy move off the log, lean back against it with Ryan in her lap, and gaze up at the sky. She wondered what the younger woman was thinking. She was torn from her thoughts when a collection of sticks appeared before her. With a smile, she pushed a marshmallow onto each one. "When you finish toasting those, I'll show you what to do with them."

Cassidy assembled a pair of graham crackers, the melted marshmallow from Ryan's stick, and a square of chocolate. Ryan gleefully ate her demonstration model as she passed out ingredients and watched several children near her make the s'more treat.

Kissing Ryan's head, she leaned back and studied the canopy full of stars. "How about *Twinkle, Twinkle*?" she suggested aloud. She heard a murmur of agreement and joined in the opening lines.

Across the fire she saw Brenna sitting alone, her mouth moving over the song extremely softly. *She's unsure of her voice*, Cassidy realized. Listening carefully, she filtered out the other voices until only Brenna's remained. Not sounding particularly trained, Brenna's voice was nevertheless entrancing, suggesting the romance of a bygone era, smooth whiskey, and hazy smoke. *Where's there's smoke*, Cassidy thought, *Brenna could certainly be the fire.*

Dropping her chin, she admired the way the firelight caught the lighter browns in Brenna's hair, making them appear more red. When she had held Brenna's cheeks as they had kissed, her fingers had drifted through the soft strands for the very first time. Even now her fingertips tingled at the memory.

She remembered the first time she had touched Brenna's skin, too, though she was just brushing away tears with the back of her knuckles. Brenna had been crying while talking with someone on the phone.

Her husband, her memory supplied helpfully.

For God's sake, she scolded herself. *The woman is married.* She put a hand over her eyes. *How in the hell could I lose sight of that?* Uncovering her eyes, she looked at Brenna again. The refrain trailed off: Twinkle, twinkle, little star, How I wonder what you are.

Cassidy had been certain that Brenna had invited their kiss. The escalation in their relationship had been Brenna's idea, too, hadn't it? She had given Cassidy the slippers. There was the physical comfort when Ryan was lost. The invitation to camping had come even before that. She paused.

Is it possible that Brenna didn't mean those things the way I took them? Her face heated at the possibility. *I need to explain.*

Just how do you plan to do that?

I have to let her know I didn't mean it.

But you did mean it.

The sounds of giggling children faded as Brenna's gaze met hers across the fire. Cassidy's heart hammered in her ears.

The gathering broke up as happy, stuffed youngsters started to fall asleep in soft laps. Brenna saw Ryan curling into his mother's body and suddenly imagined herself doing the same. *You're nuts.* She blushed.

"Mom?"

Brenna turned to find James behind her. "Going to bed?" she asked, cocking her head to the side.

"Yeah, you?"

She nodded. "After a bit." She put her arm around his shoulder and squeezed, briefly tucking her head against his. "Did you have fun today?"

He nodded, catching her right hand lightly. "I saw you getting this wrapped up. What happened?"

"Burn from the lunch fire," she said. "Doesn't hurt anymore, though."

"You should be more careful."

That's pretty good advice for more than just fires, she thought ruefully. She kissed his cheek and watched him walk away. She stood alone, an island in the sea of people moving toward their tents.

Another island emerged nearby. Thomas and Cassidy talked quietly, Ryan between them. The five-year-old did not seem happy to be spending the night in the boys' tent. Brenna listened but resisted stepping in.

"I've got cookies," Thomas offered, finally hitting on Ryan's weakness. The boy's eyes lit up; he looked less upset and more intrigued. "Cookies? For Fred, too?"

Brenna could see that Cassidy, also quiet, was grinning, too.

"Who?" Thomas looked at Cassidy, then back at Ryan.

"My monster, Fred," the boy explained with an air of "you should know that".

Brenna chuckled softly as Thomas recovered admirably. He stood, held out a hand, and assured Ryan seriously, "I have cookies for Fred, too. Come on."

Ryan trailed after Thomas. Soon Brenna and Cassidy were the only ones not inside their tent. Brenna fidgeted with her bandaged hand. The taller woman strode toward her, blue eyes soft and full lips beckoning. Brenna lifted her hand. Whether the gesture was to ward off Cassidy or pull her close, she could not decide.

Cassidy decided for her, grasping the bandaged hand carefully. With a quiet, even voice, she said, "I'll rewrap it for you, if you want."

Want? Brenna inhaled. Heat from their connection seared her. *What do I want?* She nodded, unable to break free of the other woman's gaze. "All right."

At the tent, Brenna entered first and lit the lantern. They circled on their sleeping bags, and Cassidy reached for the first aid kit as Brenna unwrapped her hand.

The silence became oppressive. They both felt the need to fill it.

"I wanted to—"

"Could I ask you—" Cassidy shook her head. "You go first." Examining the red splotches on Brenna's hand, she applied the cooling cream. She wrapped it loosely to let the skin breathe.

Brenna swallowed, alternately watching her hand in Cassidy's and the other woman's bent head. "I wanted to say that I'm sorry."

"It was my fault. I shouldn't have... I misread—"

Brenna's voice was soft, afraid of the admission she was making but unwilling to have a lie between them. "No, you didn't."

Cassidy's motion stopped. Their eyes met, and Brenna read the astonishment clearly. A cool collectedness emerged which Brenna recognized as Hanssen. "Don't. I need Cassidy here right now," she begged. "No confusion."

Cassidy shook herself, and the composure washed away. "I...I'm sorry. I...just...I don't know what to say to you."

"I don't know what to say either," Brenna admitted. "I didn't plan this."

"I'll go."

Brenna shook her head. "No, we just need to slow down."

"Are you sure?"

"I don't want to lose our friendship."

Cassidy exhaled sharply. "Thank God. I don't think I could stand it if you made me leave."

Brenna acknowledged that admission with a nod, though it was far more impassioned than she wanted to deal with at the moment. "I've never done anything like...that," she said, her voice barely audible.

Brenna was looking down at her hands, fidgeting with them in her lap again. Cassidy recognized the habit from earlier in the day. This time she did not resist reaching out. She wanted to touch this woman. And Brenna wanted it, too. "Would you do it again?" Cassidy asked.

The faint smile on Cassidy's lips drew Brenna's gaze like a magnet. Before she could demur, Cassidy had covered her hands with one of her own, pinning them to the sleeping bag between them, and was leaning forward, closing the gap between their bodies. At the same moment gentle fingers caressed Brenna's left cheek and into her hair, and Cassidy's full lips touched hers.

The earlier kiss had shocked Brenna, reducing her to a gasping puddle of mixed sensations, but this one rocketed her past shock into a place of hypersensitivity. She noted the texture, the scent, and the adoration passing from those lips to hers. She freed her hands from beneath Cassidy's and gave in to the need to touch in return. She touched the other woman's pale cheek, brushing her thumb over the satin skin, holding her still, even as they both trembled.

When the kiss broke, Brenna's head dropped forward. Cassidy's lips trailed across her forehead. "I didn't even use to like you," Brenna admitted on a deep breath, inhaling the delicate lavender again.

Cassidy's laugh, soft and lilting, washed over Brenna in absolution. The long fingers in Brenna's hair caressed the nape of her neck, spreading a delicious tingling. Brenna lifted her head. Mesmerized by her own hand lifting to Cassidy's cheek, she stroked the smooth planes. *A woman's face. This woman.*

"You are..." She couldn't find words. Cassidy turned her face into the touch and closed her eyes. A lump welled up in Brenna's throat. "It scares me that I don't understand where this is all coming from," she managed.

"You snuck inside me, too." Cassidy's hand dragged slowly from the back of Brenna's neck onto her cheek, over the arch of her nose and down over her lips, where the other woman's breath warmed them.

Brenna leaned forward to seek another kiss from the soft mouth. Cassidy's arms went around her shoulders, hugging her close. Gradually their bodies bore them down to the sleeping bags together, breasts pillowing against one another. When Cassidy's knee unexpectedly slipped between Brenna's thighs and made her groin clench, Brenna broke their kiss. "I...I can't..."

One arm instantly moved away, though Cassidy's other hand remained gentle on Brenna's lower back. Soft fingertips covered Brenna's lips. "Then I won't."

Brenna started to ease away, aware of her body's reluctance to part. Cassidy did not force her, but the gentle strokes on her back convinced her to remain partially on the leaner, longer body. She rested her head in the curve of Cassidy's shoulder, watching the pulse tick in her throat, lulled by the gradually slowing tempo of Cassidy's heart under her ear.

She felt the body under her shift. Cassidy reached above their heads and lowered the lantern's flame until they were enveloped in the night's shadows.

Gingerly, Brenna moved her hand against Cassidy's stomach, nearly jumping away when the muscles clenched in response. Cassidy's arms held her in place, tightening briefly around her back. "I promise I won't." The whispered words sifted through the hair on top of Brenna's head. The tension took some time to melt away, and Brenna was unsure what the morning would bring, but her eyes could stay open no longer. She slept.

Arms wrapped around Brenna, Cassidy stirred between wakefulness and sleep in a hazy, half-dream state. She heard a commotion outside. A glance at Brenna's face made her pause. She brushed her fingers against the woman's tousled hair, noticing up close the light freckles across Brenna's cheeks. *God, she is beautiful.*

Reaching over her head, Cassidy turned up the lantern flame, their conversation echoing in her mind. She sat up and wrapped her arms around her bent knees, considering everything.

Okay. So the kiss was consensual. She sighed, rubbing her face briskly. *What do we do now?*

The noises outside came closer, and, as only a mother could, she recognized the plaintive voice of her own son whispering anxiously to someone else. With a sigh she set aside her own problems for the time being, opened the tent flap, and looked outside.

The filtered lantern light provided just enough illumination to identify her son being led along by James. "What's up?" Looking up at the teen, she found herself suddenly transfixed by how much he looked like his mother — from the shape of his chin to the slope of his nose.

"He won't go to sleep." James' voice clearly displayed his agitation and his exhaustion.

"All right." Cassidy held out a hand to her son. "Come on, buddy. You can sleep in here."

"Thanks," James said in relief.

She held her son still with one hand and stood, exiting the tent. She could see James was uncomfortable. "I'm really sorry he bothered you."

"Well...I... It..." He stumbled to a halt. "When I couldn't wake Thomas to deal with it, I figured I better get you."

"Come to me anytime, all right?" she said. She accepted then that her feelings for Brenna were more than lust. Apparently they included insuring that her boys were all right, too.

James frowned and shrugged. "Yeah. Whatever."

Cassidy watched him walk back the way he had come. Turning to Ryan, she was startled to see Brenna leaning out of the tent. "I'm sorry I woke you," she whispered.

"I...wasn't really sleeping," Brenna admitted. She didn't elaborate, instead looking in the general direction where her son had disappeared. "Trouble?" she asked, pulling the flap aside and gesturing both Cassidy and Ryan inside.

"Not unless you count sleeplessness."

"Mine or yours?"

"Mine causing yours."

"Ah." Brenna turned to Ryan, who was curling up quickly against his mother's right leg. "Too excited to sleep, hmm?"

"Mmm hmm." He hugged his monster tighter.

"Well, why don't you lie down right here?" Brenna smoothed open her sleeping bag and patted the interior. "Come on."

He looked from Brenna up to his mother, who nodded. "Go ahead. I'll be right here." He lay down on his back as Brenna pulled the top layer up, covering his face. He laughed and pushed it away.

Brenna chuckled. Cassidy realized it was intentional, the sleeping bag becoming the mechanism for an impromptu game of peek-a-boo. Ryan was too old for it, but it clearly it amused him that this woman would play with him. Cassidy realized that's what Brenna had intended. Brenna was feeling the need to connect with her son — just as she had tried to connect with Brenna's.

"You're fun," Ryan finally declared, rolling onto his side, clearly ready to try sleeping again.

"Thank you," Brenna acknowledged seriously, smoothing her hand over his pajama-covered shoulder. When his eyes had closed, she looked to Cassidy, who displayed an adoring smile. "It's instinct," she protested quietly.

"I know. I did the same with yours a minute ago." Cassidy inhaled slowly. "This just got really complicated, didn't it?"

Brenna sighed. "Cassidy, I don't know what I'm going to do." Uncertain whether or not she should touch Cassidy, she moved away from Ryan, who was already breathing evenly, and closer to Cassidy, who remained stiff. Not wanting to be overheard but unwilling to wait until morning to address what was between them, she whispered, "I can't stop what I'm feeling. Despite everything against it, there's a part of me that doesn't want to stop," she added ruefully.

Her tone set off an alarm in Cassidy's head. Bluntly she said, "You told me about those fans talking about getting Hanssen and Jakes together, and I could tell it bothered you."

Brenna sighed. "I'm not against gays or even playing a gay. I never expected to be attracted to you, but I can't get involved with you." She swallowed hard as she looked away from the woman beside her. "Will and I... It didn't work," she admitted bluntly with a sigh. "That's probably part of why he's such a mess."

That Brenna had had an affair with Will Chapman surprised Cassidy so much that she almost missed Brenna's other admission.

"Even then I was at least single, divorced. I'm married now."

"You said it yourself, these feelings are not going away." She put her hands over Brenna's, which were resting on the other woman's stomach. The muscles quivered at her touch, and Cassidy smiled, knowing she felt the same. "We may not know where exactly they came from, but shouldn't we see where they go?"

"I'm married." Brenna bit the inside of her cheek. "I don't have another answer I can give you."

"Don't you?" Cassidy brushed her lips over Brenna's and felt the brief response from trembling lips before Brenna stopped herself and pulled back. Tears pooled in the corners of blue eyes turning them a sad gray, and Cassidy brushed at them.

"What a mess," Brenna murmured. Unconsciously she dropped her head to Cassidy's shoulder nestling closer for comfort, and then suddenly she realized what she was doing and jerked away.

Cassidy lifted Brenna's chin, guiding the mulberry-shaded lips to hers, offering the solace Brenna had been unwilling to seek.

"I can't have an affair," Brenna said in a small voice when they parted.

Exhaling across her lips, Cassidy whispered, "I don't want an affair either."

Tears streaming down her cheeks, Brenna accepted the kisses. Cassidy moaned against her mouth, and Brenna gasped as her nipples tightened, her groin pulsed, and her heart pounded hard and fast. She laid her hands against Cassidy's shoulders, drawing them up along the skin of the other woman's throat and into the fall of straight blond hair, never once breaking the contact of their lips. Finally they parted, panting softly.

Cassidy pulled Brenna into her body, hugging the other woman securely. "I remember telling myself when I first walked on set that I was going to make you like me." She nuzzled Brenna's hair and inhaled. "Honestly, this wasn't what I had in mind."

Brenna buried her face in Cassidy's neck to stifle the laughter bubbling in her chest and the embarrassing heat burning her face. "God, what am I going to do with you?"

Cassidy showed a full toothsome smile and offered cheekily, "Anything you want."

Despite her misgivings, the thought of giving up their newfound closeness actually made Brenna feel sick. She let Cassidy pull her down until they were sharing the same sleeping bag, nestled close for the rest of the night.

Lying awake in Cassidy's loose embrace, Brenna stirred as soon as she heard the faint sounds of camp activity. The soft, warm body next to her made the decision to leave the sleeping bag a difficult one. After barely a night, she was addicted. Rolling over carefully, she studied Cassidy's face only inches from her own, tranquil in sleep. Filled with awe, she traced a fingertip over the slender jaw. Her Catholic conscience took a swat at her.

Brenna Renee Lanigan, you are not thinking what you're thinking.

Glancing down between their bodies into the darkness of the bag, Brenna could not deny she was curious. *This is not the time or place,* she concluded, again hearing noises outside the tent.

She looked around the interior and sat up. Adjusting to the dim lighting, she saw Ryan obliviously and soundly asleep, tucked in her sleeping bag.

Cassidy's arm moved across Brenna's thigh as the long-limbed woman stretched, waking slowly. Brenna's body shifted into the unintentional caress.

"Oh. Mmm. Morning." Blue eyes blinked open and searched Brenna's face as muscular shoulders flexed. Cassidy's head lifted, their lips meeting for a brief kiss.

Brenna inhaled, literally tasting the natural scent of Cassidy's body. Her stomach coiled in sexual anticipation, and she broke off the kiss with a gasp. Closing her eyes to the searing sensuality in Cassidy's gaze, Brenna pulled away, despite the desire clawing at her. "Not here."

Cassidy nodded and sat up alongside her. "I know." She rose from the sleeping bag, tantalizing Brenna with the nearness of her cotton-clad hips. "I'll take Ryan and get him changed," Cassidy said, turning around in time to catch the blush staining Brenna's cheeks. Aware of the desire she and Brenna both were stifling, she kept her voice business-like. "You can change while I'm gone."

"Right."

Cassidy collected her son gently, rousing him with a kiss to his temple. "Time to dress for morning swim, buddy."

Once Cassidy was gone, Brenna pulled on a pair of thick denim jeans and a peach tank top. She was unwrapping her hand to look over the damage when Cassidy returned to the tent.

"I'll do that," Cassidy offered.

"No, actually I should be able to go without a bandage. It's almost completely pain free."

Cassidy scanned Brenna, causing her to duck her head a little at the appreciation reflected there. "Let me take care of you, Brenna, please." Cassidy's voice drew her gaze back up. "Where are your gloves?"

Brenna licked her lips. "I...uh, the gloves are in my bag." She removed the last of the white gauze from her palm. The worn leather gloves Cassidy handed her were lined with soft cotton twill. Easing her right hand inside, she flexed her fingers.

"How's it feel?"

"Not too bad," Brenna answered with surprise. "Are you ready for your first climbing lesson?"

The women joined the gathering outside that was separating into two groups. The youngest and those adults not interested in climbing were returning to the spring to swim.

In his role as co-leader of the climbing group, Thomas strode down the line, checking everyone's attire. He directed a pair of girls to go back and change into full shoes. They'd have to stay behind otherwise, he decreed in a tone that invited no argument. Standing at the end of the line, Brenna chuckled as they tried to change his mind by offering rather blunt enticements.

"He doesn't get his head turned easily, does he?" Cassidy whispered in her ear.

Brenna shook her head, then glanced to see he was only a couple of people away from them. "Straighten up," she said with amusement. "Time to see if we pass muster."

Cassidy laughed, and Brenna caught a glance of surprise from Thomas. Since the laugh had a similar effect on her, she instantly recognized the entranced delight in her son's face.

Thomas came over to stand in front of them, glanced once at his mother, and declared, "I know you're ready." He turned his attention to Cassidy, his expression very attentive. "Have you ever climbed before?"

"No."

The two were not quite eye to eye, but Cassidy only had to lift her chin a fraction to meet Thomas' gaze. His gaze swept down her attire. "Sturdy boots," Thomas said. "Thick jeans." He noted her bare hands. "Gloves?"

"I didn't think about it," Cassidy admitted.

"All right." He picked up her hand. Brenna's face tightened as she fought to keep her expression neutral. He sized Cassidy's fingers against his own. "We're about the same size. You can borrow my spare pair." He pulled them from his back pocket and presented them.

"Thanks."

Cassidy's smile made his throat turn red, and he ducked his head away, turning back to the group at large. "All right, everyone, collect your rope and pitons from the pile. Mike, we're ready to move out."

Thomas stayed at the back of the group with his mother and Cassidy, explaining as they walked how the best climbers moved up a mountainside. Keeping quiet herself, Brenna listened to both her son's voice, very animated, and Cassidy's interested questions.

They talk so easily, Brenna lamented. With a deep breath, she looked around at the scenery, trying to remember how nice it was to be in the mountains again.

Someone nudged her arm. "What?" Brenna found Cassidy had fallen back into step with her. Thomas had gone ahead as they neared the rock face.

"Are you all right?" Cassidy's smile was bright, sinking Brenna's spirits lower.

"Yes, I'm fine," Brenna lied, absurdly jealous of her own son.

Chapter 22

"Watch his rope!" Mike Connell shouted.

Thomas immediately rappelled alongside Vince, a beefy football-lineman type in a gray tank top and knee-length shorts.

"Vince! Stop!" Thomas ducked his head under the muscle-bound arm that Vince flailed as he tried unsuccessfully to regain his footing against the rock. "Hold still!" Finally Thomas grabbed the man's hand and wrapped it around his rope.

"Pull your right foot up. There's a spot for it about knee high." The big man's anxious huffing couldn't drown out Thomas' firm voice. Vince nodded automatically. "All right." Thomas checked Vince's harness again, then patted the dark shoulder. "You're fine now. Go on up to Mike."

Holding position, Thomas watched Vince's first few cautious movements, shot a thumbs up to his partner, and let out his line again, checking on the others trailing further down the cliff face. The climbers were grouped about one-third to one-half the distance up the mountainside. It wasn't a sheer drop, but roughly a seventy-degree angle to the plateau. He shouted to his mother, who looked over with a smile, flashing him a thumbs up.

Half a body length above and to Brenna's left, Cassidy looked down to adjust her footing. She wrapped her gloved hand around a higher section of rope and hauled herself another full body length before pushing her right boot into a crevice.

Cassidy tapped in a piton and clipped her belt harness to the metal loop. Looking up, then down, she absorbed the heightened sensation of freedom as she dangled between earth and sky.

A familiar auburn head crested against the rocky surface. Sure gloved hands and tanned arms snaked over the surface. A moment later Brenna stopped alongside and tapped in a piton to take a break. Her face was flushed, and sweat ran freely down her face and throat. Brenna offered Cassidy a grin, close to the expression she affected for the all-knowing Commander Jakes. "Great climb, isn't it?"

"Incredible view."

Brenna turned and looked down to the top of the canopy of trees and beyond, occasionally able to pick out the trail they had hiked from the bottom as the trees parted. Out further, the western horizon blended into blues and greens as the foothills surrounding the mountains pointed the way to the ocean.

She inhaled deeply, the fresh look at the spread-out earth making her marvel at the possibilities of life. Turning back, she studied Cassidy, who had turned her face to the sun's light, eyes closed in surrender to the sensations. Her lips curled into a cat-like smile of contentment. Brenna reached across the brief space separating them and ran her gloved fingers over the muscled wrist wrapped around the rope.

Cassidy's face turned from the sun, and eyelids opened slowly as even white teeth appeared in a sensuous smile. Then her eyes widened, and the smile dimmed slightly as she focused on something behind Brenna.

"Tired already, Mom? Come on, you're holding up the climb."

Flexing her shoulders, Brenna turned into the rock face, looking over at Thomas with a shrug. "We're coming, we're coming."

"How're you doing?" Thomas tossed his inquiry to Cassidy with a quick lift of his chin.

"This is incredible. How long have you been climbing?"

"Since I was twelve," Thomas answered, taking a moment to slip over to her side and adjust one of her ties before it twisted on her. "I learned on a scouting trip." He gestured to the north. "The ridge is north of here, called Domino Peak."

Brenna, who had moved ahead of both of them, paused and called down, "Now who's the slowpoke?"

Thomas looked away from Cassidy and grinned up at her. "Be right there." He smiled winningly at Cassidy. "That's her competitive spirit. Excuse me."

Cassidy laughed and watched mother and son for a moment before resuming her own climb. She heard Thomas laugh at something his mother said and looked up to see the woman moving swiftly away on the rocks. She particularly appreciated the firm rear and rippling shoulders as Brenna moved.

Damn this is fun, she thought, grinning as she pulled herself ever closer to the top.

When she reached the level plateau, Brenna spread out on her back, arms splayed. Breathing heavily, she could not muster energy to care about the dirt mixing with her sweat.

This is freedom, she thought triumphantly. She had beaten Thomas to the top, if only by a few seconds. He shook her hand and hugged her before he rappelled down to help others. She wondered if her competitive spirit had been in part due to Thomas' obvious attraction to Cassidy. She rolled onto her side and propped her head on her hand, watching the edge for the blonde's appearance.

Though Thomas was on the side, probably with Cassidy, Brenna hoped he would let her offer congratulations first when Cassidy completed her climb. Shaking her head at herself, she pushed to her knees and moved to the edge, peering over to find her...

Castmate? Friend?

Brenna sat up slowly as she contemplated their relationship. She could no longer consider Cassidy "just another member" of the *Time Trails* company. She had moved past the feelings of animosity, straight into... *What?* They had certainly passed "friend" with the kisses the previous evening.

Lover?

She swallowed. Despite coming very, very close the previous evening, they had not crossed that line. *Not yet.*

A hand appeared over the top of the rocks, finding purchase on the granite. Then Cassidy's face appeared, upturned and smiling as Brenna grasped her hand.

"Hey, partner!"

The eager voice filled Brenna with joy.

Partner?

"Hi," Brenna returned with a grin, pulling Cassidy the last feet onto the plateau. Stopping herself from assisting, she watched as Cassidy detached her own safety harness. Relief flooded her as they hugged firmly. Brenna could not find words to speak. She only squeezed tighter, delighted when Cassidy returned the grasp.

"Congratulations on completing your first climb, Cassidy." Mike broke free from another group that had also just reached the top.

Keeping an arm around Brenna as she steadied her legs, Cassidy flashed a huge grin. "I can't wait to do that again." She laughed, dizzying Brenna's senses.

"Well, we'll be going down in about twenty minutes." He passed her a water bottle. "Have some water. Walk around. Check out the view on the other side while we get the rest up here."

Cassidy tilted her head back and swallowed lustily from the bottle, splashing herself and Brenna in the process. She passed the bottle. Brenna drank a little, splashed her throat, and returned it.

"Want to see the other view?" Brenna asked as Cassidy's arm fell from her back.

Cassidy's eyes revealed rising passion as they lifted to meet Brenna's. "Yes."

Together they walked around some boulders and sparse vegetation and perched on a smaller boulder on the eastern rim. The panoramic view was spectacular. The Sierra Mountains sheared into the sky to the southeast, and through a valley Cassidy could see what was probably the edge of the desert.

For a while they just sat there, shoulder to shoulder. Brenna felt warmed by the sun and cooled by the breeze. She could feel the bond between them tempering, as though in a forge. Brenna pulled off her gloves and set them in her lap, studying her hands as they tingled. Cassidy did the same. Brenna's throat caught on thoughts she couldn't put into words. Brenna recalled Cassidy's earlier words. *Shouldn't we see where they take us?*

Glancing over, she saw Cassidy smile faintly at some private thought as she looked over the view. The body posture conveyed a powerful confidence, and her sweaty shoulders rippled when she rubbed her hands together.

She rose abruptly, offering her hand to Brenna. "Ready to go?"

As Brenna reached out and their fingers touched, she felt the heat of fear rising in her. A promise shone from Cassidy's eyes in reply. "Yes," Brenna finally answered, standing. *I want to see where this goes, too.* "Yes," she said again. Her heart pounded faster, and her face flushed.

Cassidy's answering smile brightened the morning sky as if it had previously been the middle of the night.

James splashed with his brother in the springs. Lunch had been spent with the two of them sitting with their mom and the Hylands. The women had talked about the climb, wondering aloud if they could find time to get together to do it again. Personally, he found that weird. They all knew Mom's contract finished up in the spring. She was corresponding with her agent to find her next project. She had even talked about going to New York, even though Mr. Shea was in Michigan.

James wasn't happy about moving anywhere. High school had proven to be fun, and he didn't relish the idea of moving somewhere else to start over again. Friends never seemed to happen quite the same way.

May would likely find the two women on opposite coasts. It seemed pointless to form a friendship that was going to end so soon. He looked over at the two women splashing one another in the shallows. They had never been chummy. He vividly remembered the things his mother had said when Ms. Hyland had been cast in the series.

Her first months on the set had made his mother, by turns, angry and anguished. She had even considered leaving the show. That had been just before she married Kevin Shea. James and Thomas had both thought the marriage sudden, but they didn't say anything. After all, it was their mother's life, not theirs. In the beginning, she had spent at least a weekend each month with him in Michigan. The visits had trailed off since spring, though. During the summer, she had built the deck out back and spent a lot of time lying out in the sun reading while he and Thomas were busy with baseball and high school friends.

Mr. Shea had come out twice, but it was clear he didn't enjoy Los Angeles. Mom had only taken them for a visit the once this fall.

Thomas nudged him. "They get along pretty nice, huh?"

"Who?"

"Mom and Cassidy."

James blinked at his brother's use of the woman's first name, then he looked at Thomas' face and groaned. He had seen that infatuated look before. *Sheesh...*

James watched his mother pick up the Hyland boy from the water and swing him around, splashing him down to squeals of delight. He realized she looked happier right then, soaking wet and laughing with Ryan's mother, than she had on the entire trip to Michigan.

"Hey, James!" Thomas climbed up onto the rocks. "Move, will you?"

James stroked out of the way and pulled himself out of the water as his brother performed a smooth, shallow dive. Thomas stroked underwater to the other side of the spring. James rolled his eyes when Thomas "accidentally" bumped into Ms. Hyland before springing up out of the water.

Holding his nose, James shook his head and cannon-balled into the water.

Thomas burst to the surface beside Cassidy, startling her into jumping backward.

"Thomas!"

He looked to his mother, who was frowning deeply. Ignoring her for the moment, he returned his gaze to Cassidy. "So, have you and Mom decided when we're going camping again?"

"No, we haven't," Cassidy answered with a laugh.

"Then how about coming over to go to the gym? They've got a climbing wall." She smiled, and he felt his chest swell. *She might consider it. Yes!* He tried to contain his excitement, unaware of how his eyes glowed with expectation.

Cassidy's gaze left him and flitted briefly to his mother. After a moment, Brenna shrugged. Cassidy nodded, then shifted her eyes back to Thomas. He straightened up quickly. "Well, I suppose I could, when my schedule gives me some time."

"Our schedules," Brenna interjected with a smile.

"Right." Cassidy patted his shoulder, and Thomas beamed.

His mother interrupted the moment. "Looks like everyone's headed back," she observed.

"We're breaking camp, aren't we?" Cassidy asked.

"Yeah," Thomas said without inflection. He was bummed, but he walked with them, pulling his body out of the water and snatching up his towel to pull around his neck. Holding the ends, he watched pensively as his mother took Ryan from Cassidy so that the blonde could pull herself out of the spring.

The three walked back to camp while Ryan ran around their legs, laughing and chasing frogs. Thomas laughed when the boy caught one and proudly showed it to Cassidy. She screamed, then laughed nervously as she stepped out from behind his mother.

"What is it?" Brenna asked. Ryan obligingly shoved it at her. She backed up abruptly, tripped, and fell over.

Cassidy's laughter was musical as she watched Brenna, on her hands and knees, wrap Ryan in a rolling bear hug. Her body protected Ryan's as they rolled over and over on the ground. Brenna looked so natural, laughing, open, and playful, it must have been a game she played with her own sons when they were small. Coming to rest, she tickled the five-year-old as he rested on her stomach. When she got back on her feet, letting Ryan scamper ahead, she had wood chips and leaves in her hair, and her damp arms were spattered with dirt.

"I think I'd better take another quick dive," Brenna said ruefully. "You two go on ahead. I'll be there in a few minutes to help you dismantle the tent, Cass."

"All right."

Thomas stepped forward. "No problem, Mom. Take your time. I've got the tent."

Hands on her hips, she scrutinized him. Finally she nodded. "All right."

Thomas looked to Cassidy and said, "Come on. I bet we can have most of the packing done before she gets there." He jogged the rest of the way to the camp, Cassidy easily keeping up with him.

Everything was tucked into their packs, and the campsite returned to its unoccupied state. The fire pits were raked over and doused again with spring water. Firewood they had cut but not used was stacked neatly at the edge of the large clearing for the next campers. Brenna surveyed the empty campsite as she adjusted the balance of her backpack.

"Ready to go?"

She looked over her shoulder at Mike. "It was a successful weekend, wasn't it?"

"Everyone had a lot of fun," he confirmed. "Thanks again for arranging this."

"My pleasure," she assured him, patting his shoulder.

He nodded, then raised his voice to address the whole group. "All right, everyone, move out!"

It was after five in the afternoon when they reached the parking lot at the bottom of the trail and loaded everything into the waiting vehicles. Brenna waved as the last vehicle drove off, then walked to the Mountaineer.

Through the rear window she saw Thomas and Cassidy talking. James and Ryan were already dozing, each head resting against an opposite side window. She opened her door and pulled out her keys. "Well, another weekend's come and gone," she said with a melancholy smile.

"Been the most amazing time." Cassidy smiled at Brenna, then apparently decided that might be too much and looked back to Thomas. "Right?"

"Definitely," Thomas replied, sitting back and securing his belt.

Definitely, Brenna echoed silently as she put the car in gear and started home.

Chapter 23

"Cameron, sit down!" Victor pulled the man back into his seat and looked toward the sole female in the room, who had spoken very little. They had called this meeting to address the specific story arc for the current episode. Will had pushed until he got the meeting, but they had decided only the key players needed to be there. He still wondered how Rich Paulson had entered the side area. Victor wished again he had taken this meeting up in the executive building where he could close doors. "Cassidy, do you have something to say?"

She looked from Will Chapman to Cameron Palassis and then to Victor Branch. "You seemed to have decided everything," she said.

"What do you want?" Will demanded. "C'mon."

She bit her lip, then sighed. "No, this is about what you want, Will. I'm just a convenience."

"You can soften Hanssen with this," he countered.

"This guts her character," she snapped. "She is not a mushball romantic. She certainly wouldn't sleep with Raycreek just because they're stuck together — temporarily — in a screwed-up timeline."

"Would you rather have Jakes?"

In her anger, Cassidy didn't check her words. "She kisses better than you do, I bet!"

Will Chapman sat down, never taking his eyes from Cassidy's face. His gaze narrowed, searching. Cassidy stood to leave.

Branch put out a conciliatory hand. "Please sit. We've got to have something to shoot. Here." He passed her a script. "Read it over. If you see any merit in it, we'll rewrite it with any slant you like. Otherwise, we'll toss it and go with our back-up when shooting starts again in January."

She pursed her lips, knowing as well as anyone what rearranging shooting could do in collateral damage to production values. "There has to be something we can do."

Will shrugged, his expression smug. "For the record, I like it as-is."

Cassidy's anger sparked again. Did he want the series to crash and burn? She turned and yelled at him, surprising everyone. "I won't crawl into that gutter with you!"

"It's not in a gutter, it's in an alley," Chapman retorted.

Can I even act like that with him? Cassidy wondered. She recalled lying with Brenna in their tent, leaning against a tree caressing her body, kissing her... She had done kissing scenes before, even on-screen lovemaking, but she had at least genuinely liked those men as friends. Chapman was making that impossible.

She realized she had to do something if she did not want to be at the center of another fight. She returned to her seat. "Can we take it more slowly, at least? Could I meet with another writer? Talk about it some more?"

Victor nodded. "I'll tell Paul to come over."

"Today?"

He nodded. "All right. Today."

She stood. "Are we finished?"

Victor stopped her as she reached the door. "Could you send in Bren? We've got the drafts of January's scripts. If we need to make changes and move things up, we'll want to be sure to get them done now."

Cassidy nodded. "Sure. I'll see if I can find her."

Rich Paulson followed Cassidy as she walked away. Though present at the meeting, he had remained silent. He spoke when they were out of earshot. "Cass?"

"Yes?"

"I'd just like to say I agree with the changes you want."

"The writing is best when it's about all of us...working as a team." She paused. "Why would only two team members go into such a situation anyway? Jakes would never allow that."

"She *is* usually much more proactive than this script suggests," Rich agreed.

"I want to put some ideas together for fixing this episode, Rich. Would you help me?"

"Anything I can do," he assured her. "Where to?"

"Not just yet. I have to find Brenna first." She rolled the script in her hands and looked back over her shoulder at him. "Would you meet me in my trailer after lunch?"

"Sure."

He looked pleased. She smiled at him warmly, then patted his shoulder. "Thanks again." He nodded, and she walked away through the rest of the soundstage.

"Rich?"

"Brenna?" He turned around and found Brenna Lanigan walking up behind him. "Victor wants you in the script meeting."

"Thanks." She looked past him. "Was that Cassidy?"

"Yeah, her meeting went badly." Brenna nodded as if she had surmised as much. He wondered if she had seen the script. "The idea of Hanssen having sex didn't go over so well."

"Sex? With who?"

Okay, so she hasn't read the script. "Apparently, Cameron wrote Hanssen into a sex scene with Raycreek in order to satisfy something Will asked for."

"That's absurd! What are we saying if we do that? This is supposed to be a family show!"

"That's what Cassidy said," Rich replied, clearly surprised. "If she can't get a rewrite done quickly, the January script gets moved up into that production slot." He gestured back to the conference room set. "That's why Victor wants to see you."

"Right. Thanks." Brenna spun on her heel and strode over to the conference room, leaving him standing alone and still a little befuddled.

Cassidy walked through the sets toward the back of the lot and the haven of her trailer. She passed the speakeasy set, still up from the previous episode. Stepping carefully around the equipment, she acknowledged nods from some of the engineers as they filmed a short business scene. She stopped, her attention caught by the closeness of Rachelle and Sean.

You wouldn't know they were just friends. Rachelle and Sean were married, not to each other, and yet their scenes exuded love and support, even now, during some simple "business".

She relaxed, enjoying the opportunity to watch others work, letting her own thoughts quiet, absorbed by Rachelle and Sean's easy friendship which was becoming so much more under the hot camera lights.

When Jeremy pulled Luria from her chair and they danced around the empty set, Cassidy felt her heart moving with them. This was what she had felt burgeoning between Brenna and herself this weekend. Too much not to move with it. Too much coursing energy not to try to grasp it, hold it, caress it. *Caress her...*

"Cut!"

Startled by the director's loud voice as the Victrola's music cut to silence, Cassidy straightened quickly, embarrassed to be caught daydreaming.

Spotting her light coloring against the dark backdrop, Sean waved at her. "Hey, Cass."

"Cassidy?" Rachelle, who had started to walk off in the other direction, turned around. "How was your weekend?"

"Nice," she supplied. "I've found a new hobby."

"Yeah? What is it?" Sean asked.

"Rock climbing."

Rachelle grinned and patted her shoulder. "That's great. I've never done it, but I like skydiving. Same thrill, I bet."

"Probably. I might have to ask Thomas."

"Thomas?"

"Brenna's oldest son Thomas was the co-leader on the climb."

"That's cool. So what'd Brenna do while you were climbing?"

"She was right there."

Sean shook his head in disbelief. "No kidding?"

Cassidy smiled. "Nope. She actually beat Thomas to the top in a challenge climb."

"That doesn't sound like Bren."

"Well, it was," a husky, amused voice intervened.

Rachelle spun. "Bren."

Brenna walked up to the group with a smile on her face. "Yes. Hi. On a break?"

"Yup," Rachelle said. "Did I hear right? You were rock climbing this weekend?"

"I've enjoyed rock climbing for about five years. When my son wanted to learn, he needed a partner. I nominated myself. A mother's work is never done."

Sean chuckled. "Man, oh man. That just boggles."

"Why?" He had the good grace to look sheepish. "Sean!" she waved her hand dismissively, "don't answer that. I don't want you to say what you're thinking."

"What was I thinking? You're fit as a fiddle."

"I'm flattered," she said with obvious irony. She looked at Cassidy. "Can I talk to you for a minute? I just got out of my meeting with Branch."

Cassidy nodded. "Let's go find someplace quiet." She looked at Rachelle and Sean. "Catch you later, all right?"

"Yeah," Rachelle said. "See ya."

Cassidy led the way outside. "My trailer okay?"

"Sure." Brenna followed her up the steps. "Are you all right?" she asked when they were inside. "They want to move up the January shoot." She sat down on the couch and Cassidy moved next to her. "I agree, by the way, about the sex."

"They insisted Raycreek be the love interest."

"I guessed."

"What should I do?"

"They gave you permission for a rewrite. So you make some changes — soften the blow to Hanssen's character, make it more logical."

"I want to toss the whole damn thing," Cassidy said derisively. "It's all about clashing egos, not about the show."

Brenna shook her head. "I know." She reached for Cassidy's hand and found the script rolled up in her fist. Gently she eased it out. "This it?" Cassidy nodded. "Why don't we see what's salvageable?"

Hands freed, Cassidy put them on Brenna's shoulders. "How was your night?" she asked, changing the subject.

"I was very happy for a mattress," Brenna mused, closing her eyes as Cassidy's fingers began a soothing massage over her neck. "I'm so sore." She reached up and grasped the distracting digits. "You'd better stop." When Cassidy nuzzled her hair, Brenna pulled away.

"What's wrong?"

"I'm just not sure yet."

"You seemed sure yesterday."

"I know," Brenna acknowledged. "It was like another world out there."

Cassidy nodded. "I felt it, too." She let her hands fall away from Brenna's shoulders. She could not keep her hands completely off her, however, and found her fingers lingering against the slight hips. "So...was it just time and place?"

Brenna lifted her chin and looked at Cassidy seriously. "My son is infatuated with you."

"Thomas?" Cassidy nodded. "Yes, I noticed."

"I don't think I can stomach competing with my own son."

Cassidy chuckled softly. "There's no competition. He's sixteen."

"Seventeen," Brenna corrected. "To his way of thinking, that's completely grown up."

"I promise I'll handle him carefully." Brenna remained silent, and Cassidy prodded her with concern. "What's wrong?" She rubbed her thumbs across the tight muscles in Brenna's lower back.

Brenna groaned appreciatively. "I feel so old right now," she admitted in a faint voice.

"I don't care how old you are," Cassidy assured her. Tucking her leg up on the couch, she drew Brenna back into the cradle of her body as she brought both hands up again to work on the muscles in the stiff shoulders. "I find you incredibly sexy," she confessed. "I think I've thought so for quite a while — even if I couldn't exactly say what it was — but the possibility of getting a negative reaction if I even spoke to you scared the hell out of me."

"And now?" Brenna couldn't deny how good Cassidy's touch felt, comforting her in a way she hadn't experienced in years.

"Knowing you don't hate me, just my character...I needed to take the chance."

"I don't hate Hanssen," Brenna said uneasily, "and I didn't hate you. I didn't want to get to know you, though. I was scared about what Hanssen's presence implied about Jakes, what you implied about me." Brenna eased out of Cassidy's embrace and turned around, holding the long-fingered hands gently away from her body as she spoke with unvarnished honesty. "I am over forty. When *Time Trails* came along, I'd had just one project in the previous five years that was worth the time I spent on it creatively. Do you know what that meant to me?"

"You are *not* old," Cassidy refuted emphatically. "The industry is a bunch of fools."

Brenna laughed abruptly. "Yeah, but this industry is still where I want to work and where you want to work. Right in the middle of a series run I was just settling into, they snatched the red carpet out from under my feet and put it under yours."

"I..." Cassidy thought about that time and what Cameron had done for her. "Brenna, I have something—"

Brenna had only paused for breath. "You're what, thirty, right?"

"Thirty-two."

"When they told me you were joining the cast..." She laughed mirthlessly. "It was two days after my birthday, actually." Her gaze grew melancholy. "I'd spent the day alone. I'd broken things off with Will, so I wasn't even dating at the time. Then they tell me you've accepted the job permanently. It was like getting slammed by a torpedo."

Cassidy's eyes shimmered with sympathetic tears. "I never meant for anything Cameron did to hurt you. I joined the cast to work with you, you know." She wiped at her face as Brenna wiped at her own tears. "Right from the beginning, I've wanted, needed, to reach out to you. Until you accepted the invitation to Ryan's party, I thought I had exhausted every means possible. I was so...grateful you came."

"Shh." Warm fingertips brushed over her cheeks. "That's in the past now." Brenna turned to the script. "Let's see if we can untangle Hanssen from her little mess, all right?"

"I had a few ideas earlier. Want to hear them?"

Brenna nodded. They rearranged themselves on the couch, Cassidy wrapping herself around Brenna, the script in Brenna's lap as she rested her hands on Cassidy's thighs. Flipping to the scene that concerned her most, Cassidy tested dialogue changes while Brenna read along.

Chapter 24

Cassidy turned her face into the setting sun while she waited for someone to answer the doorbell at the Talbot home. *God*, she thought idly, *life is wonderful.* She felt warm, exultant, open, and very positive. She and Brenna had worked on script changes for an hour — until Rich Paulson knocked on her trailer door. She and Rich had gotten some more good work done after Brenna left. They stopped only when Victor called and said Paul was available in the executive building.

What stuck in her mind, what flowed through her body, though, was the shimmering glowing happiness of talking with Brenna. Talking that had become cuddling, cuddling that had turned to kissing. The fit of their bodies, Brenna's hips pressed into her pelvis, had felt so natural and right.

The front door to the Talbot home finally opened. "Oh, hey. Come on in. We're just about to eat." Gwen smiled and pulled Cassidy inside. "You're incredibly early," she remarked in a low voice.

"I didn't have any reshooting today. I have one song to rerecord in the sound studio tomorrow. I don't even have to go in to work on Wednesday at the moment." Gwen waved her to the seat next to her son at the dinner table and placed a plate in front of her.

"Plans for the holidays?"

"I haven't stayed in town for the holidays yet," Cassidy admitted. "I thought Ryan and I could find out what it's like."

Chance piped up, "We could go to Disneyland!"

Gwen shook her head ruefully, but said nothing. Her husband, Lou, changed the subject. "Time for grace."

Cassidy linked a hand with Ryan and one with Gwen at the end of the table. The young Talbots on the other side also joined hands with their parents. Chance and Deter tried to escape notice as they thumb-wrestled. She bit her lip against a chuckle as Lou prayed, "Thank you, Lord, for the bounty your love has shown us." He paused. Cassidy looked up, catching his fleeting frown before his face smoothed over again. "Amen."

"Amen" echoed around the table, and she released Gwen's hand as she felt the woman tug slightly.

"So tell me," she asked sociably. "How's the semester finishing up?"

"My students have their first research papers due just before the break," Gwen answered.

Cassidy wrapped her mind around the idea of fourth grade research papers. It couldn't possibly be anything like her college philosophy papers. "What sort of topics are they doing?"

"Sharks, surfing, dogs, cats, that sort of thing." Gwen gave a half-shrug.

Cassidy nodded. "Good luck with that." She turned to Lou. "How are things with you?"

"Fine."

She nodded politely. He was seldom as talkative as his wife, but his tone told her that was all she would get as a response. With an internal grimace, she decided she'd have to make some inquiries with a particularly gossipy neighbor and figure out the source of the odd feeling she was getting from Gwen and Lou. *Besides, I ought to get home so I can finish working on all these script ideas.* She returned to her dinner, a casserole dish that was among Gwen's best recipes, as Lou informed her in the small talk that filled in the silence.

When Ryan had finished, Cassidy excused them, collecting his schoolbag and waiting while he put it across both shoulders, backpack style, as he had done since they had been camping. She quickly tendered their goodbyes, then paused at the door. She automatically reached for the check she had written, a regular agreement to defray some of the costs of the Talbots keeping Ryan so frequently late into the night. "I forgot it," she said. "Tomorrow, all right?" When Gwen hesitated before nodding, Cassidy thought she had her answer to their atypical behavior. Cassidy being a day late with the check usually did not bother her.

Cassidy leaned over and kissed Gwen's cheek. "Thanks for everything," she said sincerely. "I didn't expect dinner. It was lovely."

"Sure," Gwen said, a little more quickly. "See you tomorrow."

Following Ryan into the kitchen, Cassidy put her bag down and set the draft script on the kitchen table. "You just had dinner. Snack is after your bath," she said as he opened his mouth to ask.

The order of events given, Ryan ran into the bathroom. She heard the taps twist and water start to fill the tub. Grabbing a fresh towel and washcloth from the linen closet, she entered the bathroom. "Are you going to wash yourself, too?"

"Yes, Mommy."

She returned to the kitchen. Flipping on the radio to a soft volume, she sat down at the end of the table and opened the script and the notes she had gathered in her conversations with Brenna, Paul, and Rich.

Cassidy kept one ear out for alarming sounds from the bathroom but threw the rest of herself into the work. The writing staff had been more open to the actors' suggested paths for their characters since Rich's script, *Aleutian Blues,* had been accepted last season. Cassidy had remained quiet about her character's development, though — until now.

She sighed, releasing her residual anger. Most of it. The general outline of this script had to have been in the works for months. Cameron had not mentioned it to her once, even in passing, and he loved to talk about work when they were together. The original interaction appeared to have been intended to be between Chris and the other mission member, Rich's character Dr. Pryor. Cameron had substituted Chapman's Lieutenant Raycreek. He'd also expanded the interaction, taking the camaraderie, which would have been fatherly from Pryor, too far. Cassidy was working at reining it in — for Chris Hanssen's sake, as well as her own. After experiencing Brenna's touch, she could not imagine having any physical contact with Will Chapman, even if it was acting.

A spark of jealousy flared. According to Brenna, she and Will had had a brief affair. Cassidy admitted that stung, but she also knew that it was irrevocably over now, if it hadn't been before. Brenna calling him out in front of reporters certainly sealed that.

Inhaling, she put her pen down, her mind flying back to the momentous occasion: The Kiss. She was unable to forget a single nuanced movement of having Brenna in her arms, their lips pressing against each other, her own lips moving from Brenna's to taste soft skin along her jaw. She had not planned it, hadn't even really fully identified the emotion that was gripping her, until they were microseconds away from that first contact. She just knew that she'd been growing warmer and warmer all day, as she watched Brenna work on the tent or splash with Mike Connell in the mountain spring. She certainly had not expected the rush of connection she felt while innocently treating Brenna's burned hand.

Kissing Brenna had been precipitous and revealing. By then, she had needed to know. She had seen a question, and what she thought was invitation, in the gray-blue eyes. She had needed to *feel* the other woman's reaction, needed to know if Brenna experienced the same sparks when they touched or talked. During their dinner, she had decided to take a chance and had followed when Brenna left the camp. Her guess had been right, but that had only served to make things more complicated.

Cassidy burned whenever she looked at the woman. Knowing Brenna would never have an affair, Cassidy forced herself to hold her desires check. On set today she had been partly successful, mostly by staying away. *But when we were in my trailer...*

Cassidy closed her eyes. Her mind drifted back over lean muscles and conjured up the unforgettable scent of Brenna's soft skin.

"Mommy?"

Shaking her head, Cassidy straightened up to see Ryan with damp pajamas clinging to his body, anxiously looking up at her. "Yes?"

"I finished my bath."

"I see that."

"Can I have my cookies now?"

She suppressed her chuckle at her son's one-track mind, nodded, and stood. Ryan immediately sat on her vacated seat and propped himself on the table.

"What're you working on?" He reached for the papers.

"Something I have to do for tomorrow," she explained, moving the pile out of the way as she set a glass of milk and a plate of chocolate wafers in front of him. Cassidy sat down and picked up the script as Ryan munched away, dunking the wafers into the milk before eating them.

He finished with a slurp before she had finished reading a lengthy section of dialogue between Hanssen and Raycreek. She resisted striking the entire exchange and cut only one of his lines strongly suggesting that intimate relations were possible, along with her reply. *God, that one made Chris sound like a teenager.*

Finally she put down the pen, inhaled and exhaled to clear her mind, and announced bedtime. "What should we read tonight?" Together they went through his shelf of books and selected *Goldilocks and the Three Bears*.

Since he had been learning sounds and letters in his pre-K class, Ryan sounded out far more words in the tale than Cassidy expected. She ended up listening more than reading. Pride filled her, growing stronger until, when the story was finished, she praised him profusely. He giggled; she tickled him, making him laugh harder. When they quieted, she brushed his bangs back and kissed his forehead. "Good night."

"Good night, Mommy." She tucked his covers to his chin and walked out, turning off the light as she went.

Once again in the kitchen, facing an evening of quiet, Cassidy listened as a news brief concluded on the radio, then a voice announced the start of an hour of jazz. Cassidy returned to the kitchen table and picked up the pen. After another hour, she felt a more acceptable version of events was unfolding in the pages. It wasn't perfect, but she hoped it would result in less damage to Hanssen overall.

Near the end of the script, there was a rescue scene, where Hanssen and Raycreek were recovered by a second team led by Jakes. In the original version, the search party, which had not included Jakes, actually came upon the two in very compromising state of undress. Cassidy's version had already put the clothes back on. Now she changed the dialogue to a considerably more business-like, "Time to get out of here."

Trying out the new lines, Cassidy almost could hear Brenna's inflections change as Jakes' concern about Hanssen's physical injuries grew. She closed her eyes and just listened as the woman's voice played in her head. *Yeah,* she thought. *It works.*

Cassidy laid her pen aside and reread the entire act she had just finished. She bit her lip. In the action text, Hanssen gravitated toward Jakes, almost scornful of Raycreek. She realized that she had better soften that. Chapman might take exception at being shoved into the background again. She inserted a short exchange between Raycreek and Jakes, hoping it would be enough to satisfy Will Chapman's ego.

"Welcome to Dr. Swanson's Waiting Room," the radio announced, interrupting her train of thought.

Dr. Swanson's voice was soothing, his advice to callers reasonable, and Cassidy found herself sitting quietly, just listening. Twenty minutes later, her head was resting on the table, and she slept.

She knew she was dreaming, but the woods were familiar. They had to be the ones surrounding the campgrounds from the weekend. She moved deeper into the foliage, and the terrain changed, leading down to a riverbank. The water sparkled in the sunlight, and she walked to the edge for a drink.

Reaching for the water, she froze when a splash drew her attention out into the water's flow. A small reddish brown bear crossed the stream, coming directly toward her. It ambled through the water, not bothered by the current. Cassidy settled carefully to one side and watched it as it emerged onto her bank.

It looked at her, considering her for a moment, then rooted around a prickly bush full of berries. The bear's paws grew raw against the thorns and soon it stopped rummaging, soothing its paws with its tongue.

Cautiously Cassidy approached, earning a wary look from the bear. She passed by it, going directly to the bush and carefully pulled off a handful of the berries, compelled to offer them to the brown bear.

It watched her for a while, and they sat together in silence, each munching on berries. When she made no further moves toward it, the bear started watching her more often than eating from its dwindling supply.

Cassidy plucked more berries and held them out carefully, palm open. The bear sniffed, its breath washing warmly across her hand. Its cool nose eased into her palm and gentle nibbles with the vaguest edge of teeth rubbed against her fingers. She felt her heart begin to pound, nerves and excitement combining as she shared a moment with the gentle animal.

When it finished, the bear angled its head toward her and ambled forward, crowding Cassidy against the bush as she tried to back up.

It was then that she saw something else, another animal inside the berry bush. A rabbit, spotty brown fur from nose to tail, nibbled on the berries from the safety within. The brown bear watched Cassidy as she removed the rabbit, cuddled it against her chest and fed it several berries. The bear settled to the ground and watched them.

The scene was idyllic. The sun sparkled on the water, the cool breeze ruffled through Cassidy's hair. She reached out toward the bear. Head lifting and eyes wide, it held very still, as if poised to run, but it permitted her to touch its fur. She rubbed its scruff and watched it nose her thigh as it squirmed under her hand. The rabbit in her lap stopped quivering, and the soothing sounds from the bear made Cassidy sleepy.

Abruptly the brown bear lurched to its feet. It bared its teeth toward something Cassidy couldn't see. It backed up and moved around her, facing out, standing between her and some approaching threat.

She put the rabbit carefully aside just in time. The ground vibrated slightly under her as she rose to her feet.

A massive bear with brown-black fur lunged out of the bushes. It scraped the ground and air with huge claws. Its lips were drawn back in a snarl, and it bared its teeth ferociously. Rising to its hindquarters, it challenged Cassidy at her own height and scraped at the air again. It released a terrifying bellow that made her cover her ears and stumble backward. She couldn't find her voice to scream, so she looked around for a place to run.

A growl suddenly sounded beside her, and she fell to her knees. As she scrambled away, she saw the brown bear, only half the Kodiak's size, raise its hackles and growl at the monstrosity. She tried to reach for it, to hold it back, but missed as the small bear leaped into the air.

She screamed then, drawing the bigger bear's attention. It snarled at her and advanced. She looked beyond it to see the brown bear circling again. With an open-mouthed snarl, it leaped again, landing atop the Kodiak's back, snapping its jaw at the back of the thick neck.

The massive bear shrugged and easily threw off the brown bear before advancing on Cassidy again. Thorns from the berry bush behind her cut into her legs and her hands. She scrambled around it, briefly glimpsing the rabbit which had retreated inside.

Eyes gleaming, the Kodiak tore at the bush.

Cassidy realized it wasn't after the berries or herself, but the rabbit. She struggled through the bush and grabbed the rabbit, fighting to release them both from the tangle of brambles. The Kodiak's massive paws clawed down her back, drawing blood, just as she broke through to the far side.

The brown bear was there, snarling and snapping over and past her to deter the Kodiak from continuing its advance. The massive bear claws landed again on Cassidy's legs.

She curled up around the rabbit and kicked out, screaming. The sound of the water rushing nearby filled her ears and the snarling bears continued their fight.

Cassidy woke herself with her scream, her heart pounding its way out of her chest. *Oh my God,* she panted.

Shaking, she got to her feet and turned on her kitchen tap, splashing her flushed face and throat. Still shivering, she shut her eyes tightly and concentrated on bringing her breathing under control. Finally she turned around and faced her kitchen, letting her surroundings come into focus. She heard the radio playing something obscure, classical, and soft. With a gasp, she shut it off.

Taking another deep breath, she listened to the house and heard snarling coming from outside.

Grabbing a flashlight, she ran to the porch and quickly shined it into the yard. His spotted coat easy to identify, Ranger crouched in the middle of the yard. She aimed her light the direction he was facing and found a cat. She called the dog off and watched the cat leap away the instant the dog turned his back. Weak-kneed, Cassidy leaned against her house and snapped off the flashlight.

Returning inside, she glanced at the clock. It was after two in the morning. Closing up the bound pages of script and smoothing them out, Cassidy sighed and turned off the kitchen light, deciding she had better finish the night in her bed.

Despite knowing how much it would complicate things, as the last of the nightmare slowly faded away Cassidy wished she could curl up with Brenna. Hugging a pillow as a poor substitute, she closed her eyes.

Chapter 25

Brenna watched the sunrise through her front window, seated at the dining room table while Thomas and James ate their breakfasts. Dressed casually, she mentally went over her Tuesday off and made plans for what would be a quiet, at-home Thanksgiving.

"Mom?"

"Mmm hmm?" Brenna finished chewing her bite of eggs and then patted her lips with a napkin, turning her attention to James. "Yes?"

"Are you going to take us to school today?"

"I don't have a set call. I have some pages to read on another script, but I had planned to do that here. Why?"

"I was wondering...could we pick up Marcie?"

Brenna thought about her younger son's girlfriend, remembering a brunette girl who was quite shy. "What happened to her usual ride?"

"Her mom's got problems with her dad, and well, could you, please?"

Brenna reached for a half slice of buttered toast. James did not often make requests of her. He barely tolerated the times she dropped them in front of their high school. She mentioned none of that now, however, having learned it was better to just go with the flow. "You'll have to navigate to her house."

"Thanks, Mom." He seemed distracted and had since getting off the phone with his girlfriend the night before. Without another word, he finished his eggs and returned to his room.

I wonder what that was all about. She turned to Thomas. "What's your schedule today?"

"Just classes. If you're going to be home, do you want us to come here directly after school?"

"Please. We have to work on Thanksgiving dinner."

"I'm surprised we didn't plan to go to Mount Clemens," he said.

She shook her head. "It looks like I'm going to have to work with a reorganized shooting schedule. There were problems with another script being ready in time."

"Problems?"

"I don't know. Cassidy said that the changes were going over well. She had more work to do last night, but the turnaround on these things is never fast enough for the production team." She watched Thomas shift in his chair, signaling a change in topic.

"Mom, I know you had a lot of problems with Ms. Hyland when she first joined the cast. Does this mean you two get along now?"

"We're working out our differences," she answered neutrally.

"Is that why you invited her camping?"

"We had talked about camping, so yes, I invited her along." She opted not to mention that the discussion of camping had taken place after the invitation.

"I liked her."

Brenna treaded carefully. "Did you?"

Thomas finished his orange juice in one lengthy swig. "She doesn't seem like a pin-up."

Brenna quirked a smile; her eyes unknowingly turned dark blue. "No, she's not."

"Do you think she was humoring me about the rock climbing?"

Ah. Brenna suppressed a smile. "No, why?"

"I've never met anyone like her. I don't know what to make of all the stuff she said."

"Are you getting at something?"

"If I can really get her to come over for climbing at the gym, would you mind?"

"I did invite her on the camping trip, didn't I?" Brenna said with an understanding smile.

"That's a relief." The clock on the wall chimed, and he stood. "Oops, time to go."

Brenna rose, and the two of them swept the dishes into the sink. She snatched her keys and purse from the small shelf by the front door. "James!"

Her other son appeared and tossed a backpack at Thomas, who caught it handily. "Ready to go."

Twenty-five minutes later, Brenna returned home, finding the phone ringing. Catching it up, she tucked it against her ear. "Hello?"

"Hello?"

"Kevin?" She blinked, then recovered. "I wasn't expecting—"

"I wasn't expecting to find you at home."

"Oh? Um, well, what's up?"

"Shouldn't you already be at work? I was just going to leave a message."

"I didn't have a call to the set. I'm reading a script that is probably going to move up in production." She reached for it, flipping through the script idly and highlighting her dialogue.

"Oh, would that make it inconvenient if I was going to come out to L.A.?"

The highlighter went down. "Coming here? You hate L.A."

"But...I love you." There was a long pause as he formulated something else. "We haven't had much of a chance to talk. I decided you were right."

About what? she thought but did not say.

"I haven't been thinking about you very much."

"Kevin?"

"I knew when I called last time that you probably couldn't come here. So, I thought I'd come see you instead."

"When?"

"Is Thanksgiving too soon?"

"You're coming here for Thanksgiving?"

"My plane lands at LAX Thursday morning at seven. I could take a cab if you can't pick me up."

Brenna could feel her palms sweating. She wiped them before resetting the phone on her shoulder. "Of course I... Of course I'll pick you up. How long will, do you plan to stay?" She winced.

"The girls have school again Monday," he said.

"Oh, so they're coming too?"

"No, my mother's going to have them over. You'll have me all to yourself."

Brenna was silent, upset at her uncontrollable surprise.

"Brenna?"

"Sorry, I was just thinking. I'll have to add a few things to my To Do list." She walked around the living room, spotting a shirt tossed across the back of the couch. She sighed as she realized the house needed work.

"Don't go into a tizzy. Please. I don't care if the pillows aren't fluffed and the carpets aren't steamed. I just want time with you. I don't care about anything else."

She closed her eyes and pinched the bridge of her nose. *Would you care if I kissed someone else?* "All right," she said finally. "I'll see you Thursday."

Kevin's voice rolled over her. "I love you, Bren."

Brenna sat down hard on the couch cushion and put the phone aside. *What am I going to do?*

She closed her eyes. Instead of Kevin's pleasant face and soft brown eyes, she was immediately immersed in a physical memory of bodies sliding against one another in a sleeping bag. She saw the heat in adoring blue eyes and felt her own pulse race in response.

Dear God.

She rubbed her face sharply and forced her mind back to Kevin, searching for the memory of his face on their wedding day just fifteen months ago. She submerged her senses in the recall of the emotions and the event.

Brenna arranged her mother on the rocker in the small bedroom at the back of the Shea home before she pulled the summer dress from the closet.

"Brenna Renee?"

She winced as her mother used her full name. She always felt about six when she did that. "Yes, Momma?" Brenna settled on the bed, carefully tugging on white stockings.

"Shouldn't you already be in your dress?"

"Just another few minutes."

"Have you asked your sister about the bouquet?"

Brenna winced. Carefully she recited, yet again, "Evelyn can't be here."

"Still jetting with that boyfriend of hers in Paris?"

Brenna shook her head. Her younger sister was dead, having succumbed to breast cancer four years earlier. "No, Momma. Evie...couldn't break away." She shrugged. "I hadn't expected her to."

Her mother questioned, "Who's doing your hair, then?"

Evie had stood up with Brenna in her first marriage and calmed a retching and nervous bride-to-be by soothing her with a long hairdressing session. Brenna had seen her hair tugged in fifteen different styles, and she was laughing, no longer scared or nervous. Her throat caught at the memory. She missed her sister fiercely. She fluffed her shortened style. "I'm just going to twist it up."

The door opened then, surprising both Brenna and her mother. The latter looked blankly at the face peering around the edge. It was Kevin. "How are you doing in here?"

"Hi." Brenna grinned at her groom. "We're not ready yet, as you can see." She winked, raising her arms to display her slip-clad figure. She watched his face curve into a smile and felt very appreciated.

"I've got some very anxious gentlemen out here to see you," Kevin said. "Can you make yourself decent to see them?"

Something in his voice made her smile giddily. "My brothers?"

Kevin grinned back. "Tommy, Mike, Scanlon, and Gary are all cooling their heels in the living room. But they're finally here."

"Oh, Kevin. Yes." He closed the door, and she pulled a robe from the closet.

"I thought you were dressing, sweetheart."

She patted her mother's hands. "Momma, the boys are here!" Her brothers were so infrequently together in one place. No sooner had she finished tying the belt of the robe than there was a knock at the door. "Come in," she called, turning around and flipping her hair out from under the collar.

In a matter of seconds she was enveloped in the happiness of four big men, two with lighter brown hair just barely touched with the red of their Irish heritage and two with shocks of red mops and faces full of freckles. Her own coloring was the link between the extremes, as was her personality.

Scanlon, freckles on his thirty-three-year-old face still able to remind her of the gangly teen he had been, swept her up first, kissing her cheek. "Bren! Damn, you look good!"

She hugged and kissed him back, then found herself handed off to Mike, the eldest. "Mike!" Her financier brother, now forty-four, looked as he did every time she saw him: reserved blue suit, red Republican tie, and a far-too-serious look in his eyes. He hugged her back and kissed her temple.

He asked, "Happy?"

"Ecstatic," she answered. She pressed her hands to either side of his face, able to read his equal joy on her behalf despite his restrained expression. "You really need to smile more." To which he blinded her with a brief, unforgettable smile that consumed his whole face. Then it was gone, though the glow remained in his eyes.

Gary and Tommy hugged her next. "So, giving up the single life again, eh, Bren?" Gary ribbed.

"I know you never will," she prodded her playboy sibling. "Do you have a date today?"

"Just with a beautiful redhead and her new husband," he laughed, kissing her cheek. She lightly slapped his arm.

Then Kevin was in the doorway again. "Now, I'd rather she not be late to her wedding," he chided the group. "Out!"

Mike escorted their mother, leading the group back out to the living room, leaving Brenna and Kevin together.

She hugged him. "I'm so glad they're all here."

"For that smile every morning, I'll chain them to the couch." He chuckled, nuzzling her ear. "Ellie has already declared your brother 'dreamy'," he revealed.

"Which one?" she asked throatily.

"Gary."

She laughed. "Don't tell him."

"It's just a crush," he said. His hands slipped around her back, and they indulged in a leisurely kiss.

"Not from her point of view, I'm sure." Brenna leaned back in the circle of his arms. "It's got nothing on the crush I've got on you," she murmured. His mouth pressed over hers, and she felt a quiver in her stomach. "Oh, why do we have to wait?" She felt cherished in his embrace.

"Then get dressed — so we can get married, already."

Returning her focus to the present, Brenna inhaled and nodded ruefully. They had played tourist in the Bahamas for a week after the wedding, walking every morning and night in the blue-green surf, holding hands. Talking endlessly, they had dined by moonlight, and he held her tenderly, making love every moment between.

Kevin's devotion and attention had been a balm in those days. He cherished her at a time when she had been very low. Cassidy's abrupt arrival had caused major disruption and stress on the set and in Brenna's world order.

Cassidy.

Brenna's world order fell askew again at the mere thought of the slender blonde. Heat filled her, and she swallowed it down with difficulty, remembering the laughter they had shared playing in the spring with Ryan. To counter it, Brenna consciously thought of Kevin's laugh. Cassidy's returned quickly, and with it came guilt.

Didn't I promise to make my second marriage better than my first? She had started by choosing someone who supported her. Now here he was demonstrating that support again. Here he was making the gesture to come to her, when she couldn't find the time to get away and see him. Angry about a misunderstanding, she had let their relationship become distant.

Brenna castigated herself. Allowing herself to succumb to a physical attraction to someone else when Kevin was not around was not worthy of that devotion. "He deserves better." Standing, she made a decision.

Pulling out a dust rag and the vacuum, she set about cleaning up her home and pushed thoughts of Cassidy from her mind. The longer she cleaned, the more her throat tightened. Like the house, she would work on her marriage, and thoughts of Cassidy would go away.

Cassidy scanned the call board and sighed. The sets were being used for crowd shots on the previous episode. None of the central cast was required for any of them. An early Thanksgiving wish "Happy Turkey Day — See you Monday" was scrawled across their names.

Brenna was probably at home, Cassidy realized, stepping away from the wall.

"Hey, Cass. I didn't expect to see anyone else."

Cassidy turned to find Rich Paulson sauntering up, his hands stuffed in the pockets of a pair of tan Dockers. "Rich, what are you doing here?"

"Probably the same thing you are — delivering a script for approval." He grinned. "How'd the work go last night?"

"I've got most of it, I think. I think I saved Hanssen from being turned into a sexpot, but I don't know if Chapman will buy into it. He seemed really determined."

"No one blames you."

"Brenna said—"

"She'd be the first to reassure you. I remember her running through the press that day of the fight..." He thought better of continuing that line of thought. "By the way, Brenna won't be in. I was talking with Victor when she called. Her husband is coming into town."

"Oh." Cassidy lost focus for a moment, feeling a sharp reaction that took her a moment to completely submerge. "I, um, was going to ask for her advice. I changed a lot of her dialogue. Would you mind looking it over?"

"Not at all. Let's go to the conference room and have a look, shall we?"

Cassidy nodded and followed. "I hate being forced into this situation," she lamented.

"I figured that. You were more vocal than I've ever seen you in the story meeting. But," he added, "when you feel that strongly, it does nobody any good to remain silent about it."

Cassidy nodded sadly. "I guess you're right. I think I was maddest that no one thought to ask me about it before it got that far. I feel like a game show prize."

"Why did that happen?"

"I wish I knew. I thought Cameron and I were okay until that day. We'd hit a comfortable patch. Maybe Will's demands just pushed him beyond reason."

Rich sat in a chair, and Cassidy sat next to him. He opened the script. "Where do you want me to look first?"

"The ending. I want to find a way to make the story isolated. I don't want Chapman feeling there can be a continuation of this plot thread."

"That would mean finding a way to either put a halt to Raycreek's interest or..." he shrugged, "show Chris is interested in someone else." He offered Cassidy a wiggle of his eyebrows and feigned a salacious grin.

She laughed. "Sorry, I could never date a doctor. Terrible hours."

Rich chuckled. "Yeah, me neither." He dropped his gaze to the page, read through several scenes, then paused to read one more slowly. Cassidy peered over his shoulder. He looked at her curiously. "You want to leave this part like this?" In the throes of a fever, Hanssen was interacting rather openly with Jakes.

"Don't you think it works?"

"Oh, it certainly will cut Raycreek off at the knees." *And threaten other parts of his anatomy, too.* "Will Brenna do this?"

"I don't understand."

"Maybe you should have Hanssen weaker, less feverish? She's revealing a lot, perhaps too much."

Cassidy pursed her lips, studying the dialogue more critically. "You're right." Her gaze dropped, and a blush touched her cheeks. "I can't be that obvious."

Cassidy's cheeks were suddenly very pink, and Rich was stymied. He burned with questions, but he realized that this was not the time to pose them. "Maybe you'd better get that to Paul."

He waited until she was out of sight before letting his jaw drop. *Is it possible? Cass has feelings for Bren? And Bren for—?* Rich was only surprised that he had not recognized the situation before. He flashed on an image of Brenna on the big day of interviews. He had come to talk to Cassidy about a scene they were working together and found her hovering over Brenna's shoulder while the shorter woman conducted an interview. Brenna's hand had rested over Cassidy's the entire time.

Then there had been the later incident. Brenna had rapidly defused the confrontation between Chapman and Palassis when Cassidy was caught in the middle so publicly. It should have become a press relations firestorm, a real nightmare. Instead it had died, never making it to print or air anywhere that he had seen.

They certainly came a long way in a year, he thought. *From cold shoulder to warm thoughts, apparently. If not more.* He wondered if anyone else had noticed.

Cassidy stood in the doorway of the small office, watching pensively as the writer inside took the pencil from behind his ear and scratched a note in the margin of the script, mumbling, "Mmm hmm."

"Paul?"

"Hold on." Not looking at her, he held up a hand and kept reading. He scratched out a line and then made more notations.

She crossed and uncrossed her arms and leaned more heavily against the door jamb. Opening her mouth to speak, she shut it quickly. Having turned the page, he was now reading the scene that most concerned her. Cassidy watched his face, nervous about his reaction. He offered a half-smile, then a curt nod, and circled something before closing the bound script. He finally looked up at her. "Not bad."

She heard the cautiousness of the praise and swallowed. "Will it work?"

"This is how you feel? No chance of going back to the original script?"

"No." She was firm. "Chapman wanted the scenes, he's got them, but I am not sacrificing Hanssen to his ego."

"I'm probably going to lengthen the infection scene, just to draw the audience's attention, make it more obvious that's what's causing the delirious behavior. That will mean trimming somewhere else."

"Where?" Worried about where he might cut, she considered explaining her reasoning to convince him to keep the script basically as it now was. However, if the key scene was shortened, or cut entirely, at least the audience would know Chris was not in her right mind.

"Seconds here and there, no entire scenes. It's really quite cogent. I'm surprised you haven't said anything much before now," Paul mused. "We writers are going to be out of work if you guys keep doing rewrites this well."

"I heard about the union problems," Cassidy said. "I don't want to be a writer. I just want to act."

"That's a relief," he said with a chuckle.

Cassidy walked away from the office, collecting her breath a bit at a time, resenting that she had needed to "save" Hanssen. She looked up to find she was at Cameron's door. She ought to be sure he knew how she felt. She lifted her hand and knocked. The door, not completely latched, slowly opened inward.

"Cameron?" She stepped forward, pushing in, and froze.

Cameron sat on his power-napping couch. A petite short-haired blonde had her head in his lap. Cassidy's face heated when she realized the woman's head was bobbing enthusiastically. Cameron's head lolled back on the cushions as his fingers moved through the woman's short hair.

"Cameron!"

The woman abruptly fell back onto the floor as he sat up, closed his zipper, and came to his feet. "What the hell do you want?"

Cassidy straightened. "God, Cameron, here?"

"What's it to you? You dropped me, remember?"

"You are really fucked up. You take Chapman's words as some sort of dare and change a script into a horrifying character assassination, which I have fixed by the way. Now...you're into underage girls?" Out of the corner of her eye she saw the girl pulling her top together. "How the hell old are you?"

Cameron retorted, "Well, you won't have to worry about me after this. Thanks to that shit Chapman pulled last week, Victor has moved me over to another series."

Cassidy jabbed a finger at the girl. "Is she your new assistant?" Feeling absurd and angry, Cassidy swiped a hand over her face to calm herself and turned on her heel. She took some pleasure in shoving the door into the wall with a loud thud as she left.

Collapsing against the wall outside the studio offices, Cassidy waited for her heart to stop racing. She was not jealous, she realized. She was appalled, realizing that at some point that could have been her.

She crossed the open lot and re-entered the soundstage, finding a chair where she could sit quietly. If someone needed to see her they could, but the single chair didn't invite others to come and chat. She swallowed hard, accepting some of the responsibility for the situation. She had allowed herself to become wrapped up in Cameron to such an extent that she had culpability in this mess.

Her mind tumbled over the other news she had gleaned from the confrontation. *Cameron is off the series.* She exhaled. Maybe now things would calm down on the set. Chapman would not be able to get in Cam's face every day, demanding things. She wondered who would take over the writing and what the change would mean to Chapman — or any of them. It would not break the show, but some people were bound to see his departure as her fault.

With a sense of the inevitable, she covered her face with her hands. After a moment to settle her nerves, she left the set behind, along with all its troubles, looking forward to seeing her first Thanksgiving Day Parade in L.A. She had promised Ryan they finally would attend one.

Chapter 26

Moving with the traffic flowing away from the Los Angeles International Airport, Brenna watched Kevin adjust more comfortably into the passenger seat. Thomas and James sat quietly in the back, elbows on the windows, gazing out at the passing traffic. The radio played so softly she could not identify the song. She was quiet, still absorbing that Kevin was here, in L.A., with her. Her gaze kept sliding sideways to watch him.

He wore a forest green polo shirt instead of the familiar suit and tie, and she wondered why. Previously whenever she had asked him to change into something more casual, he had insisted that a candidate should always look professional. Nervously she rubbed her hand on the gear shift.

Kevin's hand covered hers. She glanced away from the road long enough to catch his smile and offer a faint one back. She turned her hand over, palm up, and briefly squeezed his fingers before looking once in each rear-view mirror. She put both hands on the wheel to change lanes. Her hand never returned to the central console.

"How are Ellie and Marie?" she asked.

"Eleanor, if you please, and Marie Curie," Kevin supplied wryly. "Eleanor's been trying to find the 'most grown-up gown' to wear to the Christmas dance at the church, while Marie can't be bothered. She's taken an interest in physics and joined a rocketry club last month. Her entire room is papered with trajectories and math equations that are years beyond me."

Brenna suppressed a chuckle. "I bet there's a boy involved," she surmised.

"That's what I thought too. She and a classmate, Kirsten, both joined up. Heard it might get them an angle on a scholarship, I think."

Shaking her head, Brenna shrugged. "If she likes it..." She changed the subject. "How's Ellie's dress hunt coming?"

"My sister took her shopping last weekend. Five hours and not a single thing she found suitable. They're going out again this weekend."

Brenna let the silence grow, but it did not feel the same. Usually silence between them was light, a time of communion. She felt anything but communal at the moment, so she concentrated on the road.

After catching the temperature on a bank sign as they passed, Kevin filled the void. "It's warm here. Barely in the mid-thirties back home."

"Oh?"

"Yeah. We had snow two nights ago. Just a couple inches, but it'll probably stick. Nice white blanket for Christmas, I figure."

"It was almost seventy when we were camping," Thomas interjected.

Kevin turned around in his seat. "When did you go camping?"

"Last weekend," Brenna supplied. "Thomas had taught the LAKE kids to climb, and this was their first chance on something other than the gym wall."

"Yeah, everyone did great, even Cassidy."

"Cassidy?"

"Yeah, that blond actress from Mom's show."

Kevin studied Brenna. "Sounds like you had fun."

She shrugged and considered what to say to that. Knowing he was not inclined to go camping, she had not even thought to invite him. *Is he bothered that I had a free weekend and didn't come to see him?* He didn't sound upset, but she could not see his face. *Damn.* Brenna wished she were not driving so she could study his face and come up with the right thing to say. Instead she shrugged again. "Yes. I think everyone had a good time." Her brow furrowed a little even as she tried to stifle it.

There was silence again; she almost reached for the radio dial to break it.

Kevin looked out the window, then mused, "I passed up riding in the parade at home today. Do you want to go see yours?"

"Hmm?"

"I was just noticing the signs blocking off the route and indicating parking. Would you like to go see the parade?"

"But, the crowds..." Brenna felt she would much rather spend the morning at home. The turkey was already in the oven, but she liked puttering around the kitchen. It always reminded her of Thanksgivings as a child.

Kevin shrugged with unconcern. "We'll just be a few more nameless faces in the madness." He put his hand on her knee as he turned around and addressed the boys. "What do you think, guys?"

"If we get somewhere near Del Ray Drive, maybe I can find Marcie. She said she and her family were going to view things from there."

"I'm sure there'll be too many people to find just one."

"We haven't seen a parade that you weren't in, in years, Mom," Thomas coaxed. "Come on."

Paused at a stoplight, Brenna looked from one face to another, then into Kevin's hopeful smile, and she conceded to the majority. "All right."

To guard against too much sun, they purchased hats from a street vendor hawking "LA 2000" downtown revitalization project logo gear. Thomas and James turned theirs backward, sauntering along with big grins until Brenna turned and gestured once with a finger. Sheepishly they both turned the caps around properly and straightened their shoulders.

Brenna pulled a golf-style visor low over her sunglasses and looked up as Kevin pulled the baseball cap brim low over his eyes. He wrapped his left arm around her bare shoulders and tilted his head to capture her lips.

She stiffened in surprise, then forced herself to rest her hand against his cheek, and willed the kiss to tantalize her. When Kevin pulled away, she blinked.

That certainly didn't work, she thought, thankful the glasses hid her eyes. She was very aware of how different his kiss was from Cassidy's — less absorbing, less able to take her to a realm of forgetting where and who she was. With a sense of loss, she turned away to watch where they were walking.

Thomas flanked her left and James took Kevin's right, slipping behind the adults when the path narrowed. Brenna worried that the boys would be bored. Adults liked parades for the nostalgia, and little kids liked them for the colors, noise, and candy at the end. She remembered herself as a teenager finding parades painfully dull unless she was surrounded by friends.

"I've missed you," Kevin whispered against her ear, brushing the lobe with his lips. His left arm moved down her back, then abruptly he grasped her hand.

She offered a tremulous smile. "So, where should we sit?"

Thomas and James forged ahead through the crowd. Brenna and Kevin followed, ducking the elbows of in-line skaters and holding their hats against the jostle of the rest of the crowd.

"Are you sure this was a good idea?" she asked.

"Sure. See?" They broke through the line, and Brenna lowered herself to the curb behind the parade rope next to a pair of preschool-age children licking fruity-smelling Italian ices. She inhaled appreciatively, identified grape and cherry, and wrapped her arms around her upraised knees as Kevin reached down, brushed a spot clean and sat next to her. Thomas and James crouched behind them.

James leaned forward, putting a hand on his mother's and Kevin's shoulder. "Mom, can I go look for Marcie?"

"There's no way you'll find us again if you leave," she protested.

He looked up and pointed across the street. "That's the Piccadilly's. Only one for miles. I'll meet you back here in one hour, I promise."

Brenna looked to Kevin, who pursed his lips, then nodded reluctantly. "I guess it'd be all right." She grasped her youngest son's hand. "Be careful."

"I will." James disappeared into the throng before she could change her mind.

Thomas' gaze was fixed on something, Brenna realized, as she turned and caught his face. "You aren't going to leave, too?"

"Well, I don't know. So far I haven't seen a prettier lady to spend my time with." He laughed. She grasped his chin and caught his kiss on her cheek as he patted her shoulder. "So, what's your favorite entry in a parade?"

Brenna opened her mouth to answer, when Kevin began offering his response. "The bands. Not that I'd be biased, having played in one all through high school myself, of course."

Thomas laughed. It hurt Brenna to see Kevin smile at her, pleased by her son's reaction to him.

"What about you, Mom? What's your favorite part of a parade?"

She fell back to a time decades earlier — a parade with her brothers. She couldn't have been more than seven. She saw painted faces, smiling, dancing eyes that made everyone laugh. Telling stories from behind masks that hid the truth. "I like the clowns," she said wistfully. "I always have."

Kevin put his arm around her shoulder, and they leaned forward to look down the stretch of road for any signs that the parade was nearing. Calliope music, accompanying the opening float, reached them over the din of the crowd laughing and hollering good-naturedly around them. Kevin's arm nudged her backward, and she felt her shoulders conform to the curve of his chest. Gradually she relaxed her posture until he was almost completely supporting her. She felt his cheek nuzzle her hair and closed her eyes, waiting for the magic.

Tears gathered instead. She did not feel a wash of protectiveness or the sudden rush of blushing affection. His hand was caressing her lower back, but it raised no tingles. Cassidy had raised so much more from across a campfire. She opened her eyes, startled that the blonde was once again foremost in her thoughts, and leaned back harder against her husband's chest. As if on cue, Kevin wrapped his arms around her, catching her hands in her lap as his body hugged hers. "Bonny Brenna's got a blush on," he said in her ear.

She was not blushing because she had shared her childhood fondness for clowns. As her mind filled with the memory of a woman who was forbidden, the first marchers turned into teary blurs before her eyes. She turned her head away, lifted her sunglasses and brushed at her cheeks.

Filled with renewed misgivings, Cassidy viewed the crowded street. She grasped Ryan's hand more firmly as the flow of bodies around them threatened to tug him away from her. She thought about just sitting right there, but the view of the parade would be less than optimal, and she wanted Ryan's first memory of the pageantry to be the best possible. She looked around and located the entrance to Piccadilly's. The route mapped in the paper had shown this as the location of the parade's second turn. She scouted the area, looking to avoid the crowd-scanning cameras. Ryan tugged her leg. "This way, Mommy."

He was gesturing toward the curb nearby, and she decided it was suitable. Tucking herself on the edge, she positioned him between her thighs. Cassidy circled her arms around him and pointed out the blue and red uniformed band marching past. "Would you like to play music someday?"

"Yes!" He jumped excitedly. "Drums!"

Cassidy ruffled his hair as the drum line marched past, feeling its rumbles clearly beneath her sneakers through the surface of the road. She resisted putting her hands over her ears and instead sat back, listening as Ryan named off the other instruments they were seeing. He paused when he could not identify one.

"What are those gold things? Tubas too?" He pointed to a golden line.

"Those are called French horns," she explained. "Don't ask me why."

"Why?"

She sighed and hugged him. "Probably because they were first made in France or something. I'll ask the score director at work."

That seemed to satisfy him. "Okay." Then he paused. "Mommy?"

"Yes?"

"Will you see that lady at work again?"

"Which lady?"

"Ms. Lan...gan?"

"Lanigan. Yes, of course." Cassidy thought of the compact woman and smiled wistfully, wondering what she was doing this holiday morning. She frowned. *Probably waking up with her husband,* she thought wryly.

"Will you tell her I like her hat?"

"What hat?" Cassidy was confused. Brenna had not worn any headgear on the camping trip, which had surprised Cassidy, actually. She still remembered the sunshine on the titian locks as they paused on the mountainside during Sunday's climb.

"The one she's wearing." He pointed.

Cassidy followed the line of his finger through the break in the parade. She recognized Brenna, but certainly not because the woman was trying to be recognized. A sun visor was pulled low over her face and her sunglasses hid her eyes. However, there was no mistaking that jaw or the soft lines of shoulders bared to the sun.

Cassidy swallowed. *Or bared to her husband's touch.* She had never met Kevin Shea, but that had to be him, curled around Brenna's body, his hands stroking her shoulders. Her throat tightened.

"Mommy?"

"Yes?" she managed.

"Will you tell her?"

"I...I'll try to remember. I'll certainly try." Cassidy sat up as the street became busy again, filling with the GE "Bright Ideas" float moving past, surrounded by dancing light bulbs, one of whom dropped candies which Ryan scrambled to get.

She caught his jacket tail, preventing him from going too far, and soon he was back in her arms, watching the rest of the parade as Cassidy contemplated how

Brenna looked, enclosed there in Kevin's arms. She looked away from the street to brush her eyes and saw couples walking hand in hand, occasionally looking at the passing parade but more often wrapped up in each other. The whole tableau made her sigh. Her gaze slipped back toward the street, and she saw a couple on the near curb from the back, one's hand tucked into the other's rear jean pocket. One brunette head turned and two sets of soft, feminine lips connected.

Normally one to glance away from public displays of affection, Cassidy dropped her chin lightly on top of Ryan's head and let herself covertly study the lesbian couple with great interest. She felt a swirl of arousal in her groin. When their kiss ended, the smaller woman tucked her head against the other's shoulder. Cassidy felt a twinge in her own arm around Ryan, which she now recognized as the need to hold, to cherish. She watched as the women caught pieces of candy thrown from the float and unwrapped them, offering the pieces to each other.

She swallowed and finally turned away, glimpsing Brenna on the other side of the street. Her arms were tucked around her knees and her mouth was open, laughing. Cassidy felt a pain in her chest. She sat back, releasing Ryan for a moment as she tried to catch her breath.

Ryan took the opportunity to bolt out for another piece of candy. Cassidy righted herself and grabbed for him, but missed. She looked at the oncoming parade and did not hesitate. She leaped for her son, now in the middle of the street as the mounted division of the Los Angeles Police Department clip-clopped past. The horses that might have stepped on them stopped instantly. The disruption of their rhythm made a few officers look down.

"Back to the side, ma'am."

Cassidy stood, walking around the two horses to reach the curb.

It was not her curb. Disoriented, Cassidy had sought a section of empty curb, thinking it was where she and Ryan had been sitting.

"Hey, Ms. Hyland!"

Recognizing Thomas Lanigan's cheery voice, Cassidy looked up as she sat, realizing she was about to sit on Brenna's feet. The other woman moved, drawing Cassidy's bewildered attention to the shadowed face. Heart hammering, Cassidy lifted her chin and met the curious expression on Kevin Shea's face.

Cassidy shook herself and looked at Thomas. "Hi. I'm sorry, I didn't see you here."

"Looks like Ryan was getting himself in trouble again," Thomas said. "Saw him dart out ahead of the horses."

Brenna could not breathe. She had stiffened against Kevin the instant she recognized Cassidy settling on their curb. She practically identified the woman by the curve of her rear in her jeans as she bent at the waist. No need to go higher and actually see her face. Mortification renewed, she tried for nonchalance, forcing herself to relax against Kevin, whose hand stroked over the muscles in her upper arm.

You ought to make introductions, her mannered conscience prodded.

Her terror issued a curt *No.*

No one's paying attention to the parade, her conscience prodded again.

Both Thomas and Kevin had fixated on Cassidy. For a measure of calm, and since no one could see her eyes clearly, Brenna focused on Ryan in Cassidy's lap. "I'm sorry, you've never met. Um. Kevin, this is Cassidy Hyland, from *Time Trails.* Cassidy, my...husband Kevin Shea, and you already know Thomas."

Brenna offered up thanks as Cassidy's gaze left her and Cassidy grasped Kevin's hand. "Nice to meet you," Kevin said politely.

"The same." Cassidy returned her hands to her son's shoulders, where Brenna watched them move slowly up and down the boy's small arms. "This is Ryan, my son."

Kevin nodded. "How old is he?"

"Five." Both women's voices mingled in the answer.

Brenna sat up and turned so she was crouched over the curb without being supported by Kevin. "His birthday was back in October. Cassidy threw a party and invited the cast."

"Oh." He rubbed her back. "So, how do you like working on *Time Trails*, Cassidy?"

"I'm sure Brenna's told you all sorts of stories."

"A few," Kevin acknowledged.

Brenna's stomach began to twist. *I'm imagining the rising tension, right?*

"I should probably try to cross back to our seats," Cassidy said.

Thomas' hand shot past Brenna's shoulder and landed on Cassidy's. "Stick around. You'll never find your spot now. At least there's room here."

Brenna turned her gaze from the slender throat swallowing nervously and the dimpled chin angling up to meet Thomas' gaze. His hand rested on Cassidy's jacketed shoulder. Cassidy's throat moved as she prepared her words. Brenna wished, just for a moment, that she had not raised such a well-mannered child, as Thomas squeezed the shoulder, silently convincing Cassidy to accept the invitation.

"All right," Cassidy finally answered. Glancing once more to both Brenna and Kevin, she settled back on the curb and wrapped herself around Ryan.

The matter decided, everyone turned back just in time to be showered by the water sprayed by the thirty-foot watering spout on the Bromeliad Society's garden float.

Wiping her face required her glasses to come off, Brenna realized. She did not want to, but the light refracting through the water droplets bothered her eyes. Reluctantly she tugged off the glasses and wiped them on the bottom of her cotton top. Lifting her head to put them back on, she caught Cassidy's sidelong glance. The other woman also held sunglasses in her hands.

The intersection of their gazes hit Brenna in the stomach, hard. Her lips trembled and her breath caught. Shaken, she looked away to the parade.

The remains of the turkey will barely be enough to cook down for soup stock, Brenna lamented, surveying the scattered dishes.

James reached for the bowl of creamed onions, then paused. "Anyone else want these?" He looked at her expectantly.

As if I have room for another bite. She shook her head. James grinned and scooped the remains of the creamy vegetable onto his plate, setting aside the empty serving dish.

"More sweet potatoes?" Brenna asked, reaching for the pan by her elbow. She cast a significant look at Kevin opposite her.

He raised his hands. "None for me, thanks." Picking up his wine glass, he sipped.

Thomas spoke up from her right. "I'll take them."

Brenna passed the pan, and soon the yams were gone as well. "We used to have leftovers," she complained good naturedly.

It had all been devoured by the boys. She herself had only a single plate, with small portions. She'd eaten reluctantly, trying to cover her lack of appetite and anxieties which lingered from the day.

"They're growing boys." Kevin chuckled.

"It's great stuff," James chimed in, reaching for the bowl of stuffing and serving himself a heap.

"I'm glad." She dropped her eyes from her son and collected her napkin from her lap. When she looked up to put it on the table, she found Kevin studying her. "Yes?"

"I was just thinking that we could leave the bottomless pits here to clear the table and do the dishes." He lifted the remains of the bottle of red wine they had drunk with the meal. "Want to sit on the deck and watch the sunset?"

The tenor of his voice bothered her, but Brenna nodded. "All right." She looked at Thomas. "When you finish in here, you can come out and join us."

"Dishes?" James pouted, still eating.

Thomas shrugged. "Sure."

She leaned forward, grasping Thomas' hand and kissing James on the cheek. "Thanks."

Kevin had risen meanwhile and stood at her shoulder when she straightened. "Ready?" he asked.

She let him pull her chair back, and retrieved her wine glass before following him out to the back deck. The light breeze picked up her hair, and Kevin slipped his arm around her, pulling her into his warmer frame. "It's a nice night," he said as she settled beside him on the A-frame swing.

Brenna didn't answer, her pulse nervously thrumming in her ears.

"So this was your summer project?" Kevin stroked his fingers over the scroll-work on one of the swing's arms. She nodded into his shoulder. "Nice workmanship," he complimented.

"Thank you." She had hunted for weeks for the right wood, and the ash had taken the stain beautifully.

"Something like this would look nice in our yard back home."

"I, well, I'm sorry I didn't come to Michigan then, but, the boys, Thomas, he had Little League coaching. James had joined the summer league through the high school." She frowned. "I was here. And I..." She trailed off wondering how to put into words the unsettled anxieties she recalled suffering. "I needed a place back here to read," she said softly. "It was stifling being inside all the time." She looked into his face for a moment and then uncomfortably looked away, noticing that her rosemary patch seemed a little wilted, in need of attention.

"Is that why you went camping?"

"The camping trip was for charity. But I like it, yes."

"I'm not much of a camper."

"I know."

"But I would have come if you'd asked."

She swallowed. "I know."

The motion of the swing gradually pushed their bodies together, hip-to-hip. She steadied herself with a hand on his thigh and felt his arm drop lightly across her shoulders. His fingers swirled against the bare skin of her arm. She tried not to feel jumpy, but the fact remained, she was. When she angled her head to study his profile, she found his eyes closed. "Kevin?"

He turned to meet her gaze. "Yes?"

"How are the girls?"

"All right."

Brenna tried to calm her mind and think only of the moment, but the sounds around them distracted her too easily. She could hear the scuffling as James and Thomas quarreled over who would wash or dry. Thinking she should help, she started to stand.

"Where are you going?"

She turned, finding their gazes level, and sheepishly shook her head. "I was thinking of helping the boys inside."

"Don't. They'll be fine. I..." He straightened slowly, and she leaned back a bit, watching him. "Here." He reached down and retrieved the wine bottle. "Help me finish this?"

Brenna held the glasses while he poured the last of the alcohol into them. She handed him his and they sat again in the swing. "This was a nice vintage with dinner," she said, letting it remain on her tongue for a moment before swallowing.

"Thanks." The only sounds were crickets. She was taking a sip when he spoke again. "Do you intend to stay out here?"

"With you, of course. I just said—"

"No, I meant here in California. After the show is over."

"You want me to come to Mount Clemens."

"Yes."

She accepted the brush of his lips against hers, tasting the light wine flavor, but ended the kiss as he touched his tongue to her lips, tasting her.

"Nice sunsets out here," he said, caressing her shoulder as she concentrated on the red-orange western sky. "Guess it won't be so tough for me to stay out here 'til the end of the show."

"You shouldn't. There's things to do back in Michigan."

"I'd be willing."

"No. That's not... Don't do that."

"Bren, I feel I need to do something."

"Why?"

"We should be together."

"It's just another five months." Brenna tried to shrug. He put light pressure on her shoulders to stop the motion.

"What about after that? I know you don't want to come to Mount Clemens, so, where do you want to go?"

"I like Mount Clemens just fine. It's just...it's not..."

"It's not L.A.," he supplied.

His expression made her hold her tongue when she was inclined to denial. "I had an offer to join a theater company here," she explained.

"I guessed. I came out here so we could at least talk about it." He sighed and sat back. "I feel like we're drifting apart. I don't want that to happen."

"Kevin, I..." Brenna bit her lower lip, unknowingly presenting a very endearing image. She was startled when Kevin groaned and grasped her hands.

"There's always regional theater, good stuff."

"I worked a long time to get where I am," Brenna said. "It's what I've wanted my whole life."

"A year ago you were ready to give it all up."

Brenna nodded. "Things change."

"Apparently. You haven't written or called much in the last several months."

"I've been busy."

"I know. So have I."

They were silent. Brenna felt crowded, as though Kevin was too close or she was too small. She wanted to get up, to get some space. She braced her hands on the wood, careful not to touch him. She tensed the muscles in her arms to push.

His voice broke the silence. "I still dream about you, Bren."

Her arms went slack. She blushed. "When the series is over..."

"That's a long time to wait." He brushed his forefinger and thumb over her chin and lifted it, bringing their mouths together. "We could make up for it." His breath caressed her lips. "I've missed you."

He pulled her back across his thighs, and wrapped his arms around her waist, nuzzling her hair as they watched the sun finish its descent. For a long time they just sat, and Kevin sipped his wine.

Brenna could not bring herself to do anything. She was frozen between rising and running and just sitting there crying. She knew that Kevin deserved a wife. She had wanted that once, too, wanting nothing more than to leave L.A. and all its competitiveness — where she was never good enough, never pretty enough, never young enough — behind her. But now, when she closed her eyes and tried to envision a future with Kevin, she felt pain grip her heart and she fought against the tears. *No, I can't.* She blinked, releasing two tears down her cheek.

In her mind's eye rose a memory of Cassidy's smile, soft fingers lifting to her cheek, the whisper of breath against her face just before they kissed...

"We haven't done this since we first were dating."

Brenna jumped at the sound of his voice. "What?"

"Just sit together, contemplating life, the universe and everything," he mused. She stiffened as she felt his lips press against her temple. "About the show. You know, I am glad to know that you're getting along at work again."

"Hmm?"

"Well, her appearance startled you, but it was good to see you smiling with Ms. Hyland. You had such trouble with her at first. Her son certainly likes you."

Brenna's breath caught at the image of Cassidy from that morning — her hair loose and blowing around her face in the breeze. She could only nod as her throat constricted with the memory of Ryan crawling into her lap and complimenting her hat. She had fallen easily into playing games with him.

"It was time to make amends. She didn't have any control over events," she explained, unable to prevent the halting as she composed her reply.

"How are things with the show itself?"

"Fine, though it feels more like the end every day. The production team is already being split between us and a new show. The questions from reporters are all about 'the end.'" She lifted her hands in the air and formed the quotation marks with a grimace. "It's depressing." She realized her melancholy showed when Kevin brushed his fingertips across her cheeks.

"I'm sorry I brought it up."

Brenna remained silent, and he let her. The sounds around them seeped in slowly, and she realized the house behind them was quiet. "Did they kill each other?" she asked in a worried voice.

"I doubt it," he whispered back.

The door to the house suddenly opened. At the sound Brenna turned with Kevin, spying one of the boys backlit in the doorway.

"Mom! Are you coming inside?" Thomas' voice reached them easily.

Brenna looked up at Kevin and raised a questioning brow. He shrugged at her silent query. "If you'd rather..." he answered, leaving the option open-ended.

"It'll get cold fast now that the sun's gone," she reasoned.

"I wouldn't want a Popsicle in bed later." He chuckled. "We'll be there in a minute," he called to Thomas. "Let's go inside," he said softly, turning back to her and pulling her against him with subtle desire.

Brenna's heart tripped against her ribcage as his hands caressed her throat, brushing over her breast and onto her hip where he tugged, lifting her briefly onto his lap for a hard kiss.

On the pretext of becoming uncomfortably lightheaded, Brenna broke the kiss. "It's not late enough to send the boys to bed." Her voice was tremulous as she laid her palms against his chest. His eyes were searching hers, and she knew what he wanted. She was unsure she could give it to him.

Arguing against the old proscription, he coaxed, "They're old enough now. We can just go into your room..." His voice trailed off when he began nibbling her throat, humming against the skin the way he knew she liked.

It didn't bring a magic rush of desire, and she began to despair. However, his hands seemed to compel her. *He's my husband,* Brenna fretted, but she couldn't think very clearly. She felt like she was betraying someone, but could not decide if it was Kevin...or Cassidy. What she did know was that her heart was not in this.

She closed her eyes, and Cassidy's face floated easily into her mind: cool blue eyes filled with a warming fire, the dimple in her chin that begged to be touched. As Kevin continued kissing her, Brenna seized on the warm desire her imagination was causing and the heat it was sending to her loins. She drew in a long breath. "All right." Shaky, Brenna found herself set on her feet. Kevin led the way back inside.

"All done?" Cassidy sighed as Ryan spread his mashed potatoes and gravy around his plate rather than eating it. "Yeah, you're done."

He looked up at her with half-closed eyes. The meal had been late; both of them had fallen asleep when they returned from the parade.

She patted his back and urged him from the table. "We should pack some of this for the Talbots, don't you think?" Cassidy looked at the leftovers and nodded.

The gossipy neighbor, Mrs. Sandsmarsh, had been less than helpful, but agreed that Cassidy's guess about the Talbots' finances might be right. "Especially seeing as it is Thanksgiving and all," suggested the older woman, a lifelong housewife who frequently hung her laundry while dressed in a bathrobe.

While Ryan settled on the floor, marching his Transformers around, Cassidy gathered a collection of Tupperware and began scooping up the leftovers. Ten minutes later she closed the last container and found a plastic bag to carry them. "Come on." She interrupted Ryan's play and opened the front door. "Let's go visit Gwen and Lou."

"And Chance!"

"And Chance." She coaxed him out the front door while he was still pushing his arms into his coat.

The streetlights were already on as they crossed to the third home on the opposite side of the street. "Now promise you'll be good. We won't stay long." Cassidy watched Ryan circling on the stoop as she waited for her rap on the door knocker to be answered. The door opened and Gwen looked out.

"Cass?"

"Hi, Gwen." She lifted the bag. "I brought some stuff over for you."

"What is this?"

"Leftovers. I made too much for our meal tonight. I thought you might like to have it. We'll never manage to eat it all before it spoils."

Gwen shifted the door wider. "Well, I... We don't really need it ourselves." She motioned Cassidy inside the entry. "Just a minute."

While waiting, Cassidy noticed the Talbot family was still at the table. Lou sat at the head of the table in view. Gwen went up to him and spoke quietly into his ear. The man shook his head. Gwen said something else. Lou's gaze found Cassidy's across the distance. She saw his jaw tighten and firm as his eyes narrowed, but he nodded at Gwen.

Gwen returned, glancing at the bags. "There's tons here. How is it you made so much? Didn't you have guests?"

"It was just Ryan and me tonight. I'm so used to Missouri spreads..." Cassidy shrugged.

"You had no one over? What about...Cameron?"

"No, we broke up."

"I didn't know that." She nudged Cassidy onto the front stoop, closing the door between them and the rest of the house. "Lou wanted me to talk to you. I don't think it's anything, but we wanted you to be aware that Ryan was telling us about your camping trip." She smiled uneasily. "He mentioned your co-star, Lanigan, is it?"

"Brenna invited us to go along on her charity's trip."

"Ryan really enjoyed himself. He kept going on and on with stories." She inhaled, then shook her head. "He told us you 'slept with Miss Lanigan'. We assume that he meant that you two shared a tent and he was just confused."

Cassidy felt her face flush and tried to joke, "Well...yes...of course. What else?"

Gwen studied her for a moment. She checked the door behind her and found it securely closed. Turning back, she grasped Cassidy's hands, feeling them shake. "My God, you did!"

Blood drained from Cassidy's face. "No, no. We didn't." She drew a breath to get her reaction under control. "I kissed her." She frowned. "It's complicated."

"I bet. I knew you felt like she didn't resent you anymore; I had no idea it had gone so far. Guess the hatchet's really buried." She frowned as apparently other implications occurred to her. "For God's sake, don't say anything to Lou."

Cassidy sighed. "You won't say anything?"

"No, I won't."

There was a long pause, and Cassidy thought that would be the end of it, then Gwen asked, "How did it happen?" Clearly "not saying anything" did not mean she would not satisfy her own curiosity.

"It was completely innocent," Cassidy explained. "We had to share a sleeping bag because Ryan couldn't sleep and came into the tent for the night. There were only two bags. He had one; we took the other one."

"Surely you could've shared with him — or just slept. So...what else happened?"

"I...I had kissed her...in the woods."

"Cass, are you serious? You're...straight. And she's married, right?"

"Yes." Her hands shoved in her pockets, Cassidy looked around, at the sky, the ground, then back at Gwen. "We haven't done anything."

"Are you still pursuing it?"

"I don't know. I don't even know if she wants to."

They looked up as Lou's voice reached them through the closed door. "Gwen!"

Cassidy shook her head and frowned. "You'd better get back inside. I can't talk about this now."

"I'll have to figure out something to tell Lou. He was disturbed by the story." Her expression told Cassidy he had been more than disturbed. "Maybe we can get together Sunday."

Cassidy nodded reluctantly. She really did need someone to talk to. "Maybe."

Kevin rolled onto his back, taking Brenna with him. Their bodies were covered in a fine sheen of sweat, and the sheet stuck. He laughed, clearly pleased, and kissed her repeatedly. Brenna turned her head aside, pretending to want to curl down and fall asleep. Kevin whispered how wonderful she was.

All the while, Brenna was emotionally distraught at what she had done. *Oh my God! I just gave my husband a sympathy fuck.* Her face hot, but not from exertion, Brenna shut her eyes tightly and fisted her hand against Kevin's chest. As soon as she felt him fall asleep, she would leave the bed.

She swallowed back a sob, knowing, even as she thought such things, that she could not invite questions from him by betraying her emotions with tears. The truth would have to come later, when she was collected and calm.

Tonight, when she could not put another out of her mind, she had learned the truth: Her heart had gone elsewhere. Kevin was still a wonderful man — socially conscious and caring for his daughters, her, and even her sons. Brenna knew, though, that she could never do this charade again. Her chest hurt from withholding the tears — wanting to cry out in passion, but finding that nothing he did moved her. The usually pleasant soreness between her legs felt instead like a violation of her soul. She needed to slip away and wash herself.

Chapter 27

On Sunday, Cassidy, waiting at the window, spotted Gwen coming across the street. She tucked the grocery list in her purse and called for Ryan. "We're going, Ryan! Come on."

Bolting in from the back of the house, Ryan drew to a sudden halt at her feet. "Ready!"

She swept an assessing glance over him. His baggy jeans and tee shirt were acceptable. "Do you have your sneakers?" He pulled up the pant legs and showed off the hidden footwear. She shook her head. "All right. Let's go."

Opening the door, Cassidy found Gwen just reaching for the knocker. "We're all set."

Gwen nodded, then looked down at Ryan. "Chance is waiting for you at my house." They watched him run down the walk and cross the street, without looking both ways. He ran up to the Talbots' front door and knocked enthusiastically.

"How've you been since Thursday?" Gwen asked as they walked to Cassidy's car.

"Right into it, hmm? I've been trying to enjoy an all-too-brief vacation."

"I'm just curious. Ryan is so fixated on you two at the camp, I figure it must've been pretty intense. I told Lou that Ryan had simply noticed Brenna because she's pretty but different from his mother. That seemed to appease him." Gwen paused outside the passenger door. "Have you heard from her?"

Cassidy slid behind the wheel. "No. I don't expect to, either."

"So...have you figured out what you're going to do?"

Shaking her head, Cassidy said, "You don't understand."

"Then help me understand. Were you experimenting, acting out something? I don't get it, Cass. You've never done anything like this before."

"Once." A sudden warmth suffused her cheeks. She had told no one else about this. Gwen was looking at her expectantly. "It was...college. We... Her name was Misty. We'd both been dumped during finals week, and we decided to take a ski trip to Colorado. It was late; we'd been drinking, snuggling by a fireplace. We... I... She..." Cassidy's blush deepened, and she lowered her voice. "The next morning, she made me promise to forget anything happened."

"Sounds like this is the same thing."

Cassidy thought about what she felt when she looked at Brenna or even just happened to think about her — the rush of adrenaline she experienced or the equally powerful flood of calm. "No comparison, Gwen. I constantly want to touch her. Talking with her is both the most difficult and the easiest thing I've ever done. She's so physical. Alive. She's intelligent, sharp-witted, private, personal, focused. When we talk acting, I can feel her passion for it. She really gets into it. She doesn't share that with just anyone."

"Passionate, huh?"

Cassidy blushed and changed the subject slightly. "She loves her family, as much as I've seen anyone could. Her boys adore her in return. That's part of the problem. I don't want her to change. If I can't find a way to live with this, it'll hurt her...not to mention her marriage."

"Is her marriage good?"

"I don't know." Cassidy had read nothing but anxiety from Brenna at the parade, anxiety that she knew her presence caused. Certainly Kevin had behaved lovingly while the group was together. *Though*, Cassidy thought ruefully, *I'm certainly not a good judge.* Mitch, and recently Cameron, had showed her that.

"If the marriage isn't good, it's not likely because of you."

"I can't know that, not for certain. That's why I have to stay away until she makes her decision. She asked me to."

"What about the parade?"

Cassidy pulled up at the store and parked. As she set the auto-lock from her key chain, she said, "That was entirely an accident. Most of this seems to happen by accident."

"How'd it go?"

"She introduced me to her husband."

They each grabbed a cart from the corral outside the store. "That had to be awkward."

"I could feel her tension."

"Nothing confrontational happened?"

"No. We all sat together. Her oldest son talked to me while we watched the rest of the parade."

"Her son?"

"We'd gotten to know each other a bit when he taught me how to climb."

"When?"

"The camping trip."

"So, the mother *and* the son?" Gwen pressed her hands over her eyes dramatically. "Sheesh, you don't do things simple."

"I'm not in love with Thomas."

"You're in love with her? You're positive?"

Cassidy delayed her answer as a man walked around them and grabbed a box of spaghetti off the top shelf. When he was gone, she whispered, "I don't just want to go to bed with her, Gwen. That's Cameron's M.O., not mine."

"Speaking of... Why aren't you still dating Cameron?" Gwen picked up two different bottles of pre-made sauce and compared labels while awaiting Cassidy's answer.

"It's over. He handled a colleague badly and really made a scene, put me right in the middle, demeaning me."

They pushed on to another aisle. "You had to have had a clue before that."

"There were times when Cam... It was more about sex and..." Cassidy finally admitted to herself what had been lingering since the night at the club with Griff Torend, "and showing me off than any emotional connection."

"Maybe what you feel for her is because you had a breakup. She's become a friend, someone to talk to. So maybe it's some sort of rebound."

"It's not all me, Gwen. I feel something back from her."

"Last year she hated you."

"She apologized."

Gwen was skeptical. "When you were kissing?"

"No," Cassidy said defensively.

Gwen nodded. "All right. Can you stay away from her and still get your work done?"

"That's a problem," Cassidy admitted wryly. "Since I touched her, I find I need that. We...fit in a way I've never felt before. When she's stressed or upset, I can feel it.

When she's happy, she glows." She thought about the time in her trailer when she and Brenna had curled up on the couch together to work over the script rewrite. Despite the sudden changes in their relationship that had prompted Brenna to request that they slow things down, they had fallen into the position so naturally and remained comfortable for hours.

Gwen sensed the awe. "Wow. You never talked like this about Cameron."

Cassidy scanned the dairy case, checking the stamped dates, and selected a gallon of milk. She nodded. "I told you."

"Does she know how you feel?" Gwen retrieved a package of sliced cheese. "I mean, *really* know?"

"I can't tell her. Not right now. She's trying to sort herself out. It wouldn't be fair of me to complicate that."

"All right. Well, may I suggest that you try not to be alone with her off-camera?"

"That's helpful," Cassidy said with sarcasm.

"Only advice I can give you. If it's meant to happen, it will." Gwen clasped her shoulder briefly, then moved away, picking up a six-pack of Lou's favorite beer. "Just don't expect it to be easy. If this breaks publicly, regardless of what you've actually done or not done, it's going to be uncomfortable — at the very least. And it won't just be tabloid reporters who will cause you problems."

"I know," Cassidy admitted. "Are you finished?" she said as they both selected apples and dropped them into bags.

"Yes, I'm finished. You?"

"Just one more thing," Cassidy said. "Wait here."

"Sure." Gwen leaned on the handle of her cart.

Going to the card aisle, Cassidy searched for her holiday season cards. One of the boxed sets had caught her eye when they passed earlier. She read the interior message of one with reindeer on the cover and decided they would do. Perusing the wide variety of individual cards, she chose more personal cards for her parents and other family members. One with a mistletoe sprig on the front and a soft gold trim caught her attention. She read the message inside and smiled, then tucked the card in with the others. *Perfect.*

Back in the produce aisle, Cassidy caught up with Gwen, who noted the box and selection of cards. "You're certainly getting an early start this year."

"I have work right up until the holiday. It's better to get them done and mailed."

"You're right." The two headed for the checkout lanes.

Stepping out of her bedroom, Brenna quietly shut the door. Out in the living room, she curled up on the couch and checked the time. It was only just after seven.

"Did Kevin already go to bed?"

She uncurled a little and looked up at James walking through from the kitchen, his hands filled with a plate of leftovers and a glass of milk. "He's going to lose a lot of sleep going back to Michigan tonight, so I suggested the nap."

He leaned on the couch back and met her gaze. "Been a pretty cool weekend."

She could not agree but nodded her head anyway.

"You just gonna sit out here and read?"

"I need to keep an eye on the time. His plane's at midnight."

"You should've come with us yesterday to Groveland Park."

She shook her head. "It was a guys' day out. But I'm glad you all got to go. It gave me a chance to do some things around here."

"Got a phone call from work, didn't you?"

She was a little surprised at his intuition. "Yes, they've rearranged production again. I have to be on the set at six tomorrow."

"Well, it won't be for much longer," he said. "Guess you're ready for it to be over. Have you decided what you're doing next?"

"No, I haven't." She paused, then asked, "What would you like to do?"

James blinked. "You really want to know?" She nodded. "I'd really like to stay here. At least until I finish school."

"Mount Clemens is much smaller, more personal," she said, playing devil's advocate.

"Yeah, I know, but five years in one place has been a long time."

Brenna considered that and realized he was right. "I hadn't thought about that."

"I don't mean to make anything difficult for you, but I really want to stay here."

"Kevin would want what's best for you," she assured him.

"Is he going to move here, or are we moving there?"

She was taken aback. Thinking it had been only a preliminary discussion they'd had on Thursday night, she hadn't expected Kevin to bring the boys into things so soon. "He told you?"

"I told you, you should have come to the park. That's all we talked about." James straightened. "He wants us to help convince you to go to Michigan as soon as *Time Trails* is over."

Brenna frowned, feeling a rush of anger that Kevin would put either of her children in such a position. "We honestly haven't even discussed it fully ourselves. I'm sorry he put you boys in the middle of this." She laid her hand on James' forearm where it rested on the back of the couch.

James pressed his lips tightly together. "You guys gotta do what you gotta do."

"I'm still glad you told me what you want. That matters to me," Brenna promised.

"Is it going to mess things up?"

She shook her head emphatically. "It will not." *Certainly no more than they're messed up now.* "No matter what happens, you must never believe that." He tilted his head, and she wondered if she had said too much.

"All right," he offered cautiously.

She accepted his kiss on her cheek and then watched him as he left the room. With a sigh of misery, she went back to the bedroom and spied Kevin rolling over on the bed. "Kevin?"

"Yes?'" His voice was filled with sleep.

"Did you mention to the boys that we were discussing where to live after *Time Trails*?"

"Yeah."

He sat up and flipped on the bedside lamp. She averted her eyes from his naked chest, trying to give the impression that the light had startled her. She turned back. "We didn't decide."

"Will you come home for Christmas? Bring the boys, and we can hash it all out as a family."

Resignation weighed heavily on her as she gave in. "All right."

"You look like you could use a hug," he said, patting the mattress beside him.

Brenna knew she did, too, but she looked at the bed and shook her head. "Get some sleep. You've got a plane in just a few hours."

She remained as still as possible while he studied her, not moving until he reached up and turned off the light. She closed the door and returned to the living room.

In the corner of the couch, she pulled a pillow across her lap, feeling the rest of the cushions hugging her back. She closed her eyes, just for a moment, sipping in a startled breath as the memory of Cassidy's scent suddenly seemed to surround her.

You should have just told him you wouldn't come for Christmas. Burying her face in the pillow, Brenna stifled her groan of self-disgust.

Chapter 28

Head down, Brenna walked into the soundstage, trying to compose herself despite the early hour. Rachelle's smooth voice interrupted her progress.

"How was your holiday?"

Looking up into the friendly face, she offered a tight smile. "Hmm?"

Rachelle blinked and lifted a hand to Brenna's arm. "Are you all right? What time did your plane come in?"

"I didn't... Kevin... His plane left at twelve-thirty this morning." She rubbed her face briskly with both hands.

"Kevin came for a visit?" Rachelle's grin held a hint of a leer, and she elbowed Brenna, patting her on the arm. "Well, now I know why you look like you hardly slept."

I did hardly sleep, Brenna thought, so she nodded. In truth, the complex tensions she had struggled with for four days had more to do with her current exhaustion. Since Thursday night she had tried several times to broach any of the many subjects she and Kevin needed to discuss. She had found herself agonizing over word choice before she even opened her mouth. It had been painful, exhausting, and in the end, she had not said anything. He was on his way to Michigan, and she had even found a way to avoid giving him a goodbye kiss. She had never before depended so much on her ability to act and yet at the same time despised it so much.

"Let's get some drinks," Rachelle suggested.

"Please," Brenna breathed. They walked along, following the faint smell of coffee. "What did you and Jacques do?"

"We took Rose home for my family's traditional blow-out — all the trimmings. Even my brother and sister-in-law flew in from Seattle."

Rachelle had clearly enjoyed herself so Brenna consciously brightened. "That's wonderful. Are you going back for Christmas?"

"Probably."

They both grabbed Styrofoam cups and filled them from the big coffeemaker. Brenna added Half and Half to hers, while Rachelle slugged it back black.

"So, where's everyone meeting?"

"Your office set."

"Why there?"

"Personally, I like the cushions," Rachelle commented, then shrugged. "Beats me. That's just where Victor said he wanted to run the meeting."

"Branch is leading the meeting?" Brenna wondered why the producer would be leading a pre-dawn meeting usually only called by the director.

"That's what he said," Rachelle confirmed, dispensing more coffee for herself and sipping at it.

Brenna followed the brunette to the office set. Many of the rest of the cast were already assembled. She exchanged grins with Terry, who sat on the desk, legs crossed at the ankles and dangling above the floor. "Morning, Terry."

Brown smiled broadly. "You look good."

Brenna's eyes dipped in acknowledgment. *Apparently a smile and coffee go a long way toward repairing my appearance.*

A semi-regular actor who filled a junior officer role darted in past her and sat on the floor along one of the couches, his muscle shirt showing off where he had spent the holiday weekend — on the beach getting sunburned. He grinned at her. She nodded back, her lips curling. "Hurt much?"

"Nah."

Scanning the rest of the room, Brenna considered where to sit. Legs spread as he sat casually, Sean Durham caught her eye and changed his position, freeing up a section of cushion beside him. Brenna shook her head.

Rachelle left her side at that moment and pounced on the space, falling into Durham's lap with a come-hither growl. He wrapped his arms around her and gave her a staged kiss as nearly everyone laughed.

Brenna however could not, assailed by the reminder of her own acting over the weekend. Instead she took advantage of attention being elsewhere and moved to the upper level, sitting on the stretch of couch under the window.

With a silent nod, she acknowledged Chapman on the other couch, sipping from his own coffee. He offered her a smile which she couldn't find in herself to return. Cheron and Durham finally sat side by side.

Shoes clicked on the bare concrete just outside the set. Branch and co-producer, sometimes writer, Lonny Nickel stepped up onto the set flooring. "Good morning."

Nickel was younger than Victor, but not much, maybe only forty, with curly black hair and a scarecrow-like build instead of a paunch. His tweed suit jacket sported large patches on each elbow. Brenna wondered why he would cultivate such a professorial look.

Just behind them, excusing herself, Cassidy slipped past, her arrival snaring Brenna's attention. She drank in the sight with a hunger she struggled to suppress. She wore a soft blue cotton pullover sweater, slightly off her right shoulder, over form-fitting cotton workout pants and athletic shoes. Brenna took in the whole and then, over the rim of the coffee cup, directed her gaze up to the other woman's face.

Cassidy looked tired, and Brenna suspected she had slept just as little she had over the last four days.

"Well, looks like we're all— Wait, where's Rich?" Branch took the chair behind the desk, while Nickel set another one for himself next to the producer.

Meanwhile, Brenna fixated on the sight of Cassidy crossing through the set, both pleased and anxious about the woman's direction — toward her. Her breath caught in her throat as their gazes met for the first time since the parade. She put her coffee to her lips to hide their trembling.

At that moment, Rich Paulson bounded in. His lean frame filled the doorway, then sagged dramatically, allowing the man to fold up on the floor in a staged fall.

The low murmuring conversations became stunned silence. Paulson rolled over onto his back and panted as if he had been running miles. "Freeway backed up. I just got out of the car and ran."

Sean grabbed the cushion next to Rachelle and pitched it at him. "Ham!"

"Salad!" responded Paulson, rolling to his feet. "Good morning, everyone!"

"We need to get started. There's a lot to cover."

At Branch's words, Cassidy spun and sat down where she stood, curling her body on the carpeting to the left of Sean and Rachelle's couch. When Brenna looked away from the blonde she discovered Chapman looking at her. She pointedly looked away, focusing on the executives.

"First off, I've appointed Lonny to be the on-set producer for the remainder of the season. Cameron has moved over to work start-up for a new fall series." Brenna grimaced. Even when she was diverting the press from printing anything about the incident between Will and Cameron, she had not expected that would resolve the problem.

There was a murmur of reaction among the others. She glanced down to see Cassidy's back stiffen, as the woman tried to cover a tension that made Brenna's fingers itch to rub it away. She did not blame Cassidy for the move, though others might. Brenna had a fleeting awareness that as recently as a year ago, she would have been one of them. All she wanted now was to hold Cassidy, protect her. She sighed.

"Brenna?"

She realized she apparently hadn't been quiet enough, as Victor looked in her direction. "Hot coffee," she explained. "Sorry."

Sean boldly asked what was on everyone's mind. "Is this because of the fight?"

Victor frowned as he shook his head. "We decided the new series needed Cameron's special touch." There was a "company line" quality to his voice. No one would say differently.

Brenna nodded. While on the surface the cover story protected Chapman and Palassis, she knew it also protected Cassidy, who had been at the center of their argument in a very demeaning way.

Two runners came in. Victor waved them over and instructed them to distribute the scripts they carried.

"These are the scenes being shot tomorrow," he explained, as everyone received one set. "We're able to go with 264 as planned. Its working title is *Crash*."

Brenna caught Victor's nod to Cassidy, who dropped her gaze to her folded hands on her knee. The Raycreek/Hanssen script. Brenna inhaled and exhaled, trying to figure out why she felt so uneasy about it. After all, she had helped Cassidy with some of the rewrite.

"You'll get the rest of the pages after we've cleared them through set production, as we finalize the filming schedule. It's a little last minute..." *Certainly not uncommon*, Brenna thought ruefully, recalling other scripts that had been extensively rewritten even as they were filming. "...so check the call board every morning. We've also got more newspaper, magazine, and wire folks coming out. As their credentials clear, they'll be sent to you."

"So, no hanging out in our undies?" Sean pouted. "Damn, I was thinking of rehearsing *The Full Monty* with the guys in the back lot."

Branch let the laughter die naturally. "*Crash* is a character piece, limited action for most of you, but there are some key moments early in the script. Let's read." Since most of the cast had not yet seen the script, several flipped pages to finding the teaser. "The director is coming in after lunch. He's checking out the sets right now."

Everyone flipped back to the start, and the scene began to unfold as they tried out the dialogue for the first time.

"Interesting opening," Will said neutrally, drawing everyone's attention to him for the first time since the reading began. He had not had a single line in the teaser.

Victor nodded. "Practice. Read. Walk the sets. We'll reconvene here after lunch, around one."

The meeting broke up quickly after he exited with Nickel. As Cassidy was standing, with help from Rich, Brenna and Will intersected as their way down from upstage.

Brenna eyed Will warily. "How was your Thanksgiving?"

"Just fine. I'm really looking forward to this, though."

Moving alongside Cassidy, Brenna vented her ire on Chapman. "We had to work pretty hard to recover from the mess you caused."

"It's all right," Cassidy said softly, touching Brenna's arm.

She looked at it a long moment before looking back up at Will. "She's more forgiving than I can be."

"I guess that's why I'm getting involved with her and you're not." His expression was significant and cutting.

As Brenna opened her mouth to respond, Rich stepped forward, landing on her foot. "Hey!" Brenna glared up at him.

"Sorry," he offered blithely. "It's crowded here." He looked at Cassidy. "Why don't we all sit down somewhere quiet?"

Catching sight of the other actors watching the four of them with curiosity, Brenna stepped out of the group. "I've got some things to do," she said. "Good luck." She looked from Cassidy to Will; he nodded.

"I'd like to talk to you later," he requested civilly.

"Fine." She strode away, the script rolled in her fist.

Cassidy watched her go, then turned on Chapman. "Why do you have to hurt her like that?"

"She's not hurt, she's confused."

"You baited her."

"She doesn't know what she wants," Will answered.

He met her gaze squarely, and realization hit her. Coolly, she responded, "It's her life, her decision to make, not yours."

Rich looked confused. "Cassidy, I thought—"

"He knows. Don't you, Will? How long?"

"Give me some credit. I have a little experience knowing Brenna's moods."

"And you use that to go around manipulating people?" Cassidy spat. "Have you been enjoying your game?"

"It created a united front, didn't it? I saw you two go off after my fight with Palassis. So, when did it happen? This past weekend?"

Cassidy ignored that. "She thinks you hate her for dumping you. You've been kicking around here like an angry mule."

Chapman sighed and looked away for a moment. "She has been seeking something for a long time. I wasn't it. Shortly after you arrived, when she went home during the hiatus, she was scared. I didn't expect her to come back married. She was so hungry for affection, for approval," he said with a quiet pain that caught Cassidy off guard. "That was when I realized how strongly she was reacting to you. I also realized I'd seen it before with..." He trailed off, took a deep breath. "With someone else. She just didn't understand what her body was telling her. She needed a push so I provided it, to let her feel you needing her. "

"*You* pushed?"

"Bren needs to feel needed."

"She *is.*"

"I'm glad you two finally connected. Her tension was going to kill her."

"It's not that simple. She's married."

"Yes, she is. She's cleared some sort of hurdle, though. She readily and openly defended you just now."

"She did look pretty upset when she walked out of here," Rich mused. "Maybe you should go talk to her," he suggested to Cassidy.

"I promised her I wouldn't pursue things. I won't hurt her." She frowned at Will, pondering his proclamation that he had purposely done things to get Brenna and her together. *Was he always acting?* She didn't know anymore. He seemed sincere. Still, it wouldn't hurt to issue a clear warning. "Don't push her again."

Abruptly, Will grinned. "Deal."

"Thank you." Cassidy leaned up and impulsively kissed his cheek.

In the shadows off set, Brenna watched the trio, unable to hear, but fully able to see Cassidy's expression transforming from anger to relief. Brenna caught her breath at the kiss. *What prompted that?* When Will hugged Cassidy and led her off the set in the opposite direction, she leaned hard on the wall and sagged down.

"Brenna?"

She quickly straightened. "Rich. I'm sorry, didn't see you."

"It's all right. Where are you headed?"

"My trailer, I guess."

"All right. See you later."

Chapter 29

Brenna was exhausted. The last reporter finally left her alone, and she signed out, already imagining the bath waiting at home. She had tried to avoid the set itself most of the day. Unfortunately, each time she got a few minutes away, she got another call to report back — for a lighting check or a technical sound check or an interview where she had to force herself to smile and be cheerful. Each time she passed the set where Cassidy had practiced with Chapman, her heart ached a little more.

"Brenna?"

Her head jerked up, and she stopped abruptly at the sight of Cassidy leaning against the wall ahead of her. "I was just going home."

"I'm sorry. I didn't mean to startle you."

Brenna noted Cassidy looked worn. "Um...how did your rehearsals go?" she asked, drawing in a breath to steady her nerves.

"It seems to be working." Brenna nodded, too tired to do anything other than register the words. Cassidy started to reach for her, Brenna even swayed toward her, then they both pulled back. "Did Will talk to you?"

Brenna shook her head. She had sidestepped him a dozen times until, she hoped, he had given up trying to talk to her. "The reporters kept me too busy."

"I'm sorry." Cassidy watched Brenna for a moment. "I should go."

Brenna looked up at her, her feelings a jumble of loss and hurt and frustration and want. Cassidy looked around at the empty area before taking a step forward. Brenna started to take a step back, then stopped. "Cass?"

"Yes?"

"I wish..."

Cassidy enfolded Brenna in a hug. She closed her eyes at the wish-fulfilling contact of their bodies. "Shh." Cassidy rubbed her hands over Brenna's tense shoulders and back. "I'm sorry about the parade. I didn't plan that. You wanted space...I didn't give it to you."

Cassidy's voice stumbled to a halt as Brenna wrapped both arms suddenly around Cassidy's back, accepting what she could no longer deny. After a long moment, Brenna's voice filled the silence. "No. Not...I couldn't...do..." Exhaustion was shattering her thoughts. She breathed in but hiccupped on an aborted sob. "I'm going to file for divorce." Brenna blinked back tears, searching the taller woman's gaze for comfort for her soul.

Cassidy leaned back and lifted Brenna's trembling chin. "What happened?"

The years of moral precepts ingrained in Brenna's upbringing were hard to overcome, but she forced out a whisper through the lump of propriety lodged in her throat. "I realized that I love you." Cassidy's arms were raising tingles where they rested on her hips. "I don't know what to do..." It was terrifying and she wanted to hide, but the heat of their touching skin and the feel of Cassidy's heart thudding under her ear fueled her courage. "Help..."

Brenna's words were a soothing balm. Cassidy bowed her head, and tears trickled down her cheeks. Will had told her during practice that Brenna would likely come around when she saw Cassidy with him in the love scenes — in the same way he had noted Cassidy's reactions when Brenna had been romantically involved as in her role as Susan Jakes.

He had not yet spoken with Brenna, not explained his actions. Nor had they begun filming. Cassidy was elated. Brenna had not been prodded into making this move.

She pulled Brenna into her body, rejoicing in the comforting touch of their curves melding once again. There was a half-gasp, half-sob from either or both of them. It didn't matter. Their mingled body heat intoxicated Cassidy as she moved her lips away from Brenna's and down the soft column of her throat. She felt the woman tremble and weaken in her arms and murmured, "I've got you."

Brenna lifted her eyes, and Cassidy saw pain and fear slide away, replaced by wonder which mirrored her own. She caressed Brenna's cheek with shaking fingers before returning to the soft mouth for more absorbing kisses.

In their groping, Brenna slid her hands under Cassidy's sweater, warm skin meeting her fingertips. She leaned back and closed her eyes, luxuriating in the sensations as Cassidy's head fell to her shoulder, and she stroked silk skin and taut muscles.

Cassidy groaned with pleasure but shook her head, lifting it to pierce Brenna with darkening eyes. "Don't..." she gasped again as Brenna's innocent touch sent a bolt of desire directly to her groin, "don't do anything you'll regret."

Brenna swallowed and stepped back. The separation was painful, more painful than she could have imagined. "How?"

"We'll do something...impulsive, and you'll wake up afterward, hating yourself...and me."

Brenna nibbled her lip. "That's what happened actually."

"When?"

"Kevin. I... He... We went to bed. I...couldn't think of anything...I...was dead afterward. Cass, I can't do that again."

"Then we wait." She grasped a trembling hand, letting Brenna lead the way as they left the set.

Out in the late fall air in the parking lot, the brisk wind helped settle Brenna's nerves. "Time to go, hmm?" Her car was closest.

Cassidy leaned against the SUV with Brenna, studying her face in the lights of the parking lot. "It is after midnight."

"Do you need to get home to Ryan?" Brenna asked.

"I should," Cassidy admitted, but she reached out for Brenna's hand in the darkness. "But I'm kind of in a daze right now."

"Me too," Brenna admitted. "I can't believe I'm doing this."

"Why did you change your mind? What exactly happened this weekend?" Cassidy asked earnestly, reaching out as the auburn-haired woman's chin dipped. "Brenna?"

"After we got back from camping, I told myself it was...the moment, the change of pace, simply getting to see you in another role. I don't know. Kevin called, and I resolved to work on things with him."

"So you have been having problems?"

"Yes...no...or at least I didn't acknowledge them. We've been finding more and more reasons to have separate lives. I haven't been to Mount Clemens in a while and he hasn't been out here in almost a year."

"What brought him to L.A. over Thanksgiving?"

"He thinks we're drifting apart." Brenna sighed. "I lied. I said we were fine."

Cassidy forced herself to be Brenna's friend first, though the ache in her arms was fierce to hold the woman, protect her from anything that upset her so. "Why lie?"

"It's supposed to be what I aspire to — a husband, two kids..."

"That's June Cleaver, not Brenna Lanigan."

"It's what I was raised to believe."

"What about your work?" Cassidy prompted.

Brenna shook her head. "I'd have to stop acting." She moved away from Cassidy and stepped carefully into the breeze that pushed her hair from her face as she hugged her arms around her chest. "I can't do that. Acting is all I've wanted to do since I was a teenager. And I'm good at it."

"You are. So is that why you want the divorce, so you don't have to give up acting? You thought you loved him once. Wasn't that why you married?"

Brenna frowned. "Kevin...made me feel...desirable when I didn't feel it from anyone else."

Damn, maybe Will actually had it right. Somehow he had managed a clear view the rest of them never got — of Brenna, the series, even her. She watched Brenna formulate her answer. The look of serious concentration created as she furrowed her brow and covered her mouth was hopelessly endearing.

"He's the perfect husband."

"Obviously not."

Finally her arms dropped, and Cassidy could see Brenna's narrow shoulders square resolutely. "I'd been alone for almost six years. Kevin cares for the boys. My mother likes him." She corrected herself. "No. Mother loves him. He and I apparently grew up across town from one another. She knew his mother through some civic organization back in the Sixties. When I was home on hiatus, she encouraged me to meet him."

Brenna fell silent.

"In the beginning he was right there, every time I turned around. Now..." She sighed, pausing as she assessed her feelings honestly. "I feel more like it's not him I fell in love with, but...the idea of his stability, the support." She groaned and covered her face with her palms. "Does that make any sense?"

"It does." Cassidy stepped away from the Mountaineer and put her hands on Brenna's shoulders, drawing the woman's hands from her face. "Still, it amazes me that Will was right."

"Chapman? What does he have to do with anything?"

Cassidy's lips curled in a grin as she leaned her forehead against Brenna's temple. "He's been trying to put us together for months."

Brenna opened her mouth to fume, but Cassidy's smile took away her sense of having been caught in a sting. "So it was all an act."

"No. He still hates what's happening in the show," Cassidy revealed. "He just didn't see why it had to ruin us, too."

"Incredible. So, he thinks Nickel will be an improvement?"

"I didn't ask him that. But, from what I discovered about Cameron, he certainly has to be." Cassidy frowned as she recalled the tableau she had walked in on in Cameron's office the previous week.

Brenna observed the frown and prodded, "What happened?"

"I'd been at Paul's office, getting the changes approved to *Crash*," Cassidy started. "I went to Cameron — to let him know how we'd changed his script and to give him a piece of my mind." Brenna smiled at that. "I found him on his couch getting a blowjob from some teeny-bopper."

"Oh my God." Brenna covered her mouth in surprise.

"I think I was in love with some facade...or dream, too," Cassidy considered. "I'd known he was...somewhat on the edge. I used to find it...exciting. And God, he did help me get away from Mitch..."

Brenna put a steadying hand on Cassidy's arm as the woman drifted back to an obviously painful time. "What exactly caused your divorce?" she asked.

As if quoting from a brief, Cassidy looked off blankly and recited, "Extreme psychological distress from physical and emotional domination."

The tone and words — so neutral, so clinical — scared Brenna. Muscles tensed, she remembered Cassidy's conversation with Mitch on the phone. *And she agreed to meet him in a park? Dear God.* "You were abused?" Brenna grasped Cassidy around the waist. "And this all happened while you were struggling to adjust to *Time Trails?*"

Cassidy nodded. "It...intensified after Chris became a recurring character. My counselor said Mitch was threatened by my success. My previous roles had been guest appearances. He thought if I really hooked up with a series as a regular that I would get away from him. Lucky for me, that's exactly what happened.

"I hadn't even seen it as abuse. He's a lot like my father — likes things 'just so', very definite about what he wants from life, and a wife and family. Mitch kept saying Ryan needed more of me, which is completely true." She took a deep breath. "When I was supposed to return home on the weekends, Cameron started finding reasons to keep me in L.A. — extra filming, a publicity event, anything. I slept on his couch for about three weeks. Then, well, he asked me once and I..."

"That's how your affair began, when you were at your most vulnerable." Brenna shook her head. "You don't have to explain." The story was disconcertingly familiar. The details were different, but both of them had felt trapped by their situations and someone had miraculously appeared to resolve everything. "So, we're both here now, I guess...losing our minds again."

Cassidy felt immense relief flood her body as she lifted Brenna's cheek in her palm. She shook her head. "Maybe it's finding our hearts for real this time. I know that I haven't been able to talk as honestly about all of these things with anyone else."

"The fact that we're both women doesn't bother you?"

Cassidy shook her head. "It surprised me, Bren, but...I'm...not unfamiliar with it." She hesitated at Brenna's surprise, then quickly went on. "When we were apart, I missed you in the space of just a few hours. Seeing you at the parade, knowing you were close but untouchable...I was hoping you'd find me today on our way out." She smiled and took a step closer, reaching out to catch Brenna's hand. "You did." When Brenna's gaze met hers, she said gently, "This might be unfamiliar territory for you, but you're here too."

Brenna's throat moved in an uneasy swallow. "I...I've never had feelings like this." Cassidy felt Brenna's fingers shifting in her hand, turning around and intertwining with her own fingers. "I've never been distracted day and night by thoughts of someone other than the one I was with."

Nodding — the words conveyed her own feelings, too — Cassidy tugged until Brenna was snug against her chest, the softness of her body warm against her own. Their hearts pounded together. She lowered her head slightly and poured her feelings out over Brenna's skin, her lips and cheeks, meeting her eyes, inhaling the sweat-sweetened scent of her hair. She returned to the soft satin of bow-like lips, delving into the sweet recesses of Brenna's mouth.

Tentative fists at first, Brenna's hands soon opened, caressing Cassidy's body, conceding to the unexpected passion between them. As Cassidy held her face with a tender finger, nuzzling and kissing the rapidly fluttering pulse point under Brenna's chin, Brenna gasped with spiraling need matching Cassidy's own. "Oh God, Cass, I want you." Brenna's fingertips worked beneath Cassidy's top, reaching the bare skin of her stomach, and she unleashed a soft predatory growl in Cassidy's ear. "Now."

Cassidy's stomach muscles clenched in sexual anticipation. The effect threw off her balance, and she shifted to find a way to make contact with Brenna's bare skin. The passion continued lapping at their awareness. They exchanged nipping kisses, chased one another's tongues, and swallowed one another's groans.

Stumbling against Brenna's car, they were abruptly reminded that they were standing in plain sight in the Pinnacle parking lot. "Oh God," Cassidy stuttered, trying to regain control. "We have to stop."

"What?"

Brenna's passionate outrage would have made Cassidy laugh if she, too, had not also been suffering the destabilizing effects of interruption. Blowing out a deep, regretful breath, Cassidy calmed herself and stroked Brenna's arms to soothe her as well. "It's just the place. I do want to make love with you, but here and now is probably not the brightest idea."

Brenna nuzzled into her. Cassidy felt her heart expand at the clear signals that she was receiving from the other woman. Stroking Brenna's hair and back, she reveled in the sudden feeling of protection. She had always been the submissive one in her relationships, used only for someone else's benefit. The men she had dated called it gallantry, but she had suffered it as domination. No way would she not go slowly with this more precious person. "Bren," she leaned back. "It's late."

"I don't want to go."

"I know."

"Cass, I want to see where this goes." Brenna's gaze followed the stroking of her hands on Cassidy's arms, upward and inward along her shoulders, then down her torso. "I don't know how, but I...I'll learn."

"It will be perfect because it will be with you...but not tonight. We have work again in just a few hours."

Brenna's hands stilled on Cassidy's chest. Slowly she nodded in agreement with some inner thought. When she met Cassidy's gaze, she asked, "Would you like to come over to the house this weekend? On Saturday?"

Brenna's passion was amazing; Cassidy felt it washing over her in waves — from her darkening blue eyes and from the sensuality of her body's caress. "That's a tempting offer." Brenna's hands moved under Cassidy's top again, the touch making her groan in renewing passion. "Too tempting." She hesitated, gently tugging Brenna's hands free. "I don't want regrets. If we rush this, that could happen."

"The whole day together." Brenna pressed her case. "What about another climb?"

"Camping again?"

"No. There's walls at the gym."

"So we would just get together, work out?"

"You could bring Ryan over. I could make dinner."

Cassidy loved how easily Brenna included Ryan in making plans. "What would he do?"

"I have a spare room at the house where the boys have all their play space, video games, television. I...don't have coloring books, or ...well, there's my sons' old primary reader books."

Her grin widening as Brenna considered turning her teen sons' space into a children's playroom for an afternoon of family-like togetherness, Cassidy realized that the depths between them were growing. Since she didn't want to rush their physical joining, a day surrounded by their children sounded like a proper start. "All right." Brenna smiled, and Cassidy kissed the curvaceous lips. "Our first date." She stepped back and opened Brenna's car door, holding Brenna's hand as she got into the Mountaineer.

Their hands met at the belt catch. Cassidy's and Brenna's happiness bubbled up into a shared laugh and another kiss.

"Drive safely," Cassidy wished as she pulled back.

"You, too."

With reluctance, Cassidy stepped back and closed the car door. The SUV engine roared to life. Holding herself perfectly still to preserve the moment, Cassidy reveled in the heated ball of joy ricocheting around inside her as she followed the vehicle's progress until Brenna was out of sight.

The house was dark when Brenna entered. Turning off the front porch light, she flipped on the foyer light and dropped her coat and purse on the small table by the door. The wall clock over the kitchen entry showed it was after two. She listened for activity in the house and heard nothing.

Keeping as quiet as possible, Brenna stepped out of her shoes and picked them up. Combing her fingers through her hair, she retreated to the master bedroom. There she turned on the light and shut the door to the hallway. She reached for the button on her pants and tugged them off her hips, leaning back to rest on the side of the bed as she pulled them over her feet.

Brenna rubbed her feet for a minute, mind wandering over the time she had done the same for Cassidy. She had been on her feet all day and then stayed in costume for the charity party afterward. Back in her trailer after things broke up, an exhausted Cassidy had fallen backward onto her small couch. Brenna had tugged her shoes off and provided a mini massage. With the clarity of hindsight, she realized the tingling she'd felt in her fingers during that incident had been lust, not nerves. Just like tonight. When it became clear they would be embarking on an intimate relationship, the same searing tingling had returned, and Brenna had become giddy with desire.

Brenna was not a sexual novice; she knew they had been engaging in foreplay. She wanted to make love with Cassidy, but from a practical standpoint, she had no idea what sex with a woman would actually be like.

Pulling off her clothes, she hung her blouse over the back of a chair to air and then lay back on her bed, tangling in her sheets, aware of their coolness against her bare skin. Overhead the fan's slow rotation lulled her, and she laced her fingers over her stomach. The light touch on her abdomen and the faint sensation of moving air over her bare nipples made her stomach quiver, much as it had when Cassidy had kissed her in the tent. Tasting the passion that awaited her fantasy, Brenna lifted a hand to her right breast and circled the nipple, closing her eyes to focus on the images in her head.

Come on, Brenna. You have a fabulous imagination. Just imagine it. Those words of advice from her acting coach two decades earlier rippled through her mind, inviting her to find her soul.

First, she found Cassidy's eyes. As Hanssen or off the set, her gaze always compelled Brenna to meet it. The eyes were not a pure blue, but swirls of blue and white, like a cloud-filled sky. Sometimes they were colorless, giving Brenna the impression that she could fall into them and drown in a soul as wide and as deep as any ocean.

Brenna imagined those eyes heating with passion as they drifted down to watch her caressing herself. She brought her other hand up, lifting her left breast and pinching the nipple between forefinger and thumb.

When Cassidy's head dropped, Brenna would see her hair falling forward around her face. Without the stage lights, the strands were more the color of honey than flax. She knew the texture was soft and fine, imagined the strands brushing against her chest and tangled in her fingers, as Cassidy lowered her head further still.

In vivid panorama, her imagination weighted her down with Cassidy's body, their breasts pressed together as they had been in the tent, the smooth legs tangled with her own. This time when the strong thigh nudged between her legs, she did not protest. The kisses she remembered so well caused her to arch into the phantasm above her, the sheets tangled tightly around her thighs and groin as she pulled at her nipples — which were swelling and rising in response to the attentions being paid to them by Cassidy's mouth.

Groin throbbing, Brenna arched spasmodically. She moved one hand away from her breasts, searching out the ache, knowing what she needed.

She started quivering even before her fingers reached the patch of hair covering her mound. Her fingertips slid through the evidence of arousal on her inner thighs, and when she finally parted her folds, she bit her lip to keep from taking herself over the edge immediately. She ran the tip of her tongue over her lips, tasting the perspiration already gathering from her effort to go slowly and fully explore the sensations.

She curled onto her side, drawing her knees up as she moved both hands to her silken heat. She imagined Cassidy against her back, arms securely wrapped around her. She imagined both their hands finding her center, and finally, stifling her gasp of reaction, she orgasmed. Lightly stroking herself as the sensations ebbed, Brenna sighed. "Cassidy."

The whisper passed her lips as she burrowed under the sheet, a satisfied smile curling her lips, then drifted off to sleep for the two hours that remained before she would have to get up again.

Cassidy knocked at the front door to the Talbot home. Lou answered it, still tying a robe around himself. "I'll take Ryan," she said.

Lou waved her off. "Leave him sleeping. We've got a change of clothes for him for school."

"I shouldn't."

"Shoulda thought of that three hours ago when you called and said you were on your way."

"Something held me up," Cassidy said quietly.

"I bet."

"I just started a pretty heavy script. Do you want me to arrange to bring him to the set after school, so you don't have to keep him overnight?"

"That set is no place for a five-year-old," Lou remarked. "I saw last week's broadcast. That farce...what was it? *Brains and Brawn*? Sick. You really want your son to see you acting like that?"

Cassidy blinked. "Excuse me?" The body-swapping script had been a fun one to do. As well as enlightening her to Brenna's physical touch, experienced as Commander Jakes had consoled the body-switched officers — her and Durham's characters. She always enjoyed working with Sean, and helping him expand on his character had been a creative challenge. She wondered exactly what Lou's problem with the story had been. Maybe it was her kiss with Rachelle's Luria...*Hmm*...Cassidy shook her head. "I don't write the scripts."

"Ah, so that makes it okay?"

"It's just acting, Lou."

"Kids don't see it that way. My kids don't." He added, "Yours didn't."

Cassidy lifted a brow. "Excuse me?"

"Don't think I believe that line Gwen told me about Ryan misinterpreting things. You aren't just acting."

"Whatever it is you're talking about, it's not your business," she pointed out.

"No, but it is Mitch's."

Cassidy inhaled. She wasn't sure why he was doing this now. "You don't like me. I get it. Give me Ryan and I'll go away."

He remained an obstacle, meeting her eyes for a long assessing moment. She felt the beginnings of real panic. "Please."

Lou Talbot finally stepped back. "Get him, then go, so I can go back to sleep."

She moved quickly to the back bedroom where Gwen typically put Ryan down on the trundle bed in Chance's room. She collected him and his school bag, cradling his sleeping form against her chest and hurrying out the door. She stood on the stoop with Ryan in her arms and watched as Lou shut the door. The front porch light was turned off, leaving her in the darkness in more ways than one. Obviously talking openly to Gwen had not been a very good idea. Resigned, she tucked Ryan in the car and quickly drove the short distance home.

As she collected him again, he stirred. "Shh, go back to sleep," she whispered. With the ease of practice, she wrangled her key into the deadbolt and let them into the house. She walked through the dim hallway and placed him on his bed. He was already in pajamas, the pair she left with Gwen each week in case he had to sleep over.

She sat on the floor of her son's bedroom for a long time after she tucked the covers up to his chin and smoothed the hair off his forehead, just watching him sleep. She hoped that, at least tomorrow, she could manage to get Ryan to and from school and then keep him at the set with a minimum of fuss.

Standing, Cassidy glanced up at the small clock on his dresser. It was almost three in the morning. With a stretch that was only slightly successful in loosening her muscles, Cassidy crossed the hall to her bedroom and pulled off her shoes. Stripping down to her underwear, she crawled into bed. Cassidy spread herself across the sheets, and her body, well-trained by hundreds of nights of knowing she would only get a couple hours of sleep, was unconscious before she had finished curling around a pillow, imagining Brenna's warm body instead of the cool linen.

Chapter 30

The next day, during a quick break from shooting, Cassidy ran to fetch Ryan from pre-school. Traffic conspired to make her return to the studio much later than she had hoped. A small backpack on over his tan coveralls and blue shirt, Ryan jogged alongside her long strides as she crossed the lot toward the tutor's trailer.

A young girl scampered down the path. Cassidy knew Sandy Tillman was fourteen, though with blond hair styled in pigtails, she looked much younger. She had a recurring role as Lilibeth, the daughter of one of *Time Trails'* base administrators. While her father frequently challenged the existence of the program, she was a proponent of the program and planned to grow up to be a Time Squad member.

"Mrs. G said you have—" The girl charged directly for Ryan. "This is your son? Cool!" She skidded to a halt as they all met on the walking path. "Hi, my name's Sandy."

Ryan looked up at his mother. "It's all right, Ryan. This is Sandy Tillman. She works with me sometimes."

Satisfied, her son looked back at Sandy. "I'm Ryan."

She looked at the paper bag in his hands. "What's that?"

"His dinner," Cassidy supplied. "We were running a little late."

"My shooting managed to speed up a little bit for the afternoon session, so I got a long dinner break. Ryan here is going to help me get out of homework, aren'cha?"

"Where's Mrs. Grinaldi?"

"Mrs. G's in Trailer Fourteen. Come on, I'll lead the way." Sandy offered her hand to Ryan, who looked at his mother uncomfortably.

"It's all right."

"Yeah. There's cool stuff. I've got my school books, but there's games and toys, too."

Ryan took Sandy's hand, and with Cassidy following behind, the trio crossed to Trailer Fourteen.

A nearby trailer door swung open, and Rachelle Cheron appeared on her steps. "Hey, Cass, glad to see you made it back. Coming to dinner?"

"In a minute. I've got to get Ryan settled first."

"Ryan?" Then the woman spotted Cassidy's son. "Oh, hey there!" She waved. "Meet you in the commissary later." Still in costume, she crossed the lot at a fast walk.

Cassidy turned to see her meeting an extra who was out of costume. Once inside the tutor's trailer, Cassidy shook hands with Karen Grinaldi. "Thank you for doing this."

"No problem. Kindergarten?"

"Pre-K."

"So, no homework."

"He usually stays with a neighbor after school, but some changes occurred recently and she can't do it any more."

"I've worked as a set tutor for a dozen years. Ten right here at Pinnacle." They turned to see Ryan had settled with Sandy on a rug near a set of shelves. The girl had pulled down a copy of Candyland which Ryan had excitedly pointed out.

"I know this one," he was saying.

"Looks like they'll get on fine." Mrs. Grinaldi set Ryan's dinner on a nearby table. "I'll get him to sit and eat when he's hungry. The rest of the staff's kids are already gone. I watch the writers' and execs' kids too from time to time. Sandy just has to stick around for an hour now until her mother can pick her up, but she's finished her shooting for the day. I'll keep Ryan here until you're done."

"It won't be too late. I just have a re-recording session and a handful of C.U.s. I'm really sorry about this. Might be ten o'clock?"

"Like I said, no trouble at all."

"Thank you, Mrs. Grinaldi."

"Call me Karen."

"Thanks, Karen." They shook hands, then Cassidy crouched and hugged Ryan. "Take care, buddy. I'll see you later."

Outside, Cassidy found Brenna standing at the foot of the steps, leaning on the railing. The way the other woman's gaze sought hers made Cassidy's breath catch. She saw so much warmth in those eyes.

Brenna's hand covered Cassidy's on the railing as she reached the bottom of the steps. "Is everything all right?"

"Yeah. I didn't even know this was here. I mean I did, but I figured it was just for the underage actors."

They walked across the lot together, and Brenna shook her head. "I used Karen's services myself. James was only ten when I started here. Thomas was twelve. A year later, I felt they were old enough to go home as long as I had my housekeeper, so I stopped needing to bring them here."

"Rachelle must use her from time to time when Rose is sick. I should've thought to ask her."

Brenna shook her head. "Rachelle has Jacques, and they have daycare in the city. Nope, it's just us single moms who need these."

"Single moms?" Rachelle was at the condiment stand when Brenna and Cassidy entered, and she'd caught the end of Brenna's statement. "What about single moms?"

"Cassidy just left Ryan with Karen Grinaldi. I was telling her that I used her services, too."

"Oh, yeah." Rachelle nodded. "Certainly didn't think you were single now."

"With Kevin in Michigan, it's still much the same thing."

"Oh. Well, come on over when you've got your plates." She finished gathering up her ketchup packets and napkins and walked across the busy commissary.

Looking out across the crowded tables, she spotted no familiar faces until she got to the cluster of tables pulled together for the *Time Trails* cast on their break. While Pinnacle was the shooting home of *Time Trails* and a handful of other first-run series, it also shot dozens of movies — both for television and theater release.

Brenna and Cassidy stepped into the buffet line and selected salads. Brenna picked up a diet cola and watched as Cassidy collected a coffee. "Are you going to make it?" she asked in a low voice.

"Yeah. I should be out of here by ten."

"I'd love to listen in. If I finish up my C.U.s before it's too late, would you mind?"

"All right."

"I'll pick Ryan up and bring him with me."

"I'll call over and tell Karen it's okay."

Brenna smiled as they stopped at the condiment counter before walking over to join the rest of the cast. They settled into the remaining empty seats, between Rachelle and one of the *Time Trails* regular extras, who played an officer in Luria's department.

"Good to see you again, Alex," Brenna offered. "How's life on the outside?"

The Amer-asian male shrugged, chewing a bite of his Salisbury steak. "I've been lucky, picking up commercials, but a lot haven't been so lucky. Projects are dying quickly and quietly. The writers' strike looks like it might happen."

"Just as pilot season is prepping?" Brenna asked in disbelief. "I doubt anything will happen. Someone's going to blink."

Cassidy shook her head. "Actually, I'm not sure. Even Paul was anxious about it last week."

"I've read the party lines. What's really at stake?"

"The way work is credited," Sean put in. He was the most experienced among them on the other side of the camera. "I haven't figured out how I'll vote yet."

Brenna nodded. "Won't get me straddling the line. If you wrote it, you should get the credit for it. End of story."

The actor-director groaned. "And a director's vision doesn't count? Many of them rewrite whole sections of scripts."

"You don't."

"I don't have to; I work with the original writer. In some cases, they're not on set."

Brenna shook her head. "I still don't see the argument as valid. Put the director's name in as co-writer then. Or as teleplay writer."

"Then the original writer gets less of the take." Sean changed focus. "And what about all the reality shows? Writers do have a decent gripe about that."

Cassidy saw that Brenna and Sean were going to really get into it and decided to intervene. "We won't solve the issue here. We'll just have to wait to see how the vote turns out." Brenna shook her head, hair falling across her face as she bent to eat. "Right?" Cassidy prompted, trying to draw up the blue eyes to look into, just once.

The woman's head came up and she smiled. "Right."

Conversation switched to catching up. While Brenna had heard about Rachelle's Thanksgiving, it was a chance to find out what everyone else had done. Across the table, Will elaborated on his time off, spent in Arizona with his sister.

"She's ready to pop," he said with a sigh. "So's her temper. Man, I don't think I've put my foot in my mouth that often since I was in junior high trying to ask a girl out. She jumped on everything."

Brenna remembered him telling her some time ago that his sister was expecting. "Pop? Your sister hasn't had her baby yet?"

"No, and she and Alex are just dying of anxiety."

"Do they know whether it's a girl or a boy?"

"Nope. They want it to be a surprise."

"Do they still need anything?" Rachelle asked. "We could get together a care package and send it to them."

"That'd be a nice gesture," Sean agreed. "They're extended family after all."

Will shrugged. "I guess they could always use things. All right. I'll give the office the address."

"We'll pack the stuff up ourselves," Terry Brown suggested. "I'll bring some wrapping paper."

Brenna looked around at the others and smiled. "Looks like your sister's going to have reason to forgive you for foot-in-mouth disease."

"Here's hoping." He lifted his cola in mock toast. Everyone laughed. The meal finished quickly after that.

Brenna found herself alongside Will in the back of the group as they returned to the set.

Finally he broke the silence between them. "I haven't had a chance to talk to you."

"I know."

"Is everything okay?"

"Cassidy told me what you did. Why, Will?"

"I'm sorry if it hurt."

"What you did was pretty strange."

"But things are working out?"

"I haven't exactly figured out what to do yet."

"You will."

"Since you're playing matchmaker, maybe you can break it to Kevin for me," she said sarcastically.

He shook his head. "You'll have to do that yourself, but I think you'll find a way."

She sighed. "I'd love to know where you get off being so intelligent about this."

"Let's just call it deja vu." He did not sound pleased but rather resigned at his knowledge.

"All right." Brenna shook her head and walked ahead, stepping up onto the set and taking her place. She watched him set up across the way and waited for the director's instructions as everyone else, stagehands aligning them, also took up their positions.

"We're going to do the C.U.s in short order, but everyone is to hold their marks to keep the background consistent."

When Brenna stepped off the set an hour later, Cassidy had already gone to her re-recordings, the close ups on her side of the set finished. Brenna changed in her trailer, removing her tunic gratefully. It was already after nine, so she hurried to Trailer Fourteen and stepped inside, drawing Karen's attention when the door latched. "Hey."

"Hello there. It's been a while, Brenna."

"Yeah. My boys are pretty much on their own now."

"How old are they?"

"James turned fifteen back in February. Thomas just turned seventeen."

"High schoolers. Geez, time flies."

"Who've you got today?"

"It's just me and Ryan. I had Sandy when Cassidy brought him, but she wasn't here long."

"Cassidy's still over in recording, I think. She said she'd call and okay me bringing Ryan."

"She did. Well, I'm on my way then. I'll walk over with you." She collected Ryan and his backpack, and they joined Brenna near the door.

"Hi!" Ryan said with a smile. "Are you going to take us camping again?"

"No. I did come to take you to your mom, though," Brenna said. "Is that okay?"

"Sure!" He freed his hand from Karen's grasp. The tutor looked on in surprise as he immediately attached to Brenna's hand.

"Let's go, buddy." Brenna caught a strange look from Karen and wondered what she had said.

When the sound booth "do not disturb" light went out, Brenna pushed open the door. Ryan left Brenna's side and charged his mother. "Mommy!"

She swung him away from the overhead microphone and onto her lap, accepting his hug as she looked up at Karen. "Thanks."

"No problem. He's pretty self-entertaining. Tomorrow?"

"At the moment, let's say yes, if that's all right?"

"Sure. Good night." Karen waved at Ryan and Brenna as she exited.

"So, how'd it go?" Brenna asked.

"Thankfully we did most of the work on the interior sets. I only needed to redo about half my lines," Cassidy declared.

Brenna laughed as she took Ryan. "Only half? When I was in here yesterday, I had over a hundred lines to redo."

"Slipping?"

"I've got a lot on my mind lately."

Cassidy nodded. "I know the feeling."

Meeting Cassidy's gaze, Brenna felt her hormones sit up and beg. It was embarrassing. She ducked her head away.

Lightening the mood, Cassidy asked, "Anybody wanna do a sing-a-long?"

Brenna held out both hands in protest. "*Happy Birthday*'s the only thing you'll get out of me."

"Whose birthday?" Ryan interrupted curiously.

Brenna kissed his head and brushed her fingers through his hair. "No one's, sweetheart. I'm just explaining my shortcomings to your mom."

Cassidy chuckled. "Not very convincingly, either," she pointed out. To Brenna she said, "I heard you at the campground. You're good."

"My first husband thought I sounded like Grable on a bad day."

Puzzled, Cassidy remarked, "Grable was never a singer."

"See, I told you." Brenna offered a toothy smile and stood. "Time to go home, anyway."

"I suppose you're right."

"Of course I'm right. That's why they put me in command." Cassidy laughed, and Brenna chuckled. "Let's go home." Ryan bounded out of the room ahead of them, and Brenna flipped off the light.

"See you in the morning." Cassidy reach out and captured Brenna's hand. Their fingers meshed for a moment, and gazes caught before they parted.

Chapter 31

Standing at her kitchen sink, Brenna rubbed a towel over the waffle iron she had just washed. Thomas and James sat finishing their breakfasts before having to run for the bus. "How's breakfast?" she asked.

"Great, Mom. Thanks," Thomas answered first.

"Sure thing," James added.

After placing the iron back in the cabinet, she leaned over the counter. "Thomas, honey, could you reserve the climbing wall at the gym this weekend?"

"I guess so. Why?"

"Cassidy— Ms. Hyland," she corrected quickly, "mentioned that she was free this weekend. She often comments on how much fun she had on the mountain. I thought that maybe you'd like to refresh her climbing lessons." Brenna tried to sound nonchalant. She need not have worried. Suddenly Thomas wasn't paying any attention to her.

He leaped for the telephone. "I'll reserve the coolest wall. There's this one at World Gym that I think she'll find really challenging."

"You can wait and call after school."

"By then it'll already be reserved. What time does she want to go?"

Brenna snatched a time out of the air. "Two o'clock Saturday?"

"Very cool. All right." He turned and plugged his left ear while listening to the call ringing through.

"Mom?"

Brenna turned and met James' gaze across the dining room table. "Yes?"

"Is Ms. Hyland coming over just to climb?"

"No." Brenna shrugged a shoulder. "I thought we could have her and Ryan to dinner afterward."

"Saturday night?"

"Yes."

James frowned and put down his fork. "Well then, I guess I'm going to miss the fun."

"What?"

"Yeah. Marcie and I have a skate date Saturday night."

Brenna studied him, getting the distinct sensation that he was lying to her. "James, what's up?"

"Well, I'm bummed I'm gonna miss seeing that cute kid," he said, returning to his food.

"When did you set up this date? I don't remember you asking for permission."

"Well, I only asked her yesterday. Didn't get a chance to mention it to you."

Brenna circled the table and put a hand on his shoulder; he tensed under her touch. "Didn't you enjoy meeting Ms. Hyland and her son on the camping trip?"

"Like I said, cute kid."

"James," Brenna prodded anxiously.

Her youngest sighed. "Mom, I don't want to spend an evening watching Thomas make gooey-eyes at her like he did at the parade."

Having been unable to find his girlfriend in the crowd, James had returned to the group after Cassidy and Ryan had joined them. She had been too caught up in

Cassidy's presence herself to notice his discomfort or Thomas' behavior. "I didn't realize you felt that way about her."

"Mom, I..." James frowned again, screwing up his face as he tried to find a way to put his thoughts into words. "I can't help but look at her and remember they brought her in to replace you."

"That's not true," she corrected sharply.

"So maybe not *replace*. But they didn't think you had 'it', and she does, and I remember how hurt you were about that." He shook his head. "You didn't used to like her, now she's everywhere." He turned his head away angrily. "What happened to keeping work and us separate?"

"James," Brenna began, not exactly sure what to say. Then she began carefully, "I was wrong to be upset with Ca...Ms. Hyland. When I realized that, I took some time and got to know her. She's...just an actress, like me, trying to do her job."

"You think 'cause you helped find her kid that makes her your friend?"

"No, I did that because she needed help. And I...*we* were in the right place to do something."

"You should've never let your guard down. She's just going to stab you in the back."

"No, she won't." She reached for him, but he pulled away. "You've never told me any of this. We should talk about it."

Frustration stiffened his body, and Brenna watched his expression fluster and sour by turns. His fists opened and closed. She hadn't seen him like this since he tried out for soccer and didn't make the third round cut to join the team.

"Damn, Mom, Thomas is so ga-ga over her. She's just some pretty face. You said so."

"I was wrong. There's no reason to get so upset."

"What happened that you've got this thing about making amends? The series is over in five months."

"I hadn't taken time to know her. Now that I have, I find she's intelligent and thoughtful. Fun. I want to spend time with her outside of work. She and Ryan are pretty special people."

James shook his head and sighed. "I just don't get it." He pushed to his feet. "I gotta get my stuff."

"James, stop. Could you please just...take some time? Give her a chance? Be here Saturday, I think you'll be surprised." Brenna leaned on the table and tilted her head back, looking up at James. She could see the tension in his shoulders as he struggled with what she was asking of him. *What is so hard? What has he been thinking about?*

He never answered. The hall clock chimed the hour, making it too late to continue their conversation. "Gotta go. See you tonight." He turned around and jogged for the door.

"James, wait!" Brenna called as he opened the door. He was gone in the next breath. "Damn," she muttered under her breath. "He's never lied to me."

Thomas rested a hand on her shoulder. "Go ahead and tell Ms. Hyland the wall's been reserved. I'll talk to him."

She patted his hand absently, then watched in silence as he grabbed up his own bag and left the house.

Picking up a fork and cutting into the cooling remains of James' half-eaten breakfast, Brenna released some frustration in silence. She bit into the waffle. *Damn, damn, damn!* The sweetness of the syrup went down bitterly.

Brenna straightened the collar of her costume's undershirt and tugged the jumpsuit smooth across her stomach. Double-checking her makeup in the mirror, she headed for the soundstage where she was expected to meet with the *Variety* people and do an interview. As she entered, she could hear the sounds of voices, and she slowed her steps. She told herself it was because she didn't want to risk making a sound that would be picked up by the on-stage microphones. Stopping at the edge of the nearest set, she listened to the dialogue between Hanssen and Raycreek.

"I prepared a fire for our meal," Hanssen said.
"Good thing I brought the wine, then," Raycreek responded.
"When do you think they'll get the vortex reset and find us?" Hanssen asked.
"If I know Susan, she's working on it right now."

Brenna swallowed. She knew from watching practice that this was the moment the two of them were huddled in a "homeless camp", an alley lit by the garbage burning in a city trash can. Curiosity pushed her slowly around the barrier. Between her and the raised area of the set, the entire film crew was scrambling around doing their jobs — adjusting sound and angle and microphone levels to catch the drop in both voices as they became more intimate.

Brenna's eyes saw past all that to the two people alone in the middle. She covered her mouth, abruptly stifling the jealousy that flared at seeing them so close. Will was practically leaning on Cassidy's left shoulder. Her *bare* shoulder, Brenna realized, seeing Cassidy's costume for the first time. *God, what a mess!* The vortex effect had taken its toll on both their costumes. Chapman wore torn uniform pants and no shirt. Cassidy's uniform was strategically torn to reveal a lot of skin.

Cassidy looked over her shoulder at Chapman's face, her hair falling across her cheeks and over her eye in a look of devastating sensuality. Brenna's stomach twisted as Chapman's face twitched into an amused smile. She tried to focus on some place other than their faces, inches apart, and found Cassidy's hands, curved together, elbows resting on her knees. Cassidy straightened as Chapman lifted his left palm to her cheek. Brenna couldn't stop staring as he kissed her.

Face hot, Brenna backed up. She shut her eyes to blot out the image. And abruptly opened them again — having found herself, during the brief moment behind the darkness of her eyelids, taking Will's place in the scene.

"Ms. Lanigan?"

"Hmm?" Brenna turned to the whispered voice that sounded just next to her right ear.

"Sanderson, *Variety*. We have an interview?"

She put her hand over his mouth and shook her head. Relief filled her as she led them out of sound range but not too far to prevent her from keeping an eye on the filming. "Now, how is it you didn't know not to step onto a live set?"

"I'm sorry, ma'am." Brenna raised an eyebrow at him. "Excuse me, I mean, I..."

She smiled at him then, completely upsetting his already precarious control. "Well, now that we've established you're new at this, how about I ask you a question?"

"I..."

He was completely flustered. Brenna almost giggled. He was a small young man, barely five-six, she guessed, and his inexperience suggested he was an intern at the industry magazine.

"Sure?"

"What's your first name?"

"Barry?"

She grinned. "Good. Now, how familiar are you with the series?"

"I've been watching since the first episode," he admitted bashfully. "I thought it was great that they put a woman in charge."

She grinned. "I don't think they knew what they were in for."

"What's it been like so many years on the same series?" he asked, warming a little to his intended topic. "Longest role you've ever had, isn't it?"

"Yes, it is. Jakes is such a full-bodied character. I've enjoyed living in her skin. It'll be hard to see her go."

"No movies?"

"They haven't made any plans."

He glanced over his shoulder as commotion from a break in filming drew his attention. "What's that all about?"

"Ah, that'd be a spoiler," she warned. "Can't print anything."

"I know, I know, but off the record?"

"What's it look like?" She was curious as to whether he saw any falseness in the acting.

"Hanssen's getting together with Raycreek? I didn't think those characters spent any time together."

"The vortex transit was rough."

"Pretty sudden, still. And," the young man went on, "doesn't Jakes have the hots for Raycreek herself?"

Brenna answered honestly, "Not anymore. He's more like the brother she never had." She scrunched up her nose. Sanderson chuckled. "Now, I bet you have other questions."

"Yeah. I, hey, would you like to do this over a cup of coffee?"

Brenna shook her head. "As you can see, I'm in costume. I can't leave the set."

"What are you shooting today?"

"Just a couple of scenes in my office."

"Could I see it?"

"All right."

During a half-interview, half tour, Brenna led the young man around the soundstage, steering clear of the shooting, and finally sitting with him on one side of her office desk and her on the other side.

He picked up a prop from the desktop. "These things really are just cobbled parts," he realized aloud. "Just...look at this, a disposable razor, a toothpaste cap? All painted gray. Funky."

Brenna laughed. "None of the science is real. We make it up. Well, the writers make it up."

"So, were you ever interested in science or space exploration?"

"No, I've always been an actor. That's what I love."

He frowned. "I got into the science. I like engineering."

"I'm glad there's an inspiration out there from the things we do."

"Anybody else in the cast like science?"

"You'd have to ask them." Brenna began to piece together the clues. "Can I ask you a question now?"

"I, well...yeah, go ahead."

"How did you get on this set?"

"Excuse me?"

"You're not from *Variety*, are you?"

"I...um, well..." He stood up quickly. She grabbed his wrist. "I'm sorry." He looked up to see someone coming toward them. "Listen, I really just wanted to meet you. I think you're great. I'll leave now. Don't report me, please?"

Brenna shook her head. "Pretty elaborate scheme to get in to see one actor."

"I'm secretary of your fan club. Really. I'm a student at UCLA. I've been following you since before *Time Trails*."

"Following me?"

"Not stalking or anything like that, honest, just always trying to find out more about you."

"I see."

"Who's this?"

Brenna looked up at Cassidy standing over her left shoulder. "Hi, Cass." She redirected her attention to the young man. "My interviewer, or so I thought. It just struck me that I was giving a tour as much as I was giving an interview."

"Really?"

"You're not going to report me, are you?" He looked at Cassidy with big eyes. "Please?"

"Bren?"

"I think he's harmless."

Barry sagged with relief. "You're not going to report me."

"No." Brenna shook her head. "If I were you, I'd get out of here, though, before someone else comes along." She stood up and pointed toward the exit. "And I'd better not hear word one of any spoiler getting out about the upcoming episode." He shook his head vigorously and scrambled toward the door she had indicated.

When he was out of sight, Cassidy said, "How could you spend an hour with him?"

"How'd you know it was an hour?"

"I noticed when he first came up to you."

"I thought you were filming."

"I was." Cassidy leaned close. "I always notice when you enter a room. I get this jumpy feeling in my stomach."

Brenna found herself face to face with a very sincere, very sensual expression. Cassidy's hand had risen from her side. Brenna intercepted it and placed it against her chest, letting them both absorb the feeling of her pounding heart.

"I looked for you before filming started," Cassidy said quietly. "You got in late."

The recollection of the morning brought several things to mind. "Thomas reserved a climbing wall — he says it's the best in the area — for two o'clock Saturday afternoon."

"That sounds good."

"Could I ask you a favor?"

"Anything."

"Would you consider talking some to James? He's...I don't know what's wrong, but he's bothered by all the visits between us. He views you as some evil, backstabbing witch."

"Sounds like an inherited viewpoint," Cassidy said drolly.

Brenna protested, "I haven't thought about you like that in months."

"That's certainly good to know," the blonde chuckled — she fingered the open collar of Brenna's vest — "because I'd like to think I've shown you another side of me."

"Rest assured, I've seen all sides."

"Not all," Cassidy teased softly. "Not yet."

Brenna couldn't help it; she leaned forward. As though pulled by gravity, Cassidy's hands moved down her sides and around her back. She inhaled the healthy aroma of perspiration caused by Cassidy's exertion under the lights.

"I needed this," Cassidy said as they hugged. "Will's definitely not my type."

"Anytime I can help," Brenna said, stepping back. "We'd better get back to work."

"Are you going to watch more filming?"

"Do you need me there?"

"I'd like it."

They stood together, bodies lightly touching, each drinking in the planes of the other's face. They heard footsteps and separated.

Will Chapman appeared around a corner, taking in the scene. "Glad I came for you instead of a stagehand." He looked pointedly at Cassidy. "Come on, we're needed back on the other set."

Cassidy left with him. Brenna remained behind, resting her palms on the desk, steadying herself from the heady rush of hormones still cascading through her body like a flash flood. She closed her eyes and absorbed the true precariousness of the indulgence she'd shared with Cassidy, breathing deeply to calm her heart. She really was going to have to find a way to stay away from Cassidy during filming. "Be one hell of a story if we got caught together," she muttered. *Damn.*

Cautiously she slipped around to watch the rest of Will and Cassidy's scenes, listening as lines were flubbed, spoken too softly, or stumbled over. Cassidy kept making eye contact with her, causing reshoots time and again.

At least there weren't any more kisses. Both Brenna and Cassidy were grateful for that mercy.

Chapter 32

"Thanks, sweetheart."

James Lanigan had known he was in for it when his mother gripped his chin, kissed his cheek, and uttered those words. She had not even asked, just assumed that he would be okay watching Ms. Hyland's kid for an hour. His mother, Thomas, and Ms. Hyland were climbing walls at World Gym.

James sighed. He was probably being unfair. His mom had not asked because of two simple facts. One, he was not climbing. Nothing could get him even four feet off the ground onto that wall. Two, Ryan was also not climbing. *Well,* James amended silently as he pulled the five-year-old off the Road Rally Virtual Racer, *he's not climbing the walls.* "Do you want to play something?"

"I want to race the cars!" Ryan responded firmly.

Feeling like his mother when he spoke, James shook his head. "You're not big enough."

"You could push the pedals," the boy answered. "Please?"

Crap. James looked with misgiving at the bucket seat, then sighed and dug into his pocket for the tokens obtained with his mother's ten dollar bill. "All right. Let me sit first, then you can sit on my lap."

Leaning forward, James dropped in the necessary tokens. As soon as he sat back, putting his hands up on the steering wheel, the boy was pushing his way onto his lap and determinedly squeezing in across his already cramped knees. *Sheesh, couldn't they make these things closer to real size?* "Ready?"

Ryan beamed. "Yep."

Obediently James only worked the brake and gas pedals as the boy steered like the five-year-old he was. Given four lives a game, Ryan quickly expended them — dumping the race car into a gorge and driving it into a spin-out with a giant sand scorpion, a river, and finally a cliff wall. They did not even make it a quarter of the way through the course.

The competitor in James took a big beating, especially when Ryan glanced up at him over a shoulder. "Can we go again?"

James sighed. "We've only got an hour. Wouldn't you prefer something else, simpler, maybe?"

Ryan's reply was uncomplicated and uncompromising. "No."

Stymied, James counted out more tokens. This time he gave them to Ryan to insert. Five minutes later, Ryan had again lost all four lives, but they made it halfway through the Desert Rally course. *Only because there are fewer things to hit,* the teen thought morosely.

Inevitably Ryan asked, "Again?"

So they did it again. This time James convinced Ryan to let him "help" steer.

Twenty minutes later, they made it through the course, dead last.

James looked at his watch. *At least we made it,* he allowed with a half smile. "Time's up. Let's go find our moms," he said, a little too cheerfully. Pushing the boy from his lap, James stood and stretched. Bending over to rub the cramp in his left calf, James was startled to feel arms around his throat.

"Thanks, I had fun," Ryan squealed directly into James' left ear.

"Hey!" He rubbed his ear to ease the ringing in his eardrum. "Yeah, yeah.

You're welcome." He stuck out his hand, and Ryan put his small one into it. "Let's go."

Standing at the edge of the gym's main room, James scanned the room for his mother. Constructed in faux rock, three climbing walls stood against the far wall. He spotted his mother and Ms. Hyland on the right two, apparently in a race to the top. His mother climbed steadily up the middle. Thomas stood at the bottom and to her right, under the blond woman, cupping his hands around his mouth and shouting encouragement. James could not tell who was ahead. He sent a bit of a wish toward his mother.

The women neared the top, both finding their handholds efficiently. In the end, due to James' wishes perhaps, his mother topped the edge first. She smacked the sensor, triggering the light and buzzer a full second ahead of the taller, younger woman. James applauded madly, then grabbed Ryan's hand and dragged the boy over to the walls. He continued cheering as his mother switched to the slide lead and quickly returned to the floor, bouncing once on her feet before turning around.

She pulled off the green bit of fabric she had used to tie her hair back, and the tresses promptly fell to surround her face, which was lit with high color. Sweating profusely, she was laughing as she caught her breath. Thomas slapped her on the back once, then turned to spot for Ms. Hyland as she began her slide down the wall face.

Ms. Hyland landed beside their mother and offered her a high-five before turning to Thomas. James' brother clasped her hand and whooped, making both women laugh. "You'll need a few more lessons to beat Mom," Thomas said. "However, I'm game if you are."

"Colluding against me?" their mother said. "My own son? Shame on you." She wrapped an arm around his neck. "Now where's my towel. God, I need water."

Laughing, Ms. Hyland walked over to a bench and fetched both their towels and gym bags. She scooped out a bottle of water. Her own skin shiny with sweat, she took a healthy chug herself before passing it over. "I'll get the right pace eventually," she warned.

"You can't beat me at handball. I'll stay ahead of you here, too." Brenna laughed.

James was surprised when she popped her towel at the other woman, making her jump backward.

"I have to point out, kindly," the younger woman teased back, "that that is scripted. *This* is not. Your days are numbered," she countered, accepting the return of the water bottle and tossing back another swallow.

The women fell silent, sharing big smiles, then realized the boys were staring at them.

"Shower?"

"Yeah." Ms. Hyland flipped her hair free of the ponytail tie and looked at Thomas. "We'll be out soon. Watch Ryan for a few minutes?"

"Sure thing," Thomas replied. He offered his hand; she shook it. "You really did great today."

"I had a great teacher." She flashed him a toothsome smile and brushed his shoulder lightly before following their mother into the locker room.

"Well, let's go sit and wait," James sighed.

"You're right. It'll probably be ten, fifteen minutes. Want to go to the Game Room?"

"Yes!" Ryan pumped his fist in the air.

"No!" James objected. Thomas shot his brother a questioning look. "I just spent the whole hour in there with him," James said defensively.

Thomas held out his hand. "Well then, give me the tokens. I'll take him."

"You just want to keep on his mother's good side," James said crossly, handing over the tokens.

"What is it with you? That night at the campsite did Cass and Ryan poke you in the ass or something?"

"No." James subsided with a pout, stuffing his hands in his jean pockets. "Fine. Let's just go."

"Come on, I'm your brother. Tell me what's up."

"Have you ever seen Mom act like this?"

"Far too rarely."

"What is it with that woman that's got you so nuts and Mom acting like last year never happened?"

"They've obviously worked things out. Shoot, you should be happy. Mom's got few enough close friends as it is. Most of them are back in Michigan. At least now she's got someone she can joke around with, do fun stuff."

"But things don't just go away like...that." James snapped his fingers.

"Maybe it's something on the set. They decided to bury the hatchet in order to get through it. Hell, I don't know. I don't care." Thomas sat Ryan in front of a space shoot 'em up and popped in the coins. "You being upset isn't going to change anything."

James frowned. "I know." He put his hand on the game console and exhaled loudly. "I can't get over the feeling something is really messed up. We're just missing it."

"You're just not giving Cassidy a chance."

"And you're giving her too much of one," James retorted. "Damn it, Thomas, she's over thirty. She isn't going to like you no matter how much you fawn over her or her kid."

"I happen to think she makes a pretty cool friend."

"So is that why you watched her butt sashay out of here just a minute ago?"

"Listen, she was telling Mom and me today just how cool all this is. How she had never gone for the Outdoors Club in college but now wished she had." He laughed. "She scared Mom nearly to death when she did her first plummet, but she had great form. She suggested skydiving might be next."

"So she's got a death wish. I'm supposed to like her now?"

"She just loves excitement. I think Mom's finding that refreshing. She's got an adventurous streak in her, too, that I think she's just beginning to let out."

"Our mother is not going to skydive."

"Maybe she isn't. But if she does, you can bet it'll be because she wants to do it."

"She's our mom!"

"But," Thomas lifted Ryan down from the game as the telltale sound of the last life lost played out, "she's a person, too."

James crossed his arms over his chest. "You are such a dweeb, Thomas."

"And you've got some growing up to do. Mom's finally breaking out of her shell, and I think it's great."

In the locker room, Brenna grabbed a full-sized towel from the courtesy rack and headed for the showers. She noted all the stalls were occupied and paused.

"Come on, let's go," Cassidy suggested, coming up behind her.

"Where?"

"The communal shower."

"I don't—"

"It's just to rinse off. That's all we need." Cassidy was already moving; Brenna automatically followed.

At the end of the row of stalls, the floor opened up to a lowered space. Spigots lined the far wall at chest height. Brenna shook her head. "I need a shower."

"Then feel free to wait." Cassidy stepped out of her shoes. Putting them up on a bench, she dropped her gym bag next to them, then pulled off her socks. Bending over, she stepped out of her shorts and dropped them on top. She remained in her white tank top and underwear as she pulled the chain under a spigot and stepped into the water flow. Turning around, she dropped her head under the spray and combed her fingers through it before tossing her head back. She looked at Brenna as she brushed the hair back from her cheeks and forehead.

Brenna drank in the sight of lean curves hidden inside the clinging wet tank. "You're soaked."

"Yes, but I'm cool now," Cassidy answered with a mischievous smile, stepping away from the water. "You ought to try it," she suggested, running a finger through the sweat dotting Brenna's near shoulder. Wrapped up in her towel, she sat down on the bench, picked up her bag, and fished out a cotton sweater, fresh underwear, and a pair of slacks.

Looking from the spigot to Cassidy, Brenna saw the blonde's smile widen slowly and her eyebrows dance. She was being challenged to drop some of her inhibitions.

Bending over, Brenna plucked off her shoes and socks. The shorts followed. There was a tingle down her back — she felt she was being watched — but when she glanced over her shoulder, Cassidy was bent over, putting on her sneakers. The blond head started to rise, and Brenna turned her face away, averting it before Cassidy could catch her looking. *So she wants a game? All right.*

Keeping her back to Cassidy, Brenna pulled off her tank top and stepped forward into the spray, flexing her shoulders as she scrubbed her fingers through her wet hair. The ice cold water teased her nipples hard before running down in rivulets to her center and continuing down her thighs.

The shower was not cooling her off. Knowing those eyes were on her, appreciating the view, made Brenna feel like a ball of fire, the white hot core of which was centered just below her pelvic bone.

She rubbed her hands down her chest and abdomen, sluicing off the excess water. Only then did she turn around. A towel was held up at face level, blocking her view of Cassidy, who was holding it out.

"Dry off," Cassidy said tightly. "Or I'll get us both very wet."

Brenna gave her a daring leer, then wiped the expression from her face as she took the towel and wrapped it around herself. Studying Cassidy, who was determinedly looking at the floor, she felt energized and said evenly, "Don't challenge me. I always play to win."

"I'm beginning to believe that." Darkened eyes, hungry with desire, flickered over Brenna's face. "Sometime you'll have to tell me where you developed that competitive streak."

"In a household with four brothers we call it a survival mechanism."

Cassidy was silent for a long moment, then quirked her brow. "You like nude sunbathing too, I bet."

"What makes you say that?"

Cassidy's smile broadened, showing her teeth before she turned away. "No tan lines."

A flush caught Brenna from head to toe as she settled quickly on the bench to cover her weakened knees. "I'm a mother," she protested innocently. "How could I dare do that?"

Cassidy watched Brenna as she covered herself in a billowy green blouse and black slacks, then stepped into low-heeled sandals. "A year ago I'd have guessed tanning salon," she mused. "But I didn't see this adventurous competitor in you then."

"True," Brenna acknowledged.

"Though I wouldn't be surprised to discover that's why you built the deck in your backyard."

Brenna's cheeks flooded with heat, and she dropped her eyes.

"I swear you've bewitched me. I can completely see you in that yard... More beautiful than any fairy princess." As Brenna's head came up, Cassidy swept in and planted a quick kiss at the corner of her lips. Aroused but wary, Brenna looked around, noting they were well hidden from others in the locker room.

Exhaling sharply, she grasped the nearby tiled wall separator and watched Cassidy leave. *God help me, I've never felt anything this totally consuming in my life.* Collecting her wet things and rolling them into her towel, Brenna stuffed them into her bag, tossed the bag on her shoulder, and strode out.

When she stepped out into the gym again, Brenna spotted Cassidy standing among their children. Ryan was in her arms as she spoke with Thomas on her left and James looked at them from her right. A sensation of family slammed into her with the force of a physical blow. At that moment, she resolved to make that snapshot a permanent picture in her life.

Wrapping her arm around James' shoulder, she addressed the group. "Everyone ready for dinner? I'm starved."

Chapter 33

Brenna stood at the stove, tending a skillet of chicken strips sautéing in a white wine and mustard sauce. She glanced at the timer, noting the wild grain rice still had ten minutes. *Just enough time to finish the chicken thoroughly.*

She looked over her shoulder at the kitchen's other occupant. Cassidy's face was in profile as she skillfully chopped vegetables on the cutting board. *Odd enough for a first date,* she thought with a smile. *Dinner with my kids and me.* Cassidy looked far from daunted. When all three boys disappeared into the game room, she had offered to assist. Right now she was cutting mushrooms to add to the salad in a bowl by her left elbow. The fall of her hair obscured her face somewhat, so Brenna shifted to catch the profiled chin and nose, admiring the smooth features.

"Salad's almost finished." Cassidy spoke without turning, alerting Brenna to the fact that she knew she was being watched. "You'll burn your hand again if you don't pay attention to what you're doing." She turned her head slightly until their gazes met. Brenna blushed under her amused smile.

You're distracting me, she thought. She tried to hide her blush and covered it with, "The chicken and rice are almost done."

Cassidy nodded, pushing the mound of cut mushrooms from the board into the bowl, then tossing the salad briefly. "Well, why don't I tell them dinner's up?" She flashed a quick grin, dropped the knife into the sink, brushed off the cutting board, and put it back on a hook over the sideboard.

"All right." Brenna returned to minding the chicken, pleased with the ease with which they'd divided the responsibilities.

Cassidy had learned how to walk silently in order to get herself in and out of the house while tiptoeing around her ex-husband's rages. She employed the talent now, to get a peek into the game room before the boys knew she was there.

Peering around the edge of the doorway, she surveyed the room. Thomas coached Ryan through a flight simulator video game. Both were seated cross-legged on the floor, control pads in hand. Ryan bounced frequently, giving Thomas a running commentary. The older boy cocked his head and listened. He maneuvered his own ship through the same obstacles on the split screen with the other half of his attention. As he had with her at the gym, Thomas was encouraging, prodding Ryan into making better choices. *He would probably enjoy being a camp counselor,* she thought, wondering exactly what he thought he might do with his life, knowing he would be graduating from school in May.

Brenna's younger son, James, was a different story. In the corner of a small futon couch, lowered so that she could barely make out the top of his brown hair, he read a book propped on his bent knees. He seemed pretty absorbed by the contents of the small paperback. Noticing his exhaustion when she collected Ryan before the group left the gym, she had tried to talk to him. He had rebuffed her, politely, but it had been a rejection all the same. She wondered if it was personal or if he was just mad at the world, as some teenagers were wont to be. He did not seem the "mad at the world" type. His mother was just too involved in his life to let it get that far. *No,* she thought sadly, *it must be me.* She thought about how Brenna had said the same thing when Cassidy had been shivering on set one day. *Well, not everything has to be about us.* It was interesting to think that Brenna had been seeing the relationship that interconnected them even then. She smiled and stepped into the room.

"Dinner," she announced. Three sets of eyes turned to her, expressions ranging from interested to excited to wary. She smiled as Thomas and Ryan stood. The seventeen-year-old flipped off the game console, and James rolled to a sitting position, still warily watching her.

"I'll set the table." Thomas stepped past her and left.

Ryan looked up at his mom. "Can I help?" When she nodded, he ran after Thomas.

Amused, Cassidy turned back to James. "Coming?"

"In a minute."

He returned to the page he held open, and it was clear to her that he'd become interested in the reading again. "Good book?"

He shrugged, trying to tuck the book out of sight. "Just something I picked up."

"Something for school?"

"No." He stood up, pushing the book aside. "Come on, before Mom comes looking for you."

She remained in the doorway, studying him. She wondered at his choice of words: looking for her, not for him or for both of them. Meeting his gaze, she waited until he broke the connection and said, "I may not have said it, but I sure did appreciate you watching Ryan this afternoon."

"Yeah."

The silence spread like a fog, making it difficult for her to gauge what he was feeling. She was put in mind of Commander Jakes' stoic mask. It was a phrase that director after director had used while coaching Brenna. "*Nothing's supposed to get through the mask. When it does, that's the drama.*"

On the other hand, Hanssen was supposed to be a contained but forthright individual. Getting at the unflappable Jakes was her form of rebellion. Cassidy was frequently instructed, especially during her first months on the series, to deliver lines with the intent of breaking the mask.

Brenna's "mask" was a tight jaw, and eyes that wouldn't look quite at you. She always looked as if she were holding her breath. Cassidy saw that now in James' face.

She tried to break through. "James, tell me something." He looked at her, but the mask stayed in place. "Do you watch the show?"

"No."

She judged the response to be too quick. "Your mom doesn't like you to?" Silence again as he, again, wouldn't look directly at her. "So," she poked carefully, "what do you think of her portrayal of Susan Jakes?"

His gaze snapped to hers. Defensively he said, "I told you, I don't watch."

"Maybe you should," Cassidy prodded. "She's very good, you know. I've always thought so."

"What do you know? You're just a..." He cut himself off and turned away from her. "Dinner's getting cold."

Careful to avoid any expression that she was startled by the unfinished comment, she stepped back. "I may be anything. That's what acting is all about. I happen to be your mother's friend. That," she assured him, "is not an act." Stepping out of the doorway, she returned down the hall. She found Brenna at the end of it, gaze upturned to meet hers.

"I was beginning to wonder what happened to you."

"Just turning off the stuff." James edged his way around them.

"Oh." Brenna watched him stride out of sight. She turned back to find Cassidy studying the spot at the end of the corridor where her son had last stood. "Are you all right?"

"Yeah. I'm fine. Let's go eat before the food's cold." Cassidy rested her hand companionably on Brenna's shoulder, then gradually dropped it away as they entered the dining room.

Until she started a conversation with "Ryan loves baseball", Brenna was sure the group would have been content to remain silent. Even the normally sociable Thomas had alternated between watching Cassidy and watching his plate. Brenna knew Cassidy was uncomfortable; she had stopped meeting Brenna's gaze across the table.

Responding to the cue, Thomas began regaling Cassidy's son with the stats from his latest season of baseball. Ryan *ooohed* and *aaahhhed* and asked many knowledgeable questions.

Thomas asked, "How'd he learn all those stats?"

"TV," Cassidy explained. "I've started letting him get the cards, but mostly he just listens to the commentators."

"That's very cool," Thomas praised. "Have you ever seen a live game?"

"Mom took me to one this year."

"Who was playing?"

"Oakland A's and Baltimore Orioles," Ryan reported proudly. "A's lost."

"That was a great game," Thomas said. "What position would you play?"

Ryan grinned. "First base."

"There's an active Little League in L.A. Besides playing for the high school team, Thomas helps coach one of them. Perhaps you could let Ryan join up." Brenna prompted an expansion of the conversation with a look at Cassidy. "The new season starts up just after our filming finishes," she added.

"Please, Mommy?"

Cassidy nodded. "I guess you could."

"It's T-ball until age eight, but I think he'd have a lot of fun," Thomas said.

Cassidy chuckled. "Between climbing together and Ryan's games, you may see too much of me."

"Don't forget, we'll all have to go watch Thomas play," Brenna responded with a smile. Her smile faded as James stood. "James?" He looked toward her. "Done already?"

"Yeah. I've got stuff to do."

"We've got cobbler for dessert," she said.

"Call me." Then he was gone.

"All right," Brenna said to his back. Disconcerted, she slowly picked up her fork.

Disheartened and confused, James listened as his mother, Ms. Hyland and Thomas started up the conversation again as he left. He bristled at the woman's inquisitiveness. He really wished she would just go away. Now his mom was talking about seeing the Hylands more often, inviting them to Thomas' baseball games, even getting her son involved in the Little League.

Flopping down on the couch in the game room, James sighed. She had seldom brought any of the *Time Trails* cast to the house, except for hosting the occasional holiday party when she had briefly dated one of the other actors. That had all stopped when she married Mr. Shea.

Cassidy Hyland was the last person James had ever expected to see sitting at their dining room table. In the beginning, when she was alone in her room when she thought no one could hear, his mother had cursed the blonde. Socializing with her should be the last thing on her mind. Now, that seemed to have all changed. He just did not get it.

Thomas was right; it was his mother's life. However, she was changing rapidly, right before his eyes. She barely spoke to her husband any more; weekly calls had dwindled to less than once a month. James hadn't seen her writing a letter in weeks. It made no sense. Thomas said he had seen them kissing out on the deck before they disappeared into her room at Thanksgiving.

He immediately terminated that line of thought. Thinking about his mother having sex was just *icky*. He had only just gotten into petting with his girlfriend, Marcie. He knew what he wanted to do with her, but thinking about his mother and Mr. Shea doing the same thing was just...He groaned and closed his eyes, shoving the heels of his hands against them to rub out the images. *Ew.*

She was more enthused about physical stuff lately, too. She worked out and swam a lot when she first got the job on the series. That had tapered off as the series itself provided her with more than enough exercise. Now she was actually racing Thomas when they climbed. Thomas seemed unsurprised, saying her competitive spirit was reawakening.

Why was it happening now, just when he thought she was ready to leave this role behind? Why hadn't this happened when she married Mr. Shea?

Damn it, he cussed. *Why the hell do I think Cassidy Hyland has everything to do with it?*

Pulling the remote control from the table, he lost himself in television.

"Thomas, would you please take him out of here?" Brenna held Ryan's hands to prevent him from sticking them in the sink where his mother was washing dishes. Brenna had turned around to say something to Cassidy and nearly tripped over him for the fourth time.

She herself was finding containers to store the leftovers. Since James had left the table early, more food than usual remained. He had always been her most robust consumer.

Thomas, who was bringing the dishes in from the table, put down the glasses he carried and held out a hand to Ryan. "I could show you my baseball cards. Come on. Let's leave the moms to do the tough stuff." He grinned cheekily at his mother as Ryan trotted over and took his hand. "Right, Mom?"

She blew him a kiss. "Thank you." He laughed, and in a moment the two boys were gone.

Cassidy stepped back from the soapy water. "I have never seen Ryan worship anyone so fast."

Brenna reached over and flipped on the radio, grabbing a towel to dry the pans filling the dish rack. The quiet music was a pleasant backdrop as they continued to work. "Thomas has always been great with kids."

"Has he thought about being a camp counselor?"

"He has. Until he has a car of his own, it's just not feasible."

Finished, Cassidy dried her hands and leaned against the counter, crossing her feet at the ankles and easing herself back on both hands. "You could get him a car."

"I don't work that way," Brenna said. "He'll get a job in the summer and earn his own."

"I guess you're right."

"I'd rather Thomas earn something himself, than for me to get him something he won't appreciate."

"You didn't raise him to be shallow."

"No, I didn't."

They fell silent. Brenna reached into the refrigerator and drew out two wine coolers. "Drink?"

"All right." Cassidy took one, glancing at the label. "Raspberry. Nice." She opened it and sipped, then paused as she listened to the tune on the radio. "Wow, that brings back memories."

"What?"

"This song."

Brenna listened to the tune. "I don't recognize it."

"It's an oldie, but that was all the Armed Forces heard overseas."

"Armed Forces?"

"My dad was...*is* retired military. Marines. I was born in France."

Thomas had come back in with Ryan and asked, "We were wondering. Wasn't there supposed to be dessert?"

"Oh, right," Brenna answered distractedly, caught up in the image of Cassidy as a small girl, probably in pigtails, running around a military base. "Go on," she encouraged. "Sit down and I'll get things together."

Thomas, Ryan and Cassidy settled at the table. Brenna grabbed the vanilla ice cream and set it on the counter. "We should probably tell James," she said, recognizing that her younger son was still absent. She looked to Thomas, who got up quickly and went on a search. Then she turned back to Cassidy. "You said you moved around a lot."

"I did, but from birth to six, I lived just outside Paris. Since I started school there, it's still the best foreign accent I do." She chuckled. Easily changing her accent to reflect a French influence, she said to her son, "Don't you think so?" He giggled.

"So you traveled a lot as a child." Brenna emerged with the tray of plates. The smell of warm peach cobbler filled the air, and steam rose from beneath the cool splashes of vanilla ice cream that she added on top.

"There were two bases in France. We lived in Texas, Tennessee, then Missouri — where he retired. There were also stops in San Francisco, London, and Bremen. Though I didn't go, since he was posted there only two months, he was stationed in Thailand for a training assignment when I was fifteen."

Thomas returned at that moment with James, and they both sat down. Brenna passed James a plate. "Cassidy was just telling us about growing up on Army bases."

"Uh huh."

Cassidy decided it probably would be best to go while things with James were just strained instead of completely out of hand. He clearly had issues specifically with her, but she was getting nowhere with resolving them. "I learned a cool language out of it, I guess." She sat up. "Maybe it's time I took Ryan home."

"It's only eight o'clock," Brenna protested.

"Can't we stay?" Ryan looked at her pleadingly, cobbler dribbling from his spoon as he lifted it to his mouth. "I'm not finished."

"Let him finish his dessert, Cass. You, too." She tapped the edge of Cassidy's untouched plate with her spoon.

Relenting, Cassidy fell silent, trying to enjoy the cobbler. James finished quickly and left the table even as he was putting the last bite into his mouth.

Watching Ryan take his last bite, Cassidy wanted to end the evening on an up note, to try and make Brenna feel less like she was being driven off by James' indifference. She stood, grinned at Thomas, and nodded at Brenna. "*Merci. Vous semblez délicieux. J'ai eu l'amusement dans la douche.*"

"What'd you say?" Thomas asked curiously. "That sounded really nice."

She chuckled. "I said, 'Thank you. The food was delicious. I had fun...at the gym.' Impress your friends, confound your enemies — learn a second language."

"Of course, you're right." Brenna stood. "I guess I'll see you Monday, then. Would you like some of the leftovers?"

"No thank you. Why are you going in Monday? There's no shooting."

"It's just for a little while. I have interviews and a meeting with my agent."

To spend a moment alone with Cassidy, Brenna waited until she had said her goodbyes to both boys. Thomas flushed a bit at Cassidy's hug, taking a quick step back after she let him go. Brenna bit the inside of her cheek to prevent a chuckle from escaping.

She walked Cassidy and Ryan out to their car and leaned on the open driver's door. Ryan secured his own belt over the booster seat in the back. Cassidy started into the driver seat. A soft hand over hers on the top of the door made her pause. Brenna's eyes were slightly obscured by windblown hair. Cassidy's hand reached up and brushed her face free. "Yes?" She appreciated the heat that rose in Brenna's cheeks and the way her lips parted, her breath caught, and the tip of her tongue came out to wet her lips.

"What did you say? Really."

Cassidy glanced at the front door, then leaned closer to Brenna and whispered, "I said, 'Thank you. You look delicious. I had fun in the shower.'" She leaned back, meeting Brenna's gaze again. The smile widened, and the intention was overtly lascivious.

"That can't possibly be something you learned when you were six," Brenna said breathlessly.

Cassidy could see that her words had piqued Brenna's desires. "I took a refresher course in college."

"What else did you learn that I should know about?" Brenna asked coyly.

She leaned close again, surprised by how much she wanted to kiss Brenna, right there in the open, in front of God, Creation, and the kids. Instead she issued her words across Brenna's lips in faint puffs of breath. "One weekend in particular comes to mind. I'll reenact that with you some other time. Privately." Clearly her words had an effect. Brenna's pupils widened with desire.

"Would you like to get together again sometime? Soon?" Brenna's invitation was hopeful.

"There's the 'office' Christmas party on the seventeenth," Cassidy reminded her.

Pursing her lips, Brenna nodded. "I forgot."

"Aren't you going?"

"I have to, but I haven't...Kevin escorted me last year."

Gambling, Cassidy suggested, "You could go with me."

"A date, you mean?"

"I'm willing," Cassidy said. "But we could just tell the reporters we're friends. I'm going stag. No Cameron this year."

Brenna's brow knitted in sudden anxiety. "I...I need some time."

"Are you unsure of the press, us, Kevin, or the kids?"

Nibbling her bottom lip, Brenna was the very definition of adorable. "It's...I have to talk to Kevin first." She lifted her gaze to Cassidy's. "Can there be another time during the hiatus?"

"I'm not sure yet whether Ryan and I will be headed out to St. Louis to visit my parents for Christmas."

Brenna nodded. Cassidy's hand brushed hers lightly in parting before Brenna had to step back and watch the other woman get into her seat, fire up the engine, and back out of the driveway. She watched until the taillights disappeared into the evening.

Chapter 34

When Brenna returned inside, James and Thomas were in the kitchen polishing off the remains of the cobbler. "That was pretty cool," Thomas remarked when she walked in to check things. "You think we'll be able to do it again?"

James shook his head. "It seems to me from what Mr. Shea said that we should be cutting ties, not making more of them."

Brenna put a hand on his shoulder. "We're not leaving L.A. tomorrow; there's all spring. A lot could change."

"Are you planning to stay here after *Time Trails*, Mom?" James asked.

"There are a lot of options," Brenna replied noncommittally. "I'm just saying that you shouldn't get anxious about it. I thought you said that you wanted to finish school here," she said.

"Yeah, I do. Come on, Thomas, get with me here. I don't want to start over totally someplace else."

Thomas shook his head. "Mom, I...is Kevin going to escort you to the Pinnacle Christmas party? Maybe we could all talk then."

Brenna frowned. "I haven't talked to him about it."

"I'll escort you if you want."

"Sorry, that's not possible." She hesitated. She would rather go alone, making it possible to meet up with Cassidy, but she knew that the press could have a field day with that. If Kevin came out to L.A. for the party, they could talk, and she could end it then. She was afraid. If she went to Mount Clemens to give him her decision, surrounded by their families, she wasn't entirely certain she could hang on to her nascent resolve. Looking at her sons awaiting her decision, Brenna knew guilt. She was looking for them to supply arguments for her to avoid telling Kevin the real reason she wanted a divorce.

Well, that is going to stop. She wanted and needed Cassidy, needed to make her own way. Out on the driveway, she had been a breath away from Cassidy's lips, wanting to kiss her, only stopped by the sight of the lights in a neighbor's house across the way. She decided convention would no longer hold her back.

"I'll call him right now and see if he can come," she said sharply, reaching for the phone. Her eye caught the clock, and she unconsciously converted the time ahead. "It's almost midnight there." She put her hand down, only to be startled when the phone rang. She snapped it up and hit the button. "Hello?"

"Hi, Bren."

"Kevin?" She blinked, looking from Thomas to James. "It's late."

"I hoped I'd find you in," he said. "I know it's late for me, but this time differential..." He seemed to shake himself. "Anyway, I called to... We didn't get a chance to finish talking about everything."

She felt her stomach get queasy. "I know. We've got a weekend coming up."

"You want to come here? I can make up the boys' room."

"No, Pinnacle's got a party, like last year's, our final one — press and everything. The execs are throwing it for the cast and crew."

"Oh."

"It's the seventeenth." Thomas and James sat on the couch, watching her. She turned slightly aside, expecting anger at the lateness of the notice.

Instead Kevin was unnaturally calm. "That's this Saturday."

She winced. "Yes. I know."

After a long pause, he answered, "I'll fly in Saturday morning."

"I could go alone."

"I will fly in."

She felt a frisson of anxiety as she heard the deliberation in his tone. "All right."

"We can talk more when I get there."

"I know." Brenna pulled back the receiver and swallowed back her nerves. *Come on, Brenna, seize the brass ring.* Returning to Kevin, she said simply, "Bye."

"Good night."

"Mmm hmm." She dropped the portable back onto its cradle and sat down on the couch.

Thomas spoke first. "Mom, what's wrong between you two?"

She shook her head. "I'm sorry, Thomas, but our problems... I have to talk to Kevin about them." She started to her feet, but her son's hand grasped her arm and she settled back down, meeting his light eyes.

"Mom, can I let you know one thing?"

"What?"

"It seems like all fall has been a real roller coaster for you. Whatever is going on, all I want is to see you happy."

James nodded. "Me, too."

"I'll be all right," she responded. "Kevin and I will talk, and things will be resolved." That was as much as she was willing to say. She went to the calendar. "Your school dance is the sixteenth," she realized.

Thomas leaned over the couch and looked at her. "Yeah."

"Looks like we go tux shopping tomorrow after church."

James and Thomas groaned. "Can't we just wear suits and ties?"

"What's the attire requirement?"

"Formal," James supplied with a grimace.

"Then it's tuxedos. Have your dates picked their dresses yet?"

"Yes."

Brenna nodded. "Tomorrow's a busy day. You'd better get to bed." She crossed the room again and accepted a kiss on the cheek from each son as they passed her. She kept a lingering hold on James. His reticence around Cassidy bothered her. "Are you all right?" She rubbed lightly between his shoulder blades, feeling the layer of tension there.

"Just anxious about all the changes," he stated. "I'll get over it."

"Promise me you'll tell me if anything gets to be too much." She brushed her fingers through his hair. "Yes?" He nodded but said nothing. She pulled him into her body and rejoiced at the way he clung to her for a brief moment. *My son.* "I love you. Good night, James."

Letting him go, she stood quietly, watching them both walk to their rooms. With a small smile, she had a moment of faith that everything might actually work out. She went into her room and closed her door, picked up the phone and dialed a now-familiar number.

Cassidy stepped into the house, putting her keys and purse aside. Ryan charged to the bathroom. "A quick bath," she reminded him. "Then it's story time."

"Will you read me a story?"

"Sure," she answered, leaning in the doorway. She grinned as he splashed into the filling tub. "Keep the water off the floor."

"Okay."

"Did you have fun today?"

"Yes." Cassidy started out the door to get his pajamas. "Mommy?"

"Yes?"

"Are we going to see Ms. Lanigan again?"

"Probably." She smiled warmly at the memory of Brenna's face in the twilight.

"Are we going to be able to see Daddy anymore?"

"What?"

"Now that you're dating Ms. Lanigan, will I get to see Daddy?"

"What makes you think Brenna and I are dating?" Cassidy knelt at the side of the tub and soaped a washcloth, helping him by washing behind his ears and over his back. "We're just friends."

"You don't kiss 'just friends', Mom," he said, rolling his eyes.

Cassidy carefully stifled her inclination to deny it. *He must have seen us kissing in the tent during the camping trip.* Obviously he had continued to think about it. At least he was finally talking to her about it. "Does that bother you?"

Ryan shook his head. "She's really nice, and Thomas is a lot of fun. James doesn't like me."

"So, what's bothering you?"

"When you were dating Mister P'lassis, I didn't get to see Daddy. I want to be able to see Daddy."

"Who I'm dating doesn't affect you seeing your father."

"Does that mean I can see him again?"

"Why do you want to see him?" Cassidy had kept Mitch's image as pristine as possible for Ryan. During the divorce, the youngster had not been old enough to understand anything other than that he no longer saw his father every day.

"I asked Thomas if he ever saw his dad, and he said no. He hadn't seen him since his mom married Mister Shea."

Cassidy wondered if that was Brenna's doing or her first husband's. "I don't know the reasons," she admitted, "but we shouldn't guess. It's not nice."

"Okay. So, are you dating her?"

Were they dating? Tonight could be considered a first date, even though they had been surrounded by their children. Or had the camping trip been the first one? She wanted to take Brenna out on a date sometime, just the two of them. That would be their first date, she decided. She finally shook her head. "No, we're not dating."

"Would you like to be?"

Smiling at her son's "cut to the chase" manner, she said, "Yes. But it's our secret, all right — yours, mine, and Bren's. Okay?"

"Okay." Ryan nodded and turned away from her, standing up in the tub. "I'm ready for my story."

At her son's typically abrupt change of subject, Cassidy stood and wrapped him up in a towel as he stepped out of the water. "I'm glad you approve." She laughed, rubbing his hair briskly under the terrycloth. He giggled when she tickled him and helped him into his pajamas.

Together they went into his room and pulled out *Jack and the Beanstalk*. They shared the reading and oohed and aahed together over the various mishaps and marvels in the giant's home and the final triumph as Jack cut down the beanstalk.

When they finished, she tucked him under the covers. "Good night, Ryan."

"Good night, Mommy."

The phone rang. Hurrying out to the living room, Cassidy settled into the corner of her couch and answered it. "Hello?"

"Cassidy?"

Brenna's voice slid through the phone and wrapped around her. It was soft, Cassidy realized, likely in order to keep their conversation private. She pictured the woman in her bedroom, lying across her bed. She shook herself to damp down the desire aroused by that simple image. "What's up? I don't think I left anything at the house."

"You didn't. I just wanted to tell you, I got off the phone with Kevin a few minutes ago."

"You didn't tell him over the phone!" She brought her voice down to a more normal pitch and volume and said again, "Brenna, don't tell me you did that."

"I didn't. I...chickened out. He's coming here, though. He'll escort me to the Christmas party."

"Oh." She stifled her disappointment. "Everyone will expect that, I guess."

"I know. We'll talk after the party, though. I...wanted your permission...to tell him about us."

Cassidy was torn. "Do you really want to do that? I thought you had other reasons that were precipitating the divorce."

"I do, but I realized they're all excuses, reasons to avoid coming right out and saying I don't love him. He recognized at Thanksgiving that we've been drifting apart. So, that's what I should tell him."

"Brenna, I don't know. My divorce was very messy because I'd had an affair. That's part of the reason I agreed we shouldn't do anything until you were...able to." She gripped the phone. "Besides, have you thought what that would be admitting? Are you really ready for the publicity? He's a public official, if a small-town one. The firestorm would be—"

"Oh God, unbearable." Brenna sighed. "I don't want to hurt him like that. I just want to be able to tell someone how much I love you," she ended with a whispered pledge.

Cassidy blushed at the lowered, enticing tone. "Brenna, I—"

"I had an incredible time today. All day," Brenna admitted with soft amazement. "I felt like we were a real family."

"James might have a problem with that," Cassidy pointed out.

"I think he'll come around. I had a talk with them."

"About us?"

"Not exactly, but I told them I was unhappy, that Kevin and I have problems."

"But you didn't actually mention divorce."

"No."

"What did they say?"

"That they want me to be happy." Brenna sounded a little stunned.

"I love your sons," Cassidy said. "We have a lot in common."

She heard the bedsprings as Brenna shifted on her bed. Imagining activities she could share with Brenna on that bed made her weak in the knees. She could almost imagine Brenna breathless and writhing under her touch.

"I, uh, should get some sleep," Brenna said reluctantly. "I have to take the boys to a men's shop tomorrow and rent tuxedos for their dance next Friday."

"Tuxes? That must've gone over well. I bet they'll look smashing, though. They've got their mom's genes, and you looked incredible in that men's suit in *Wild*

Horses."

During a time jump, they had all been swept through a vortex to the American Old West. A fun romp, the episode had been a breather from their usual characterizations. Jakes had portrayed a Calamity Jane type and Hanssen, one of the "upstairs girls". One of Hanssen's johns was supposed to be stopped from killing the town sheriff. Creighton had insinuated himself as the bartender and provided the modern, untraceable compound slipped into the drink. Jakes delivered the poisoned drink to their suspect during a high stakes card game.

"How long did you say you've been attracted to me again?"

Cassidy could just picture the sensual smile curling those kissable lips. The same look had innocently met the gaze of the sheriff, the man they had saved, though without his knowledge. Cassidy countered with a question of her own. "And what's the favorite outfit you've seen me in?"

"As Chris?"

"As Chris."

"I rather liked the flight jockey look on you in *Brains and Brawn*," Brenna replied huskily. "Before that, the gown from *Wild Horses*."

Cassidy grinned and chuckled softly. "See you Monday?"

"I'll be there."

"Good night, Bren."

"Good night, Cass."

Chapter 35

Crossing her feet at the ankles, Brenna leaned forward to get a better look at the script just laid in front of her on the small table in her trailer. "You really think I should consider it, Ray?"

Raymond Aruth, a slim man with brown hair and eyes, adjusted the lapel of his gray suit jacket. "Yes, I do. It's got an energized group already assembled. The script is original, bold."

"It's shooting in England."

"Tops you'd be there only...four weeks." He put a hand on her shoulder to close the sale. "They loved the clips I sent. They want you."

"When?"

"May. However, you have to go out before that specifically to read for the part, otherwise the government won't issue the work visa."

Brenna groaned. "Good thing my passport's up to date. When do they want to do that?"

"As soon as possible."

She looked at the opening pages. Ray had highlighted the role he had considered for her. The plot was elemental fantasy. She wondered what the pages would reveal.

"Read it. Think it over." Ray patted her hand. "Now, tell me how it's going here."

She set aside the script. "Good."

"Really?"

"Yes."

"Anything you need? I heard there was a top-down shake up."

Brenna nodded. Cameron and Will's fight still unnerved her. "Positive results from that so far."

"All right. How are Thomas and James?"

She smiled. "We had a good break together camping. I've gotten the time I wanted with them."

Ray stood. "That's great. So, it's still working. Happy?"

Brenna had an image of Cassidy the last time she had seen her. "Yes." She grinned. "It's proving to be a good season."

"I like that smile, Brenna. I do. It's been a while since I've seen it." He reached for his briefcase. "I've represented you for ten years, and that smile is a promise that I'll do it for a lot longer. Right?"

She stood and hugged him. "I promise I'll look at the project. England's daunting, though." She winced. "We'll see."

Opening the trailer door, Brenna let Ray hug her as he passed onto the steps. She leaned on the railing as he moved down to the sidewalk. Suddenly she joined him. "I'll walk you out."

They passed several crew members headed out to other soundstages. On another walkway, she glimpsed Cassidy and caught a small wave.

"I was looking at some of your recent tape," Ray said. "I'd like to add a couple of scenes from *Brains and Brawn* to your audition reel."

Brenna smiled, remembering the shoot and how hard she had worked on it. "Go ahead." They stopped on the path. "I'll call you after Christmas with my verdict on the movie proposal."

"Excellent. Give my love to your family."

"I will."

With quick strides, Brenna returned to her trailer to pick up her scripts. She was looking forward to the holiday break.

An unexpected visitor rose from her couch. "Cassidy?"

"Forgot what I looked like already?"

"I mean, what are you doing here?"

"I had to be here for a few meetings myself. I saw you with..."

"That was my agent, Ray Aruth."

"I thought I'd see how you were."

Brenna pulled her door shut. "I'm good."

Cassidy sat back on the couch, and Brenna watched her getting comfortable. In deference to the cool temperatures, she wore a light blue sweater and wool slacks. A jacket lay over the couch arm next to her. "I thought about what you said," Cassidy interjected into the silence.

"What?"

"About telling Kevin about us. I'm still not sure you should, but I don't want to tell you how—"

Brenna knelt on the couch cushion, one knee on either side of Cassidy's thighs, and put a light hand over full lips. "You didn't. You expressed an opinion that I asked for. And you're right," she added, "about the press it would generate. I won't let you or Ryan be hurt." She leaned forward, removed her fingers, and kissed Cassidy soundly.

"So now, tell me about what Ray brought you?"

Brenna chuckled as Cassidy tugged her down until she was sitting on her lap. "It's a script to be filmed in England," she said.

"Sounds interesting."

"It sounds far away," Brenna countered.

"Well, read the script before you decide. If it's worth a look, you'll find a way."

Brenna blinked. She had thought with them feeling their way into a relationship, her leaving the States right now would have been at the bottom of Cassidy's suggestion list. "You're serious."

"Don't I sound serious?"

Cassidy's fingers combed through her hair, and Brenna couldn't deny how wonderful it made her feel. "What about us?"

"There isn't any us...yet," Cassidy pointed out. "But even if there was...Brenna, you're a brilliant actress. We'll find projects together or close to one another, or I'll wait while you work, and...I hope...you'll wait while I work. I won't ever tell you that you can't do a project that you want."

Cassidy was in earnest; Brenna saw the proof of it in her face. A lump of emotion lodged in her throat. She rubbed her eyes to avoid the tears burning in them. Hands slid up her arms to her shoulders and pulled her against a warm, soft chest. "Thank you," she murmured against the soft skin of Cassidy's throat.

Fingers brushed against her chin, lifting it. "So...tell me, was the tux hunt fun?"

Brenna laughed at the change of subject. Obviously her getting emotional over the statement of support made Cassidy uncomfortable. *Well, damn it, no one had ever just said, "Do it" before.* "They suffered, but now Thomas and James are properly outfitted for Friday."

"Have any pictures?"

"In my bag."

"Let's see." Brenna withdrew the Polaroids, and Cassidy encouraged her to recline into her chest to share the viewing. Her fingers moved gently over Brenna's shoulders, raising tingles, then down her sides under her arms before tucking around her stomach.

The first picture was of James. Cassidy traced the outline of his frown as he fidgeted with the cummerbund. "He doesn't look pleased."

"James would rather curl up with a book than dance, but he's going because he's totally in love with Marcie."

"Do you like to dance?"

"I love it," Brenna replied, as Cassidy's hand slid across her abdomen. "I took a little time on Sunday night to show them both how to lead." She grinned, remembering the awkward moments as they stepped on her feet or just stumbled on the idea that their mom was teaching them to dance. However, she had seen the pride in their eyes when she declared them "fit to serve". She switched to another picture — James adjusting Thomas' bowtie. "They managed passable ties, too."

Cassidy looked more closely at Thomas' figure. "He really takes after you," she murmured. "I love that smile."

"Thomas has always been...more balanced. Maybe it was the fact that he was already in school when I divorced Tom. James...cried for months, upset at the least little change in plans or routine." Brenna fell silent, pensive as she recalled those difficult days.

"What happened with your first marriage?" Cassidy nudged her into the curve of her shoulder. Brenna lifted a knee and adjusted her position to be more comfortable. Cassidy's chin dropped gently onto her right shoulder, faint breathing sounding reassuringly in her ear.

"I was becoming miserable. I love my boys, but I wasn't working. I hadn't worked in almost three years. I felt a part of myself dying." She sipped in a breath. "Tom said it was for the best. I should just quit entirely, he said. Stay home and raise the boys." She swallowed the bitterness that still rose at his total lack of support. "He did not understand at all. There he was with his work; I had nothing." She pursed her lips and frowned, then inhaled and exhaled slowly. *God, it still hurts — feeling that alone.*

"So, I got out. Custody was tougher. He was working; I wasn't. I knew that without Thomas and James, something in me would die."

Cassidy brushed her cheek against Brenna's. "Mitch did the same to me. I'm so sorry."

Soft lips traced over her brow, and Brenna turned into the touch. Finally she felt surrounded by someone who honestly could understand. Their lips met; Cassidy's mouth soothed over hers. Waves of desire washed over her, through her. There was no shooting to interrupt them, no script demanding rehearsal. No time constraints at all.

Putting aside the pictures, she curled into Cassidy's body and murmured, "I've thought about you, about this. If you have time," she went on, tilting her chin to bring her lips into contact with the smooth curve of Cassidy's jaw, "I'd love one of those lessons you promised."

Cassidy nuzzled her ear. "If you like."

Beneath her hands, Brenna felt Cassidy's heart rate pick up, confirming her interest. She turned around and straddled Cassidy's knees, resting her hands on the slender shoulders, looking down into an upturned face. "I'd like." She ducked her head to capture full lips. Cassidy's hands remained on her hips as Brenna balanced her weight onto her knees to either side.

"You said you've done this before," Brenna pointed out. She trailed her fingers under Cassidy's top, watching Cassidy's eyes drift shut as Brenna warmed her hands against tight muscles and delicate skin. "You'll have to tell me if I'm doing it right." Cassidy's eyes opened as Brenna found a spot along Cassidy's ribs that made the other woman jump. She moved her hand away from the ticklish spot, and her fingertips grazed the soft weight of another woman's breasts for the first time. She inhaled, entranced by Cassidy's direct and intensifying gaze.

Cassidy's hands moved from resting on her hips to resting just below Brenna's bra. Brenna felt the difference in touch like an epiphany. The fingers were slender, soft, and smooth and made her arch into the contact. Cassidy moved her hands around Brenna's back and undid her bra, moving it aside. The edge of the fabric abraded a nipple, hardening it. Silk soft fingers moved over the outline of her breasts, while Brenna maintained eye contact. Slim fingertips trapped her nipples as she did the same to Cassidy's. The intense connection she always felt around Cassidy, and had never quite understood, strengthened as they both tweaked sharply.

Brenna was startled by the intensity of the shock that shot to her groin. Her fingers flexed unconsciously, and Cassidy arched into the contact, encouraging exploration. She felt the nipples harden against her palms and huskily asked, "Will you take it off?"

Cassidy smiled. Her marvelous hands left Brenna's skin for a brief moment as she tugged off the top. When her arms came down, she found Brenna studying her torso. "The costume changes the look," she explained bashfully.

"You're beautiful." Brenna was surprised by her sharp desire to taste the nipples hardening under her fingertips. She met Cassidy's eyes. "Please tell me they're as sensitive as mine."

Cassidy laughed, and there was a sign of patience and restraint in the catch of her voice. "As sensitive as yours, I can't say, but you're welcome to find out." Covering Brenna's hands with her own, Cassidy moved their hands together over her breasts.

Brenna considered what turned her on and tentatively followed imagination with action. To her delight, Cassidy writhed, offering up moans of pleasure that Brenna stole away with kisses. The textures were familiar, yet not. She was surprised how much she felt deep in her own groin as Cassidy continued to voice her appreciation. The gentle scent of arousal, both hers and Cassidy's, rose between them. Slowly she pulled one hand away, and down, feeling Cassidy's stomach muscles constrict as she passed over them. She captured an abandoned nipple in her mouth as her fingers pulled at the waistband of Cassidy's pants.

Massaging Brenna's scalp and hair with languid pleasure, Cassidy's hands left tingles in their wake. Despite the definite wetness between her thighs, Brenna felt no need to rush, only to indulge. Cassidy's body was responsive, but again there was no push from her to move faster, nothing like she had experienced from men who wanted to get down to business.

Brenna moved her attention up Cassidy's body once again, capturing her lips briefly before returning attention to Cassidy's breasts. The woman's reactions thrilled her as she indulged both their desires.

Cassidy's pulse thrummed hard in her throat, but she only continued to stroke Brenna's hands, cheeks, and hair as Brenna explored her breasts. Brenna found she liked the weight in her palm, lifting it and licking the hardened nub before returning it to between her teeth and sucking on it. Moans and cries of her name wrapped Brenna in more love than she thought she could hold.

Brenna pulled back and met Cassidy's gaze, finding the same hot blue gaze she had inadvertently caused in the gym shower. Slender fingers cupped her chin.

"You..." Cassidy began unsteadily, pausing to moisten her lips with her tongue, "don't need lessons."

Brenna rested her palms across Cassidy's stomach and felt the quivering muscles. The sensation slowly dissipated, and Cassidy's eyes stopped looking quite so glazed.

"Is that good?" Cocky pride edged her voice as she realized that, even in her inexperience, she could move Cassidy to such an intense reaction.

"Brenna, cockiness is very attractive on you." Cassidy sat fully upright and stripped Brenna's shirt off, along with the bra.

"Must be why they made me commander," Brenna teased back, trying to mask her anxiety as Cassidy looked at her, studying her body intensely. "Like what you see?"

Cassidy loved what she saw. Brenna's breasts were just a handful. Much to the other woman's enjoyment, she tested their fit in her palms. Brenna closed her eyes and bit her lower lip endearingly. Freckles liberally dotted her upper chest. The nipples were taut, and a golden tan blended into wide areolas. "I was right," Cassidy said, dragging her eyes up to Brenna's face.

Brenna's eyes opened with surprise. "About what?"

"You do sunbathe in the buff." Drawing her fingertips down evenly tanned skin from sternum to stomach, she felt the muscles jump as she nudged her fingers under the waistband. "Don't you?"

"Yes." Brenna's blush spread down not only her throat, but her upper chest as well, making the freckles, which Cassidy now kissed, stand out.

"How could you chain this free spirit for so long?" Cassidy asked, honestly curious. "It's incredible. I only glimpse it when you're beyond exhausted at the end of a day of shooting." She lifted her chin to nibble Brenna's lips as their bared breasts brushed together. Brenna's open-mouthed moan slipped hotly between her teeth.

Gasps of delight blew softly through the hair on Cassidy's temple as she lowered her mouth to taste Brenna's sun-kissed skin. She watched the muscles flex in Brenna's shoulder as the woman's arm encircled her neck. Cassidy nudged her nose into the tendons in Brenna's throat. The jumping pulse under her palm on Brenna's left breast told her she had found a ticklish spot. She kissed the skin more firmly and licked the mild salts.

Moving Brenna off her thighs, she arranged the woman against the couch pillows. She trailed a fingertip over Brenna's throat, cheek, lips, and nose, drawing their gazes together. A low quiver started in her own stomach again, and she realized she wanted to go all the way — right now, right here. Aware of other limitations, though, she inhaled and exhaled, catching sight of a clock on the nearby table. "I'd better stop," she murmured. "I have to meet with my agent in twenty minutes."

Rising onto her elbows, Brenna nodded. "Okay, but that gives us, what? Fifteen?" She offered a searing, passionate expression.

Cassidy would have willingly burned to a crisp had Brenna been actual fire. However, she did not want to explain to her agent that she was late for their meeting because she was having sex with her co-star. It would cause far too many questions too soon. Cassidy acknowledged she was willing to face those questions eventually. She would have even escorted Brenna to the Pinnacle party and weathered the questions then, but Brenna was right to hold off. They did not want press, not right now when this was so new for the two of them.

She indulged them both in the distraction of another absorbing kiss. Brenna's mouth was flavored by her morning coffee and her teeth were pearl smooth. *Her tongue...*Cassidy sucked the little muscle into her mouth and felt her head spin when Brenna initiated a sensual duel. She broke the kiss, panting softly. "God, Brenna." She found herself captured by a grin, seduction narrowing Brenna's eyes and curving her wine-shade lips.

"Later?"

Regretting now that she really did have to go, Cassidy nodded. "Not too much later." She sat up and reached for her top. Pulling it on, she watched Brenna do the same. "I'd like to take you on a date," she said abruptly.

"What? Where?"

"Somewhere away from work, away from kids. Just you, me, and an open evening."

Brenna thought for a moment, "I don't know when we could work that out." They stood, with Cassidy at her shoulder bestowing a kiss behind her right ear. She leaned against the taller woman, feeling her breasts pillow against her back. Together they drifted into a zone of sensation as their body heat rekindled. "But I'll come up with something."

"Your husband will be here Saturday."

Brenna's hand slipped from the doorknob, and the door opened slowly. Without thought, she turned hotly into the mouth and hands that drew sensation out of her every pore. She wrapped her arms around Cassidy's neck and pressed wantonly against her. While tasting the full lips, she offered a hungry promise: "I'll call you."

Cameron Palassis grumbled. He had to cross the whole lot these days to reach the sets being built for Pinnacle's newest series. He was supposed to oversee the PR shooting they would use to entice the rest of the actors they wanted, now that their principal was in place.

Looking up, he realized he had reached "trailer row" behind the *Time Trails* soundstages. He frowned, still angry about being pulled off the dramatic series. *All because of that asshole Chapman,* he bitched. The sound of a door opening, coming from the end where Chapman had his trailer, drew his attention. Cameron's hands flexed. What he wouldn't give to rearrange the man's face. He walked closer.

The open door was not Chapman's trailer, but Lanigan's, and she was not alone. It took less than a breath for him to identify the blonde standing with her. *Cassidy?* Stepping back in surprise, he saw Brenna's arms slide around Cassidy's neck and pull her head down.

Cautious but curious, he edged around the trailer and looked on as Cassidy's hands slid down Brenna's butt. He had never thought of Brenna as attractive, really, but watching the long-fingered familiar hands stroking over the small ass, he grew hard.

Son of a bitch! his mind screamed. *Brenna and Cassidy, his Cassidy, were kissing!* He could not deny the total turn-on as he reassessed his thinking that Cassidy was prudish. Obviously, he had been mistaken. *What a fucking turn-on. Hmm.* He wondered if Cassidy might be persuaded to invite him to their playtime.

Not now, he thought with some sense. *There will be a better time to make a deal.* So he held his knowledge close and retreated quickly before either woman saw him.

Chapter 36

"Front and center," Brenna called, standing by the front door. Still adjusting his bowtie, Thomas appeared first. James appeared at the end of the corridor, his shoes in his hands.

"I'm not ready yet," he protested.

"Well, you're going to have to be, young man," Brenna teased. "Never keep a lady waiting."

He leaned against the couch arm and tugged the shoes on. Standing, he held his arms wide. "Better?"

She grinned and held his cheeks between her palms, kissing him soundly. "Perfect." Brenna turned to Thomas and looked him over with a loving, critical eye. She reached out and adjusted the lapel of his jacket. "There."

"Thanks, Mom." Thomas stuffed his hands in the pockets of the jacket. Almost immediately, his mother tugged his hands out. "This cummerbund is awful." He grimaced but resisted adjusting it. "Mom, do men really wear this stuff?"

"All the time. It's not the throwback you think it is." She patted his cheek. "I promise."

James straightened up and grinned at Thomas. Stockier than his brother, who had the lean build of a runner, James was considerably slimmed by the formal tailored suit. "I like it. Thanks, Mom."

"Kiss up," Thomas snorted.

"Hey," Brenna warned.

"Sorry."

"You both look wonderful." She lifted the camera pulled out for the occasion. "All right, line up."

Thomas and James rolled their eyes, but they stood in the entryway, in front of the door. Arms around one another's shoulders, with the occasionally bunny ears over one another's heads, they posed for their mother. Brenna snapped the shutter a dozen times and then finally set the camera aside.

"Now," she picked up the Mountaineer's keys, "one a.m.?" Thomas nodded as his hand closed around the fob. "I'll be waiting up," she promised.

"Yes, Mom."

She feathered her fingertips through his hair, setting it to rights. She turned her gaze to James, combed her fingers through his hair as well, then trailed them down his cheek and chucked his chin. "You look really handsome," she said, pride and love filling her chest. She swallowed it down and patted his cheek. "You'd better go. You don't want to be late."

She hung at the door, watching Thomas back them out of the drive and head off to pick up the girls. Dinner would be first. The boys had reservations at Michael's. The dance would be at the Radisson ballroom starting at eight p.m.

Offering up a prayer for their safety, she sat down on her couch and reached for the script from England. With a soft exhalation, she pushed her slip-ons off her feet and sank deeper in the cushions seeking a comfortable position. She tried to concentrate on the pages of dialogue, but they blurred. Rubbing her neck, she let her head drop back to rest against the couch arm.

Brenna's body told her loudly exactly what was missing. Or, rather, *who* was missing. Not going to the set for four days had felt terribly strange. Before, set breaks had simply induced boredom. The additional duress of not seeing Cassidy each day had brought her close to stir crazy. The boys were going to be gone almost seven hours. Looking longingly at the phone, she asked herself if it would really hurt anything to spend those hours with Cassidy. *Conversation, a movie maybe?* She nodded, agreeing with herself, and picked up the phone.

As it rang, she wondered what to say. *What if Cassidy can't find a sitter?* She would enjoy having Ryan, but she recalled Cassidy's request for a date, just the two of them.

"Hello?"

"Hi." Pleasure filled her voice at the sound of Cassidy on the other end of the line.

"I just finished reading to Ryan. What's up?"

"I just sent Thomas and James off to their dance. You, um, don't have to, but...I've got movies, or popcorn?" She shrugged at the phone as her nervous tongue stuttered to a stop. "I would love to see you." Brenna bit her lip, waiting.

"I'd love to see you, too." There was relief in Cassidy's voice. "How's seven sound?"

"Think you could arrange it?"

"I'll be there," Cassidy promised.

Cassidy hung up the phone, dazedly considering her good fortune. The series was on hiatus until after New Year's and she had heard nothing from Brenna since their tryst in her trailer. Nearly a week had passed, and Cassidy had begun to wonder if she'd dreamed their mutual explorations or if perhaps Brenna had simply decided it was all too much.

Looking down at the coveralls she had worn while refreshing the all-weather white paint on her back porch, she decided she'd better change. She had come inside on a break from the project, and Ryan had asked for a book, leaving her only the chance to pull off the paint-spattered smock. She reached for the phone again and took it with her when she went into the bedroom to search her closet. It had been two weeks since Gwen had last looked after Ryan. She hoped the time away had settled the Talbots' situation. "Gwen," she greeted as the line opened.

"Hello, Cassidy. What's up?"

"I need a sitter."

"Going out?"

"Yes, can you? I don't know how late I'll be out. I know it's last minute, but I'd rather he be with you for the night rather than ask one of the Treacle girls down the street." Cassidy waited, counting her heartbeats in the silence.

Finally Gwen responded, "We'll keep him all night. I'll return him in the morning."

"I'll call tonight around ten." Feeling butterflies in her stomach, Cassidy realized she was nervous about seeing Brenna. She, unlike Cameron, would have no problem at all if Ryan had to come along, but honestly, what would he do at Brenna's with her boys gone? She wanted time with Brenna, and the woman had made a point of reminding her that her own sons were at a dance for the night.

"No problem," Gwen assured her. "I'll deliver him in the morning. You have a good time."

"Thank you."

"Leave an emergency number?"

"My cell is always on."

"All right."

"See you in a few minutes." Cassidy hung up the receiver and looked through her open doorway into Ryan's room. "Ryan?"

"Yes, Mommy?" He appeared at the doorway, Legos in hand.

"I'm going out for a while. Pack up so I can take you to Chance's house."

"Okay."

He handled the change in plans with such calm it made Cassidy wonder. *Have I spent that much time out?* "Ryan?"

"Mmm hmm?"

"We'll be going to Grandma's for Christmas, okay?" She had not wanted to leave town for the holidays, but maybe a little concentrated time with Ryan would be good for both of them. Certainly she could not sit here in L.A. wondering how Brenna was faring with Kevin's visit. She had no idea how long he intended to stay. Besides, she did not want to get in the way if Brenna decided to use the time to talk to Kevin about a divorce.

Cassidy sighed. *Why'd I have to fall for her after she married?* she asked, knowing that she had barely known Brenna prior to her marriage, not only because of her abrupt arrival to the series, but because of her own problems, affair, and divorce.

Melancholy words of a romantic song tripped across her brain. "*It's sad to belong to someone else when the right one comes along.*" Desperate to get away from Mitch, Cassidy had decided Cameron was "the right one" and jumped from one ship to another, completely overlooking the woman who was the reason she had agreed to join the series in the first place. She paused, realizing the implications of her thoughts.

She recalled the tapes her agent and the Pinnacle executives had shown her to convince her to accept the role of Lieutenant Hanssen. She even remembered the scene that had clinched it. Commander Susan Jakes had been injured, and Brenna played opposite a very talented actor, Brett Heslip, who portrayed a man who believed the injured commander was his daughter.

The range of emotions on Brenna's delicate, determined face had immediately captured Cassidy's attention. Brenna had played the lines written, but Cassidy recognized that what made the words work was Brenna's special gift — portraying the riveting emotional turmoil of a woman torn with real love for her rescuer. The Pinnacle people had not needed another session; Cassidy agreed to the part. She wanted the chance to play opposite that kind of depth.

But instead of working closely as allies, their characters were set against one another, and life seemed to imitate art. Despite that, though, Cassidy had intensified her attempts to break through Brenna's icy reserve toward her off-camera.

Standing in front of her closet considering her choices, Cassidy recognized the nervous indecision that accompanied going on a first date. Brushing her hair back from her face, she shook her head. *Come on. This is Brenna.* The agenda was a movie and popcorn, which strongly suggesting a casual evening, so Cassidy reached for a pair of Capri pants in a neutral taupe. She stepped into the comfortable cotton Lycra mix, then looked through the sleeveless tops she favored and finally decided on a v-neck in pale blue cashmere that was not form fitting. She dusted her hair off her face and examined her appearance in the mirror. Shaking her head, she went to replace the Capris with dark blue jeans.

Splashing water on her face, Cassidy studied her features in the small bathroom mirror, hoping Brenna would approve. She chuckled as she rubbed her damp palms on a towel. *God, I am so nervous about this. What's up with that?* She thought about the compact woman and the glimpses of skin she had seen in the gym and in the trailer. *Because I want something to happen tonight.*

Thinking back to her one college experience, Cassidy was suddenly plagued by self-doubt. Would she be able to make Brenna's first same-sex experience pleasurable? Just thinking about it made her stomach swirl with desire.

Her time with Misty had been an experiment, a solace for both of them for losing boyfriends. She had enjoyed herself, but the feelings had been ultimately casual, not emotionally entangling, no matter that she had been in a daze for an entire week. Her feelings had not even been hurt when Misty abruptly announced she was going to bed a fraternity brother who had caught her eye.

With Brenna, it was not going to be a game, and it was so far from casual as to feel in another universe entirely. Cassidy wanted to make Brenna cry out with pleasure. She wanted to have Brenna lie in her arms afterward and for the two of them to whisper together of future dreams and wishes. She wanted to share a life with Brenna for years to come.

Walking out to the front door, she called for Ryan. "Come on, buddy." With his small hand in hers, Cassidy felt steadier. She glanced in her front hall mirror and frowned. Grabbing a brush from the table, she stroked several times through her already perfect locks before ushering Ryan into the evening air.

No car sat in the Talbots' driveway. Cassidy knocked; Gwen answered.

"Lou's out," she said when asked.

Cassidy handed over Ryan's bag. "Are you sure you want him all night?"

"It'll be easier on him. If you get home early, just get some sleep. We'll see you after breakfast." Gwen patted Ryan on the back and sent him to find Chance.

"When will Lou be home?"

"Sunday. He's checking a job lead upstate."

"So he did lose his job."

"Yeah."

"I'm sorry."

Gwen shook her head. "Somebody will pick him up." She leaned over. "So, is this a date with Brenna?"

"Snacks and a movie."

Gwen pursed her lips. "Friends? She's still married."

"Yes."

"Be careful."

"Thank you, Gwen. That means a lot." Cassidy grasped her friend's hands briefly, then hurried out to her car.

Eagerness to see Brenna drove her across town quickly. She stopped at a florist shop on the outskirts of Pacific Palisades and chose two perfect roses surrounded by baby's breath before proceeding to Brenna's home.

Gripping the roses in one hand, she raised her empty one and rapped with the engraved knocker. *This must be why men bring something on a date,* she thought, hiding her shaking hands under the tissue paper. She had a sudden carnal image of grabbing Brenna as soon as she opened the door, pushing her against the wall, and kissing her hard. Excitement warred with anxiety as she waited.

Brenna had stepped out of the shower twenty minutes earlier. Aside from brushing her hair, she had managed to decide on her underwear and not much else. Seated at her vanity, she looked to the closet open to her left and at the array of clothes scattered on the bed — and wished the butterflies in her stomach would go away. She stood and shook her head at her image in the mirrored door.

Her little voice prodded with uncertainty, *You really want her to see you?* Her gaze swept her figure. Forty-plus years glared back at her — from the uneven sag of her breasts to the extra swell at her stomach. Tiny crow's feet shaped the corners of her eyes.

Cassidy, on the other hand, was young, fit, and trim. Brenna sighed with pleasure, reliving the feel of soft breasts nestled in her palms. She fisted her hands in her lap. Cassidy was not just a body, though Brenna had thought that when Cassidy first arrived. Since that original erroneous assessment, Cassidy had more than proven she was smart, forthright, and not at all arrogant, as Brenna had also wrongly assumed. Cassidy had gifted instincts as an actress and a giving nature.

That she could have fallen in love with a woman shocked the Midwestern Catholic part of Brenna. Trying to set that aside, she was clinging to the possibility that she had finally found someone who accepted her completely.

She scooped up her black sweater and stepped into her favorite steel gray slacks. *Informal*, she staunchly told herself. She stepped into sandals and crossed through the living room and from there to the refrigerator, where she checked on the bottle of wine she had chilling.

There was a knocker rap at the front door. Drying her perspiring hands on her hips, Brenna went to welcome her guest. "Hi. Come on in." She looked at the short, deep brown leather coat Cassidy wore. "Can I take your coat?"

"Thanks." Cassidy pulled it off, and Brenna opened the front closet, pulling down a hanger for the coat and then placing it back inside. Wondering at her brief thought of it never leaving, she left the coat with a lingering stroke down the arm.

As she turned around, Cassidy stood close over her shoulder. "How was the drive?" Brenna asked, feeling like her heart was doing a marathon.

"Fine."

Cassidy's arms moved, and Brenna jumped as something appeared between them. She looked down in wonder. "Roses?" She studied the entwined pair, a red rose and a golden rose. "Where did you find these?" She looked up into Cassidy's face. "They're incredible."

"I thought of us when I saw them." Cassidy blushed. "God, I've never said that to anyone before." She leaned in for a fast kiss.

When they could part, Cassidy still nuzzling Brenna's hair, Brenna took Cassidy's hand and led her into the living room, her stomach aflutter with nervous butterflies. She couldn't tell who was shaking more as they gripped hands and settled on the couch.

"When I invited you, I had every intention of just sharing a movie and popcorn with you."

Cassidy curled on the couch and looked back at her steadily. "A first date," she replied, "never goes too far. I grew up with the same mores."

Their grasps on one another's hands tightened, and they leaned closer. "So, do we start the movie?" Brenna's voice quavered.

"What's the movie?" Cassidy's voice was even less steady, and she did not break contact with Brenna's eyes.

"*The English Patient.*"

"I hear it was good." Cassidy's mouth was only a breath away.

Brenna's breath was short. "Very good," she barely voiced. "One of my favorite movies." Their mouths fell together as she finished. Hands and arms tugged bodies close.

"Four days." Cassidy hid her head against Brenna's shoulder as she murmured her fear. "I thought... Four days and you didn't say anything. I thought that you had decided you couldn't—"

"I never stopped thinking about Monday," Brenna replied, still keyed up and slightly raspy. "I couldn't find any time alone to talk to you."

Cassidy leaned back, and Brenna turned so their bodies settled together, her arm across Cassidy's stomach. "So, um..." Cassidy's fingertips circled over Brenna's forearm in a slow manner as they both caught their breath. "How about that movie?"

"All right." Brenna slipped from her cozy spot and put in the tape. "The movie." She handed Cassidy the remote. "Popcorn?"

Nodding, Cassidy turned on the television and then the tape player, amused by the absence of up-to-date equipment. It was a VHS player, not even a combination DVD/VHS machine like she had in her own home. Brenna had a turntable, too, obviously a classic, for records that were on another shelf. As the previews played, she adjusted the sound level then turned to watch Brenna in the kitchen. "Need help?"

"No." Brenna paused and turned around. "Well, yes. I...there's something in the refrigerator I thought we might enjoy."

Cassidy was immediately on her feet with an eager smile. "Chocolate?"

"Ah, the perfect aphrodisiac," Brenna remarked. "I've never had to think like a seductress, so no, chocolate never occurred to me. It's a bottle of wine."

Cassidy opened the refrigerator, found the wine bottle, and read the label. "Wine and popcorn — a first for me."

"Well, it *is* a first date," Brenna quipped. "Lots of firsts," she set the pan of kernels over the gas burner, "in lots of things." Concentrating on the popcorn, she felt Cassidy come up behind her.

The younger woman's hands caressed her shoulders. "You're shaking as much as the pan."

"I guess I am."

"How late are Thomas and James going to be out?" Cassidy asked. "Just for reference."

"Their curfew is one a.m." As Cassidy did not move, Brenna began to relax. Their bodies were close but not touching. The heat was incredible — addictive, seductive. She moderated her breathing to concentrate on not burning the popcorn. When the silence was broken by the first kernels exploding, Brenna stepped back directly into Cassidy's chest.

"Careful." Cassidy's hand closed around Brenna's and steadied the pan. "You have this nasty habit of acquiring burns when you're around me."

Brenna chuckled and more of the expectant tension broke, leaving her closer to the lightheartedness that characterized their easiest conversations together. "I'm glad you came over."

"Are you all set for tomorrow?"

"Yes." Brenna nodded soberly. "Kevin arrives in the morning." She pulled the pan away from the fire and poured the popcorn into a large earthenware bowl. "I don't want to think about tomorrow. Let's just think about tonight."

"If I do that, we won't be doing much talking," Cassidy said, popping a puffed kernel into her mouth. "But if you're worried about Kevin...are you going to be okay while he's here?"

"I haven't figured out what to say to him. He's... I mistook need for love," she said sadly. "He was stability when I needed it."

"Do you think you ever loved him?"

"Once, maybe. I'm not sure anymore."

"What's different with us?"

Brenna shook her head. "I'm not any better at putting that into words, but I feel...like you might understand me...all the little parts that don't make sense sometimes...even to me."

"I can't wait to discover all those little parts," Cassidy said with a smile. "Ready for the movie?" They returned to the living room, wine and popcorn in hand. Brenna and Cassidy sat together on the couch, and Brenna found the remote and pushed play, keeping the volume low.

Easing her arm around Brenna's shoulder, Cassidy asked, "Have you looked over the English script?"

"A little. I like it."

"I read somewhere you'd done another movie overseas before," Cassidy said.

"A mythic romance." Brenna sipped her wine. "I was twenty-five. It was in Scotland. Tom hated that I was gone for a month. After that, he wouldn't let me do anything unless it was shot in L.A. Understandably, the project offers tapered off."

"But you liked that movie."

"I loved it," she enthused. "It was epic. How I carried the role really mattered. He just didn't care." She took a long swig.

Taking the bottle from her, Cassidy nodded. "Tom was a director, right?"

"Still is, though he does fewer projects."

"So, Kevin is totally opposite. I can see it."

"So could I. It was the only clear image I had during those days."

"I really am sorry we didn't get a chance to talk like this when I first joined the cast," Cassidy said. "I gather I was the devil incarnate for much of the first year?"

Brenna winced. "That wasn't fair of me."

"I could have told Cameron to stop setting up all those PR appearances. All that extra publicity work kept me away from Mitch, but that build-up wasn't fair to you."

Brenna waved that off. "Even if he had ulterior motives, he actually did help you. It doesn't sound as if your marriage was ever good. How did you meet Mitch?"

"At a cabana bar when I first got to L.A. after graduation," Cassidy said. "I did a little modeling. He was working the beach bar, and going to school. After he finished his master's in finance, we moved back to his hometown, Highland, Illinois, which was across the river from St. Louis. My parents liked having us closer, too, and for a while it was all right.

"Like you, though, I wanted to get back to L.A., to maybe do some acting. At first it was all right with Mitch. I'd stay with Gwen and Lou when I came out to do some modeling and a few walk-on parts. Then I became pregnant with Ryan. Mitch really began working at holding on to me. Forbidding me from leaving, and, well, hitting me when I didn't listen. When I got the vampire movie, he managed to make it look like a simple accident, but he broke my foot in three places. A director here saw footage and wanted me to screen test. I missed three calls from my agent because Mitch erased the voicemails."

Brenna and Cassidy eased together as they talked more about their early marriages, about what they had done to their lives as they discovered what they really wanted. About how marriage and motherhood had changed them and their expectations of what was important. About all the missteps they had made anyway.

Shaking her head, Brenna lamented, "I ran away from the anxiety your arrival generated in me and walked right back into a marriage — and all out of fear. Kevin should have a woman who loves him. I can't be her."

"Do you think he'll understand?"

"I don't know. He may feel like I've been lying to him. Trouble is, I'm not certain I wasn't. I certainly was lying to myself. Doesn't that mean I lied to him?"

Cassidy hugged her and kissed her temple. Caught by the scent of Brenna's hair, she continued nuzzling the fine strands. "I don't know the answer."

"It's enough that you listen," Brenna replied, her hand stroking Cassidy's leg as they sat in a half-dark room illuminated only by the television's flickering. "Really." She moved closer and melded their torsos together, pressing a tender kiss to the full lips.

Cassidy didn't let her pull away, instead wrapping her arms around Brenna's back while she explored Brenna's mouth. Both their heartbeats ticked up a notch. "First date?" Cassidy asked breathlessly when they parted briefly.

Brenna found it so easy to slide her hands under Cassidy's sweater. "Um. Maybe... There was..." She brushed Cassidy's lips, remembering their first kiss in the woods. "Camping...we shared a sleeping bag. Then there was...um, the gym and dinner? So...third?"

"Certainly kissing is permitted on a third date," Cassidy murmured, pressing her lips to Brenna's and then sliding her tongue into wet warmth.

"Absolutely," Brenna concurred breathlessly as she pulled back. Slowly her fingers edged the cashmere up Cassidy's ribcage. "We've showered together already," she pointed out. Hands shaking slightly, she eased the top higher, "And seen each other nude."

"Partially nude," Cassidy corrected.

"Maybe, we could just...satisfy our curiosity?" Brenna murmured the question against Cassidy's breastbone, inhaling the scent of skin and light perspiration.

"Are you sure?" Cassidy pulled back and watched the need clear a little from Brenna's face. "I don't want you to regret anything. I don't want to regret it either."

Brenna exhaled. "I know that I want to connect with you completely." She bit her lip. "You excite me," she pointed to her heart, "in here. It's lust, and love...I think. For the first time I'm not really able to articulate everything I'm feeling, and it's a bit frustrating. I'm no novice, you know, but it feels...wonderful and scary. But right. Does that make sense?"

Cassidy pulled Brenna to her to place a tender kiss on her nose, cheeks, and then finally her lips. "It does. It's not something I understood either, until I looked at you and wanted the same thing."

"So, um..." Brenna licked her lips, aware there was a precipice looming, "does this mean we should move to the bedroom?"

"We could sit here," Cassidy mused, "if you want your sons to find a wet spot on the couch."

Brenna shivered and her groin convulsed at the thought of how they might cause that wet spot. "Let's clear this stuff into the kitchen."

"We should wash our hands." To illustrate her point, Cassidy traced a popcorn-greased finger down Brenna's cheek.

They made quick work of putting away the bowl and bottle and turned off the television, taking turns at the kitchen sink with soap and water. Warm, damp hands brushed together, and Brenna, still trembling, led the way to the bedroom.

Closing the door carefully, Brenna and Cassidy looked at the array of clothing covering the bed. "It took me three outfits to figure out what to wear, too," Cassidy confessed with a hint of laughter.

Scooping the clothing to the vanity chair, Brenna turned to find Cassidy sitting on the bed. Her hands splayed across the sheets, tracing their whimsical blue and white flower pattern before she looked up. Brenna reached up and tucked her hair behind her ear as Cassidy's gaze lingered. *She's here. She's really here. In my bed.* She started to tug her sweater over her head. Suddenly hands wrapped around her waist, and she was falling to the bed. Cassidy completed the removal of her top, tossed it aside, and rolled half over her body, warm fingers stroking over her stomach.

"I was taking too long making up my mind, wasn't I?"

"Oh no, not at all. My body heat was just about to set your bed on fire. You could've stood there as long as you wanted; I'd have just burned up the bedroom around you." Cassidy chuckled and pulled off her sweater, tossing it to the floor with Brenna's.

Brenna's hands slid up Cassidy's arms and shoulders, then down, slowly circling the breasts. "Partial nudity achieved," she reminded with a grin.

Cassidy's hand caressed Brenna's thigh and calf to tug off her sandals. Their gazes locked. Reversing direction, she moved her hand up the inside of Brenna's thigh until the heat from her center guided her the rest of the way. Softly she covered the area for a moment, reveling in the heat and her own rising passion, then reached for the top of Brenna's pants.

Lifting her hips as the slacks were removed, Brenna felt Cassidy's touch along the bare skin of her inner thighs for the first time. She hooked her fingers into Cassidy's waistband and tugged in return. Warm skin, smooth and familiar in an unfamiliar way, met her palms as she spread her fingers across the taut abdomen. Braced over her, Cassidy copied the touch against Brenna's stomach.

They looked their fill for several minutes. "Touch me." Cassidy lowered herself onto her side on the mattress and combed her fingers through Brenna's hair as the other woman's fingers explored over peaks and valleys. With whispered encouragement, she told Brenna how each touch made her feel.

Brenna moved against her, and Cassidy's tremors quaked through her as Brenna first brushed her fingers through the hairs covering Cassidy's mound.

Cassidy's hand slid over the roundness of Brenna's butt, nudging her fingers toward her intimate flesh from behind. Brenna arched into the contact and they kissed as they each found wetness for the first time. Nervous laughter served as a vent to their passions.

Brenna felt the penetration in detail. An intimacy far keener than simple sex, Cassidy's fingertips circled in her wetness. "Cass." She moved her hips into the contact, encouraging it deeper. She felt her muscles ripple around the digits as her own fingertips explored between Cassidy's folds. She kept her eyes open, watching intently as Cassidy's chin dropped and the muscles around her fingers convulsed. She moved her fingers slightly and slipped deeper without conscious intent. The blond head fell back, and Brenna tasted the perspiration shining on the exposed throat. Appreciative moans spurred her arousal.

Cassidy arched abruptly and pulled away from Brenna's fingers. With her mouth she sought out Brenna's taut nipples. Crying out and curling in reaction to the hard suckling, Brenna lodged her knee between Cassidy's thighs, bumping her groin. As her own orgasm spiraled closer, Brenna felt Cassidy rub herself against the protruding leg.

Cassidy's orgasm was a beautiful thing — primal, wild. Golden hair fell in disarray around her face. Eyes shut tight against the acute sensations, her body became rigid, then collapsed bonelessly against Brenna.

Gently, rhythmically, Cassidy rubbed her knee between Brenna's thighs. Fingers in her hair drew their gazes together. "Mmm," Cassidy murmured unintelligibly against Brenna's lips, then the fingers and knee moved again. Brenna gasped as her idling passion surged. She groaned, her voice rising into a keening as her orgasm crashed through her.

Chapter 37

They were both covered in a thin layer of perspiration. *At least that's not new,* Brenna thought. The sensations flooding her body held her suspended in a pleasurable daze. She rubbed her fingertips together, and viscous fluid coated the pads of her thumb and forefinger. She remembered the delightful feel of moving inside of Cassidy and wondered what the other woman tasted like. Lifting her fingertips to her lips, she flicked out her tongue and experimentally tasted. When she lowered her hand, she found Cassidy studying her.

Cassidy's lips wrapped around the fingers, tasting Brenna's skin, saliva mingled with her own essence. The gesture was incredibly intimate and arousing, Brenna thought, feeling a fresh rush to her groin. "How'd you know what I was thinking?" she asked when Cassidy let her fingers go.

"It's the first thing I thought about, too," Cassidy confessed.

"You, um, never told me about your first time." Brenna eased into Cassidy's shoulder, resting her chin against the back of her hand over the other woman's breast. "Who was she?"

"A classmate in college."

"How did you...did she seduce you?"

"We were drunk. There wasn't much seduction involved."

"Did you enjoy it?"

"It was experimentation," Cassidy admitted. "As long as something didn't hurt or wouldn't get me kicked out of school, I was game to try it. This was a case of 'broken hearts', though. She and I had both been dumped, and it was a way to still feel wanted."

Brenna nodded. She could easily picture it. She had sometimes gone to bed with some director, or another actor, just to feel connected. Easing her thigh over Cassidy's, she brushed her knee against her center. The other woman's eyelids drifted closed. She felt the smooth arms tighten around her back. "Let me assure you, you are very much wanted," she said. She nibbled down from the known quantity of kissing and conducted teasing forays on her breasts, which had Cassidy writhing beneath her.

"I keep finding more and more things to like about you," Brenna said with a smile. She pressed a hand between their bodies, and while it was awkward with their slight difference in height, she found Cassidy's center again as the other woman's fingers curved up inside her.

They withdrew with gentle touches, caressing whatever skin lay within their reach. She traced her own fingertip across Cassidy's lips and inhaled sharply when Cassidy sucked the finger into her mouth. Sharing the experience, they rubbed one another's essence on their lips and kissed. Cassidy replenished her wet fingertips frequently, and Brenna was surging toward another orgasm from the intermittently interrupted and resumed sensations.

She tasted both of them strongly in their next kiss, as Cassidy filled her with three fingers. Gasping, she moved her hips in rhythm. "Oh, God," she groaned appreciatively.

Cassidy's palm splayed across her stomach, holding her down, and the full lips trailed kisses from her mouth to her breast and back up again. Brenna tried to pay attention, but the woman clearly had her number, as every touch drove her higher and higher. She rapidly lost focus and just gave over to the sensations.

When Brenna, panting and covered in perspiration, opened her eyes, Cassidy was intently studying her. Her groin clenched as she watched Cassidy inhale and leisurely lick and suck at her wet fingers.

Cassidy rolled onto her back, bringing Brenna with her. "Did you enjoy yourself?"

Cassidy's curves were softer and the skin smoother than any other body Brenna had cuddled. "Yes, I did." The love connecting them expanded in Brenna's chest as she watched Cassidy lift her arm across her eyes, panting lightly.

Brenna remained keyed up in a way she found exciting, yet comfortable. She decided she could either do it all over again or simply fall asleep with a contentment she was uncertain she had ever truly felt before. She almost thought she had drifted off when Cassidy spoke.

"I have a confession to make."

Brenna cupped her palm against the underside of Cassidy's breast and murmured, "What?"

"I'm very happy right now." Cassidy's lips smoothed over Brenna's forehead. "I think I've been wanting this a lot longer than just the last couple of months."

Perching her chin on Cassidy's chest, Brenna wondered what that meant. So she asked. "I'm not sure what you mean."

Cassidy sat up and skimmed her palms over Brenna's skin. She could not get enough of how smooth and warm it was. Brenna's hands covered hers on her breasts. "I wanted to work with you, but now I'm thinking I really wanted to *be* with you." Moving back into the circle of Brenna's arms, Cassidy heard regret in Brenna's response.

"I'm sorry I didn't let that happen."

Looking back over her shoulder, Cassidy captured Brenna's palm and kissed it. Brenna curled toward her, her breasts lightly pillowing against Cassidy's back as she intertwined their legs. "When you finally did...I really enjoy the person I've met. I loved watching you with the kids at Halloween, the way you dealt with the police for me when Ryan was lost." She sighed as Brenna kissed away the fear that passed over her features. "I enjoy just sitting with you, munching on a lunch bar and arguing out a piece of script, climbing in the state park, watching you swim, and," she concluded softly, "Ryan loves you, and that means you're perfect."

"I'm far from perfect." Brenna brushed her fingertips across Cassidy's nose, amused by the crinkle that formed in the bridge as Cassidy smiled. "Ryan is a handsome little boy, and I think you're doing a wonderful job raising him. It's not easy doing it alone. I know."

"Cameron could never be bothered with Ryan. Mitch uses him against me." Cassidy sighed. "I just want..." She faltered.

Brenna brushed her hands over Cassidy's hair. "I know," she said with a soft chuckle. "Why can't life just be normal?" She lifted Cassidy's chin. "If it had been, though, would we have met?"

"Probably not."

Brenna heard the distraction caused by her nuzzling Cassidy's ear. "Are we done being serious?" she asked. "We've gotten so much out in the open," she said. "I was thinking we could get back to some *fun*." Brenna lifted her chin and offered a sensuous smile.

"Fun, hmm?" Cassidy asked, smile returning.

Cassidy grasped her wrist and guided her fingers. Torn between watching Cassidy's face as she touched her and watching her fingers moving over the intimate flesh, Brenna darted her eyes back and forth. She began inserting two fingers, but Cassidy shook her head. "No, just..." Voice strained, Cassidy repositioned the touch until Brenna was just on the edge, massaging her center.

Cassidy's back arched, and Brenna licked dry lips as nipples pebbled before her eyes. Cassidy reached for one of her own nipples, pulling and twisting it tightly. Brenna dropped her chin and sucked on the other, trying to keep her fingertips in contact as Cassidy arched with growing need, her moans the sweetest music.

Moving down further, Brenna's lips drew circles on the quivering stomach. She offered kisses across the skin to soothe the tension she felt gathering in the body beneath her. Fingers threaded through her hair — Cassidy appreciated the increased tempo — and she rubbed more determinedly. Brenna slipped her middle finger inside and continued with her thumb across the bundle of nerves.

Then inspiration struck as Cassidy's breast bumped into her cheek. Brenna twisted the nipple in her teeth, recalling Cassidy's reaction to this same action in her trailer. *Brilliant!* She congratulated herself as Cassidy's chest expanded suddenly. The woman gasped for breath, whimpered, and then scared Brenna by growling and bucking.

Gradually, the flutters slowed under Brenna's palm and finally Cassidy's heart rate slowed. Brenna's groin throbbed with empathy. Cassidy's palm slipped down and found the wetness. They lifted their fingers to one another's lips and both comforted and aroused each other with their juices mingling.

Brenna traced the tear streak on Cassidy's cheek. "I'm sorry. Did I hurt you?"

"No, it's okay." Cassidy swallowed hard and captured Brenna's hand in her own, kissing the knuckles.

Brenna wrapped around her, feeling the light aftershocks. Squeezing a little, Brenna felt the gentle touch of an arm stealing across her waist. "What was that?"

"Beginner's luck," Cassidy replied whimsically. Then she kissed Brenna until she was dizzy.

"Do you always come like that?" Cassidy shook her head, hiding her face in Brenna's shoulder. "Good, because that would make it really hard to hide that we're...together." She kissed Cassidy's tear-stained cheek. "Thank goodness the house is empty."

Adjusting their positions to snuggle, they had to move when Cassidy's thigh landed in a wet spot. They laughed, dozed a little, and talked a bit more. The sound of gravel crunching under tires abruptly shattered the tranquility. Headlights illuminated the cul-de-sac outside. Brenna sat up. Beside her, Cassidy moved off the bed. "The boys are back," she said.

Brenna stood quickly, finding Cassidy's clothes mingled with hers on the floor. She passed them over and pulled on her own top and pants. "I'll go see. You can use the bathroom."

"But..."

Putting a finger to Cassidy's lips, Brenna iterated clearly, "Popcorn and movies." Cassidy started to speak, but Brenna quickly left, dusting her hands through her hair to set it in a semblance of order and pulling the door shut behind her.

In the living room, despite her nerves, Brenna moved methodically to the couch and turned on the TV. *The English Patient* was about thirty minutes from the end. She looked at the time; it was just after midnight.

Seconds passed, but the front door did not open. Brenna stood and walked into the foyer. Finally she opened the front door and stepped out onto the stoop. Only Cassidy's hatchback sat in the driveway; her Mountaineer was nowhere in sight.

When she came back in, Cassidy was half standing and half sitting on the couch as she turned toward the door.

"Nobody," Brenna said. Cassidy collapsed on the cushion and laughed, making Brenna chuckle as well as she sat down on the couch beside her. "Look at us." She reached out and grasped Cassidy's hand.

"Well, if you'd rather explain things..." Cassidy left the thought unfinished as the front door opened and light from the porch poured onto the foyer wall. Their hands dropped apart, and both turned to face the door.

James stepped into view first, bowtie hanging loose around his neck and cummerbund askew. "Your car?" he asked Cassidy.

"Yes."

"Thomas parked on the street so you could get your car out." James turned to his mother. "He thought it was Ms. Hyland's. I wasn't sure."

"I decided on a night of popcorn and movies," Brenna said. "I called Cass to see if she was interested."

Thomas appeared at the entryway. "Hey, Cassidy."

"Hello, Thomas." Cassidy stood at Brenna's shoulder and watched the boys with a faint smile. She could feel Brenna's nervousness, so she tried a diversion. "Was the party fun?"

Grinning, Thomas nodded. "Yeah, it wasn't bad."

"So, do you forgive me for the tuxedo?" Brenna asked.

"Okay, I forgive you," Thomas said. "Cheryl said I was the hottest thing on the dance floor."

Brenna laughed. Cassidy questioned in astonishment, "Should you be telling your mother that?"

He looked at Cassidy and blushed. "Sorry."

Brenna patted his shoulder, "That's okay. I'm glad you had a good time."

"Is Ryan in the spare room?" Thomas asked.

"No, he had a sleepover, so I took your mother up on her invitation."

Brenna moved into her younger son's path. "You're awfully quiet; didn't you have fun?"

"It was okay. Thanks for the dance lessons earlier."

She rubbed her thumb over his cheek as he met her eyes. Behind James, Brenna saw Cassidy smile at her. Hoping her blush was invisible, she turned back to James. "Well, get yourself comfortable and get some sleep." She leaned in and kissed his cheek. When he sniffed, she stepped back. "Okay?"

"Yeah. Whatever." He looked at her and frowned, then shook his head dismissively. "Good night."

"Good night." Brenna watched both boys disappear down the hallway and then felt a tentative hand on her lower back. "Wait," she murmured.

The light in the hallway went out, and Brenna turned around, facing Cassidy. "They looked all right. I guess the dance broke up early."

"Guess so."

Brenna sat down but Cassidy remained standing. "It's all right to stay a bit," she said. "It would look odd if you left right now," she added quietly, pulling Cassidy to the couch. "Something to drink?"

Realizing her mouth was quite dry, Cassidy nodded. "I don't think the wine."

"Iced tea?"

"All right."

Brenna stood, and Cassidy followed her into the kitchen, where they took a few moments to pour the drinks. As they stood together in the kitchen, sipping in silence, they realized the mood had fled.

"Any ideas?" Cassidy studied the dark hallway where the boys had disappeared.

"None," Brenna admitted.

"Still shaken?"

"A little."

"We ought to say something eventually."

"I know." Brenna put down her glass and idly traced her thumb through the condensation. She glanced at Cassidy. "Thomas' statement about Cheryl gives me hope that he's getting over his crush on you."

"It does seem that way."

They walked to the front door. Brenna retrieved Cassidy's coat from the closet and helped her into it. The natural motion of Cassidy adjusting the leather on her shoulders pulled Brenna in close, and she was assailed again by the scent of their lovemaking. Cassidy turned into her, and Brenna barely restrained herself from a kiss. Cassidy grasped her hand and turned her lips into the palm. She inhaled and whispered, "Step outside with me?"

"All right." Brenna followed her onto the stoop, rubbing her arms against the cold air. "I'll see you tomorrow...tonight, I mean, at the party."

"What time does Kevin fly in?"

Brenna shook her head. "I don't know. He's going to call from the airport."

Cassidy kissed her fingers one by one. "You might want to shower."

"You, too."

"I mean before Kevin gets here." Cassidy slipped Brenna's fingertips into her mouth for a brief moment, conveying her message without words.

Mortified, Brenna closed her eyes. "That must've been what James sniffed." Her cheeks turned pink with embarrassment.

"I do think you smell wonderful, it's just..."

"I know." Brenna watched Cassidy get in her car, start it up, and back out of the drive. Pensively, she returned inside, closing the door and setting the bolt.

Thomas was at the refrigerator in shorts and a tee shirt. She stopped at the counter. "I thought you were in bed."

"Just getting some milk." He pulled out the carton and poured it into a plastic mug he'd already set on the counter. "So, Cassidy came over for movies?"

Brenna nodded. She considered how to explain it. "Who wants to sit around the house all alone on a Friday night, right?"

"Yeah." He studied her a moment as he drank his milk. She watched him set his glass in the sink, then, as he neared her, he stopped. "Good night, Mom."

"Good night, Thomas."

After giving him a few moments to clear the hallway, Brenna entered her room and began tidying up her space. She opened the window to let the air circulate. Hanging the clothes strewn on the vanity back in the closet, she found a pair of lace underwear under the untidiness and blushed, tucking them into her own underwear drawer. *How on earth did Cassidy forget these? Too easily*, she concluded, remembering the speed with which they had dressed.

She stepped into her shower and washed her hair and face. Running the washcloth over her shoulders, neck, and breasts, she sighed wistfully as she recalled Cassidy's touch. Nude, she stepped into her room and pulled on her satin nightgown.

The clock told her it was nearly one-thirty in the morning. Tired, she crawled between the sheets and closed her eyes.

She was next aware of voices in the hallway.

"Thanks, Thomas."

It was Kevin just outside her bedroom door. Brenna stole a glance at the clock, alarmed to find it was after seven. As the door opened, she rolled over and sat up. As Kevin approached the bed, she shivered in the cool air blowing in the open window.

Leaning in as his weight shifted the mattress, he kissed her cheek as she turned her head. "Good morning. Thomas says you all had a late night last night."

"Yes." She rubbed her eyes and watched as he crossed the room and pulled the window shut. "Thanks. I wanted a little fresh air last night."

Kevin sat on the mattress almost on her feet. She bent her knees and wrapped her arms around them, then looked up at him. "How was the flight?" she asked, her voice burring groggily.

"Wow. You are tired. Why don't you get yourself together? I'll fix you breakfast and bring it in here." He put his arm around her waist, balancing his weight with his opposite hand. "With all the frequent flyer miles, we'll probably be able to take a free round trip to Singapore by summer." Usually the comment would have elicited a chuckle. She simply nodded. He kissed her quickly. "I'll see to that breakfast." He paused, then leaned in close for a kiss. After a moment, he smiled. "Smells like you missed me last night," he said softly. "I could send the boys out."

Brenna quickly rose. "No. We've got little enough time to be together today as it is," she said, moving toward the bathroom. "Just give me a minute to tidy up, and I'll join everyone at the table."

"All right."

He stood, and Brenna watched from the open door of the bathroom as he let himself out. With a quiet exhalation, she girded herself for the day ahead.

Chapter 38

Brenna had long ago realized that she could no longer attend any party resembling a simple cast party like those she cherished from her younger acting days. The Millennium Holiday Gala was part formal ball and part public relations for Pinnacle Productions. Attendance was mandatory for all actors and even most of the creative staff. As Commander Susan Jakes from *Time Trails* Brenna was expected to literally give a command performance. Stepping out of the limousine, she stood for a moment at the end of a crowded walk carpeted in blue-gray that led to the Hyde Hotel's Grand Marnier ballroom. It was sunset, and the photographers' flashes popped randomly as she discreetly checked the smoothness of her full length gown. Tucking her black purse under her arm, she placed her hand inside of Kevin's elbow.

She heard the buzz of national entertainment reporters recording their segments and local personalities from radio and television news reporting one of the city's most famous studio-sponsored events. The entire block was cordoned off. She nodded to the dress uniformed L.A. police officers as one of them requested her purse and checked its contents.

Accepting her bag back, Brenna allowed Kevin to lead her inside. The high-ceilinged ballroom was festively decorated for the holiday in greens and reds, mistletoe, and Christmas wreaths. The company's theme colors of blue and purple were also prominently displayed throughout, decorating the mounted placards proclaiming the various series and movie projects sponsored by Pinnacle and its parent company.

At her shoulder where they stood outside the entry doors, Kevin asked, "Ready?" Passing through the velvet brocade rope barrier would mean officially joining the party and submitting to the interview-hungry press.

Spying Victor Branch dancing with his wife, Brenna steeled herself for duty. "Let's do it," she said. Kevin led her down the two steps into the pandemonium.

Cassidy had escaped the stir that ensued when she arrived at the event alone and had sought out Rich Paulson and his wife, Linda, in the throng. They were presently discussing Linda's work as a Department of Children and Families foster placement specialist. The conversation had turned to the topic of what exactly constituted a nurturing environment.

"It seems to me that all varieties of family models will work," Cassidy observed, "if a child's needs are put ahead of those of the parents."

"It's more of a balance, I think," disputed a woman with short brown hair and a happy air about her. Her date leaned easily against her shoulder, a younger woman with feathered short blond hair. "If you're not happy, your kids won't be either, no matter what environment you try to provide for them. There are an awful lot of miserable rich kids. And a hell of a lot of happy poor ones."

"It seems we put a lot of pressure on people to conform to some ideal," Rich said. "When in fact, there is none. A lot of ancient civilizations provided communal childcare, a small percentage of the females doing the caretaking while everyone else worked to provide for the other needs of the community."

Cassidy reached for a wine glass from a passing tray. "Only the women should be responsible for the caretaking?"

Linda shook her head. "No, many men are very capable. I've argued for custody being given to several fathers following messy divorces. They were simply in a better position to provide the appropriate care."

The brown-haired woman nodded. "Equal opportunity."

"Just so," Linda agreed.

Conversation around them ceased for a moment, causing nearly everyone to look toward the entrance to identify the new arrival. Cassidy's chest squeezed in surprise. On Kevin's arm, Brenna stood scanning the room. Alarmed that the heat rising in her face might be noticed, she took a step back from Rich and Linda to assure that she remained inconspicuous and could observe Brenna without the press observing her.

She sighed with pleasure. Brenna looked wonderful in a floor-length, tank-style, red silk gown. The daringly low décolletage was covered by a red, gauze-thin wrap that hugged her upper arms while leaving her shoulders bare. She had swept her hair up into a softly gathered twist of curls that brought out the red highlights. *God, I want her.* Her fingers itched at the tactile memory of the softness of Brenna's hair and how satin her skin felt. With a dry swallow, she diverted her attention to observe the man at Brenna's side.

Kevin Shea was built along the lines of a defensive lineman and towered every inch of six feet. His broad face was weathered and framed by wavy gray hair, only hinting at the dark brown it must once have been. Not unkindly, Cassidy compared him to her father and found him a handsome man.

She watched him lead Brenna through the photographers and executives. He lightly put a hand on her lower back, as if afraid she would break. The doting glances he gave her when the smaller woman was not looking were embarrassing to observe. The tenderness brought a lump to Cassidy's throat. It was clear to her that Kevin loved his wife.

As Brenna and Kevin started down the steps, Rich moved forward to greet their titular leader. Cassidy hung back, wishing she dared to approach but not trusting her body, much less her voice. Brenna's smile, she noticed, was tense. The photographers were the usual bunch, but still she ducked away from two photographers whose flashes went off less than a foot from her face. Her mind was apparently on something other than publicity.

Cassidy felt a presence come up on her left side. Taking a sip from her wineglass, she offered quietly, "Evening, Cameron."

He sipped from a small tumbler, and she recognized the sharp smell of a Triple Sec Speeder, a drink for which Cam had a penchant when his sole professed purpose was to get rip-roaring drunk. It was likely his first, since the evening was still young, but she knew it wouldn't be his last. When he spoke, his words were the unmeasured tone of someone not interested in watching his language.

"Bitchin' cool party, I guess."

"Mmm hmmm," she replied noncommittally.

"Hey," he said, pointing as he slithered an arm around her waist. She stepped away from the embrace. "I've only been off the set what, two weeks? Chapman's looking buffer than usual."

She nodded. "He switched gyms."

He looked to another cluster of celebrities. "Isn't that Spellman? Look, Brenna and her husband are headed over to say hello to him. Why don't we join them?"

Cassidy was stunned. He was acting as if they had never broken up. "What's going on, Cameron?"

"Oh, I'm just thinking we could spend some time together — you and me. Can't I be sociable?"

"This isn't sociable. You're drunk, and you're fawning."

"Ah, but I've seen the woman I love in the arms of another. Shouldn't I fight for her?"

Cassidy froze. "What?"

"That was a very hot kiss on her trailer steps. Which of you did the seducing? I've always wondered how dominance works in a relationship like that," he went on, deliberately ignoring her discomfort.

"I think you've had too many drinks, Cameron. You're imagining things."

"Not tonight. I just wanted to get my facts straight — pardon the pun — before I go over and share them with her husband. Now, it was...just last week. Right? On her trailer steps..."

Cassidy's eyes widened with alarm. "You're fishing. There's nothing," she tried bravely.

Cameron didn't buy it. "What is it worth to you for me to keep your secret?"

"Secret about what?"

"I can blurt it out right here and now if you like."

Cassidy grasped the hand he raised to gesture to Kevin and Brenna. Through clenched teeth, she drew him to a quiet corner. "What do you want?" she asked cautiously.

"Just what Chapman said. You can act, right? So, I want you to act like we never parted ways. I came to this damn thing alone, and that got me dozens of stares. I'm not going through that again."

"You want me to be your date tonight?"

"Not just tonight," he corrected. "However, it'll be a start. I rather like everyone in the room envying me."

A reporter drew a bead on them at that moment, directing his cameraman to follow. "Mr. Palassis, Ms. Hyland, having a good time tonight?"

"Pinnacle knows how to throw a party," Cameron replied. "Right, sweetheart?" He pressed his mouth over Cassidy's and boldly licked her lips.

Cassidy exhaled carefully through her nose to keep herself from doing something publicly she would later regret. She put a hand on his arm so he could not wrap it around her shoulders. She collected herself when the reporter addressed Cameron.

"There was a rumor that you'd been moved from *Time Trails* because of some differences between you and the cast."

Cameron shrugged. "Rumors. My expertise was needed on the new sets. *Time Trails* gets along fine now that I've set her on the straight and narrow. But the move has meant less time together for me and Cass, and you know how rumors are."

The reporter nodded. "I guess so. Well, you two enjoy your evening."

The reporter moved off. Cassidy exhaled sharply when Cameron's elbow happened to "bump" her ribs. "Do a better job," he warned. "You don't get multiple takes, so I suggest you get into character."

"I can't do this, Cameron."

"Well then, let's see, where's... Oh yes. Looks like the cozy couple is dancing. Shall I cut in for you?"

Cassidy grimaced. Cameron took her silence as agreement and immediately pulled her into a dance embrace. She looked toward Kevin and Brenna and relaxed when Cameron started them off in the opposite direction. "Why do you want to hurt her?" she whispered.

"She seduced you; my manhood must be avenged," he declaimed dramatically.

He was playing with her. Whatever his true motivations, he would not be sharing them. "What if I told you it wasn't like that? Maybe I seduced her. Maybe I'm the one with a broken heart because she turned me down flat."

"You are anything but flat," he said pointedly, rubbing against her as they danced, drawing her attention to her chest with the salacious maneuver. "Absolutely anything but."

Cassidy gambled, "Well, I did. She's lovely. It's true. I hungered for her. Approached her. The kiss you saw? She left me begging afterward."

"Poor darling." He nuzzled her cheek with his nose and whispered harshly in her ear, "If I believed you for one second, I'd be furious on your behalf. You are completely irresistible. I don't believe it. She's defended you too ardently lately. That was really spectacular how she helped you rewrite my script so quickly," he added. "Everyone was buzzing about it."

"She's married."

"Didn't stop you from taking up with me. Come on, you women are all alike — take your thrills where you can get them and play coy when it suits you." He changed their direction. She followed his lead and tried not to stiffen as they moved alongside Brenna and Kevin.

"Hey, there," Cameron opened.

"Cameron?" Brenna looked over her shoulder at them. "Hello, Cassidy." Brenna's smile managed to be both welcoming and cautious. She glanced up at Kevin. "You remember Cassidy Hyland and Cameron Palassis?"

"Ms. Hyland, a pleasure to see you again. Has your son gotten in any more trouble since Thanksgiving?"

"No, thankfully." Cassidy felt Cameron tense beside her, and she smiled genuinely at Kevin. This affable exchange was exactly what he had not expected to see. "Has winter hit Michigan yet?"

"Yes. We had a light first snowfall just after I returned home. It'll be a white Christmas, for certain." Kevin glanced down at Brenna. "I'm trying to convince her to come home with me for the holiday itself. Maybe you can add your persuasions?"

Cameron smiled at Brenna's unease, so obvious to Cassidy. "Got plans in town?" He leaned forward and kissed Cassidy's neck as Brenna studied them.

Brenna's eyes flashed dangerously, but her voice was calm when she responded. "There's too much chance I'd get snowed in and stuck out there when filming is supposed to resume. Like I did our first year, Cameron, remember? I've always just found it safer to stay put. Summer's better for trips anyway." She stopped dancing. "I think I should go freshen up."

Kevin nodded. "All right." Cassidy stood beside him watching Brenna move quickly off the floor to the alcove containing the powder rooms. "Mr. Palassis, would you mind if I took your lovely lady for a spin around the floor?"

Cameron inhaled sharply, and Cassidy almost laughed at the triumph she felt. "I'd love to," she answered, taking her hand from Cameron and putting it in Kevin's. She followed the older man easily, feeling a burst of joy. Cameron could not possibly continue clinging to the idea that she and Brenna were involved if Kevin were this congenial. Certainly a man would know when his wife was unfaithful. *Right?* She looked at Kevin, suddenly uneasy.

He smiled at her. "I have to admit I didn't ask you to dance just to pass the time," Kevin said in the lengthening silence. "I have a question to ask."

Cassidy steeled her jaw to keep her mouth from gaping. Carefully she nodded, then cleared her throat. "What is it?"

"I need to know what's bothering Bren. She won't tell me. Maybe I'm just not able to understand, or so she thinks. Do you think you could — if you know what it is — tell me?"

"Are you bothered that she's not going to Michigan?" He nodded. "She is right about the shooting demands. She's heavily featured in the next episode. There are a lot of lines and a lot of scenes. It would mess up shooting if she got stuck because of a storm. I used to have to avoid going home this time of year, too."

The forthright answer seemed to pacify Kevin. "I guess you're right. It's just..." His voice trailed off as he kept the changing thoughts to himself. "Never mind."

Cassidy found herself in the unenviable position of dancing with the spouse of her lover, expected to sympathize with the estrangement that he could feel but for which he could not see an apparent cause. "She's uncertain about a lot more than just being here when shooting resumes," she allowed.

"You're her friend. Has she told you what?"

Cassidy hesitated, uncertain whether she would be breaking a confidence. "She's been offered a job in England. She has to make a decision soon, I think."

"England?" Kevin sighed. "We'll have to talk."

"Apparently they want her badly enough to wait until she's finished with the series in May."

"Oh." Kevin's frown deepened. The song to which they were dancing came to an end. "Well, I'd better return you to your date."

"All right." Cassidy squeezed his shoulder. "Have a good holiday."

"You, too."

They returned to the side of the ballroom. Cassidy did not dare leave Cameron and Kevin alone. Though derailed abruptly and thoroughly, Cameron was no doubt planning another way to use his knowledge to his benefit. She immediately pushed him out to dance, leaving Kevin on the side of the floor waiting for Brenna's return.

Brenna found the restroom a quiet haven. The loud music was muted there, and the strain of conversing with Kevin was also gone. Seeing Cassidy in Cameron's arms had startled her, but it was when Kevin took Cassidy off to dance that she understood exactly what she was feeling. She was not jealous that Cassidy was dancing with Kevin because Kevin was her husband; she was jealous that she could not be dancing with Cassidy herself.

You're going to tell him tonight. Brenna knew what she had said to Cassidy the night before, and yet, she had continued to wrestle with how to tell Kevin it was over. She was in love with someone else. Remaining married to Kevin would be wrong. She would just have to come out and say it.

She emerged back into the ballroom and scanned the crowd. Cassidy and Cameron were dancing. Kevin was coming toward her, as were Will and Terry. *It would be better in private,* she reasoned. She turned and greeted her co-stars first. "Hi. Having a good evening?" She looked up over her shoulder as Kevin stopped behind her. "Kevin, you remember Terry Brown and Will Chapman."

"Terry. Will." He shook their hands in turn and then rested his hands lightly on her shoulders. She shivered. "Why don't we get something at the buffet?"

"All right." She eased away from Kevin's hand on her lower back guiding her lightly through the milling crowd. Cameron and Cassidy were also at the buffet.

"Hello again."

Brenna caught Cassidy's startled look and noted that Cameron had his hand wrapped tightly around her wrist and the knuckles were white. It made her look at Cameron more closely. He did not release Cassidy's wrist. Instead he pulled her against him.

"Nice spread," he said, looking directly at her as his hands roamed Cassidy's butt. Cassidy's face was growing steadily redder.

Whatever was going on, Brenna knew she had to stop it. Obviously Cassidy was not with him by choice. The realization that there was manipulation going on also clued Brenna into something else. Cameron knew, or thought he knew, there was something to tweak in her relationship with Cassidy. A year ago she would have said he was doing it to see her get mad because Cassidy was stepping into her limelight. Now though, she wondered if he actually did know something.

"Excuse me," she said, easing forward to collect a plate. "Looks delicious. What do you think we should try, Cassidy?"

"The capers?"

"All right." Brenna smiled and edged along the table, guiding Cassidy along in front of her, Cameron preceding them, unwilling to relinquish Cassidy. She felt her husband step into line behind her. Brenna took in the layout of the table, taking particular notice of the punchbowl at the end, its red juice and floating balls of ice cream beckoning. She speared the capers and nudged a few onto Cassidy's plate. "Here you go."

"Thank you."

Caught between Cameron and Kevin, Brenna and Cassidy exchanged grimaces. *I will get you out of this*, Brenna vowed, moving along the table. Walking backwards as he kept his eyes on them, Cameron did not notice he was next to the punchbowl until his hip bumped the table and he stumbled. The punchbowl rocked unsteadily and splashed. Brenna grabbed Cassidy's hand out of his and stepped back, unerringly kicking her own shoe forward and under Cam's foot.

Chapman and Brown were behind Kevin when Cameron toppled. They stepped out and around, offering Cameron a hand up.

The reporters and nearby guests all caught the commotion and turned. Several flashes went off as Cameron stood, his suit dripping with punch. "Cameron, let's get you cleaned up," Will offered.

Cameron hesitated and looked around. Straightening, he walked out. Terry and Will moved to flank him as he left.

Terry discreetly kicked Brenna's shoe back to her and she slipped her foot inside, exchanging a quick nod with the dark man, who then followed Will and Cameron out to the restrooms.

The distraction was over almost before it had completely built up. Brenna mentally patted herself on the back.

Cassidy nodded and squeezed her hand, excusing herself. "I'll say good night, now. Kevin, good to see you again." With a brief smile at Brenna, she turned and made a graceful solo exit.

Brenna ached as Cassidy left, wanting to follow the other woman out, to assure herself that she was all right, that Cameron had done nothing more untoward than coercion. She started forward. She saw Terry come out of the corridor with the restrooms and cross to follow Cassidy out. *Should I follow?* Then she felt Kevin's hand on her elbow and the flashes of light receding and knew she had to stay to deflect everyone's attention from Cassidy's early departure. The notion was reinforced by Victor Branch leading his wife to their side a moment later.

"Get out there," he hissed.

Kevin looked to her. She knew he would do whatever she asked, even if he did not know immediately why. She was grateful for it even as she recognized she was using it to advantage. "Just a dance or two."

She smiled disingenuously and followed Kevin's dance steps out to the center of the floor, circling several times before other couples joined them and they could slip to the fringe once again. They stopped for the cameras, and she answered the pertinent questions from reporters about the series, sounding excited for all that she was far from it.

Kevin's expression grew more confused as the evening's performance wore on. He said little. He drew them to a stop as Will Chapman approached. "You had probably better perform a little more," Kevin said, handing her off to Chapman. "I'm going to get a drink."

Brenna realized Kevin sensed she was off kilter, though he seemed to think it was caused by her responsibility to 'perform' for the press tonight. "Just one dance," she assured Kevin before she took Will's hand, wanting to talk with him about Cameron and aware that the wagging tongues might be quieted even more if she spread her attentions around.

Stepping out with her, Will smiled, and Brenna saw in his eyes a brotherly affection. "Thank you," she said earnestly. "And Terry, too, for the save."

Will nodded. They circled in the dance, pausing near a flower-bedecked column for photographers. In a low voice, he acknowledged her words. "Terry saw she got to a limo fine and told the reporters who followed them out that she had been caught in the punch spill also."

Brenna exhaled, most of her questions answered by Will's quick explanation. "How did she seem?" she asked anxiously.

Will's reply took a few moments, as they were stalled by Victor and his wife. Though they exchanged greetings, Brenna declined Victor's request to swap partners, asking him to catch her for the next dance, pouring on the charm as he frowned. "I'd rather have an entire dance with you."

Will offered his assessment of Cassidy's departure low, for Brenna's ear alone, as they danced away. "She seemed anxious to be away; otherwise Terry would have pulled her back onto the dance floor, too."

"I know." *Always with the appearances*, she thought with a frown, though she quickly replaced it with a winsome smile up at Will. The deliberate posing was caught forever on film as a camera flashed.

She danced next, as promised, with Victor, Will taking Victor's wife Melanie out for a spin to the quick, jazzy number. Brenna was grateful that the tempo limited the conversation.

"Word about is that your husband is running for office, and you've got a job offer from England."

"He actually has already been elected. And yes, I've been shown a movie project."

His brow furrowed. "Have you been happy with *Time Trails* overall, Bren?"

Genuinely surprised by his question, she nevertheless answered honestly, "It's been a learning experience."

"I read your interview with Sci-Fi Magazine. You didn't sound like everything was peachy."

"Working was tough, Victor."

"Was? You do seem to be enjoying rehearsal a little more. Well, except for that fiasco with Palassis."

"He's got quite a hot temper," she concurred, and added, "I'm glad he was moved off."

"Is that what tonight was about?" Victor asked, clearly having talked her around to the topic he most wanted to discuss.

"Tonight?"

"That mess at the buffet."

Brenna shook her head. "An accident."

"Nothing you do is accidental, Bren." She could say nothing to that, realizing she had just been told that he viewed her as calculating.

In the strained moments that followed, Victor's dance steps led them back to where Kevin stood sipping from a small glass with ice. He put it down on the tray of a passing waiter as they approached. "Mr. Shea, thank you for the privilege."

Bren found her hand placed into Kevin's. She looked up between the two men and wondered what her producer would say further.

"You may go," Victor said coolly. He turned away without changing expression and took his wife back out onto the dance floor for the song just starting.

Kevin studied her quizzically. She lifted a shoulder in a shrug though she was far from feeling at ease. But, she had been granted her reprieve. For now. "Ready to go?"

It was nearly midnight when they returned to the house. Brenna remained quiet as the limo driver wound through the neighborhood streets and pulled into their driveway. Relaxing at her side, Kevin loosened his bowtie. "Bit of an odd evening."

"Mmm hmm."

He took the keys from her hand and opened the front door. "Are you going to tell me what that was all about?"

"Pinnacle's annual meet 'n' greet," she said.

"No, that bit of sabotage you did."

"That was an accident."

"You aren't that clumsy."

She pulled the wrap off her shoulders and put a hand on his left arm. "Me?"

"Yes, you. Whenever you saw him tonight, you bristled. Has something happened on the set that I should know about?"

"No. He's been reassigned, actually," she said, perhaps with too much of a smile. "He's working exclusively on a new series." She led the way to the deck in the backyard, and Kevin sat on the swing.

"So you don't see him a lot?"

"Nope. One thing about this set I will not miss is the politics that play off-camera."

"Are you finally thinking about afterward? Ms. Hyland said you have an offer from England."

"I do." She smiled. "And I'm thinking of taking it."

"I thought we were going to settle down, take a break from things."

Brenna shook her head. "You've got your life to live, and I've got mine."

"That's rather harsh," he said. "Just come home for the holiday, see Ellie and Marie. We'll visit with your brothers."

"I'm not going to Michigan with you. Not now...or in the future."

"What are you saying?"

Brenna exhaled, girding herself for a fight. "Kevin, you said you felt we are drifting apart." She nodded. "I agree. It's not fair to you to be distracted like this."

"You mean how you're distracted by set politics?"

She shook her head. "You deserve someone who can focus on you, who *will* focus on you. I...I tried to, I wanted to, but...there's..." *No, not good to tell him about Cassidy.* She started again. "I can't go back to Michigan with you."

"You're still working, I know." He lifted a hand and laid it gently over hers on her lap. "There'll be other jobs. I...I'd like you to take a little time off for a while, just be...a mom." He paused. "My wife." He nodded. "Get the anxiety about all this out of your system. We can just *be* for a while."

Brenna shook her head. "Kevin, I shouldn't be with you at all." She looked at her hands — small, nearly hidden by his one big one. Gingerly she pulled free of his light touch. The wedding band on her left hand, put there for tonight's publicity event, glinted in the deck lighting. She pulled it off.

She lifted his hand and pressed the ring into his palm. "I was wrong to take this from you," she said, afraid as her voice cracked. She wanted to do this; it was the right thing to do. *So why am I about to cry?* She looked up from his hand into the stunned expression her words had put on his face. "I want a divorce."

"Bren... I... We...we're married. You're my wife. I love you—"

"But I don't love you," she interrupted, forcing her voice to remain even.

"This is just a rough patch we're going through. You're lonely." He cast about for words. "I'll move out here. We'll work it out." He tried to press the ring back into her hand. She pushed back. "I'll support—"

"No, Kevin." She stood abruptly, causing the bench to rock erratically. "You are...a wonderful man, but...I can't. I can't lie any more...to myself or to you."

"Lies?" His shock was palpable.

Brenna nodded. "I married you because I was too afraid to face things on my own. That was wrong. I... You're a strong, steady rock. You...were everything I thought I should need." She blinked away tears. "But I was lying to myself about some very important things I needed to face."

"I'll help you face them. What's brought this on tonight — the weird encounter with that writer?"

She shook her head. "No. I just realized tonight what I want and what you are for me...I was using you to be able to avoid...someone."

Kevin shook his head. "I don't understand, Bren. You're avoiding someone? Who?" He started to his feet. "If it's someone at Pinnacle, I'll make it right. That's what I'm here for — for you, for whatever you need me to do."

Brenna exhaled. She was going to have to say it. "Kevin, I have been trying to avoid this, but...please, listen to me. I don't deserve you; I have been unfaithful to you."

"We've barely been married a year!"

"Yes, I know. I spent our first anniversary waiting for you to come home from a political rally."

"Were you with him that night? Were you upset I was gone?"

She shook her head. "You know I wasn't. And I wasn't angry with you," she hastened to add. "I used to wonder why. I should have been, if I loved you as much as I professed." She sat down on the swing. "I've been unhappy so long, I didn't even know I was faking my happiness."

She looked into his face. "The bottom line, Kevin, is I don't love you. I admire you a great deal. You're a great family man, the kind of person my mother was right to point out to me, and I should love you. I think you're smart, and I've been treating you very, very stupidly." She shook her head at herself.

"You're at least admitting the affair. It's over. We can recover from this."

"It's not over, Kevin. It's only just beginning."

"You swore you needed fidelity, not the least because Tom never gave you his."

"That's why I have to let go, Kevin. You're right — I want fidelity. I asked it of you, and I can't let you believe you have it from me, when you don't."

"Can I at least know the name of the man? Is it that writer? Is that why you were so abrupt with him — because you wanted to cover up in front of me how you lust for each other?"

The notion of her being interested in Cameron Palassis was so absurd, Brenna laughed out loud. "No, no, Kevin. He is nothing to me, not even a colleague I have to suffer for the sake of the job. No, Kevin. Cameron was, however, acting an ass for an entirely different reason, and she is why I tripped him, risked complete public humiliation, and now must confess and end the charade with you."

Kevin's brow furrowed as he processed what she'd said. Finally he seemed to deflate. "You're having some sort of intimacy with Ms. Hyland?" He looked utterly confused.

"Yes."

"But you're not gay. We've made love and I'd...know."

"I've had sex with you. I thought it was...all I was supposed to feel." She struggled to explain. "But...until I...she...it's different," she finished lamely, aware that explaining further would just hurt him unnecessarily.

"Am I that bad a lover that you would go to a woman?"

"Kevin..." She shook her head. "No."

"Then why the hell are you leaving me for some lesbian?"

"I didn't *know* Cassidy felt the same."

"Did she seduce you?"

Brenna shook her head. "It was mutual."

Kevin stood up looking sad, angry, confused. His posture went rigid, hard. Brenna leaned forward, clasping her hands together, arms braced on her thighs, looking at her now bare finger, not even a mark to indicate a ring had been there. She really had never worn it honestly. *God, how could you make me so blind?*

"I'm truly sorry," Brenna said. "Whatever you want in the divorce, I'll...pay it."

Kevin's brows lowered angrily. "I want *you*," he snapped. "I married you for love, Bren. That's what I want."

She nodded. "I know."

"I'll have a lawyer draw up the papers." He threw the ring into the darkness; they both heard it hit the pool surface with a plop. *Down the drain*, she thought as he walked away, leaving her in the yard alone.

When she went inside later, reluctant to face him but driven in by the chill, she found he had left. His overnight bags were gone. She heard a car drive up and looked out her window in time to see him bend down and get in the back seat of a cab. Gone.

Chapter 39

Cassidy removed the pins from her hair with relief and dropped them on her bathroom counter. Finger-combing her locks, she caught her gaze in the mirror.

I wish we'd had a chance to talk privately, she lamented. She had fully felt overwhelming love and protection in those few seconds surrounding Cameron's "accident". It made her want to curl up in Brenna's embrace.

Just twenty-four hours ago she had indulged that want. She had touched Brenna in the ways she had imagined, even tasted her. Rubbing her cheeks as they heated with the memory, she inhaled slowly.

So why did I feel Brenna's love just as palpably across the separation tonight as when surrounded by the scents of our passion?

Indulging in the quiet since Ryan would not be returned by Gwen until morning, Cassidy relaxed on the couch and relived the evening with the perspective of time. The conversation had been pleasant and stimulating. Rich and his wife, of course, Cassidy had known. The brown-haired woman had been a new acquaintance. A singer by trade, as soon as she'd learned Linda's profession, she had turned the topic to childcare by bringing up one of the segments from a women's issues program that she hosted.

At the time, Cassidy had not thought about her conversation companions. In reflective retrospect, she saw the sandy brown hair, the warm brown eyes, and remembered her from a recent news story. *Something about her children. The woman and her previous partner... Lesbians.*

She thought about that word. She'd been referred to so often as a blonde bombshell, treated like a dumb blonde. What would being labeled again do to her career?

She loved Brenna. De facto, the press would label her a lesbian. *Well,* Cassidy thought with a slight quirk of her lips, *at last something they say about me will be true.*

Immediately Brenna's features coalesced in her mind — the rounded chin, softly slanted eyes nestling above smooth high cheekbones, and her dainty, kissable lips. Her heart expanded with acute joy. When Brenna had entered the ballroom, Cassidy knew she had stopped breathing. The older woman was compact, luminous, gracious, and scintillatingly sexy. And later, in her eyes, Cassidy recognized what love really looked like.

Cameron's face interposed itself over Brenna's, with the half sneer he had worn when talking to her about witnessing the kiss. "*I know. I saw,*" he taunted. Cassidy sighed. She may have prevented the publicity from breaking tonight, but that grace period would not last forever. She had overheard the light buzz concerning Brenna's husband's political aspirations. His wife wanting a divorce would be popular news. That same wife having an affair with a woman would give the tabloids fodder for page one stories for months to come.

Cassidy knew that the timing of advancing her relationship with Brenna to a physical union could have been better chosen. She could foresee the coming difficulties. She wondered if the storm clouds on the horizon, formless and swirling, might blow everything away.

She suspected that if the publicity caused any problems with the roles she was offered, the effect would not last long.

She briefly considered that Mitch might cause a problem if he knew about her relationship; his continual badgering that she was a poor parent might gain new traction, though his abuse and her financial independence would likely still prevail. However, Ryan would probably be all right with Brenna being around a lot more. He was too young to understand everything, but he had seemed genuinely unconcerned by the concept of his mother "dating" Brenna, however his five-year-old mind might define "dating".

Brenna's sons, on the other hand, were old enough to have definite opinions about it, and those were not likely to be favorable. But they loved their mother, and they wanted her to be happy. If they accepted Cassidy, it would be because Brenna asked it of them.

Shaking her head and not understanding why her stomach twisted, Cassidy flashed back to the previous evening. During their lovemaking, Brenna had been indulgent, offering Cassidy her passion freely, finding numerous ways to give pleasure. While Cassidy had been shaky, Brenna had responded to the possibility of discovery with utter calm. She had regained herself with quicker aplomb.

Has Brenna not fallen as far, or as deeply? Will our one night together be enough to convince her to not turn her back on what we have when the press breathes fire down our necks?

Another thought sprang to mind, and the crushing weight of it made it difficult for Cassidy to breathe. *She's already expressed fears about her ability to continue her career because of her age. How much more fear will it create if she is branded a lesbian and alienated from her family?*

Enveloped in sudden depression, Cassidy finished with the cloth on her face and splashed in the water. Going to her bed, she burrowed under the covers, reluctant to face the dawn.

Morning coffee percolating and still wrapped in her full-length thermal robe, Cassidy stepped onto her stoop to fetch her newspaper.

"Mommy!"

She looked up from her crouch in time to catch Ryan, dressed in a pair of jean coveralls and a plaid long-sleeved shirt. His arms slipped around her neck, blocking her view of Gwen walking up behind him.

"Lazy morning?" Gwen asked.

"Not too bad." Cassidy stood. "I've got coffee on. Want some?"

Ryan raced past her into the house, and Gwen entered ahead of Cassidy. "Do I get to hear all the details before they show up in the paper?"

Cassidy shrugged. "It was a press party," she said wryly. "I went. I talked — mostly to reporters mind you — and that was that."

Gwen helped herself to a cup from the coffeemaker. "What I wouldn't give for a night out among all those hot names." She leaned on the counter while Cassidy poured a bowl of cereal for Ryan at the kitchen table. "So, who was there?"

"You met some of them at Ryan's party. Rachelle and Jacques Cheron, Rich Paulson and his wife Linda..."

Gwen shook her head. "Who *else* was there?"

Cassidy lifted an eyebrow and nodded, knowing Gwen's tastes among the other actors who worked at Pinnacle Studios. "Kyle Gramercy was there. Daniel Pettigrew, too. Oh yeah, and Spellman. Brenna talked briefly with him and his wife..."

"So, she was there?"

"Of course."

"Did you..."

"We had a brief conversation with her husband Kevin, then he took me out on the floor dancing. After that we went to the—"

Gwen grabbed her arm. "You danced with her husband?" The brown head shook in disbelief. "My God, that is just plain weird."

Cassidy smiled broadly, recalling a similar reaction. "It was strange, but I'd do it again, just to see that stymied look on Cameron's face."

"Why would Cameron care? I thought you broke it off with him."

"He decided to play a little game of blackmail," Cassidy explained with a grimace. "I was supposed to pretend we were still together, or he'd tell Kevin that he saw Brenna and me kissing." Gwen looked alarmed. "Don't ask me how. I was positive we were alone, but—"

"Oh, Cassidy, please tell me she's already gotten separation papers, something. She hasn't?" Gwen shook her head again. "Shit, Lou is gonna flip."

"No, Gwen. You can't tell him. I know, I just know this is going to break soon, but please — you know how he gets about these things." Cassidy shivered. "I need time to figure out what to do about Mitch myself."

"He'll find out."

"I just need a little time to prepare." Cassidy was determined. She brushed her hair back from her face in exasperation. "Somehow."

She watched Ryan climb down from the chair, his empty bowl left on the table. "Ryan, clean up."

He had gotten halfway to the sliding door. "Yes, Mommy." Ryan moved his bowl to the sink with a clatter. Cassidy grimaced at the sharp noise. "Can I play with Ranger now?"

"All right. Then we'll figure out what to pack for Grandma's."

"Going to Missouri, then?" Gwen asked as Ryan ran outside to the excited barks of the four-year-old Dalmatian.

"Might be the last chance I get for a while."

Oh my God. Brenna rolled slowly over onto her back, blinking into the morning sunlight cascading into her bedroom. She swallowed against a painfully dry throat and rubbed the heels of her palms gently against her eyes, which felt puffy from crying.

She stretched her shoulders and back, achy from sleeping across bunched covers all night. *I'd better clean up.* Standing and stretching with several groans, Brenna stripped off the wrinkled remains of her gown and stockings. Then, with a gasp of shock, she stepped under the stinging spray of gradually warming water.

Her heart thrummed fast, making her breathless as she opened her mouth and gargled.

Well, here we go again. Divorce. She recalled her mother's reaction to the news eight years ago that she and Tom were divorcing.

"You're breaking a contract God made, Brenna Renee Lanigan. Who are you to question God's will?"

Brenna's throat tightened at the sharp note of disgust in her mother's voice. However, she tried to defend herself. "I didn't break it, Mama," she said. "Tom did."

"You've obligations. He's your husband, father of your children."

"You want me to forgive him? Mama, he took another woman into the bed he shared with me!"

"Don't you talk to me like that! You have a duty."

Her mother had raved about damnation and excommunication. Brenna had stopped regularly attending church several years earlier, but the sense of disappointing her mother had stuck. She had disappointed her before. Divorcing Tom had been strike one. Divorcing Kevin might be strike two. As for partnering with Cassidy... She shook her head.

Stepping out of the shower, Brenna dried slowly. Standing at the sink, she checked her face. The puffiness was almost indiscernible. She conjured up Cassidy's face, and her lips curled up at the corners. The sensation of a reassuring hug across her shoulders made her stomach twist, her nipples tighten, and her groin heat.

She thought about the party and wanting to escape with Cassidy to the bathroom, even for just a moment to talk. The touch of winsome blue eyes had steadied her. She had done what was necessary.

Thinking about Cassidy led to thoughts of Cameron, whose behavior at the ball had been beyond the pale, even for him. His direct gazes while pawing Cassidy had been designed to taunt her specifically.

Brenna did not regret backing him into the punchbowl. She wondered what happened after he was escorted away. She sighed. No doubt she would learn all in great detail when she returned to the set.

Holding her robe closed at her throat, Brenna stepped into the mid-morning sun and went down the front walk to collect the Sunday paper. On their small cul-de-sac, she could see two girls playing on the front drive of a nearby home. She smiled and turned back inside.

She worked through much of the newspaper and was about to get herself a second cup of coffee when James appeared in the kitchen. He poured himself a glass of pineapple juice and settled next to her at the dining room table. He was barely conscious. She brushed his hair out of his face and commiserated. "Rough night?"

Busy draining the glass, for a moment James did not speak. Mouth wet and eyes blinking, finally he nodded.

"Anything you want to talk about?"

"No." He looked at one of the discarded sections of paper and picked it up, flipping through the sports news. "How was the party last night?"

"Nice."

He seemed to straighten, then. "Is he still asleep?"

Brenna shook her head. Abruptly there was another presence behind her. She jumped when Thomas' hands caught her shoulders and he kissed her cheek. "Good morning," her elder son greeted then crossed through to the kitchen.

Sighing, Brenna knew there was no sense in putting off the announcement. "Kevin's not here."

"Did he go out?"

"He went home. About three o'clock this morning."

James frowned and shook his head. "Mom?"

Thomas stepped in from the kitchen, his orange juice clutched in his hand. "What's up?"

"We had a fight last night. I asked for a divorce." James got up and walked into the kitchen. She could see him leaning on the counter while he poured his cereal. Brenna winced as she saw him slam the box on the counter with a sharp thump.

From the kitchen, James asked, "Does this have something to do with Ms. Hyland coming over Friday night?" The question made Brenna look up at him in surprise. "It does, doesn't it? You become friends with her, and suddenly everything you have isn't enough for you, is it?"

"Kevin and I have had problems for a while now. I talked sometimes with Cassidy about them, but she did not make me do this."

"You're such a doofus, James."

"Shh." Brenna laid a quieting hand over Thomas' on the table. She studied James' face, trying to gauge how much he should understand. Obviously the divorce was angering him. *Is it this one, or recalling the first one?* Telling him at this point that she was involved with Cassidy would be inappropriate additional information.

"Some things just can't be gotten past. Kevin wanted things I couldn't give to him and still have the things I want. We'd thought it would resolve itself when *Time Trails* finished. I learned that's not going to happen. Our goals are too different. I really want to keep working. He doesn't see that as important."

"Why didn't you know this before you got married?" James let his frustration and confusion show, stalking away from the counter and out of sight.

"Because nobody's perfect." Brenna entered the kitchen and found James standing away from her as if staking it out as a defensive location. He cringed when she reached for him but when she pulled him into a hug, he collapsed against her. "Kevin's not. I'm not." She kissed his hair. "I've always told you that things have a way of working out the way they should."

James' arms slowly moved between their bodies, and he pushed away. She let him go. "I saw this coming. Damn." He turned away. Brenna looked to Thomas, who had gotten up and walked to the outside of the counter.

"So what happens now?" he asked.

"Our lawyers will be getting together. Kevin and I actually didn't have a lot of joint property, so it won't take long." *Or at least it shouldn't.*

James suddenly looked up at her with concern. "Will Dad have to be involved?"

"Your father? No. Why?" Brenna suddenly wondered what her first husband's reaction would be. "You two are staying with me. That's not up for negotiation."

"So you'll have to go to court," James asked.

"At least once. In Michigan."

Thomas grimaced. "Will we?"

"I doubt it. Unless you want to come for support. It's your choice." She wasn't certain they did support her, but she wanted them to have the option.

Thomas rested a hand on hers on the counter between them. "Mom, are you going to be okay?"

Old habits died so hard. She was tired of causing so many people so much pain. "I'm just sorry to be putting you through this again."

"It's a shock," Thomas replied honestly. "But, we're older. It's not like divorce isn't common, y'know?"

Sighing, Brenna agreed, but she didn't want either of her sons to feel that divorce was the predictable end to all marriages. "Don't think it has to be this way for everyone." She picked up her coffee mug and looked into its emptiness. "You can do better." She exhaled and filled the cup. "The most important thing is that you don't lie to yourself about who you are or what you want."

Pretty smart words, she castigated herself. *Too bad I have to drag my sons through my lessons. Twice.*

"Mom?"

"Yes, James?"

He pinned her with a questioning look. "What do you really want?"

"Cassidy" immediately came to mind, but she held the name back. *In a while*, she thought, *after they've adjusted a little more.* But James needed an answer. "To be loved for who I am and not what someone wants me to be."

He bit his lip. She reached out and pulled him against her, feeling him squeeze lightly around her waist. She looked over to Thomas, who nodded. "Thank you," she said quietly.

Chapter 40

Cassidy put her and Ryan's suitcases on the end of the full-size bed that took up much of the space in the cozy corner bedroom. Two windows draped in gingham that matched the bedspread opened on the view of the modest backyard of her parents' suburban St. Louis home.

The squat dresser was dominated by a large mounted oval mirror. Looking into it, seeing the room's reflection, was like dropping back in time. Cassidy plucked a picture from its carved wood frame. She smiled at her self at sixteen on horseback. After living several years in one place and finally feeling settled, she had learned to ride. By high school graduation she had become an adept horsewoman and spent some of her happiest hours in the saddle. It had been a true break from her heavy academic load and the extracurricular activities of Key Club, Student Government, and drama.

Maybe when the snow cleared she could come back out and take Ryan across these hills for his own equestrian experience. He was old enough now. *Actually, Brenna might enjoy it, too.*

Cassidy smiled at the thought of introducing Brenna to her family. She would probably get along well with Cassidy's mother. With a sigh, she set the picture back in the frame and wished anew that she had been able to see Brenna one last time before the holidays. She'd had to settle for a brief phone call as she rushed for the airport. As she shuffled clothing from the suitcase to the dresser drawers, she pulled off the long-sleeved blouse she had worn out of L.A. Reaching into the left-hand dresser drawer, she pulled out the North St. Louis High School River Rats sweatshirt and donned it, completing her homecoming ritual.

"Cass?" Her mother appeared in the doorway. "Oh, good. I see you found everything."

"Of course I found everything. You and Dad haven't changed a thing in this room since I left for college."

"Always good to have a place to come home to." Her mother, Sylvia, sat on the bed. "Are you sure you don't want to put Ryan in with Jimmy?"

Cassidy shook her head. "This way I'll be able to read his bedtime stories." She turned back to the clothes in Ryan's luggage, pulling them out. Setting the pajamas to the side for the night, the rest she tucked in the top drawer of the empty dresser.

"But it isn't right you should sleep with your son. He's old enough to sleep on his own."

Leaning back against the dressing table, Cassidy waved off the concern. "We're comfortable with it. He likes knowing where I am."

Sylvia frowned. "Well, if you change your mind, we'll pull out the trundle." She stood. "I have to get back to the kitchen. There's cocoa and coffee available."

"I'll be out in a minute to help with dinner."

"We'll be going to the service tonight," Sylvia said. "What's Ryan wearing?" Cassidy pulled out a red turtleneck and long pants from Ryan's things. Sylvia asked, "Didn't you bring a suit for him?"

After a moment of confusion, Cassidy shook her head. "No."

Her mother's frown deepened. "I'll see if I have one of Jimmy's old suits in the basement trunks." Shaking her head, Sylvia left the room. Cassidy looked at the turtleneck, finding it perfectly suitable.

She moved from her son's things to her own, pulling out an off-white pantsuit and forest green cotton scoop-neck blouse. She hung each in the closet after a quick shake to loosen the travel wrinkles. After hanging the rest of her things, she moved to tucking away her undergarments in another drawer.

She frowned at a small shallow box wrapped in shiny maroon paper trimmed with dark green velvet ribbon. "I thought I left this at home." It was Brenna's gift, but with the change in her flight time, Cassidy had not had a chance to take it by her home. "I'll just have to give it to her when I get back to town." With a fond smile, she tucked it back into the suitcase, hoping Brenna would like the silk scarf and small rose clasp. Brenna favored scarves as final touches on her outfits, and Cassidy hoped her selection would be an acceptable way to express her private feelings for Brenna without being obvious to the public.

She was looking forward to presenting Brenna with the gift. She'd been smiling ever since purchasing the gauzy red scarf, and her fingers tingled at the prospect of pinning it on her.

"Something for under the tree?"

"Oh, no." Cassidy turned to find her mother standing in the doorway, now holding a small stack of folded clothes.

"For Ryan. Hopefully everything will fit." Sylvia passed the clothing.

Cassidy looked at the gift box, considering again whether Brenna and her mother might like one another. "Mom, the next time I come for a visit, would it be all right if I brought someone?"

Sylvia's gaze lit up. "Are you considering marrying that fellow from L.A.?"

"Cameron?" Cassidy shook her head. "No. I—"

"Mommy! I ran all the way to the fence and back and didn't fall once!" Ryan pushed enthusiastically past his grandmother and plowed into his mother's legs, wrapping his arms around them and looking up her body as he gave a rambling recounting of his adventures outside in the snow-covered yard.

"Stephy got a snowball, but Jimmy hit her first."

Sylvia asked, "Jimmy hit Steph?"

"She was all wet. Jimmy ran away from her and fell down, but I didn't. I didn't, Mommy!"

"That's very good." Cassidy ruffled his hair, pleased by his high color and excitement. "It's time to clean up for dinner now. Change to dry clothes."

Sylvia nodded and left before Cassidy could re-address the topic of her bringing a guest.

Despite the request to change, Ryan kept pausing in the task and telling his mother how to pack the "best snowballs", demonstrating with his hands while his pants remained around his ankles. Cassidy finally grasped his hands, kissed his nose, and helped him finish changing — helping him step out of his pants, pull on new ones, and change to a long-sleeved green shirt.

"Do you want a cup of cocoa?"

"Yes!"

With a smile, Cassidy led the way out of the bedroom, into the main area of the house, joining her gathering family. As an only child, and traveling as much as she had with her father's military postings, extended family was the one constant.

Her Uncle Travis, her father's brother, looked up as she entered and then sprang to his feet. "Hey, Cassie girl! How's it going?"

Across from him, leaning back in a big stuffed brown leather recliner, Uncle

Floyd, her mother's brother, chimed in. "When'd you get in?"

"A couple of hours ago."

"Cutting it a little close, ain'cha?" Travis wrapped one of his linebacker arms around her shoulders and ruffled Ryan's hair as her son wrapped his slender arms around the man's tree-trunk thigh. "Howdy, squirt."

She kissed Travis' clean-shaven cheek and accepted a kiss on her own cheek before stepping back. Travis sat down and pulled Ryan into his lap. "I'll be right back with cocoa."

"We've got it all together, don't we, Ryan?" Travis chucked him under the chin and tickled his stomach.

Cassidy heard the creak as Floyd lowered his chair. "Stay," she encouraged. "What can I bring you?"

"Nothing, thanks." He followed her into the kitchen. "Just hoping to catch up with you." Floyd, her mother's younger brother by two years, watched her move around her mother in the kitchen, finding the hot kettle on the stove top and pouring cocoa mix into two mugs, one for herself and one for Ryan. "Wasn't sure we'd see you this year."

"I did have some trouble getting a flight, but at the last minute a space came through."

"You still happy out there among all them stars?"

Cassidy stirred the cocoa and put down the spoon. "Just working hard like anyone else."

"Are you going to be finishing up soon?"

"They tell us it'll be done in April. We aren't being renewed."

Moving the turkey from the oven to a platter on the counter, Sylvia interjected, "That's good, then. You can move back here so Ryan can start school."

"I wasn't planning to move home."

"You can't raise Ryan out there all alone."

"I'm not alone, I've got friends, and I will get another job." By rote, Cassidy took the turkey platter from her mother's hands, walked out to the dining table, and set it in front of her father's seat at the head of the table. "Is that the last item?" At Sylvia's nod, she said, "Excuse me, I'll take Ryan to wash up." Feeling unsettled by the discussion, Cassidy left her mother and uncle and took Ryan to the bathroom, where they washed their hands for dinner.

While she was doing that, Sylvia called the rest of the family to the table. Cassidy found Steph and Jimmy — her Uncle Floyd's children — washing up at the kitchen sink, directed by their mother, Lydia. Floyd, her father, Gerry, and her mother were already moving to their seats. Travis entered from another room. "I've got Brenda down," he reported, taking his seat.

Cassidy pushed Ryan's seat in and took the one next to him. "How is she doing?" she asked.

"Bren? Oh, fine. She's too little yet to know much about what's going on."

Cassidy reached over and gave his hand a light squeeze in silent support. She felt him squeeze her hand back. Virginia "Ginny" Hockman, Travis' wife of only two years, had died of a staph infection, leaving Travis with their newborn daughter, now just seven months old.

"Travis is moving into the old Arbor place down the street so we can help him out," Sylvia said.

"Time for grace," Gerry said, as he held his hands out to either side. Ryan took his right hand, Steph took his left. Everyone at the table grasped hands, and Gerry dropped his eyes, closing them briefly before speaking.

"Dear Father in Heaven, You have gathered us together to witness the birth of the Living Word as the Wise Men foretold. We bless You for all that we receive in this world and in the Kingdom to come."

Cassidy echoed "amen" with the rest, surprised at how awkward she felt inside at the sentiments her father expressed. She didn't recall grace at the table being so religiously formal. There had always been thanking God, but it had not seemed so much like an invocation.

Her father carved the turkey, and plates began to circulate. As the dinner items moved from person to person, from cranberry sauce to cornbread stuffing to the creamed string beans, Cassidy served herself and Ryan, remaining quiet as she listened to the conversation that started up around her.

Steph had entered junior high in September; Cassidy marveled at her poise. She sat quietly, unhurriedly eating, back straight, hair pinned up tidily. By contrast, at that age a pigtailed Cassidy had been always been in a hurry to get back outside, whether it was to run around the Army base playing tag or act out the skits she and the other military children had scribbled out. When she had gotten to high school and found the drama department, it had been an epiphany. She had been ecstatic when her father retired and she was told they would finally be staying put.

Jimmy, at ten, seemed unusually quiet. He did not look up as the adults talked. He ate quickly, clearing his plate. Instead of asking for seconds, he asked to be excused. Lydia nodded her permission, and he was quickly gone from the table.

Ryan ate with energy, commenting on everything — from the decorative lamb-shaped holiday salt-and-pepper shakers to the "stringy beans" catching in his teeth. And of course he had to show everyone the one missing incisor he had that made it "hard to chew right".

Several times as Cassidy reminded him to eat, she caught her mother studying them. She felt a surprising amount of disapproval coming from her, despite the fact that she never said anything directly.

Her father was less restrained. "Ryan, sit down." Ryan sat with a frown. "So, Cassie, tell us when you'll be done with this television thing."

"*Time Trails* taping ends in April."

"So will we see you in the summer? Do you want us to come help you move home?"

"I wasn't planning to move back to St. Louis," she said again.

"Your divorce is final. Without Mitch supporting you, you obviously can't raise Ryan by yourself. Your mother tells me that you're no longer dating that writer," her father said.

"It's time to give up this silly thing and come home," her mother added. "Your room is still as you like it, and the other room will be Ryan's."

"That won't be necessary." Cassidy shook her head. "Ryan will be starting school next fall. Our life is in L.A. now. We're doing fine." The sensation that she had already had this conversation with Mitch was unnerving. "Have you talked to Mitch recently?"

"He did call here to wish us a happy holiday."

"He did?" Cassidy chewed quietly as she considered why her ex-husband would be contacting her parents.

"He seemed rather concerned about your arrangements for Ryan."

"I've got that all worked out. After school, he's on the set with me." From the expressions on their faces, that seemed to be the wrong thing to say. "He spends the time with a professional caregiver, and I get to see him on my breaks."

"And you plan to continue doing things like you've done on this show?" Her mother sounded the word distastefully.

"Until April, certainly."

"And you'll find another job from the friends you've made on this one?"

Cassidy nodded. "There's a theater run by one of them. I might try that for a while. I haven't decided yet."

"Ryan can't live in that kind of environment."

"Is your problem with me, with L.A., or with something on the show?" Cassidy asked.

"We object to the content, yes."

"What content?"

Her mother looked pointedly at Steph and then Ryan across the table. "We'll discuss it later."

That brought the topic abruptly to a close. Too abruptly. Cassidy looked from her mother to her father, then to Travis and Floyd to inquire silently if they felt the same. No one said anything. She returned her gaze to her mother. "It seems to be something everyone agrees on."

"In this house," her mother said.

"I see." Not sure what to say and aware that whatever it was they did not want it discussed in front of the children, Cassidy pushed herself away from the table. "Excuse me, I'm finished. Ryan, come on; time to change our clothes."

She led Ryan from the dining table. In the room, she looked at the size of the pants her mother had provided. Realizing they would be too long for him to wear, she put him in the clothes she had brought. Pulling the turtleneck over Ryan's head, she sent him to the bathroom with instructions to potty, wash his hands, and brush his teeth. While alone, she quickly changed and joined him in the bathroom, brushing his hair and then her own and cleaning her own teeth.

They were finished and emerging as Steph and Jimmy walked up, changed as well — Steph in a short jumper dress in green plaid, a crisp white turtleneck underneath. Jimmy wore a pair of green slacks, with deeply pressed creases down each leg, and a white oxford-style button shirt, a hunter green tie finishing off the semi-formal appearance.

Lydia stood in doorway of the other bedroom holding a dress jacket in her hand.

"Lydia," Cassidy sent Ryan off with a nudge to his back, "can you tell me what's going on?"

"It's not my place."

"What isn't?"

"Floyd told me it's none of our business what you do, but we don't have to watch it."

"What did I do?"

"I didn't see it," Lydia said sharply. "I was at choir practice with Steph."

"Something on *Time Trails*?" Cassidy asked, beginning to understand somewhat. "They're upset about one of the episodes? For that they think I can't run my own life and need to come home?"

"As I said, it's not my place." Lydia stepped back as Steph and Jimmy returned to the room. She shut the door to tend the final preparations of her children, leaving Cassidy staring at the wood.

During the church service, Cassidy put the issue from her mind and tried to enjoy the pageantry of the holiday service. She lifted Ryan to see as they sang *Good King Wenceslas, On a Midnight Clear,* and *Silent Night*.

The assembly filed out past the live manger scene, several members portraying roles in the hay-covered, rustic barnyard-style scene. She knew something about the landscape of Judea at the time and knew that it was more likely to have been a cave than a barn, but she thought the distinctly Midwest interpretation would have appealed to Brenna. She left the church smiling after shaking hands with the minister and his wife.

Out in the parking lot, she looked around to find the rest of the family. She noticed none of them had Ryan in tow. Hearing chuckles and sounds of a disturbance, she realized he had climbed inside the manger area. She found him petting the lamb that was curled up on the floor. "Come on, my little farm boy." She picked him up, laughing easily.

Thomas watched his mother curled up on the couch. Her gaze, though supposedly on the book in her lap, was a little vacant and lost as she reclined, propping her chin in her palm. Wanting to help but not sure how, he waited another moment before crossing through the living room to the kitchen. As he'd expected, she jumped at the noise of his passing. "Mom?"

"I'm sorry. What is it? Has James come home yet?"

"Not yet." He set his cup on the counter. "Are you sure you're all right?" He reached into the upper cupboard for the cocoa mix. "I'm having some cocoa. You want a cup?"

She started to shake her head, but he tilted his head in question. "All right," she conceded. She started to rise.

"No, I've got it. You sit." He put a teapot on and set out another cup of mix. "You've been awfully quiet," he began. "Everything okay?"

"What makes you think something's wrong?"

"Well, let's see." He stepped out from behind the counter and tapped off his observations on his fingers. "You've been sitting there reading the same page in that book for the last twenty minutes. Before that, you sat in the chair and read the comics page for half an hour. Before that, you sat at the desk and worked on a letter for almost an hour."

His mother waved off any further commentary. "I get the point. If you've been watching me, what have you accomplished in the last two hours?"

"Finished wrapping presents," he said proudly.

"I see." The teakettle whistled, and he turned away to pour and stir. When he carried the cups into the living room, offering her one as he sat down, she blew on it and took a sip, then asked, "When did you have time for shopping?"

He shook his head. "Who says I shopped?" Thomas grinned at her. "Don't ask me what I got you, and I won't ask what Santa's bringing me."

She laughed heartily. "You and James haven't believed in Santa in almost five years."

"So why is there a package marked 'From Santa' under the tree?"

His mother pursed her lips. "I got a little something for Cassidy's son."

"Pretty big box."

She swatted his arm. "Now who's being nosy?" She lifted the mug in her palms and sipped, then exhaled. "It's a kid-sized hiking pack, if you must know. He liked yours so much, I thought I'd get him his own."

"Was that phone call you took from Ms. Hyland?"

"Yes. She took Ryan to Missouri for the holidays."

"Well, I guess I'll hold her present until she gets back then."

"You bought her a present?"

"Well, yeah, I did. I got her a pair of climbing gloves," he answered sheepishly. She frowned at him. "What's wrong?"

"Thomas, she's... I'm sure she'll love the gloves, but, sweetheart, you shouldn't continue this infatuation with her."

Thomas felt his face get hot. "I like her."

"She's twice your age. It's not healthy." She hesitated as she decided how to continue. "I thought you were doing well with Cheryl."

"Cheryl's nice, but she's more interested in dances and going shopping than things that matter."

"Thomas," she patted his arm, making his frown deepen. "Yes, you are more mature than the average teen. I admire that. But there is such a thing as growing up too fast."

He pulled away from her and stood, pacing away from the couch. "I don't want to spend time with empty-headed girls, worrying about my clothes or my hair." He wanted to convince his mother of his earnestness. "I've been thinking about Ryan, too. I'd be good for him. We get along so well. I can show him things he should know."

"Thomas, you can't possibly be thinking that you could be a father to that boy. You aren't even responsible for yourself yet." Brenna stood, squeezing a couch pillow between her hands. "I know you find her fascinating and she's very engaging, but Thomas, she'll never feel the same way about you."

"I thought we really hit it off," he said, sitting down, deflating a little in the face of his mother's objections.

"You did...as friends." She drew a short breath, sat beside him, and put an arm around his shoulders. "You taught her to climb in a single afternoon. That takes incredible talent. You impressed her, but that's very different from love."

He leaned forward over his knees and braced his elbows on them as he covered his face. "You're telling me I've been obvious?" When he turned his head toward her, she nodded. "God, she must think I'm such a—"

"I just told you — she thinks you're talented."

"But I'm only seventeen to her."

"You *are* seventeen. That's not a bad thing. You've got a lot of choices ahead of you." She leaned back and rubbed between his shoulder blades; he shrugged off the touch. "Come on. What's wrong with being her friend? I enjoy that role myself."

"Mom, it's not the same thing."

"No, it's not." She straightened. "It's not going to be. She and I are peers. But you two can be friends. I'd like you to be. If you're comfortable around her, she'll be comfortable around here. That's important to me." She grew wistful.

Thomas hated when his mother got uncertain. He quickly assured her, "Don't worry, Mom. I'll figure it out. I promise."

"Thank you, sweetheart." She hugged him. "Someday you will find someone suited just for you."

He pursed his lips and nodded tightly. It felt unlikely at the moment. Cassidy Hyland was, as his mother had said, both captivating and engaging. She also stirred him in ways Cheryl or his other girlfriends never had. When he was around her, he felt smart, thoughtful, respected. She made him feel mature, though he knew there were many things he still needed to understand. He took a deep breath. Maybe there would be only friendship for them, but he suspected he would always harbor a love for Cassidy for sharing that with him.

Brenna stood as he did and touched his shoulder. "It's Christmas Eve. Would you like to attend midnight Mass?"

"What about James?"

"Curfew's in another few minutes," his mother said. A vehicle pulled up outside even as she spoke. "Probably him now. Let's get changed, and we'll all go."

"All right."

The door opened, closed, and James swept into the living room. Thomas noticed immediately something was wrong. When his mother called to him, James only dropped his head and waved before quickly passing through to his room.

"James?" Brenna tried again. She brushed past Thomas, turning back as she reached the hall. "Go on and get changed. I'll talk to James."

She hurried to James' bedroom door only to find it shut tight. "James, sweetheart?" She tried the knob and found it locked. "Can I come in, find out about your evening?"

"Go away."

His voice was muffled enough that she could not discern any particular emotion in it. "If you're hurt about something I'd like to help."

"You can't help. I just need to be alone."

Brenna swallowed hard, fighting the emotions stirred by her conversation with Thomas. She had come so close to telling him more, much more, than he should know about her relationship with Cassidy.

"James, unlock the door." There was a long silence while she waited, then came the telltale noise of the lock disengaging. She reached for the knob and turned it, pushing inward. James straddled his desk chair, his head down on crossed hands on the back of the chair.

"Mom..."

She heard the pain lancing through his voice now that it was no longer muffled by the door. "What happened?"

"Marcie dumped me." He pulled something from his pocket and tossed it on the desk. "I've been walking around downtown for the last hour trying to figure out what I did wrong."

Her heart clenched with sympathy — and with fear. "That's so dangerous, honey." She stood close but didn't touch him.

"I know; I'm sorry. What did I do wrong, Mom?"

James turned, and Brenna saw the tearstains on his face. "You didn't do anything wrong; sometimes it just happens." She crouched next to him and put a hand on the desk, looking into his face. "I know it hurts. It won't make this any less painful, but, there will be other girls."

James' jaw hardened, just like his father's did when he was trying to suppress emotions he thought inappropriate to display. She rubbed her thumb over his chin, feeling it tremble slightly. His gaze cleared just a little at the familiar, comforting touch. Knowing him as she did, she changed the subject. "It's Christmas Eve. Thomas and I were going to attend mass."

"I don't want to go out. People will laugh at me."

"No, they won't. You've always enjoyed the music. It might ease the pain, just a little." He nodded briefly. Quickly, as he preferred, she caught up his head and shoulders in a hug, no more than a squeeze, and stood away. "Get changed and I'll see you in a few minutes, all right?"

Brenna left him and went to her own room. She wanted to tuck the last presents under the tree before the boys came out. Quickly she changed for the service, pulling on a jade green pant suit and draping a diaphanous emerald scarf around her shoulders. Then she pulled two objects from her closet shelf — one wrapped in navy blue with a mistletoe print and the other, a round cylinder, papered in metallic red. Putting on soft leather green pumps, she carried the presents out and set them beneath the tree that glowed in the far corner of the living room.

She was just standing when her sons appeared, ready to go. Each had chosen a simple green dress shirt to wear under a blue suit jacket. Thomas' was a vertical striped forest green and black. James wore a solid aquamarine. She grinned at both of them and stood.

"Presents?" James asked.

"You'll see them in the morning." Brenna saw that James had washed his face and looked better than he had a few minutes earlier. She put a light hand on each shoulder. "Let's go."

Putting the children to bed after hanging up their stockings, the adults gathered in the living room. Some had coffee, Travis with a shot of whiskey in his, and Cassidy had chosen cocoa. The stocking stuffers, little baubles and toy knick-knacks, were pulled out. As they parceled out the treats, filling the children's stockings, Cassidy was surprised at the unusual solemnity. Normally this task, the adults' last one on Christmas Eve, was joyful, and even though they couldn't talk loudly, they would usually whisper back and forth. No one tonight was saying a word, and Cassidy was disturbed to feel that she was the reason why.

"Can we talk about what the problem is?" she asked. "I can't address it if I don't know what I'm supposed to have done wrong."

Her father scowled at her. "As if you didn't know."

"Well, I don't know. Obviously it's something I did on the show, or something someone else did. But I thought I didn't have to remind you that it's all a fantasy. I act for a living. I'm not a secretary or a teacher; I'm an actor."

"So what you do is a game?"

"I take it very seriously. You know that."

"Then how could you participate in something like that? You kissed a woman, and all our friends think you're a *lesbian*." Her mother hissed the last word.

Oh boy. Cassidy exhaled. "An accident had switched our bodies. It was supposed to be seen as Luria — that's the other character — kissing her husband."

"That doesn't excuse it."

"Did you even see it? Do you understand what it was actually about, or are the neighbors your judges now?"

"How dare you!" Her father's voice rose angrily. Her mother put a hand on him quickly to quiet him. "You blindly think we'd accept such a display? Homosexuality is a sin against God."

Cassidy hung the stocking she had been working on, a sinking feeling making her chest feel heavy. She strove for a calm response. "I'm sorry that you've been embarrassed by your narrow-minded neighbors."

"They're our friends."

"I'm sorry."

"You're sorry; that's all? You're sorry?"

Her father stared at her with an angry expression and Cassidy felt her adrenaline start to flow. The longer he stared at her, the more hurt and surprised she was, feeling just as she often had just before Mitch hit her. Her father hadn't struck her since disciplining her as a very young child. Abruptly, he backed up, pushed away Sylvia's hand, turned, and walked away. Travis reached up from the couch and tried to grasp his arm. Gerry brushed that away as well.

"I'm going to bed."

"Dad," Cassidy called after him.

"Everyone," Sylvia said, "I think we're all tired. Time for bed."

One by one the family left the living room. Cassidy looked after them. Travis was the last to stand to leave. "Uncle Travis?"

"Hopefully there won't be any more shows like that one," he said. "Gerry was not happy."

"But it's just a show. You know that, don't you?"

"Yes, I do," he said gently. He rested his hand on her shoulder and kissed her forehead. "Good night, Cassie."

Restlessly rolling around beneath the covers, Ryan woke. His mother lay beside him, and from the quiet sounds he knew she was sleeping. Uncle Travis had read the story about Santa Claus, and Ryan still had the pictures in his head. He had to see. Getting to the floor, he stumbled over something. When he looked, he found another present his mother must have forgotten to put under the tree. He thought he could do it for her and carried it with him out to the den. The fire glowed orange and the stocking Grandpa had helped him hang bulged in the dim light. *Santa's already been here!* he thought excitedly, putting the box under the tree.

"Mommy! Mommy!" He ran back into the bedroom and launched himself onto the bed with a squeal. "Santa's been here!"

His mother rolled over and sat up, brushing her hair from her face. "What? Ryan, it's..." she squinted toward the bedside clock, "it's only three a.m. At least wait until six. Jimmy will be up then, all right?" She pulled him down with her under the covers and murmured, "Now try to go back to sleep."

Obediently, he closed his eyes, but sleep did not come. He squirmed. "Mommy?"

"Yes?" She sounded tired.

"How much longer?"

"About three hours. Please go to sleep." She brushed his hair with her fingers and kissed his forehead.

"I can't. Can I wake Jimmy up now?"

Cassidy moved away from him, and then suddenly the room was filled with light. He blinked as she looked down at him from the edge of the bed. "I know it's Christmas and I know you're excited, but you really need to sleep."

"Read me a story?"

Sitting up in the bed, she pulled a big book out of the nearby bookshelf. "Just one story, all right?"

"Okay." He settled between her legs and helped her open the book to a story. "Little Red Riding Hood," he read carefully. The squeeze on his shoulder told him he had gotten it right.

A tale unfolded of a little girl hunted down by a wolf who pretended to be her grandmother. Ryan was excited by the end of the story where the woodcutter killed the wolf with his axe. "He saved her from the mean old wolf," he cheered at the end. "He saved her."

"Yes, he did." She kissed his cheek and pulled the book away. "Now, that's your one story. Let's try to go back to sleep." He yawned, and after she turned off the light and pulled him down across her chest, he closed his eyes as she patted his back, with her heartbeat strong in his ear.

"I love you, Mommy."

"I love you too, Ryan."

Her voice was soft, sleepy. Ryan found it easy to succumb to sleep himself.

Chapter 41

Comfortably ensconced on the couch, Brenna sipped her coffee as she watched Thomas and James opening their presents. Gift cards from their father were already tucked in their wallets for the holiday trip to the mall tomorrow. Shaking her head about the absurdity of a father who neither called nor wrote except to send money, Brenna watched James opening his last gift from her. It was the package she had tucked under the tree at the last minute, but the one she'd worked longest on in preparation for the holidays. She hoped he would still like it. Music tastes changed so fast.

He unfolded the white tee shirt, looking blankly at the back for a moment before turning it around. His eyes widened, and he yipped, "Lifehouse! This is so cool! How'd you get all the autographs?"

She grinned as two oblong pieces of paper fluttered from the folds of the fabric. "There's more," she said.

He set aside the tee shirt and snatched up the strips of cardboard. "Tickets to their concert! Cool!" He tucked the tickets into his shirt pocket and turned back to the tee. "How *did* you get the autographs?"

"They *are* an L.A. band, you know," she said with a smile. "I...ran into someone who knows them."

"No way."

Laughing, she responded in teen parlance, "Way." Obviously boggled at the autographs, James immediately pulled the shirt on over his other one, which made her grin broaden.

Thomas, who had watched quietly through the exchange, finished opening the small present from his Uncle Gary, her brother. "Thomas, what have you got there?"

"Uncle Gary sent tickets to spring training exhibitions for the Dodgers. Says he got me some batting and pitching practice with them, too."

Brenna looked at the tickets. "There's two here for each game."

"Yep." Thomas read more of the note his uncle had included. "Says he's going to take me. Looks like he's coming for a visit."

"There's a half-dozen games here. That's...what — three weeks worth?"

"Yeah, probably. It's usually two games a week." He tucked the tickets safely in the small box and then turned to open the present from her.

Brenna suddenly realized there might be some conflicting dates. Biting her lower lip anxiously, she awaited Thomas' reaction.

His brow furrowed as he read, "U.S. Department of Forestry."

Brenna's heart sped up at the slow-building smile, finally laughing when he burst out, "I'm going to co-op with the Forestry Service!"

"What?" James asked.

"Yeah. Mom? How did you do this?"

"I had a talk with your counselor about how interested you were in hiking and climbing and how much fun you have with the LAKE kids. He looked up the contact information and the requirements."

"I've got enough credits to do this?"

"You'll get two credits, as well as get paid. Mr. Thierry can tell you more, but I've already set up an account for you on the bus line." She gestured to the tube. Thomas looked inside and when he shook it, the credit card bus pass dropped out into his palm. The magnetic strip would debit the account, allowing him to not always have to travel with change for the bus. "After lunch you take the bus to the forestry office and get home around eight o'clock." She hesitated. "I was just thinking it might make getting to some of your Dodgers games a little tough."

"Don't worry about that! This is fantastic!"

He skimmed the letter again, and she registered with pleasure the wonderment on his face. "I'm glad then that I thought to talk to your counselor."

"I can't believe Thierry didn't tell me about this opportunity himself."

"Apparently it's not a widely publicized program," Brenna explained. "I guess that my asking if there was something along those lines caused him to go looking in the right places."

Thank you, Cassidy. Cassidy had mentioned the idea of Thomas being a camp counselor in the first place. The Forestry Service co-op would give him a chance to see all the related outdoors careers and let him find his own place, if he chose. She would have to tell Cassidy how well the gift had been received. *Actually, I would like to tell Cassidy a lot of things.* She suddenly missed her very much.

"More coffee, Mom?"

At Thomas' question she looked up, only then realizing that she had been staring into her empty mug. "Thank you." She passed it to him for a refill.

James stood up and retrieved a present from under the tree. It was square — about a foot long on a side and an inch deep. He passed it to her. "For you."

"James?"

"Just a little something." He shrugged and sat down, looking nervous as she took it carefully onto her lap.

It was quite heavy. She tore through the plain navy blue paper. Inside was a framed piece of art, a portrait, she realized, identifying a shoulder before she removed the last of the paper and revealed the face. Her face.

Awestruck, she looked at a portrait of herself rendered in pastels. The figure was in three-quarter profile, from the shoulders up, and the skin tone was flawless, shadowed well enough to suggest the muscles in her throat and face as she smiled. *He really sees me this way?* "It's...beautiful," she whispered.

"I had a good subject," James said, smiling. "I did it in art class."

Still studying the portrait, Brenna realized the shadows above the figure's left shoulder were not just random swirls. "There's another face in here."

"It's you...as Jakes," he said.

She picked out the shadowy face and shoulders of an almost ethereal rendering of her on-screen alter ego. It was..."Truly amazing," she breathed. "Thank you." Looking at the picture, she said, "I didn't know you could do anything like this." She traced the swirled 'JL' signed in the lower left corner.

"We had a portrait unit in class. Mrs. Vetter thought this was good enough to enter in the district art fair."

"Did you?" When he nodded but remained silent, she patted his arm. "Well? Are you going to tell me, or make me drag it out of you syllable by syllable?"

"I won second place in the pastel category."

He grinned at her, and she squeezed his hand. "That's wonderful!"

"Thanks."

"Thank you." She pulled him down for a kiss. "Let me know when you do another show." James looked surprised. "I'd really like to go."

"Uh. Sure." He blushed and stepped back.

Thomas appeared over her shoulder with her coffee. "Here you go, Mom." He caught a glimpse of the portrait. "Man, James, that's nice." James accepted the praise with a nod. Thomas looked at his mother. "You might not want mine now."

"Of course I will." She reached up and patted Thomas' cheek. "Go on." As Thomas retrieved a package from under the tree, she noted the similar dimensions; it looked suspiciously like another picture.

He introduced it as he passed it over. "I know you've seen some of the pictures I took on the camping trip. I thought you'd like this one to remember it best, though."

Brenna tore aside the paper and found another framed image, this one a photograph, blown up to 8 x 10. It was a picture of the mountain they had climbed, shot from above. Framed centrally between golden brown rocks and the green forest, Brenna and Cassidy had their arms wrapped around their ropes, resting in the grandeur. The sunlight seemed to beam on them both, illuminating them against the tan of the craggy surface. Looking up at Thomas, she said, "But you were on the mountain with us."

"That was taken on my second stop at the top. I pulled out the camera and captured it, then rappelled down to meet you." He dropped his chin, swallowed hard, then returned his gaze to her. "I'm giving Cassidy a duplicate of the shot."

"She'll love it." Knowing he was concerned she would be upset with him, Brenna reached out a hand. When he leaned past his brother and took it, she assured him, "It's an appropriate gift." He smiled with pleasure, and she let him go.

"Thanks, Mom."

She looked to James, then at the pictures. "I'm going to have to build on a gallery room," she said with a chuckle. "Both of these deserve more of a display than the living room wall." She squeezed their hands. "Thank you. And, you know, I love you."

Predictably, her younger son sidestepped the mush. "If we're finished, how about some lunch?"

"A snack," she suggested. "Dinner is early today." She stood. "You two get something together, and I'll hang these."

It was two in the afternoon when the Hockman family began to wind down the opening of presents. The last ones around the tree were being distributed by Steph and Jimmy. Ryan was playing with a new race car. Cassidy looked up from unwrapping a sweater from her parents to see Jimmy carrying a familiar-looking box. "Jimmy, what have you got there?"

"It looks like it's for Brenda." He crossed to Travis, who was giving his daughter a toy he had just unwrapped.

Cassidy reached for it, but Travis got his hands on it first. Brenda, having heard her name, pulled it from him.

Travis looked at the card, "To Bren, love Cass."

She cleared her throat. "That's not for Brenda. I'm sorry, Travis. It got mixed in by mistake."

"That's the present I brought out, Mommy," Ryan said proudly.

"Thank you, Ryan, but it's for Brenna back home."

"Oh." He brightened. "Is it pretty?"

At that moment Brenda tore into the paper, and the box was opened. Gerry reached over the back of the couch and pulled the box with the scarf and pin from

Brenda's hands. "It certainly is pretty." He fingered the silk. "Who is this for?"

Cassidy was unnerved by his tone. After last night's very one-sided exchange, she could not them know she was involved with Bren. "Brenna Lanigan, a woman I work with." She stood up to take it from him. As he plucked out the note, she remembered what she had written. Everyone else found out, too.

Obviously surprised by what he read, her father read it aloud, as if asking her to confirm it. " 'A silken embrace to remember me.' " His eyes darkened in plain anger and disgust as he continued reading silently. He looked at her with suspicion. "Rather intimate for an office gift."

Her heart beginning to hammer, Cassidy saw the terrifying glint of steel in her father's blue eyes. She reclaimed her property. "I'll just go put this back in my bag."

"You'll explain who this woman is to you." His voice was deep and dark.

"Cassidy, what kind of trouble have you gotten into?" Her mother's tone was anxious.

"What trouble?" Cassidy exhaled. "Yes, it's a present for my friend on *Time Trails*. We work together sixteen hours a day!"

Her father's voice exploded through the room. "It looks like a note to a lover!"

Little Brenda wailed at Gerry's shout. Travis bent to soothe her even as he was rising to stand between Cassidy and her parents. Cassidy had also taken a quick step backward at her father's loud exclamation, almost tripping over Ryan. She righted herself as her mother exclaimed, "Gerry!"

"I told you she'd get perverted ideas out there!" Gerry accused. He threw the scarf box down on the couch.

Cassidy quickly retrieved it, tucking the contents gently back inside, holding it tightly. "Get ideas?" Cassidy was jolted by his patronizing tone. "I've been in L.A. eighteen months working on my job. I've been on my own working since I was twenty. I'm thirty-two, not ten or twelve."

Her father shot back, "We sent you to college to get an education."

"And I earned my way all by myself." Her scholarships for academics had paid the bulk of her tuition, and the money from a few small beauty pageants — and commercials as she was cutting her teeth in acting — paid for the rest of the fees at the state university. She hadn't asked her parents for anything. Apparently they remembered things differently.

"I told your mother that place would corrupt you. First you take up with that playboy and get a divorce!"

"Playboy? Cameron? He's just a writer."

"We've heard all about casting couches," her father retorted.

"Well, I've never auditioned on one," Cassidy replied evenly. "I got the job on *Time Trails* through hard work, and I've kept it the same—"

Her father's hand landed hard against her cheek. "You don't talk to me like that."

Cassidy's eyes watered as she gingerly touched the stinging hot skin of her face. Biting the inside of her cheek, she kept the tears at bay. Silence blanketed the room. Taking a step back, she looked for Ryan, finding him being held by his grandmother.

"Mommy?" he said, anxious eyes on her.

"I'm all right, Ryan. Just—" She gestured for him to relax. "Stay still." She stared at her father, angry at him for instigating this display in front of Ryan. "I didn't think you were the same as Mitch," she said with cold fury.

"It's your own fault. He wouldn't have done anything to you if you hadn't made him jealous," her father retorted.

"My fault?" Cassidy shook her head. "Not my fault."

"You get it in your head that you want to act — instead of being a mother to your son — and you claim that your husband getting tired and jealous isn't your fault?"

"And so it's okay that he hit me? For you to hit me? Something you've never done before, I might add," Cassidy retorted. "Why are we discussing this?"

"If I'd been less lenient with you as a child, maybe you would've paid more attention to how things are supposed to be."

"You're talking nonsense."

"I should've beat all those fool ideas of acting out of you in high school, but your mother thought it was 'harmless.'" He turned to Sylvia again. "Harmless, hmm?" He jabbed at the note.

"I'm not a little girl."

"No. But damn well you're my daughter and I won't have it." Gerry turned his back abruptly.

Cassidy had never heard her father spew such vitriol. "I'm no different than I was just yesterday when I came home to spend some time with my family for Christmas."

"*Christmas?*" He tried to grab Cassidy, but she backed away and he stumbled forward, knocking around the furniture noisily. "You are no Christian, behaving like this! No respect for your parents, all we've done for you! Sleeping with a man while you were married!"

Travis stood. "Gerry, please. Shh. You're scaring the baby." Gerry shook off his brother's hand on his arm.

"I'm sorry, Uncle Travis." Cassidy apologized though she had not been the one yelling. Her father said nothing. She looked from her father to her mother and back again at her father's sternly set jaw. She set her own jaw and then exhaled. "It would be better, I think, if we went home. This obviously isn't the best time to talk about this."

"I don't want to hear you say anything but that you're giving up all these damn fool notions," her father retorted.

"You've made that perfectly clear." Shaking inside, Cassidy drew on her acting skills to maintain an outward appearance of calm. "Which is why we have to leave." She reached out for Ryan, who pulled away from his grandmother. "Time to go," she told her son with forced lightness, though she couldn't bring herself to smile.

Her mother's voice stopped her. "You can't leave now, we haven't had dinner," her mother protested. The request made Cassidy stare at her a moment in disbelief.

She considered responding, but caught sight of her father, who gave every appearance of not relenting. He stood with his back to her, his arms over his chest. He seemed proud of himself as he walked away and settled — in what Cassidy could only characterize as a "king-like" manner — on his recliner, his arms splayed outward over the padded arms, hands wrapped around the ends. He looked like he was waiting.

Abruptly Cassidy recalled how he would do the same thing to her when she was younger, his silence conveying disapproval of something she had done. She would buckle under that look and apologize, promising profusely not to do whatever it was again. Though today was the first time he had struck her, the rest of the situation made her feel like she was twelve again, being grounded for some unspoken infraction.

Only now she wasn't twelve. She was not going to be cowed into apologizing for doing something wrong when she felt she hadn't. She had learned a great deal in the last year about herself, particularly when it came to making her own choices and directing her own life. Mostly from Brenna. She smiled at that, and her spine straightened with resolve.

"Maybe I'll see you in the spring after *Time Trails* finishes up." She saw her father's eyes narrow and felt vindicated that she had surprised him by not capitulating. She tried to lean in and kiss her mother's cheek, but the bewildered woman pulled away, eyes wide. Stepping away, Cassidy took Ryan and went to pack.

"Cassie?" Her Uncle Travis stepped out of the doorway of the second bedroom, where he'd just put his daughter down for a nap.

She stopped, gauging his expression but finding nothing but the question...and love. "I'm going home," she said quietly, continuing past him.

Travis followed her into her bedroom. "Do you need a ride?"

"I can call a cab." She pulled out the luggage and set it on the bed, haphazardly repacking what she had unpacked only the night before.

"Most likely double the price today."

Cassidy automatically went through the process of changing Ryan's clothes while she responded. "I can handle it."

"I could see you safely on the plane."

"I've got to change my flight. It'll probably be a few hours before we can find space to L.A."

"I wouldn't mind waiting with you and Ryan."

"Dad wouldn't take it kindly."

"Doesn't seem right — you leaving on Christmas Day."

"I won't let them continue to treat me as if I'm a child. Besides I've got someone who will be happy to see me back in L.A. just as I am."

Cassidy finished securing the lock, and Travis grabbed the luggage. "You can tell me about her on the way." She exhaled and felt a single knot of tension release in the back of her neck; she smiled at him gratefully.

The tension thickened as Cassidy, leading Ryan by the hand, followed Travis out through the living room. Her father stood, and they regarded one another warily, Cassidy not moving a muscle and keeping her face expressionless and her father frowning deeply. Her mother stood beside him, a hand on his arm, not restraining him, but the gesture suggested that she was holding him in place nonetheless.

"Cassie, please don't go. Let us help you."

She shook her head. "I don't want, or need, the help you want to give."

"We're your parents. We know what's best for you."

"When I was ten, maybe. You seem to have forgotten I grew up."

Her father took exception to her tone. "Don't talk to your mother like that," he growled.

Cassidy nodded. "Goodbye."

Uncle Floyd and Aunt Lydia, each with a hand on a shoulder of their two children, remained seated on the couch. Cassidy directed a "Goodbye" to them. Travis said nothing, but the suitcases in his hands spoke volumes. She followed him to the hallway, put Ryan in his warm coat, and pulled on her own long winter coat. Sylvia followed them but didn't say anything more.

Travis addressed himself to her. "I'll be back when I've seen her safely off. Maybe after dinner. See to Brenda, will you?"

Sylvia nodded, and Cassidy watched her close the door, leaving them outside standing on the porch. The silence was oppressive, and Cassidy felt suddenly as heavy as the door barring her from her parents' home. She exhaled. "Let's go."

"Where are we going, Mommy?"

"Home."

"Christmas is over?"

Cassidy nodded. Ryan took her hand as they walked down the snowy wet front steps. She belted Ryan into the back seat of Travis' large four-door gray sedan. The car rocked a little as he closed the trunk lid.

"Got everything?" he asked as he entered the front seat.

Cassidy checked her purse for the tickets she would have to exchange. She considered the keepsakes she had left in her old bedroom — the pictures in the mirror, the yearbooks in the closet. St. Louis was only the last stop in her family's many moves, but it was the home she remembered most. Now it all felt like her things belonged to someone else. She now understood that her parents had believed she was supposed to stay that same amenable girl. She wasn't, and she would have to wait them out until they realized that as well.

She shook herself, rubbing her cheek where it still hurt from her father's hand. "Yes, I've got everything." She got in on the passenger side of the front bench seat and secured her belt. "All right. Let's go."

The doorbell sounded as Brenna, Thomas, and James were finishing their holiday cleanup and sampling a fruitcake sent by Rachelle Cheron. James went to the door.

Looking through the peep hole, his face took on a puzzled expression, and he opened the door. "Ms. Hyland?"

Brenna paused in folding together her wrapping paper collection. *Cassidy?* She pushed to her feet and dusted off her hands. "Cass? I thought you were in St. Louis." She pushed the door open wide and watched as Cassidy nudged Ryan forward first. Cass looked tired, and her face seemed a little drawn. Her left cheek was bruised.

"We were in St. Louis until this morning. I decided to come home early."

"Well, we're just finishing cleaning up. Come on inside; I'll make some coffee."

"I'd like that."

Brenna watched as Cassidy crouched and helped Ryan off with his coat. Sensing something unsettled about her, Brenna gave in to the impulse to put her hand on Cassidy's shoulder. Cassidy rose with Ryan's coat in her hands and turned to meet Brenna's gaze.

"We need to talk," Cassidy said quietly.

Chapter 42

Thomas and James stood as Cassidy and Ryan entered the living room, Brenna walking in behind them. "It's good to see you," Cassidy said to them.

"Mom told me you were in St. Louis visiting your family," Thomas said with concern.

"I was. We had...a problem." Cassidy looked to Brenna. "They don't like what I'm doing," she elaborated vaguely.

Brenna wondered exactly what Cassidy meant, but clearly the woman didn't want to speak in specifics without a private word first. "Thomas, would you take Ryan into the game room? I'll make some cocoa with our coffees and bring them in a minute."

Thomas looked as if he were about to balk at the request, and Brenna noticed how he fidgeted toward Cassidy. "Just a few minutes," she added.

Finally he nodded. "All right. Ryan, c'mon. Let's see how you do on my latest Playstation game."

James actually led the way, clearly eager to leave the whole group.

Brenna nodded toward the kitchen once she and Cassidy were alone. "It's not perfectly private, but obviously something's on your mind."

Cassidy followed her to the kitchen and helped pull out the makings for coffee and cocoa. "I'm sorry. I didn't really think about this; I just knew I needed to see you."

Shaking her head, Brenna flipped on the coffeemaker and then reached over to grasp Cassidy's hand. "You should feel you can come to me about anything. So, what happened at home?"

"My parents didn't like the same sex kiss I did with Rachelle. I mean, *really* didn't like it. I found that out Christmas Eve."

Brenna pulled down mugs with a light clatter to the counter. "Controversial stuff. We knew that."

"Unfortunately, that was not all. They've decided that somehow L.A. has corrupted me. They basically demanded I come back to St. Louis to live with them."

"That's nonsense. You're thirty-two and have a great job."

"They don't care about that; they think they need to 'fix' me."

"What?"

"They... We had already argued about what I was doing out here in L.A. I had a present for you. It accidentally got mixed in with the others under the tree. When my father intercepted it, well, he..." Cassidy's explanation trailed off as she recoiled from the memory of her father's contorted angry features. "He hit me."

Brenna closed her eyes and inhaled, caressing the bruise. "So that's where you got this. Damn."

"This is not about you and me, I swear I didn't tell them. Too much could go wrong. You and I together only can decide who learns what and when. But my father... I've lived meekly... I didn't realize it. My few visits home were relatively quiet. I didn't suspect they harbored these kinds of feelings. They apparently felt...or at least my father felt, that my acting is a game. My mother called it a phase I was supposed to grow out of."

"I'm sorry."

Cassidy nodded. "Their narrow-mindedness and lack of understanding hurts. I actually thought for a while that you might like to come to St. Louis the next time I visited. There are a lot of things that I'd like to share with you from my growing up." Cassidy shook her head. "But I won't be going back to see them for a while. At least until they understand that I won't change to suit them."

"That bad?"

"My father was...unrelenting. I decided to leave, but more to prevent being thrown out and making more of a scene in front of Ryan or the other children." The teapot whistled, and Cassidy poured water into three mugs of cocoa mix, stirring each.

"I remember saying something about our families when we started this." Brenna sounded regretful.

Cassidy shook her head. "It matters, yes, but we're adults, Bren. It's our life. My parents don't get to tell me what to do with it."

"But your family is all you have."

Taking Brenna's hands, Cassidy pulled her against her body and kissed her. "No, please. Ryan and I have you." Trying to convey her conviction, Cassidy lifted Brenna's chin and kissed her solidly.

Thomas stood in the kitchen doorway staring at the two women as they parted. A shocked moment of silence was shattered by his "What's going on?"

Brenna exhaled and swallowed, then felt Cassidy's arm around her back and the long fingers wrapping around hers. "I think it's a good time for a family meeting."

Thomas turned sharply, striding quickly down the bedroom hallway. Before they could catch up to him, he pounded on his brother's bedroom door. Brenna shushed him. "Stop!"

James, half-undressed, appeared at his doorway. "Mom has something to discuss," Thomas said quickly.

"Can't it wait until morning?" James asked, leaning against the doorframe.

"I'm not listening to this alone."

Thomas pushed open the door, and James' exhaustion fled instantly, replaced by anger. "What the fuck's up with you?"

Brenna cleared her throat, reminding them she, and Cassidy, were right behind Thomas. "Family meeting. Now."

James grabbed a robe and arrived in the living room as Brenna was directing Thomas to sit on the couch. "Being angry won't change what I have to say," she started.

"About what?" James sat in nearby chair, looking up expectantly. With her hand on Brenna's arm, Cassidy was moving both Brenna and herself onto another seat, the divan, and foot stool. Cassidy sat up behind Brenna, who leaned forward on the stool.

"This is nuts!" Thomas' outburst was emphasized by him jumping to his feet.

"Sit down!" Brenna ordered. "Sit down, please," she added more softly.

Thomas did as she asked. James continued to wait and watch, with growing curiosity.

"Ryan?" Cassidy asked.

"Busy with Mario Brothers," Thomas answered curtly.

Brenna looked over her shoulder, meeting Cassidy's gaze, squared her shoulders, and turned back to face her sons. "Cassidy and I have grown very close over the last few months. We didn't realize at first what was happening." She reached for Cassidy's hand. "*I* didn't realize what was happening," Brenna amended. "But I couldn't...didn't want to stop it."

Thomas ground out, "When?"

"When what?" James asked.

Cassidy answered, "It started getting really serious on the camping trip."

"When you were flirting with me?" Thomas snapped. He turned on his mother. "Why you?"

"What's wrong with me?" Brenna retorted sharply.

"I was not flirting with you, Thomas." Cassidy sighed. "I genuinely think you're a great guy, but it's not... I'm in love with your mother."

"You're in love with Mom?" James blurted. "How the hell did that happen?"

Brenna's gaze darkened in dismay at his language, but he was uncowed. So was Thomas. "She... You..." He shook his head and stormed to his feet. "So all that stuff you told me, about being her friend?"

"It's all true, Thomas. I am Cassidy's friend. When I opened myself to that much, I realized I felt more than just friendship."

"So you... This is why you're getting the divorce?" James asked.

"Kevin and I were a mistake I made."

"The fight you had, you said he left."

"I had to tell him the truth."

James nodded. Thomas countered, "And the gym climb, dinner — that was a...a...date?"

Cassidy answered. "Dating is part of being together."

"Together? So...you...you have been...physical?" Thomas closed his eyes, rubbing them quickly. "Forget it, I don't want to—" He cut himself off again. "I'm going out." With quick jerky motions, he stalked to the front door, grabbed a coat, and slammed out of the house. Brenna was on her feet after him, watching in dismay as he took off on foot.

"Thomas!"

"Bren, wait."

"But it's..."

Cassidy turned her back inside. As they reached the living room, James was just entering the hallway. "James?" Brenna asked.

"You've said what you need to," he said with a shrug. "I'm going to bed." The door to his bedroom closed loudly in the sudden silence.

Brenna sat down heavily on the couch where Thomas had been just a few moments earlier. "Well, I can see that wasn't the best way to do this." Cassidy sat next to her, wrapping her arms around Brenna as she turned into her chest.

"You should get some sleep while I go after Thomas," Brenna said after a few minutes struggling for calm.

"Any idea where he would go?"

Brenna thought. "It's late. It's Christmas. I don't know."

"He knows that, too."

"He was still in love with you," Brenna said ruefully.

"I gathered."

"I'm sorry. First you have the scenes with your family, then here."

"I've been gifted with a lot in the last few months. I'm not giving it up easily." Cassidy stood, pulling Brenna up with her. "Let's go look for Thomas."

They helped each other into light coats, then got into Brenna's car. "There's a park down the street," Brenna suggested.

"All right."

They were just out of the cul-de-sac, reaching the first corner to turn when Brenna's headlights picked out a figure walking on the south sidewalk toward them. The light caught his face and Brenna quickly stopped. She was out of the car on her side as Cassidy strode across the grass.

"Thomas?" Cassidy called.

"Yeah." He sounded winded.

"Your mother was worried."

He looked toward Brenna, then up at Cassidy. "I just needed some space."

"Are you all right?" Brenna asked.

"With this?" He gestured between the two women. "No."

"I'd like to think you are smarter, and kinder, than that," Cassidy said gently. "Can you at least give us a chance?"

Thomas' ears reddened. He looked away from Cassidy but nodded.

"That's all we're asking."

"Will you come home?" Brenna asked.

He nodded again and moved to the back door of the SUV. Reaching for the handle, his hand met Cassidy's. They said nothing, but Thomas let her open the door for him and close it after he was inside.

Cassidy put herself in the front passenger seat as Brenna went back to the driver seat. They were silent for the short turn around to the house. Thomas said nothing to them as he entered. He disappeared into the bedroom hallway before they could ask him for his coat.

Cassidy hung both her and Brenna's coats. "I should probably take Ryan and go home."

They walked into the empty living room. Brenna nudged Cassidy into the couch cushions. Then she also sat down, pushing herself further back, coaxing Cassidy to turn her back into her chest. As they nestled together, Brenna stroked her fingers through Cassidy's hair, untangling it with her fingers but also relishing the feeling of its softness against her skin.

They settled into an embrace, arms around one another, each breathing in the other's scent and sinking slowly into the sense of warmth and peace being together generated for them. Out of the corner of her eye, Brenna caught the twinkling of the Christmas tree lights and remembered her present for Cassidy. "I have something for you." She brushed her lips over Cassidy's and sat up.

"No, it's—"

Brenna's fingertips silenced her. "Shh. Humor me?" She retrieved the small cube-shaped package and watched anxiously as Cassidy studied it. "Do you remember one of the first real conversations we had? In my trailer?"

Cassidy's brow furrowed. Now curious, she tore the wrapping and withdrew the unmarked cardboard box. The top lifted easily after a fingernail was judiciously applied to the bit of tape sealing it.

Brenna smiled, love shining from her eyes as Cassidy tipped the box to the light and looked inside. Slender fingers withdrew two ceramic figurines, and Cassidy smiled. "Rocky and Bullwinkle?" Her voice filled with amazement and amusement.

"Friends through thick and thin," Brenna explained, kneeling on the couch cushion. "A promise." She bent toward the uplifted face and kissed the full mouth with infinite love pouring through their connection. "I do love you," she murmured as their lips barely separated for a breath.

Cassidy put the figurines aside and grasped Brenna's shoulders, and then, unromantically, she yawned. "I'm sorry," she said, dropping her face away.

"You don't have to collect Ryan now." Brenna shook her head. "Please stay?"

"Thomas isn't going to handle that very well."

"I missed you." Brenna reached for Cassidy's hand. "When I saw you on the doorstep, it was... I thought about you so often today."

"Me, too." They wrapped their arms around one another. In the relative privacy, they reveled in the contact and kissed lightly.

"Then please, stay. We'll have breakfast tomorrow. I'm taking Thomas and James to the mall with their gift certificates. Maybe we can...I...it might feel 'normal' for them."

As Cassidy considered the offer, her brows knitted then relaxed slowly. "All right." Brenna smiled and quietly led Cassidy to the bedroom. As she was being guided inside, Cassidy stopped. "I should go sleep with Ryan."

"We can put him to bed." Brenna led Cassidy to the game room, and showed her how the sofa folded out to a single bed. She watched Cassidy change her son's clothes to pajamas, and waited at the door as mother and son said good night. When Cassidy got to her feet and came to the door, she grasped her hand. Cassidy looked to protest.

Brenna kissed her. "We'll be up long before anyone else," she whispered persuasively. Cassidy let herself be led into Brenna's bedroom.

Passion was there, riding a hot crest in Brenna's stomach as Cassidy undressed. However, she only reached for Cassidy to position them both in the middle of the bed, arranging the covers around them. She brushed her lips across Cassidy's nose and closed her eyes. "Go to sleep."

Gradually their bodies curved and settled into one another. Their breathing quieted, evened out, and finally slowed into sleep.

Chapter 43

Edging away from the dark anxiety of her dreams, Cassidy moved closer to Brenna as early morning sent rays of light through the gaps in the curtains. With a deep breath, she inhaled the soft sweet scent of the woman next to her. Her uneasiness faded away, safely closed off to be dealt with another time, and she opened her eyes. A smile curved her lips when another gaze met hers.

She blinked sleepily into blue eyes that were almost indigo in the indistinct light. Lips met hers again, filled with love and comfort. Brenna's fingers splayed over her back, the tips circling along her spine and raising tingles. *All in all, a pleasant way to wake up.* It was then she realized that her borrowed tee shirt had been eased up and Brenna's hands were moving over her skin, not through the shirt.

"Good morning."

Brenna's words were breathed against her ear. Pleasure coursed over Cassidy in sauna-like waves of wet heat. "Good morning," she offered back, concluding on a groan as Brenna's knee grazed against her center with just the right pressure. Brenna rose and loomed over her for a moment, just studying her, and Cassidy rolled onto her back to meet her gaze. She found desire and a soul-deep connection looking back. Fingertips trailed through the long locks of hair at her temple, eyes following with a reverent intensity. The contact filled Cassidy with the contentment of being cherished.

Even when the light touch skimmed over her bruised jaw, there was no pain, only healing. Listening to Brenna's murmurs of disbelief and comfort regarding her parents' treatment, Cassidy felt the rawness of her spirit being mended as if it were being rewoven in a loom. Torn apart by her parents' revulsion and rejection, Cassidy felt Brenna's love and support making her whole again.

Satiny lips soothed over hers, and an invitation was issued by the gentle nipping on her lips. Cassidy met Brenna's eyes and found the dedication, protectiveness, and all those qualities she so loved in their out-of-bed moments that moved her so much. The realization that she was a whole person to this woman who had so completely captured her heart ignited Cassidy. She answered the invitation as it was given — with a kiss. She poured her feelings into the connection and was gathered up and held safe in her arms.

Tenderly she held Brenna's face above hers, bringing their mouths together from the faintest to the deepest of kisses. When Brenna's arms shook, unable to hold her weight steady any longer, Cassidy welcomed the soft curves against her own and moved her attention to Brenna's face and throat, bringing their bodies into fuller contact.

They both gasped as hardened, sensitive nipples brushed against the inside of fabric. "Take it off now," Cassidy growled, pulling at Brenna's shirt. When the blue eyes widened at the rough huskiness of her demand, she swallowed down the keenest edge of her passion and added softly, "Please?"

With a grin, Brenna sat up, straddling Cassidy's abdomen as she pulled her shirt off over her head. Before she could lower her arms, Cassidy was on her, kissing hard against her throat and shoulders and across the swell of her breasts where she covered a nipple with her hot, wet mouth.

"Ah," Brenna gasped.

Cassidy felt soothing arms come around her shoulders and massage over them and down her spine. She pressed Brenna down, trapping her between the cool sheets and her own heated body, then tugging Brenna's shorts from her hips. She slid them off her legs and tossed them to the floor. "I'm glad I came home early." Her voice thrummed with a low growl, as she undressed herself. She pulled Brenna sharply against her body, surging skin on skin. She sighed at the feel of the down between Brenna's thighs brushing against her stomach.

Her mouth moved from Brenna's breasts down the firm plane of her abdomen. The muscles quivered. Brenna's hips surged beneath Cassidy, and she spread her hands wide across the peaks and planes of Brenna's chest.

"My parents are nuts if they think I'm ever going to give this up." Cassidy's voice was harsh, firm in its defiance of the parental disapproval that had hit her so hard.

Brenna's heart ached. She understood Cassidy's instinct to distance herself from the hurt, but family was so important. *How could they treat you like a child?* Only wanting to soothe, she drew Cassidy up and swirled her tongue in the woman's mouth as they kissed.

"Don't...don't think about it," Brenna murmured against her lips, then treated Cassidy's face to tender kisses from chin to temple to nose and back again. Her voice hummed against Cassidy's throat at the juncture of her shoulder. "I'm glad you came home early, too. It wasn't right without you and Ryan here."

"I feel the same."

Cassidy's head fell back, and her hands encouraged Brenna down with her. Skimming her touch down Cassidy's sides, Brenna felt the stomach muscles contract pleasurably with each kiss she placed down the woman's chest. When she swirled her tongue in the slight depression of belly button, Cassidy arched her hips. Brenna did not linger there, instead returning to the full-lipped mouth, letting her hands smooth over throbbing muscles. They sat up again, kissing devotedly with patience not present in their first joining.

"I love you." Breathing the words across Brenna's shoulders, Cassidy turned her in her arms until the lean back was pillowed on her chest and rounded hips rested between her thighs. Brenna's heart thrummed a rapid tattoo under her palms. *We are one body,* Cassidy thought wildly, as their heartbeats matched and sped up together. Strong fingers pressed into her thighs as her hand skimmed down Brenna's stomach and soft wiry hairs met her fingertips. "Let me show you how much." As they experienced the first feel of silky wetness, their sighs mingled and combined into one voice.

"Cass."

"Bren."

To still her own voice and listen to her lover, Cassidy closed her mouth over Brenna's shoulder, sucking lightly on the velvet soft skin. With a reverent devotion that she mirrored in her strokes below, she swirled her tongue over salt-sweet skin.

Brenna turned her head and lifted Cassidy's face, inhaling as she climaxed on warm fingers. When Cassidy subsided and rested her hand on the inside of the damp thigh, Brenna turned around and held Cassidy close for a lingering kiss. Embraced in a tight hug, Cassidy felt Brenna's hands splayed on her lower back. Cassidy's quivering rocked through both of them.

Brenna rolled them over until she lay on her back on the sheets. Cassidy gazed down as the fine-boned hands guided her hips until their mounds were pressed tightly together. The sensation of hairs tangling made Brenna's back arch in an aching sensuality. She kept her eyes locked on Cassidy's to witness every emotion playing across her features.

All Brenna's love seemed poured into their connection; tears pooled in her eyes. "So beautiful," Brenna said.

Her voice filled Cassidy with so much emotion, much as Brenna's fingers filled and satisfied her ache and longing inside. At the feather-light touches, like capturing a live wire, an almost electrical feeling passed between them. Cassidy arched as Brenna's fingertips pressed between their bodies. Her climax engulfed them both in its flashpoint heat. Tearfully biting her lip to keep little more than a whimper from escaping, Cassidy bonelessly collapsed. Brenna welcomed her into a sheltering embrace. Soft fingertips brushed over Cassidy's cheeks, drying her tears.

As Cassidy's heartbeat slowed, her lips moved reverently over the breast pillowed under her cheek. She heard Brenna's heartbeat slow, too. *That was...so different*, she thought dazedly.

Arms tightened around her shoulders when she would have moved off. "No. Don't go," Brenna murmured with noticeable hesitance in her voice. "Stay."

Cassidy's whispered reply came against Brenna's lips. "I'm not going anywhere." She moved only enough to settle her weight mostly on the bed and intertwine their legs, then her head fell back to the curve of Brenna's shoulder.

The auburn-haired woman looked down into Cassidy's face as she looked up. They both spoke softly at the same moment, the same words. Their hands intertwined, and they kissed their joined fists at the same instant. "Thank you."

Bemused, they moved their hands aside and drank wonderingly of the sight of one another, combing fingers through locks of soft hair — dark and light. With light touches they explored damp bodies, not out of arousal, but for contact.

"I need you so much," Cassidy whispered. "You make me whole." She soothed her palm over Brenna's breast, cherishing the heart beating so strongly within. "You were wonderful," Cassidy commented softly. "So different." She nuzzled Brenna's throat and reveled in the strong arms moving over her back in a secure hug. Sure hands moved to her nape and coaxed her head back up for a leisurely kiss which went on for several minutes.

When Brenna bent her knees, Cassidy rested naturally in the cradle formed by her hips. They floated in the daydreaming world of mutual heat and, for the moment, completion. Her eyes were almost closed, her body lulled, when Brenna's voice wrapped around her, strong and soft.

"With everything I am, I love you," she said.

To Cassidy, the inflection was clear in a way she had not heard before...from anyone. *You.* The totality of who she was. *Friend. Lover. Daughter. Mother.* Here, in this woman's arms, she felt, for the first time wholly Woman as well. *Nothing ever will or could be wrong with that.*

"Hey, are you awake?"

James vaguely registered the whispered question before rough hands were shaking his shoulder. "Go away," he grumbled.

"Come on. I need to talk." More insistent shaking followed.

"Is the house on fire?" James pushed the hands off his arm, then pulled the covers around his head. "No? Then leave me alone."

A pleading whisper came back. "You can't leave me to face them alone."

He furrowed his brow. "What the hell are you talking about?"

"Mom and Cassidy."

Rolling onto his back, tucking the covers under his arms, James stared up into the shadows. His brother loomed over his bed, hands on his hips, fully expecting him to get up and participate in this conversation. "What about them?"

"Do you think they're out there?"

James glanced at his bedside table and the LCD clock. "At five o'clock in the morning? Not unless there's some emergency...like this is *not*," he grumbled, turning away and pulling his pillow over his head. His muffled voice issued up from beneath the pillow. "Besides, it's a holiday. You know how much Mom likes to sleep in when she gets the chance."

"Yeah, but what about Cassidy?"

"She doesn't strike me as a morning person. She's probably still asleep, too."

There was a long moment of silence and James hoped that Thomas had left, though he hadn't heard the door closing. His brother's voice broke the silence.

"Do you suppose they're sleeping together?"

Damn. From beneath the pillow, James bit out, "I. Don't. Care."

Thomas' voice became agitated. "Why are you taking this so calmly?"

James rolled toward his brother again and answered sarcastically, "Maybe because it's five o'clock in the morning?" He sighed. "Just go back to bed."

"I can't. I had to go to the bathroom, and then I..."

Groaning, James pulled the covers over his head, blocking out the rest of whatever his brother was saying. *What is it lately with people sharing much more than I really need to know about their personal lives? First Mom, now this.* Firmly, to be heard over his brother's rambling, he bit out, "Shut. The Fuck. Up."

His brother did fall silent, but instead of leaving, he dropped to the end of James' bed. The mattress jostled. James groaned. Thomas moaned, "I don't know if I can go out there."

"I'm not sharing the bed," he said dryly.

"You saw how they were last night."

True, James acknowledged silently, then muttered, "Mom is more sensible than that." When Thomas asked him to repeat it, he did, adding a few choice words for effect. "They are not *fucking* on the *damn* couch."

"But..." Thomas paused; James could imagine him shaking his head. "What if I—"

"Go and look?" James threw off the pillow and rolled to his feet enthusiastically. "*Great* idea. You go look and report back. Later. *Much* later. Like after noon, okay?" He pushed his brother toward the door. Thomas pushed back.

"This only gets more complicated if you make it that way. Frankly, I'd rather you not upset the balance by getting into a pissing match with our mother." He opened the door and pushed Thomas out. "Go. Do whatever. Just leave me alone." He firmly closed the door in Thomas' face.

Turning around, Thomas realized he was stranded in the hallway, in nothing but shorts. *What do I do now?*

Too keyed up to go back to sleep and uncomfortable about possibly encountering their houseguest, who would undoubtedly be tousled and painfully beautiful fresh from sleep, Thomas retreated to the only safe haven he could think of — the game room. Too late he recalled that was where Ryan had been put to sleep. The five-year-old stirred even as Thomas was closing the door as quietly as possible.

James returned to his bed and flopped down, pillowing his head on his hands as he tried to empty his mind and return to sleep. Thomas' visit bothered him. Even though James had ribbed Thomas about it, apparently his brother really had fallen for the blond actress who, it now appeared, had been gradually becoming involved with their mother.

While James did wonder how his mom had come to the conclusion that she returned those feelings, the explanation made sense of many things he had been observing over the last several months. That was really the only thing he required, since emotionally he had no attachment one way or the other to anyone other than his mother in this little drama. Considering his mother in a lesbian relationship was only slightly more unsettling than considering her as any kind of sexual being at all. Definitely it all fell into the category of "too much information", and he preferred to ignore it, so long as the situation was ignorable.

Thomas however was reacting out of his emotions concerning Ms. Hyland, which meant he was jealous of their mother. When the relationship had been revealed, Thomas had even asked, "Why you?" making their mother defensive with her "What's wrong with me?" James recalled the camping trip and what he'd heard about the challenge climb between Thomas and their mother. Now he realized it had been a competition for love, like Romeo and Tybalt in *Romeo and Juliet,* which they'd been reading in English class.

James sighed. As a matter of fact, Marcie had dropped him because he wouldn't become jealous over her. She had told him that another guy had asked her out. James had shrugged and said if she wanted to go, she should. He had thought that giving her the space to do as she needed was most important. That's what his mother had said she had most wanted from Mr. Shea.

Marcie had wanted him to react more possessively. He didn't see the intelligence in fighting a football player who could easily pound him into the turf. So, Marcie told him they didn't need to see each other at all. *Why wasn't she pleased that I left the choice up to her? Isn't that what they all want — no man making all their choices for them?* He frowned and closed his eyes, admitting it was all too confusing to be unraveled at five-thirty in the morning.

"I should go."

The whisper in the dark lured Brenna from her half-dream state. She was feeling content with her choices, wrapped up pleasantly in the circle of Cassidy's arms as they languidly stroked each other's skin. "You don't have to," she murmured back, lifting her chin. Unerringly, Cassidy found her lips with the kiss she had sensed coming. She purred into the contact and turned until their breasts touched when the kiss became deeply arousing.

Cassidy's chuckle tickled her lips, voiceless as it was. "I think I had better not be coming out of their mother's bedroom when I first see your sons today. I didn't really think how it would complicate things for you when I came straight here from the airport instead of going home." She indulged them both by stroking down Brenna's hip and then over her buttocks, tugging until they were perfectly fitted together, breasts to breasts, stomach to stomach, and hips to hips.

A knee nudged between Brenna's thighs, and the slight pressure against her center made her want their interlude to continue. "It had to happen eventually," Brenna pointed out. "I needed to tell them." She reminded Cassidy of her words the night before. "We told them. Together. That was right to do."

"Ryan had already guessed." Cassidy sounded pleased.

"I'm not surprised. He's seen us together a little more often than Thomas or James." Brenna sighed. "And clearly Thomas still thinks he's in love with you."

"There is at least one thing we can do," Cassidy said solemnly, withdrawing from Brenna slowly. "Give him time. I really should go to the guest room." She sat up and slipped her legs off the bed.

Brenna studied the long lean line of the other woman's back and moved a hand over the muscled surface. She nodded. Cassidy was right. Their children's acceptance was important. Brenna's sons would need time to adjust, and, because they both cared deeply about those affected by their decisions as well as each other, they would have to take things slowly in making a family together.

"It wouldn't hurt to shower first," she said, moving across the mattress to press herself indulgently against Cassidy's back and place a kiss behind her ear. At the touch the woman's back arched in a sensual shudder. Brenna reached around and filled her palms with the soft fullness of warm breasts. She squeezed lightly. "What would you say to that?" she whispered hotly.

"I...could do that." Cassidy's voice was halting, the woman clearly and quickly affected by the sexual play. She turned her head slightly and inhaled Brenna's breath before sealing their lips together in a hard kiss. "You so don't play fair," she said breathlessly when she tore herself away. "Come on, before we lose any more time."

Brenna's small smile turned into a confident grin as Cassidy pulled her to her feet. Already nude, they stepped into the master bathroom together. After letting the water warm, Brenna switched the flow over to the showerhead, then drew the sprayer off its mount, and they soaped and washed one another.

Cassidy knelt in the tub and soaped down Brenna's thighs, then rinsed them by directing the sprayer. Brenna shuddered when the spray hit her center. She reached out to steady herself on Cassidy's shoulder. The blonde set down the showerhead, leaving its water spraying up slightly around their ankles, then she leaned forward.

Brenna thought Cassidy was going to wrap herself around her waist, but then full lips trailed quickly over her stomach and— She gasped when the grip firmed on her butt, and Cassidy nuzzled through the hair covering her mound. "You shouldn't...Oh...God..." she groaned. She threw her head back as Cassidy used her mouth to pleasure her. *Kevin never did this at all,* she thought wildly, *and Tom was never this good at it.*

She felt every little movement of Cassidy's tongue and lips, as if the area were sensitized tenfold; the sensations consumed her. Her fingers moved through Cassidy's wet hair, which grounded her and steadied her nerves. She was panting and groaning with the pleasure rapidly spiraling out of control. She shifted her feet to remain upright. Her hands found the towel rack over her head. Cassidy's hands moved to steady her as well, spreading wide to support her back. As the waves overtook her, her essence pulsed into Cassidy's avid mouth and her entire chest vibrated with a cry of ecstasy.

Almost instantly, Cassidy's mouth retreated. She rose to muffle Brenna's cry of frustration with a kiss, but her fingers deliciously drove Brenna through the orgasm until she was panting and spent. "Shh," Cassidy murmured quickly. "You don't want to wake the boys."

The hell with that, Brenna thought rebelliously when Cassidy's touch continued to ignite small fires throughout her body. When the sensations ebbed and she was wrapped up in Cassidy's strong grasp, Brenna sighed. Cassidy was right, though. Had she done as she wanted, the screams would have awakened their sons. The kisses that

280 ÷ Lara Zielinsky

followed, where she tasted herself on Cassidy's lips, made the aftermath so much sweeter than she could have imagined.

Cassidy watched Brenna dress. From her own bags, she had retrieved a long-sleeve cashmere sweater top, and jeans. Brenna was pulling a sweatshirt on over her bare breasts. The logo swept Cassidy back through wonderful memories. She reached out to caress the lettering. Brenna looked up at her curiously.

"I remember the first time I saw you in this," Cassidy said with touch of melancholy. "I knew I was seeing the real you."

"I don't understand." Brenna hugged her quickly. "Is something wrong?"

"Remember Ryan's birthday party?" Cassidy began. Brenna nodded against her shoulder. "You came in this sweatshirt, a pair of blue jeans, and with your hair in a ponytail. You took my breath away."

"I don't understand why that should upset you."

"I love sweatshirts," Cassidy answered. "I even have a ritual at home where I slip into one of my old high school jerseys the minute I get into my bedroom. It's my way of saying 'I'm home.'" She gasped in sudden distress and tried to pull away, but Brenna held her firmly. "I guess that won't be happening anymore."

In Brenna's embrace, Cassidy safely cried until the tears stopped. Brenna pulled the sweatshirt off and held it out, her meaning clear. Cassidy leaned back, stripped off her sweater top, and pulled on the sweatshirt. Brenna helped her smooth it over her chest. As their gazes held, Brenna said, "Welcome home."

It was after six-thirty when the women finally peeked out of the bedroom doorway, looking up and down the hall before stepping out together and walking to the kitchen. Cassidy leaned on the counter and watched Brenna grind the coffee and prep the coffeemaker. "Anything I can do?"

"If you want some juice, the glasses are in the cabinet to the left of the sink," Brenna said.

"Would you like some?"

The "yes" that replied wasn't Brenna's voice.

Together they turned and saw Ryan standing in the entry to the kitchen, looking up expectantly at them. A welcoming smile curled Brenna's lips as she took in the sight — still in his pajamas, looking only mildly sleepy. "Good morning, Ryan."

"Hi," he said to her, then turned to his mother. "Good morning, Mommy."

"Good morning." Cassidy scooped him up in a tight hug before releasing him. "You're thirsty, hmm?"

"Yes."

"One orange juice coming up." Brenna collected the small glass, poured the juice, then passed it to him. "Got it?" She watched him carefully put his hands around the base of the glass before she released it.

He nodded. "Thank you."

"You're welcome." She brushed her fingers lightly over his hair. "Why don't you go sit at the dining room table?"

Brenna leaned next to Cassidy, who gazed across the counter into the dining area, following Ryan's progress. She put a light hand on Cassidy's back and held the blonde briefly against her shoulder before stepping away and pouring them each a glass of juice.

Thomas stood just out of sight in the bedroom hallway, listening to the exchange between Ryan and his mother. He ached at the affection in her voice. *God, she's really happy.* Nudging around the end of the wall, he remained silent, the position allowing him a chance to watch them without them seeing him.

It wasn't anything overt, but he saw Cassidy's face as she handed his mother a glass of juice. Clearly, Cassidy was in love with his mother. He thought back to the times the three of them had shared together. He winced, realizing that the laughter and the looks they'd exchanged had been more than camaraderie. He had not seen it before because he had not wanted to see it. Feeling foolish and hurting, he wondered if he could fall out of love as quickly as he seemed to have fallen into it.

He stepped forward, and the noise of his entrance drew their eyes to him. Thomas squared his shoulders and affixed a careful smile. "Good morning."

"Good morning." Cassidy answered first; she was sitting at the table next to her son.

His mother's greeting preceded a pat on his arm. "Have a seat. Here." She set her glass of juice in front of him and returned to the kitchen to pour herself another.

"So, what's on the agenda today?" he called to her.

"I'm going to drop you and James at the mall to spend your Christmas money. I'll be taking Cassidy and Ryan home."

Chapter 44

The mall was already busy when Brenna pulled to a stop in front of an entrance. She had decided against parking at all. News vans were everywhere, covering the post-Christmas shopping crowds.

"Can I come?"

Cassidy turned around and put a restraining hand on Ryan's thigh to discourage him from following the older boys, who were getting out of the backseat. "Don't you want to go home?"

"I want to play video games with Thomas."

Cassidy looked wryly at Thomas, then Brenna, who shrugged and left the decision to her. It was Thomas' expression that decided her. Standing on the curb, he had his jaw set carefully, and though he looked at her son, he wouldn't look at her. "You two go on and have a good time. Ryan and I really need to get home."

"Mom?" Thomas drew his mother's attention.

She fished in her purse and handed a twenty dollar bill to each of them. "Don't spend it all at the arcade. Eat some lunch, too. I'll be back at five to pick you up right here."

"Okay, Mom." James looked at his mother, then briefly to Cassidy. "See you."

"Bye," Cassidy responded with a faint nod. From her place in the front passenger seat, she kept her hand on Ryan until both rear doors were closed. He squirmed and pouted but remained quiet. Brenna did not drive off immediately. Her gaze followed her sons until they were inside. Cassidy watched her face. When the blue eyes darkened, indicating she was getting upset, Cassidy asked, "Are you all right?"

The upset vanished quickly, and a smile turned to her. "Yeah." Patting her knee lightly, Brenna went on, "Yes, I'm fine. Ready to go?"

As Brenna drove north to Cassidy's side of town, Cassidy said, "You can park at my house. The Talbots are only on the corner." Directing Brenna to make a left, she added, "Gwen's been feeding and walking Ranger while we were gone. Right, Ryan?"

"Can I walk him when we get home?"

Cassidy shook her head. Disconcerted, Brenna said, "I didn't see a dog at the party."

"We left him at the Talbots' that day so he wouldn't misbehave with all of the excitement. Ranger's a Dalmatian. I got him when Ryan was three."

"Dalmatian's a big dog, right?"

Cassidy chuckled. "Brenna, are you afraid of dogs?" The other woman did not answer. "Ranger's a softie," she assured. "That's why I chose the breed — because they are obedient but active enough to keep up with children."

"I didn't know that." Brenna pulled into Cassidy's driveway. "Well, we're here."

"Home!" Ryan unbelted himself and was in the yard in a couple of bounces.

"Keeps up with kids, huh?" Brenna laughed. Cassidy chuckled, coming around. "You know, I think I remember meeting Gwen at the birthday party. I remember thinking you were...rather intimate," she added the last under her breath as Cassidy led her across the street.

"She's just a friend," Cassidy said, sealing the assurance with a kiss just before she rang the doorbell.

Brenna felt the appraisal begin as soon as introductions were made. Since

Cassidy did not make mention of their changed relationship, she suspected that somehow Gwen had already learned about it. It was the oddest sensation to be aware that another person was skirting a subject that she wanted, just as desperately, to broach.

She looked around the modest home as Cassidy shared the first part of her trip to Missouri. Those events — getting to spend time with her uncles, aunts, cousins, and their children — brought a fond smile to her face, Brenna noticed, particularly when she mentioned Travis and Brenda. Each time a story veered close to referring to her parents, though, Cassidy shifted the subject to another relative or one of Ryan's snowy adventures.

Brenna hurt for her. She also acknowledged to herself that rejection by her family was a very real fear of her own. If Cassidy's family had responded so violently, what could she expect, with her family being almost another full generation older?

She suspected how her mother might react, but she and her siblings had never had cause to discuss such an issue, so she had no basis on which to figure out what their response might be. Despite his political stances, when it came down to her personally, even Kevin's biases had come out, with him believing she was "not like that" and "not one of those people".

Preoccupied by her jumbled thoughts, Brenna started nibbling her bottom lip. She did feel different. She was sure it wasn't because her lover was a woman, though, but rather because she was finally, really, truly in love. The discovery made her feel calmer about everything.

"Bren?"

Cassidy's voice drew her from her thoughts. "I'm sorry. What were you saying?"

Cassidy turned to Gwen. "I think I'll get the house key now, then Bren can go home."

"No, I...It's all right. I've just been thinking."

"About your work? I catch the show frequently," Gwen offered. "You're quite good."

"That wasn't actually what I was thinking about, but thank you." Brenna stood as the other two did. Gwen excused herself.

"Brenna, are you all right?"

"Just learning to live with secrets," she whispered. She fell silent as Gwen returned and passed the key to Cassidy.

"Well, it was nice to meet you," Gwen said.

"You, too. Thank you."

"Ryan!" Cassidy called.

He came running out with a boy Brenna now remembered from the birthday party as well.

"Say goodbye to Chance," Cassidy said. "Time to go."

"Mommy!"

"Sorry, but it's time."

Ryan turned his blue eyes on Brenna. "Ms. Lanigan, tell her I want to stay."

Brenna knew her eyes sparkled with amusement, but she kept her voice serious. "Honey, if your mother says it's time to go, then I suggest we listen to her."

"Yes, ma'am." He hung his head, dropped the toys in his hands on the floor, and, shoulders slumped, exited the Talbots' home.

"Good budding actor you've got there, Cass," she said with a chuckle. "I don't think I've ever seen a pout quite that perfect."

Cassidy sighed. "Come on. Let's go." She turned to Gwen. "Thanks for looking after things."

"Anytime." Gwen looked Brenna over once more as she showed the women to the door.

Brenna paused on the stoop after the door was closed. Cassidy had already started down the walk. She turned back, her expression curious. Nervously Brenna asked, "She's your friend. So, what's the verdict?" Cassidy smiled, and it untied the knot in Brenna's stomach.

"She likes you."

They walked across the street and up to Cassidy's home. "She knows, though — about us, I mean — doesn't she?" Cassidy nodded. "She's burning with questions. It was unnerving."

Cassidy keyed the knob, then the bolt, and stepped back, letting Brenna enter first. "When I was pretty confused, she was good to talk to."

"You were confused?" Brenna tugged off her light jacket, and Cassidy hung it in her closet.

"Very."

Ryan ran past them. She watched him enter what she presumed was his bedroom. The toys he poured onto the bedspread with a clatter confirmed it. She turned back to find Cassidy in her bedroom across the hall opening the luggage and sorting clothes into drawers, her closet, and a wicker basket by the bathroom door.

"Are you going right back to the mall?" Cassidy asked.

"No. James and Thomas would really hate if I joined them so soon. I should give them some normal space and not go back until the time I said I'd pick them up."

"How about some Irish coffee?"

"I'll make it," Brenna volunteered.

"Supplies are in the kitchen. Help yourself. I'll be out in just another minute."

Ryan joined Brenna in the kitchen when he heard her clattering around. "What'cha doin'?"

"Making something for your mom to drink."

"You're being very nice to Mommy. No wonder she likes you."

"She said that?"

"Yes. I knew already, though."

Cassidy had mentioned Ryan had already guessed about them. Brenna crouched down to talk to him. "What do you think you know?"

"I know you kissed. I saw that."

"When?"

"When you took us camping. In the tent."

"I thought you were asleep."

"I wasn't."

"Are you okay with your mom and me kissing?"

"I like when Mommy's happy."

"That's all?"

"Yes."

"I like when your mommy's happy, too." Brenna could not stifle her amusement. She looked Ryan squarely in the eye. "Your mother raised a very smart boy."

"Me?"

"Yes." She hugged him. "I love you."

"As much as you love Mommy?"

"Just as much." He smiled broadly at that. She stood and ruffled his hair.

"Would you like a snack?" He grinned, and she saw his mother's features so clearly, she felt her heart beat faster. "Let's see what we can find, hmm?"

"Okay."

Together they raided the refrigerator, locating a pair of apples. While she ate hers whole, she cut the second into wedges for him. They sat together at the kitchen table. When she'd finished and was rising, Cassidy appeared from her room. "All unpacked?"

"I ran across this," Cassidy said, holding out the unwrapped box. "Sorry, it's a little worse for travel."

Brenna took the box, lifting off the top and withdrawing the scarf.

"There was a note with it, but I think it got lost in the..."

"Confusion?" Brenna supplied an innocuous descriptor.

"Yes."

"It's a beautiful gift."

"I was hoping you'd like it enough to wear it...around."

Brenna looped it around her throat, tucking it into the neckline of her blouse. The blouse's color was not really suited to the silky red, but the effect caused an immediate and broad, lust-filled smile from Cassidy. "Done."

Cassidy reached out to caress the silk, lightly brushing the skin beneath. "You're beautiful."

"Want an apple, Mommy?" Ryan held up his last apple wedge.

Smiling at Brenna, Cassidy dropped her hand from the silk and took the apple piece from her son. "Thank you."

"Ryan says he's happy we're together."

"One down, two to go?"

Brenna nodded. Despite the anxiety clouding her eyes, she bestowed a loving smile on Ryan and brushed her fingers through his hair. She turned to Cassidy abruptly. "I was just about to finish the coffee. Still want a cup?"

"I'll get the whiskey." She moved toward the cabinet over the stove. "The whipped cream is in the refrigerator."

With Ryan in his mother's lap, Cassidy and Brenna sat on the couch, sipping their coffees. Brenna had cut more apples, which the trio nibbled as the women talked.

"Have you heard anything more from the British production?"

"I have to contact them after the first." Brenna sounded pensive. "What with everything, I haven't finished reading the script." She thought for a moment. "What are you planning to do after *Time Trails*?"

As much as she wanted to talk about all of them making plans together, Cassidy carefully kept her news neutral. "A few series pilots have been dropped off, but I'm not interested in a starring role. I'd like another ensemble. The hours can be much better for Ryan and me."

Brenna nodded, then finished her coffee with one final swallow, and patted Cassidy's thigh. "Well, I should probably be going."

Cassidy heard the strain. "Brenna, do you want to talk about doing something together?" From the averted eyes, she had her answer. "Ryan, look over there, okay?" She pointed to the porch. Preceded by such an absurd request — what five-year-old would look away when told? — Cassidy leaned forward and kissed Brenna quickly on the lips, stunning her. She felt the other woman's tension gradually melt away under her nibbling kisses and finally leaned back.

Brenna blinked, clearly gathering her so-pleasantly-scattered wits back together. "What was that for?"

"To relax you. You don't have to be nervous. I would love to do something with you."

"That probably won't happen."

"Neither of us thought this would happen, either. Obviously anything is possible," Cassidy said earnestly. A buoyant energy streamed through her as Brenna accepted her optimism with a careful nod. To be able to provide someone else support made her feel good. It was not something she was used to. Setting Ryan on the floor, Cassidy stood up. "We've never just hung out. How about we go back to the mall together?"

"Do we dare?"

"I'm not going to ravish you over the perfume counter," Cassidy assured her. "I don't want to hide away, either. Besides, we'll have Ryan with us."

Brenna took her hand. After spending a moment clearing their few dishes into the dishwasher, Brenna drove the three of them back to the mall.

Brenna felt as if she hadn't smiled and laughed so much in years. She, Cassidy, and Ryan started at the end of the mall furthest from the food court, looking through the racks in a designer store. She purchased a blouse that would go perfectly with Cassidy's scarf. When she stepped out of the small dressing room wearing the combination, having kept the scarf in her handbag, Cassidy's expression, so full of fiery passion, almost buckled her knees. The touch of their hands was electric.

Standing at the counter waiting for the purchase to ring up, they chatted about nothing in particular and everything — clothing, fabrics, decorating, early apartments, Cassidy's college dormitory, getting too drunk on a date, not getting drunk enough — all the time wishing that half the people they had known over the years had been half as easy to talk to.

At the perfume counter, Brenna discovered her favorite scent on Cassidy was Emporio White Elle by Armani. The floral woodsy scent transported her immediately back to November. When she leaned close, inhaled deeply, and whispered the direction of her thoughts, Cassidy's laughter sent sensual shivers through her. Cassidy acquired the scent in a body lotion, promising under her breath to let Brenna apply it any time she desired.

To reward Ryan for his patience while the two women tried on clothes, they next stopped in a toy store. The five-year-old headed immediately for the baseball equipment. Though Cassidy protested weakly, they eventually split the cost of a regulation-size baseball, junior wood bat, and glove, not forgetting the oil, as Brenna told him that Thomas always worked his gloves for weeks before ever using them.

They talked about the Little League team Thomas helped coach. Brenna found her phone book, and Cassidy programmed the head coach's number into her cell phone.

They talked a bit at that point about the spring and working out the situation with their sons.

"I found Thomas an internship with U.S. Forestry," Brenna revealed. "It was your suggestion actually that led me to go and talk to his counselor."

"Camp counseling?" Cassidy asked.

"No. The group, as I understand it, will survey many of the jobs available through the National and State Park systems."

Cassidy smiled. "He'll love it."

"He did seem pretty excited. The news even trumped his uncle's tickets. My brother Gary always sends him spring training tickets and comes to town to accompany him," she explained.

Ryan pulled at his mother's hand excitedly. "Thomas!"

The women looked up to see they had reached the arcade. Inside, Thomas stood at one of the games, wrestling with a joystick, several shopping bags piled at his feet.

Thomas turned at hearing his name called. As she let Ryan run to Thomas, Cassidy asked Brenna quietly, "Ready?"

Ryan "helped" Thomas with his purchases, opening each bag as he asked, "What'd'you get?"

Without answering, Thomas picked up the bags. He didn't seem angry at Ryan or at either of them as they walked up.

"We're early," Brenna said. "Sorry."

"I was done."

"Is James in here?" Brenna looked around.

"No. I did run into him coming out of Blick's with an armful of sponges and grease pencils."

Cassidy was surprised. "James dabbles in art?"

"Draws mostly, but there's a new art teacher who has been encouraging him to work in other mediums," Thomas answered. "For Christmas he gave Mom this fantastic portrait he did of her."

Brenna blushed, and Cassidy decided she would have to see this portrait. "Where are you going to hang it?"

"I have to completely rethink the living room wall," Brenna answered. "Thomas gave me a photograph he took on the mountain."

The foursome turned out of the arcade and started for the food court tables when Cassidy spotted James coming out of an odds'n'ends shop, just putting away a receipt in the bag in his hand and readjusting the bags under his arms. He looked up just as they reached the tables. "Oh, hey."

"Fruitful day," Brenna remarked.

"Yep."

They all put their bags down. Brenna conferred with Cassidy while Thomas and James went off to choose their food. Cassidy stayed at the tables, pulling two together to give them enough space, and watched Ryan while Brenna picked up two salads at Salad Express and a burger meal at Hokey Joe's for Ryan. Thomas and James returned with barbecued beef stacks, fries, and super-sized sodas.

Ryan informed everyone about his acquisitions, explaining that he would be the "best player on Thomas' team". He tried to pull out his bat to show it around. When his mother intercepted it, he showed the vial of oil and the new glove instead. Thomas took it from him and showed him how to work the oil into the leather. Before long, he was finally smiling easily and laughing as Ryan irrepressibly rattled off the statistics he believed he could rack up when he began to play.

Brenna quickly took a forkful of salad, but Cassidy did not miss the gleam of tears gathering in her eyes, or the way the tension finally left her shoulders. Under the table, Cassidy nudged Brenna's knee as they sat side by side, giving her a smile when she looked up. The corners of Brenna's lips turned up, and her eyes dipped in acknowledgment.

Epilogue

Nudging open the door with her hip, Brenna balanced the champagne flutes and wine bottle in her hands. Stepping into her back yard, she turned at the first crack of fireworks and spied Cassidy with her head tilted back, eyes skyward. The bright sparks of blue and red faded from their blossoming formation. Cassidy turned at the sound of the screen door slamming into its frame.

"Thought we might celebrate the start of the year properly," Brenna said with a shrug, nodding at the glasses and wine.

Cassidy met her halfway along the garden walk and took the glasses. "All that will take is the traditional New Year's kiss. First one of the year always brings good luck to the relationship." Cassidy chuckled, kissing Brenna's ear, making the other woman shiver in reaction and fumble as she started to work on opening the bottle.

Finally wresting the foil and wire mesh from the bottle's neck, Brenna paused at another explosive crack. The two of them watched a pair of green fireworks blossom overhead. The light display altered the shadows over Cassidy's face. Brenna was entranced by the delicate bone structure and the look of peaceful repose.

"Thank you for inviting me," Cassidy said, her gaze on the fireworks.

"I'm glad Thomas thought to take Ryan to the park to see the display from there so we could have some time together."

"He's...adjusting well," Cassidy remarked, turning to look at Brenna. "He bolted with Ryan after twenty minutes instead of five." She turned back to the fireworks. "Where's James?"

"He went to the park earlier. I think he's trying to get back together with his girlfriend."

"Did he know Ryan and I were coming?"

"I didn't hide it from them."

"You would tell me if there were problems, right?"

Brenna sighed. "The shock has worn off. I was working with my lawyer on the divorce papers. James didn't like it. He said I was being selfish. I told him it would be more selfish to stay with Kevin just for appearances." Brenna sighed. "Until I said it, I didn't realize that's what I'd been doing all along, letting appearances govern my actions. My reaction to you, in the beginning, was like that. You appeared to be everything I should fear, and yet, even in the beginning I couldn't stop focusing on you. I hated it, and that made me lash out."

"I've lived for appearances, too," Cassidy replied. "I had to be the perfect actor, fit in here without raising any questions." She took the bottle from Brenna's hands, trading her the champagne flutes. Pressing the sides of the plastic cork with her thumbs, she turned away and worked it out of the neck. A little bubbly spilled as the cork popped free. Tucking it in the pocket of her pants, she filled both glasses as Brenna held them up.

Cassidy lifted her glass. "To two thousand one, a new century."

"That was last year," Brenna pointed out.

"Last year was the end of the twentieth. Nothing against it, but it was a tough one. I'd rather the century start with a good year."

"To a good year." Brenna tapped her glass against Cassidy's.

Cassidy watched Brenna sip from her flute, the muscles in her throat moving gently, tantalizingly. As Brenna's glass lowered from her lips, Cassidy could no longer resist. She leaned in, caressed Brenna's cheek, and claimed her lips, tasting the light flavor of the champagne lacing over Brenna's own unique taste. The moan that met her kisses thrilled Cassidy endlessly. "I love you," she murmured, trailing away from Brenna's lips to nip and suck at the skin where her jaw met her throat.

Brenna's husky voice made Cassidy's heart skip. "Oh, God. I love you too." There was a soft thump as the champagne glass slid from Brenna's fingers and hit the grass. *No shattering*, Cassidy thought, pleased, as she let her own glass slip free so that she could wrap both her arms around Brenna. Brenna's arms encircled her neck, and she lifted the small woman up. Their eyes met, both reflecting their rising passion.

Cassidy's fingers skimmed a warm and now familiar path to arousal over Brenna's shoulders and down her stomach. Moving her fingers beneath the hem of the low-cut black cocktail dress, she recalled her first sight of it — as she was let in the front door. Brenna's figure was shown off to full effect, even more than it had been the night of the Pinnacle party.

She had wanted to say it then but had been too tongue-tied. "I want you." She said it now, pulling the smaller woman closer still, supporting her fully as she felt Brenna's knees give way. She slowly sank to the ground with Brenna, the grass soft and cool against their flushed skin. Her fingers found the clasp of Brenna's garter. She gasped at the bolt of lust that shot through her own groin.

Brenna dislodged pins from Cassidy's hair. "Now, let's see about starting the New Year off right with a really big bang."

The fireworks in the sky faded into the background as they melded in their own explosions together under the stars.

Printed in the United States
75385LV00007B/142